"How can I be of service to you?"

"Service to me?" Marcus echoed, making the offer sound anything but innocent.

Her cheeks burned, and she decided that at least one of them needed to be frank. "You obviously want something. What is it?"

His brow lifted at her discourtesy. "I'm recently back in Town. Can I not stop by to pay a visit to an old friend?"

"You are very good at rewriting history," she charged, crossing her arms. "I wonder why. What are you up to, Marcus Dunn?"

He leaned back, his palms wide. "Must I have a hidden purpose?"

"You show up after years of stalwart silence and suddenly wish to make amends? Don't forget, I knew you as a lad."

"Ahh. Old hurts still sting. So what was it? A frog in your pocket? A pine needle in your chair?"

Digging her nails into her arms, she fought to cool her mounting irritation. "I have no concern for the past. My thoughts bear only to today." She would not allow him to turn her aside.

"Whatever your game, I will not be so easily duped."

Other **AVON ROMANCES**

SARI ROBINS

More Than A Scandal

AVON BOOKS
An Imprint of HarperCollinsPublishers

This is a work of fiction. Names, characters, places, and incidents are products of the author's imagination or are used fictitiously and are not to be construed as real. Any resemblance to actual events, locales, organizations, or persons, living or dead, is entirely coincidental.

AVON BOOKS
An Imprint of HarperCollins*Publishers*
10 East 53rd Street
New York, New York 10022-5299

Copyright © 2005 by Sari Earl
ISBN: 0-06-057535-2
www.avonromance.com

First Avon Books paperback printing: July 2005

Avon Trademark Reg. U.S. Pat. Off. and in Other Countries, Marca Registrada, Hecho en U.S.A.
HarperCollins® is a registered trademark of HarperCollins Publishers Inc.

Printed in the U.S.A.

10 9 8 7 6 5 4 3 2 1

In memory of my father,
Sheldon C. Katz,
a true hero in every sense of the word.

I miss you, Daddy.

Acknowledgments

I will be eternally grateful to my family and friends, especially my mother, sister, and brother, who continue to enthusiastically champion my efforts. I want to specially acknowledge the following people for their wonderful support:

Dorothy Rece
Bill Eubanks
Deb Brink
Marilyn Simes and Digitalinstincts.com
Joahnna Barron of Athena's Salon and Spa
Willa Cline
Barb and everyone at Romance and Friends
Emily Cotler and the Waxcreative Design Team
Julia Quinn whose graciousness knows no bounds
Frances Drouin
The Paradies Shops
Lowenstein Yost and Associates
Susan Grimshaw
The incomparable Avon Books team, including but not limited to: Brian and the entire Merch Sales Team; Mike, Carla and the rest of the Field Sales Team; International Sales; Darlene Delillo; Adrienne, Nicole

and Julia in Marketing; Pam in Publicity; Lara and Laurie in Foreign Rights/Subrights; Tom and Gayle; Managing Editorial; Carrie, May, and most especially, Lyssa—so glad you're back!

Finally, my husband and children, who gave me the opportunity to follow my passions and meet my deadlines.

Chapter 1

Spring 1811
Ciudad Rodrigo, Spain

"**T**hank you for considering me for the privilege, sir," Major Marcus Dunn demurred with a smile. "But wild horses couldn't drag me back to London."

"Oh, but your talents are particularly suited to this mission, Dunn," Major General Henry Horace replied, seemingly not at all put out. Yet, two high spots of color tinged his pale, craggy face and his stormy hazel eyes were bright, indicating some discomfort at Marcus's refusal. "Proof of guilt must be ironclad, in this instance, and if what we suspect is true, then Wellington wants the nails hammered in the bastard's coffin."

"An excursion to London *is* a much-sought-after assignment these days." Marcus scratched his chin, pretending to consider it. "Say, Lieutenant Geoffrey's mother's been ill. I'm sure he'd jump at the chance for a visit home and it would be most appreciated by his family." *Espe-*

cially by his older brother, the influential Lord Derbyshire.

In his seven years of serving in the King's army against Napoleon, Marcus had learned to be firm but to deliver any refusals with a coating of honey and an alternative. That, and he'd mastered the task of procuring difficult-to-come-by items for the officers, ensuring that at one point or another a gentleman found himself in Marcus's debt. It made for a much smoother jaunt through the war.

"But you've such a talent for securing confessions," Horace replied cheerily, as if he were describing a gentlemanly sport.

Looking down, Marcus toyed with the white plum on his crimson shako. Once a mission was over, he tried not to reflect upon the lies, murder and treachery he'd faced. It was enough to make one feel soiled to the soul if you let it.

"And," Horace continued, "we're dealing with a certain peer of your acquaintance—"

Marcus looked up. "Willoughby's the officer you want, then. He knows every noble, their lineage, their connections—"

Horace frowned. "We don't need a diatribe on pedigree—"

"Then Kirkland's your man. In polite circles he harvests acquaintances like a dog collects fleas—"

"Yes and likes the tipple for breakfast—"

"Everyone knows that I'm not exactly one of the club, sir." Marcus tried to make his voice sound regretful that he wasn't born with a sterling pedigree. "I don't hunt—"

"But you deal well with targets of influence," Horace interrupted, raising a bent bony finger. "You don't let them browbeat you, and likewise don't try to bully them." Turning, the major general eased his wiry frame into the canvas chair behind his brown wooden desk.

The airless tent smelled of mold and damp and Marcus

wished they could open the flap. But Horace did not like the mountain air; he said it made his mind empty when he needed it full.

The major general scowled. "I still take grief over that Marquis Valdez disaster. Major Redstone was like a raging bull at a soiree." His brows lifted. "Remember that business with Viscount Brent's son, the shamming bugger? You managed that handily without a hint of the nasty affair tainting his innocent family. Stunningly well-done."

Marcus knew that he was being buttered for toast, but a gratifying swell of satisfaction rushed through him just the same.

"Then that foul Spanish lord. What was his name?" Horace scratched his head. "You know of whom I speak. The one who you ensured kept up his correspondence for Napoleon long after you'd turned him into our informer." His rheumy eyes twinkled as he nodded approvingly. "Capital win there, Major. I still say that misinformation is the most untried soldier in this war."

Marcus had to agree that was one of his better successes. But that didn't mean he was going to let Horace shuffle him off to the city of sycophants and timeservers. He was a field man who relished his freedom. Marcus tried not ruminating on his other reasons for avoiding London.

"What was that Spanish lord's name?" Horace's slate gray brows knotted in concentration as he stared at the far corner of the tent. The man often had the air of an absent-minded academic, with his thoughtful gazes and tendency to mutter to himself, but under that wiry gray hair was one of the sharpest minds Marcus had ever encountered. He would recognize sense in this matter, Marcus was sure.

"Was it Leone? Larose?"

Lorenz, Marcus provided, but only in his mind. Without even trying he could recall the face and charge of every last traitor who he'd helped experience Lady Justice. The nightmares didn't bother him much, not really. It was only the ones with the relatives demanding to know *why* that stole his slumber. *Ask your father, or brother,* he would say to those apparitions when he found himself awake in a chilly sweat. *I am only the blade; they laid their own heads on the guillotine.*

"Lorenz!" Horace smiled, deepening the rivers lining his mouth. "Knew I'd remember it eventually." His eyes scanned the multitude of papers scattered across his desk. "No, Major, you're the perfect man for this job. Especially since your father is the headmaster of Andersen Hall."

Marcus felt as if the world was shifting beneath his feet. "What the hell does my father . . . or a lousy orphanage have to do with the war?" He hated the pitch he heard in his voice.

"I'm sure you'll do your usual bang-up job, Major," Horace declared, reaching for a folded piece of paper. "Ah, here are your orders."

Marcus had spent seven years separating himself from the hornet's nest of his past; he wasn't about to get dragged back now. His mind raced almost as fast as his heartbeat, as he desperately scrambled for a way to dodge this bullet. Devastatingly, nothing came to him.

Reaching for the void he used in battle, the one that got him through the cannonball volleys, the musket shots and the screams, Marcus gritted his teeth. Dear Lord, he was going to have to explain. He hated having to explain. "There's something you need to know, sir—"

"You leave on the next ship." Horace picked up his gold-rimmed spectacles and a sheaf of papers. "Good day, Major."

Marcus's face burned, almost as much as his indignation at being dismissed. "If I could only enlighten—"

Horace kept reading. "You have your orders."

"But there are complications." Marcus barely kept the panic from his voice. "I'm the worst possible man for this assignment—"

"Nothing that you can't handle, I'm sure."

"But I can't go back there!"

"You will go where we determine it's best to send you. Dismissed, Major." Horace resumed reading once more, pointedly ignoring Marcus.

Marcus gripped his shako so tightly, the plume shook. "Please, sir." He swallowed. "I'm begging you, sir. Please listen—"

Looking up, the major general whipped off his glasses. "I've no more patience for your excuses, Major—"

"Please don't send me back to Andersen Hall!" Marcus hated begging, he hated explaining, and at this moment, he hated having to answer to someone who clearly didn't understand or even want to understand him. "I don't care if Wellington himself orders me to, I can't—"

"If I'm reading you right, Major," a deep aristocratic voice drawled from behind Marcus's shoulder, "then you are being insolent to a superior officer."

General Wellesley stood on the threshold of the tent, his black-winged eyebrow raised in inquiry. "The only question is: to which officer?"

"My lord!" Marcus snapped to attention, whipping his crumpled hat upon his head. His face burned hot and his heart hammered in his chest. He felt as if he'd been sucked into a macabre nightmare and couldn't figure out how to claw his way out.

"Major General." Wellington nodded.

Horace stood. "Good day, General Wellesley."

As usual, Wellington's uniform bespoke impeccable elegance, from the tips of his tall black riding boots, to the shining brass-buttoned red uniform coat, to his lofty gold-fringed red shako.

Wellington fixed his penetrating blue-gray gaze on Marcus. Marcus felt frozen, like a mouse caught in a hawk's sights. And a hawk is exactly what Wellington reminded Marcus of at that moment, with his sharp beak of a nose, blue-gray icy stare and predatory air. "Well, Major Dunn, what have you to say for yourself?" Wellington drawled.

Marcus began to sweat. If he was lucky, he might get off with a lashing. On the other hand, they couldn't send him to London if he was impaired. Staring at the far corner of the stained ivory tent, Marcus declared, "I apologize for any impertinence, sir."

"Apologizing is very good of you, Major Dunn," Wellington replied, waving for Horace to sit. "Given that a court-martial could be the alternative." He strode to the canvas chair next to the major general and sat. His shiny leather riding boots crinkled as he crossed his long legs. "And I wouldn't want you joining your friend Captain Hayes."

Marcus felt as if he'd been punched in the gut. "Hayes?"

An inscrutable look seemed to flash between the men. "I wasn't intending to tell him about it, my lord," Horace supplied.

"Well he's soon to find out anyway. Can't keep a blasted thing under wraps in this army."

Marcus reached for that abyss, but it remained appallingly out of reach. "What, exactly, happened to Captain Hayes?" His voice was thin.

"Well, first he struck a superior officer," Wellington replied.

"That was the challenge." Horace shook his head sadly. "The glove cuff across the face."

Marcus's mouth went dry as sand. Wellington strictly

prohibited dueling. Anyone caught was to face a court-martial, or worse if there was a fatality. "Who was it?"

"Blackstone," Horace explained. "No one likes the bugger but he *is* a major."

Months ago, Blackstone had wanted a Portuguese beauty named Paloma, but Paloma had preferred Captain Hayes. Ever since then, Blackstone had tried to make Luke Hayes's life a living hell. Marcus had thought that matters would have eased once Hayes had been transferred to Colonel Courtland's regiment, but apparently not.

"Courtland?" Marcus asked, reaching for any hope.

"Nothing for him to do. Captain Hayes was caught right in the middle of it."

Marcus distantly wondered if it was swords or pistols, but it didn't matter. "And how was Blackstone punished?"

The men exchanged a resigned glance. "He's been re-assigned."

So Blackstone had used his connections to save his hide. Not surprising since the man was a prig of the first order. His father was the Earl of Kenterling.

"But Hayes was the one to issue the challenge," Horace added, as if it made a difference. "So arguably he was . . . more culpable."

"Blackstone could have apologized," Marcus countered, knowing that it was futile. An apology would have ended the matter then and there. But Blackstone would have known that he'd likely get off.

"Blackstone apparently decided that an apology was not in order," Horace proclaimed. "Said that the lightskirt deserved what she got."

Something inside Marcus chilled. "What did Blackstone do?"

"We've wasted enough time on that matter." Wellington scowled. "I want to hear about Major Dunn's assignment."

"About that, sir—" Marcus began.

"At ease, Major." Horace shot him a quelling glance.

Marcus took the hint. He needed to settle down. His military career, if not his life, could be in jeopardy. He repositioned himself and turned, standing before both men but not relaxing by a hair. Somehow he needed to get Wellington to help him negotiate out of Horace's trap. But the general was not a man easily swayed. "If I may—"

"I just received a new shipment of Scotch whiskey, my lord," Horace interjected, reaching inside his desk and pulling out a snifter and three glasses.

Marcus couldn't decipher the major general's actions as a warning not to cross him or as a caveat to be circumspect with Wellington. Or both.

After giving a glass to Wellington, Horace pushed one across the desk. "Here, Major. You look a bit parched."

Woodenly, Marcus gulped the tipple. It tasted like sawdust, even though it was some of the finest Scotch whiskey one could buy this side of the Channel. He knew, since he was the one who'd procured it.

Sipping from his glass, Wellington watched Marcus over the rim. The man could take your measure in a half second and at the moment, Marcus felt as if his assessment was wanting. "Odd turn of event, you serving on the board of trustees of the orphanage from where you hail?"

On the Board of Trustees! Marcus almost dropped his glass. "That requires a vacancy, my lord. And a vote of the full board."

"Can you believe our luck?" Horace nodded. "A board member dropped dead a few months ago and they've yet to replace him. Fancy that."

The men smiled at each other and Marcus broke out in a sweat. They couldn't have manipulated that vacancy, could they? Marcus pushed away the notion; these were men of honor, not so brutally cold-hearted as to murder an innocent Englishman for their own ends. The thought bolstered his confidence.

"I am a good officer, my lord." Marcus kept his gaze fixed above Wellington's hat. "I've never forsaken a mission." *Stepped around one or two, but never disobeyed a direct order.* "And in this instance, there are facts that, once you know them, will make you reconsider my suitability for this mission."

"Then inform us," Wellington intoned, setting his glass aside. He rested his elbows on the canvas chair and steepled his hands before him. "Why our good judgment is in error, if you would."

Marcus heard the "our" and realized that this was Wellington's trap, not Horace's.

He was in the jakes for sure. Distantly, he wondered if they'd expected his protests. That Horace was to load the cannonball and Wellington to light the fuse. Problem was, Marcus didn't like explosions in his face. He worked to get his mounting anger under control; this skirmish wasn't over yet.

Marcus cleared his throat. "I left London on *exceedingly* bad terms, sir. My return would raise undue suspicion and imperil any chance an agent had of securing information." Not half-bad, he allowed himself, knowing in his heart he was not the man they needed. "Moreover, I was known as a hotheaded lad—"

"You don't say," Horace interjected with a smile.

Ignoring him, Marcus continued, "—who had no interest whatsoever in Andersen Hall. Truth be told, I was quite adamant when I left that I would *never* cross that threshold again. For me to suddenly take an interest in serving the institution is, if I may be frank, absurd. And would be viewed as suspect."

"Well, Horace," Wellington turned to the major general. "What do you think, now?"

"It's water under the bridge." Horace waved a hand. "We can craft a story where you almost died. The brush with death brought you around, made you see the error of your ways."

"But why would I take my leave from the army?"

"Your injuries, of course," Wellington supplied.

A chill slithered up his spine. "But I have no injuries, sir."

"Which shall it be, Dunn?" the general inquired, smiling like a cat that's cornered a mouse. "A hand or a leg?"

Horace opened his snuffbox, sniffed, then sneezed into his bandanna. "Don't give the man a seizure, sir. Dr. Wicket can be creative so he can easily pass for injured. Sergeant Tam will serve as his batman, so there should be no difficulty there." He looked to Marcus, his eyes red and watering. "Still, you will have to play the part, Major."

Marcus felt like the walls of the tent were closing in on him, smothering the air from his lungs. Yanking at his collar, he muttered, "I'm a terrible actor, sir."

The general wagged a lanky finger. "I like this close call with death story. Napoleon's lackeys tend to be sentimentalists." He turned to Marcus. "Any more issues, Major? The way you are going on, I might begin to think that you doubt Horace's competence."

Horace sent Wellington an irritated look, as if to say, *Why must you make this even more difficult than it has to be?*

"Isn't there someone closer, say at Whitehall, who can handle the mission?" Marcus desperately reached for straws.

"We need an outsider," Wellington intoned.

"Two agents have been compromised already," Horace supplied. "We cannot take any more chances."

Except with my life, Marcus thought bitterly, feeling inconsequential to these men. "But what about my father? As headmaster of Andersen Hall, his challenges will raise all sorts of trouble for this plan, rendering it precarious from the start."

"I have to agree with your assessment, there," Wellington replied. "Which is why I wrote to him and informed him of your return and the reason for it."

The world swayed in and out of focus for Marcus. Blackness swirled at the edges of his vision and for a moment he wondered if he'd heard correctly.

"We needed your father's help," Horace admitted. "Or else the plan would never have hatched. Luckily he and General Wellesley are well acquainted."

"And your father, in his typical fashion, has taken the charge like any good soldier." Wellington added smugly. "The man's positively a saint, with his good works for London's street children. Can't say no to the man when he comes calling for donations, but who would wish to with the admirable job he does running Andersen Hall? I'm just glad that it's not me supervising those unfortunate children." He grimaced. "Although there are times when I'm overseeing a pack of unfortunates of another variety."

"You wrote to my father?" Marcus knew that he should not be shouting at his commanding officers, but he was a hairbreadth past caring. His breath was shuddering and his hands were quaking so violently he thought he might explode. "Without even asking me you contacted my father about my coming back?"

"Now see here, Major." Horace stood.

"I put my life at risk, willingly, every single day!" Marcus snarled. "And yet you can't be satisfied with my blood sacrifice alone. You must dig into my personal affairs as if you own me? Well, you don't own me! No one does!"

"Major Dunn!" Wellington stood.

"You can take your bloody assignment—"

Wellington glared. "I do not suffer insubordination lightly! You will do exactly as we say or bear the consequences!"

"I'd sooner dance a jig for Napoleon than be a puppet on your strings!" Marcus ripped his insignia off his coat, thrust it on the desk and stalked from the tent, knowing that he had just signed his own death warrant. And he didn't even care.

Chapter 2

Spring 1811
London, England

Catherine Miller stepped gingerly over the threshold to Andersen Hall Orphanage, cautious even after having crossed the very same doorsill a thousand times before. Although her leg was much better than it had ever been, she always feared that it would give out on her at an embarrassing moment. It was a constant reminder to be cautious in all circumstances.

Now was the dinner hour, the perfect opportunity for a moment of solitude on the veranda. Dusk had fallen and the air was thick with the ring of crickets and the shadows of impending darkness. The air smelled of musty leaves and approaching spring . . . and the cloying scent of smoke. Catherine surmised who must be puffing on the end of that pipe. This was her opportunity to know once and for all if her suspicions about Headmaster Dunn's health were correct.

"It must be hard to be Mrs. Nagel," Catherine remarked, as she crossed the wooden porch and joined Dr. Michael Winner by the banister. They watched the stout gray-clothed matron progress across the courtyard from the orphanage's main building to her residence. Even in the gathering darkness you could not mistake the matron's gray topknot, snowy cap and white apron.

"Why do you say that?" Dr. Winner asked, chewing on the tip of his black pipe and narrowing his eyes to watch Mrs. Nagel. He was a tall, portly fellow with a tuft of brown hair ringing his receding hairline. He had kind eyes and loose lips that slipped easily into a smile. He'd been the doctor to every child and staff member at Andersen Hall for as long as Catherine had been there. He'd been the one to try to reset her leg upon her arrival at the orphanage ten years before.

"She must discipline the children," Catherine explained, "keep the kitchen running, the orphanage cleaned, and," she continued boldly, "all the while the man she loves above all others is dying."

The doctor's russet brows lifted in inquiry, but his gaze was veiled.

"There is no need to pretend with me, sir. I know that Headmaster Dunn is ill."

Winner was silent a long moment, watching puffs of white drift out of his mouth and upward. "What makes you believe that?"

"I have been acting as his secretary now for two years. It's hard not to notice that he is wrapping up his affairs. He's been uncommonly secretive. Making all sorts of confidential arrangements with the board of trustees. And he is corresponding with General Wellesley, I mean Viscount Wellington."

"So Wellesley's a viscount now? I did not know that."

"And a general—"

"Well, regardless of what you call him, he is a patron, as you well know. It's not unnatural for the headmaster to correspond—"

"Wellington is on the Peninsula, for heaven's sake. He's a bit occupied with the war. The only reason I can surmise Headmaster Dunn would correspond with him is because of Marcus."

Winner pursed his lips. "One can't be too certain of these things . . ."

"Please, Doctor. Just tell me, is he dying?"

"Not that I'm aware of."

None too steady on her feet, Catherine let out a long breath. Relief didn't come close to describing her feelings. Headmaster Dunn's generosity of spirit, moral fiber and clever humor drew others to him simply so they could orbit in his radiance. His loss would be . . . immeasurable.

"Thank the heavens," she breathed, pressing her hand to her heart. "Andersen Hall, the children . . . I'm so relieved."

"But," Winner added, tapping his pipe on the edge of the railing and frowning, "something is going on."

She sighed. "So long as he isn't dying, I almost don't care."

"Well, I am more curious than a fox teased with a scent of hen."

"So that's why you've been hanging about these last few weeks?"

His cheeks tinged pink. "I am the official physician, and on the board . . ."

"We love having you near, you know that, sir." Seeing his discomfort and suspecting the reason, she squeezed his arm. "Don't take Dunn's secrecy to heart, Doctor. You know him; he holds his cards close to his chest until he has a winning hand."

He scowled, looking off into the descending twilight. "Annoying habit, actually."

"But an effective one, as we both well know."

"He should have at least confided in you. You certainly wouldn't tell anyone his secrets."

Her smile was bittersweet. She didn't have anyone to tell.

They stared off into the darkening trees, the silence between them comfortable, yet sober.

Winner scratched his chin. "So Dunn is corresponding with Wellington . . ."

"I shouldn't have said anything, sir." Now it was her turn to blush. "Nor should I have pried. It's none of my affair."

"You were worried." He pursed his lips. "Did you ask Dunn about it?"

"Of course." Quoting Dunn, she explained, "It's the straightest way to an answer."

"What did he say?"

Her cheeks heated and she crossed her arms, feeling foolish. "He assured me, with great emphasis I might add, that Marcus was not dead."

"Ah, child. Your infatuation was no secret."

Oh, she had been so green. So idiotic. Granted, she had not really understood her feelings. The irrational desire to jump and hide whenever Marcus Dunn had strode past. The impulsive yearnings to brush the dark curl from his forehead when he sat near her in the dining hall. How many hours had she wasted staring longingly at his broad shoulders in chapel? She wanted to die for all of the heated fantasies of his dreamy azure eyes, and those smooth peach-colored lips, too sumptuous for any lad rightfully to own. Her solitary saving grace was that no one knew about the secret dreams that had lulled her to sleep at night. It seemed, however, that they were the only things that had gone above notice.

"It was ages ago." She exhaled loudly, trying to expunge the humiliating memories from her mind. "You'd think that everyone would have forgotten it by now. I certainly have."

A sudden thought jolted her. "You don't think he's married?"

"Who?" Winner asked, an innocent grin splitting his face.

She hadn't realized that she'd spoken aloud and now she had trapped herself into a corner. Slowly, Catherine cleared her throat. "Marcus. Perhaps that is the reason for Headmaster Dunn's correspondence?"

"Then why the secrecy?" Winner shook his head. "No, Dunn has always feared that Marcus was not one for commitment. He would be delighted to share such a happy event."

Catherine tried not to let her relief show. Somehow if Marcus had married, it would mean that she would never have a chance . . . But that was ridiculous wasn't it? He'd hardly known that she existed when they'd lived under the same roof. Now he was across the ocean and worlds away. Just considering the possibility was patently absurd. Still, she was reassured.

"Mrs. Nagel says that Marcus swore he'd never return to Andersen Hall," Catherine stated slowly. "What happened to make him leave in such anger?"

"That, my dear, is one of those sleeping dogs I let lie." Winner shifted uneasily. "Dunn has never spoken of it, and he likely never will."

"It grieves him still. He tries to hide it, but on May 9 every year he sits in the cemetery the whole of the day. He does not eat or take water. Simply sits by his wife's grave."

Winner's brow furrowed. "Mrs. Dunn died in the winter. A lingering fever. Why May 9?"

"Marcus's birthday."

"What a terrible shame." He shook his head. "And Marcus is more stubborn than a three-headed bull. So I doubt we will ever see Marcus Dunn cross this doorstep again. More's the pity."

Something on the edge of the green near the chapel moved, catching Catherine's attention. Her eyes narrowed. "Did you see that, sir?"

Dr. Winner stuck his pipe into his mouth and leaned against the porch railing, squinting. "I have trouble seeing in this dratted twilight. Plays tricks on my eyes."

"Everyone is supposed to be in the dining hall having dinner," she muttered distractedly. Straining to hear, she could not discern anything above the birds serenading the dusk and the leaves rustling in the trees surrounding the orphanage.

There it was again, a movement near a ring of bushes. A pale-haired youth popped up from behind the hedge. Recognizing the fourteen-year-old lad who belonged to that blond mane, Catherine wondered where his cohorts were. The hedge shivered so violently that Catherine could almost see the leaves shudder from across the lawn.

"Excuse me, sir." Lifting her skirts, she quickly descended the steps and strode across the lawn, doing her best not to be heard. She'd grown quite adept at making herself move noiselessly, the better to help her deal with naughty children.

"Kirby Jones!" she cried, catching sight of the rascal.

The sandy-haired lad stopped midstep, hunched his shoulders and turned. "Ah, good evening, miss."

His voice was so "I'm innocent" as to assure her that he

was up to no good. Moreover, where Kirby Jones was, so were his puckish cronies, all aged around thirteen or fourteen, and all as mischievous as two-month puppies.

"Come out, boys," she demanded. "This instant."

Slowly, forms emerged from the shrubs. First fourteen-year-old Jack O'Malley with his shocking red hair, freckled face and truculent scowl. Next, raven-haired, tea-skinned, sheepish twelve-year-old Benjamin Bourke. He was always hanging about the older boys. Followed by . . .

"Jared Miller!" She wagged her finger at her brother. "I thought I told you to stay away from these boys!"

"Bloody hell, Catherine . . ." Jared mumbled, his pink cheeks obvious even in the descending darkness.

"Don't you curse at me, young man. You know better than this . . ." She glared at the lads, young men, really, and crossed her arms. "Why aren't you at dinner?"

"We were done—" Jack began.

"Then you should have been helping clean up," Catherine interjected.

"Yes, miss," Benjamin replied, shooting his comrades a telling glance. "We can go right now if you wish . . ."

"Yes," Jared added, shuffling toward the main house. "We'll be on our way back to the kitchens . . ."

The lads seemed so intent on leaving the area. What had they been up to? They were about fifteen paces from the chapel, but did not seem focused on the building. They appeared more interested in getting away from the hedge . . . Or in getting *her* away from the hedge.

"Stop right there." Slowly, Catherine skirted around the bushes and looked around. There, in the twilight, a pear-shaped gray jug sat shoved under a shrub.

"She's as bad as bloody Mrs. Nagel," Benjamin muttered sourly.

"No, she's worse," Jack retorted. "She's smarter."

"And she's my sister," Jared finished with a slight groan.

Circling back to the lads, she uncorked the jug and sniffed. It felt as if a thousand bee stings were piercing her eyes and nose, it was so wretchedly potent. "What is this?" she cried, slamming the stopper back in and blinking back harsh tears.

The lads shrugged, almost in unison.

"Better yet," she grimaced, "where did you get it?"

Silence. Apparently, only the crickets were chirping willingly this evening.

Shaking her head, she sighed. "You might as well tell me now, for I will only make it worse for you if I discover the truth on my own."

Kirby stared off into the distance, feigning innocence. Jack and Ben looked to Jared. Jared was busy looking down at his scuffed boots.

Jack whispered to Jared, "It can't be worse than the last punishment."

"Oh, cleaning the chapel's eaves of bats and droppings is nothing compared to what you will have to endure next," Catherine assured them.

A scoffing noise emanated from Jared's glowering lips. She might have considered boxing his ears if he wouldn't have hated her forever for embarrassing him in front of his friends.

Well," she stated slowly, "if I do not see the appropriate level of cooperation, I might be forced to ask Headmaster Dunn to reassess your training duties."

"No!" Kirby shrieked. He took great pleasure in working as a soap maker in Mr. Shafer's shop. Who would have known that the lad was a born salesman for perfumed wares? Headmaster Dunn, of course.

"You can't do that!" Jared cried. "It's not fair!" Although Jared was not well pleased with his role assisting the Latin tutor, he clearly knew his friends' positions meant the world to them.

She shook her head. "You all are well aware that Headmaster Dunn does not allow spirits of any kind on the grounds. He will be most disappointed in your actions, *should he learn of them . . .*"

The boys exchanged a look. They worshiped Dunn, as wolves did a pack leader.

"It was Mr. Graves," Jack mumbled.

Catherine frowned. It seemed the gardener, Mr. Graves, was breaching the rules of Andersen Hall. Knowing Headmaster Dunn, the man would likely lose his position, which was a shame, really, after so many years of service. She wondered if Mr. Graves would think it worth it in the end. But that was not her problem. Protecting the children and keeping the orphanage running smoothly was.

"Do you all confirm that Mr. Graves gave you the . . . whatever is in this jug?" she asked.

"He didn't give it to us." Kirby kicked the dirt. "He bloody sold it."

Overlooking the profanity, she asked, "How much?"

"Two shillings." Jack looked up, interest gleaming in his brown eyes. "A deal, he said."

"You were cheated," she replied brusquely. "And now you have nothing but a punishment and empty pockets to show for it."

"The bugger!" Kirby cried. "I used my last pence on that stuff!"

Catherine sighed, seeing the sense of betrayal flash across their faces. What they did was wrong, but hadn't they already paid with their lost coin? Lesson learned, perhaps?

Jack shoved his cap back on his head, imploring, "So you won't tell the headmaster?"

"I am beholden to tell him about Mr. Graves's infraction. But that doesn't mean that I have to name names."

The lads' shoulders sagged with obvious relief.

"So what's our punishment?" Kirby asked, scratching his privates.

Ignoring his indelicacy, Catherine considered the situation for a moment. She needed to remain firm with them, but could hardly fashion something onerous at this point. "I will let you know once I've come up with one that suits the offense."

Kirby groaned.

Jack muttered something unintelligible under his breath.

"Go back to the dining hall," Catherine instructed. "I'm sure that Mrs. Burton would appreciate some assistance with scouring the pots."

Slowly, the lads shuffled off, sulking.

Catherine eyed her brother. "Jared, you remain here."

Her brother stopped and waited, watching his friends drift off as if he would have eaten his own arm to have been able to join them.

Chapter 3

~ ❧❧ ~

"**W**hat is the matter with you, Jared?" Catherine demanded of her younger brother once the youths were out of earshot. "You continue to flout my instructions about those lads. They're no good for you and drag you into trouble at every turn."

"But they're my friends," he ground out.

"They are not in your league and you know it."

"Don't be such a snob."

Frustration filled her so powerfully she yearned to yank on his golden brown hair and scream in his ear until he finally understood her. Instead, she gritted her teeth. "I'm not talking about social status. I'm talking about intelligence, prospects—"

"Just because they don't like books or music doesn't mean that they aren't honorable."

"It's more than that and you know it. You might be living here amongst the other charges, but you are expected to behave in a manner befitting your station."

23

He crossed his arms, glowering. "What station is that, Catherine?"

"Don't be a buffoon." She lowered her voice. "You are Baron Coleridge and you need to start acting like it. How can you expect to travel in higher circles if you have the manners of a street hooligan?"

"I thought you said I was supposed to fit in." His voice was taunting.

"Don't take my logic and twist it around." She scowled, irritated. "Not announcing to the world that you are a peer of the realm does not mean that you are at liberty to act like a ruffian. It's beneath you. It's beneath all of the boys here, in fact, but they don't know better. You do."

Tense silence encased them as she waited for a response, some semblance of responsibility for his actions. Her patience was met only by the crackle of shrubbery whipping in an agitated wind.

Jared crossed his arms, pouting like a three-year-old instead of a lad of fourteen. "Can I go now?"

Her hand began to throb and she looked down, realizing that she was clutching the jug handle in a viselike grip. She set it down on the grass and crossed her arms, trying to make sense of the only flesh-and-blood relative that she acknowledged. "I don't know what to do with you, Jared. I try to give you the opportunities to be the best man you can be. To be prepared for the next phase in your life. The extra money for books, the tutor whom I can hardly afford—"

"What if I don't want it?"

"Don't want what?" she cried exasperated. "The tutor?"

"Any of it."

"What *do* you want then?"

His hands fisted by his sides. "You to stop yanking on my tails."

"Tails?" Frustration made her voice pitch up. "What on earth are you talking about?"

"Forget it," he muttered as if she were the one speaking gibberish.

She looked around, then grabbed his arm, heaving him into the side door of the chapel and into the vestibule. No one should be in the sanctuary at this hour. "I am trying to give you the education that Mother and Father would have *wanted* you to have. That you would have had if the blasted Caddyhorns had not been so wretchedly insidious," she whispered harshly. "You need to be prepared for when you take your rightful place in Society as Baron Coleridge."

"Why, Catherine?"

She sputtered a moment, flabbergasted by his obtuseness. "Why, because it's your just due."

"And how the bloody hell do you suppose that fantasy is going to happen?" His voice was full of contempt. "We are orphans, Catherine. We have no means of stopping the Caddyhorns or reclaiming our money. My title is nothing more than an empty designation, one that I heard the Caddyhorns were going to get anyway, since everyone thinks that the real Baron Coleridge is dead."

"They *presume* that you are dead, but they cannot have the title if you are alive . . ."

He glared, not even bothering to state the obvious paradox. They could not let Uncle Dickey and Aunt Frederica Caddyhorn, their legal guardians, know of Jared's existence or they might try to resurrect their plan of locking her brother in Bedlam. Or, worse, Catherine wouldn't put it past them to try to kill Jared. Yet, if she and Jared did not speak up, the title might be declared vacant and all would be lost.

Jared shrugged. "At this point I don't see the purpose in banging our heads against the wall for a dream that will never become a reality. It's gone, all of it. The money, the title, life as nobility. Accept your lot and learn to live with it. I know I have."

His pessimism shocked her. He had made feeble protests in the past but now he seemed so *certain* of failure. It almost broke her heart.

"Mother and Father would never have given up," she replied carefully. "They would not wish for us to either."

"Mother and Father aren't here now. Nor were they ever forced to deal with life served up on a chipped platter. They were born to a station of privilege and lived a life of plenty."

"You say it as if it's a crime."

"Well, they never had to deal with the things we've had to face. Don't try pretending you don't think of the Caddyhorns every day, Catherine. I know I do whenever I see you limp."

Involuntarily, her hand flitted to her leg, broken during their escape ten years before. Thank heavens only she had suffered from the fall; a rhododendron bush had saved four-year-old Jared.

"I don't know that in similar circumstances Mother and Father wouldn't have stopped pining for fantasy either." Jared scowled, anger marring his boyishly handsome features. "Face it, Cat. This is our lot now. Going up against the Caddyhorns is a fool's game. You've tried and failed before, as you will if you try again."

"I don't agree," she snapped, crossing her arms as if to ward off his charges. "We simply need to bide our time."

"Until what?" he scoffed, pain haunting those familiar gray Coleridge eyes. "It's been ten years already. We have no money. We have no allies. Hell, you wouldn't even tell Headmaster Dunn, the man who knows every gilded family in London!"

She let out a long breath. "Dunn can't help us until you are older. To tell him now will only expose him to all sorts of legal challenges of guardianship from the Caddy-horns." Moreover, Headmaster Dunn could be bullheaded and unpredictable when it came to matters of "justice" and Catherine didn't want to take any chances. "We agreed ten years ago, anonymity is our staunchest ally."

"I didn't agree. You decided," he scoffed. Turning away, he muttered under his breath, "You're just afraid."

"Of what?" she almost screeched, yanking him to face her.

"Of trusting anyone."

Her mouth opened, then closed. "Why, that's the most preposterous rubbish I've ever heard. I love Headmaster Dunn like a dear father. I admire him more than any man on earth. I trust him with my life, our lives in fact."

"Well, maybe it's not *just* that," he shrugged. "You're also afraid he'll try to set you up in Society . . . and that you'll fumble." He said it as if it was a *fait accompli*.

"That's . . . that's . . ."

"For good reason," he continued mercilessly. "Look at yourself, Catherine. You're a spinster, long on the shelf and thin in the purse who has no connections and hardly a decent dress to her name." His tone was scathing. "I'm sure you'd be the toast of the town."

She stared at him a long moment, feeling an ache in her chest that her brother could be so spiteful. She *was* getting on, but she was only two-and-twenty years old. She still had time yet, didn't she? But for what? She'd always known her life would have no romantic storybook ending, but she'd be damned if she let Jared lose his chances because of the Caddyhorns.

Sticking his hands in his pockets, he scoffed, "Face it, Catherine. Reclaiming my title is a fool's quest. If you need the hope to get you through your lackluster existence, then by all means keep it up. But don't pretend that you are doing it for me. And don't try to force me to be someone I'm not."

"When did you become so cruel?" she whispered, wondering who had stolen her dear baby brother and put this monster in his place.

He strode off into the now darkened evening, calling over his shoulder, "About the same time you started acting like a nagging witch."

In the shadow of the chapel arbor, Headmaster Uriah Dunn's fury was so white-hot he was quaking. He had come to the sanctuary for some quiet contemplation when he thought it would be vacant. He had not meant to eavesdrop, but had heard snippets of Catherine and Jared's argument. Not wishing to intrude on the family squabble, he had stayed in the shadows, ready to skirt the building and head back to the dining hall. His steps had frozen as the truth barreled into him harder than any cannonball.

Jared Miller was Baron Coleridge! Catherine a gentleman's daughter, a lady of quality.

He'd always had his suspicions about Catherine and Jared's origins. But as a rule, he never pressed children about their pasts. Where was the point when there was no going back? But for Catherine and Jared it was not about choices, but of crimes against them. Crimes where reparation was long overdue.

He clearly recalled their arrival almost ten years before. She'd been twelve, shaking with fear and pain from her broken leg. Dr. Winner had tried his best, but she'd been walking on the broken leg for so long . . .

Dunn's fists clenched. He could only imagine the terror

she must have felt to have run away in the dead of winter, to have traveled on a broken limb . . . Jared had been only four . . . To drive off helpless children into the cruel world like that . . . when there was family . . . means . . .

Caddyhorn. The name seared itself onto Dunn's list of scoundrels to be dealt with. Lamentably, that list was growing a bit long these days. But Dunn was not one for misgivings when it came to correcting wrongs. He would do what he must to see Justice wear her gilded crown of glory.

His first order of business was to safeguard Jared's title. That could be done without anyone knowing of Jared's existence. Scratching his chin, he nodded. Digging up dirty skeletons and whispering them into the right ears was a nice way to stifle a title petition. Somehow Dunn doubted that it would be too difficult to unearth misdeeds regarding the Caddyhorns, given Catherine and Jared's experience with the clan.

But what to do about the children who seemed unprepared to claim their rightful places?

No matter how much Jared maintained that he was content with their lot, Dunn knew the lie for what it was: fear. He was afraid to face the Caddyhorns. He was frightened of going into Society after living the majority of his life in an orphanage. Moreover, Jared was terrified of failure. For him it was easier to give up than to try and not be up to snuff. For all of its disadvantages, Andersen Hall was safe. To Jared, the thought of leaving his home with little promise of success made him want to surrender from the start.

Jared could not be alone in his misgivings, about going back into Society, Dunn recognized. Catherine had to be anxious about the prospect of facing the *ton*'s whispers and the scandal of having lived penniless in an orphanage, especially as an unmarried lady almost past marriageable age. But knowing her, she wouldn't let it stop her, especially if her conduct could help her baby brother. She would do anything for him, her sense of duty overwhelming concern for herself.

Such sense of sacrifice was not healthy, Dunn knew. And could only lead to discord. Catherine would give up everything for her brother, but would expect him to make the world of himself in return. Jared would resent his sister's demands and flout her at every turn. It was a match destined for failure unless someone moved to stop the cycle of antagonism. This, Dunn knew, because the interaction was disturbingly familiar, given his fractious relationship with his son Marcus.

Dunn sighed, feeling like an old warhorse trying to learn a new march. Staring up at the moonless night, he lamented his mistakes with his only son. And bemoaned the fact that he might never have the chance to rectify them.

His recent hopes had been dashed that morning when he'd received a cryptic missive from Wellington saying that there was a problem and that Marcus might not make it back to London after all. The tone of the letter did not sound optimistic.

Doubt plagued Dunn's consciousness as a vulture circles a carcass. He hadn't expected Marcus to rush home after their terrible parting or to receive his father with open arms. All cannot be water under the bridge when you've had so many years of strife. But Dunn had hoped . . . given the chance . . . they could meet on fresh ground.

Part of him prayed the threat regarding Marcus's original mission still existed so that Wellington would send him home; part of him prayed that there was no menace at all.

Dunn sighed, feeling suddenly very old. "My prayers seem to conflict with each other these days," he muttered. If only one or two of them might be answered.

Chapter 4

"**B**last," Catherine muttered to herself, then sneezed in the dusty room. She tried to ignore her irritation at being inside on a glorious day like today, cleaning a closet, no less. But it was her own fault, really. She'd put off asking someone to do the tedious task for four days, wanting to spend time with Jared before his departure.

Catherine had been surprised by Headmaster Dunn's sudden decision to send Jared along with his tutor to a family in Reigate and wondered if it had anything to do with the misadventure involving Gardener Graves's spirits. She had not mentioned any of the lads involved, but the headmaster had decided to send Jared off the very next day and had packed him and his tutor off just four days later. Moreover, the headmaster had assured her that the Hartzes were a family of quality and that they would be a good influence on Jared.

Headmaster Dunn had to know about the spirits, she decided. But in his usual capable fashion, he'd figured out a way to calm the situation and teach Jared a lesson. Although glad for the opportunity this mischief had provided for her brother, she couldn't help but miss him. For all of his sulking and insults, this was their first parting in over ten years.

Now he was off to Reigate, most of the staff was away on an excursion with the children and she was left cleaning dusty closets on the nicest day in ages.

Sighing, Catherine dug through the trunk of clothing, seeing an aspect of Headmaster Dunn that was not usually apparent. As she had always suspected, the man was a sentimentalist. Yet he hid that side of himself, appearing in public as a paragon of principle with not a sappy bone in his body. It was a good tactic, she realized, given how many people—especially in the *ton*—saw sentimentalists as weak-willed, inconsistent and romantic.

Feeling something long, she tugged the fabric free. A muted jingle rang in the air. Leading strings, of all things, knotted around a baby's rattle. Unwinding the rattle, she shook it gently. A clear tinkle rang in the small closet. She smiled, fingering the plaything and finding ridges and dents marring the handle. Marcus's tooth marks, she supposed.

She gently placed the rattle back in the chest and the cloth beside her. Undoubtedly Marcus would want none of these items, dare he ever deign to return to Andersen Hall. He had never been interested in anything of a sentimental nature, as different from his father as oil and water.

Whereas Headmaster Dunn was steady as a rock, Marcus had been more like the wind—free-spirited and always up for a storm. Catherine had secretly envied his devil-may-care attitude, longing for a bit of abandon herself. Marcus had only lost that lightheartedness when he'd gone up against his father. Oh how they'd fought. The walls fairly shook from their tempestuous arguments. Marcus had always completed his punishments with a fiery intensity, then he would sulk for days. His darkly handsome looks and brooding mien drew the girls like barnacles to a ship's bow. It was enough to make one ill. Catherine had never joined them, always watching Marcus from afar. Thank heavens, he'd never given any of the chits the attention they'd longed for. Including her.

But he'd been away in the military for seven years, and according to Mrs. Nagel, had sworn never to return to Andersen Hall. Not that it mattered. She would never marry, or do much else, it seemed. She would shrivel and die, a decrepit old spinster . . .

Irritated by her morose thoughts, Catherine shoved aside the trunk with greater force than she'd intended and it crashed into something behind it. A cloud of dust swam in the air. She sneezed so loudly that her ears rang. Pressing her white apron to her nose, she reached forward and righted the chest, only then noticing a piece of wood wedged between the angled ceiling and the wall. Lifting the candle for better light, she realized that behind the lumber rested a trunk, jammed into the small space, purposefully difficult to access.

Curious, she raised the candle, careful not to let it near anything flammable. Setting it down, she yanked at the board, ripping it from its post. Then, positioning herself on hands and knees, she leaned forward, trying to grab the chest. It would not budge. She stood, leaning over, trying for better purchase.

"Now that's a sight to make a man weep," a deep voice murmured from behind.

Catherine straightened so quickly her head smashed into the pitched wall of the closet.

Rubbing her aching skull, she turned, glaring. "Blast you, Pres."

"Lovely to see you, too, Cat," her childhood tormentor replied easily.

As usual Prescott Devane sported a beautifully tailored coat, today in primrose yellow, that outlined his broad form. He was not bulky like the laborer his father was supposed to have been. Those firm-muscled thighs, narrow hips and broad shoulders he'd grown into reminded Catherine of an equestrian's build more than a manual worker's. He must have had more of his mother in him. She supposedly had been a lady of station who had fallen upon hard times before dying of a disease of the lungs. Prescott never spoke of his life before the orphanage, so it was hard to know.

"I've been off at a friend's country house," he drawled. "I hadn't realized how long it's been."

"Never long enough as far as you're concerned," she retorted, but her tone was good-natured.

"It's wretchedly dusty in here." Prescott eyed the chests and crates with a look of dismissal. "It's no wonder your skin is turning to ash. You stay inside on a glorious day like today."

She bristled at the comment about her complexion. "The headmaster needed the closet cleaned."

"Why, it's spring, for heaven's sake," he interrupted, yanking a handkerchief from the pocket of his primrose yellow coat and waving it about like a dandy. His musk perfume was an unwelcome addition in the dusty space. "It's depraved to be inside today."

"Headmaster Dunn said that it needed to be cleaned out posthaste," she replied, trying to make it sound important.

"As always, stiff upper lip and such, our Cat. Never one

for making waves. But have you no thought for your delicate health? Like an exquisite blossom, you need sunshine, fresh air . . ."

"Leave your hogwash for your lady friends, Pres." She
shook her head. Prescott had been a monster as a child,
plaguing her with his antics. Now, she simply attributed
them to the frolics of a troubled lad. There had been a
fierceness to him, not a meanness of spirit but a steely determination that had set him apart from many of the other
boys. When he fixed his mind on something, he moved
heaven and earth to see it done. Problem was, he'd set his
hat on becoming a dandy and living a high life, and he'd
achieved it with aplomb. The ladies loved him, and unaccountably, he didn't seem to mind when they lavished him
with gifts and supported him. The man was a *cicisbeo*, a
Gallant to married women. And, astoundingly, he was
quite open about it.

Wrinkling his nose, Prescott patted it with his handkerchief. "You can't deny you'd rather be outside, even if it is
just reading one of your tomes."

She glared at him. "If I stop chattering with you, I
might actually finish my work and make it outside before
night."

"Take a breather, Cat," he pleaded. "Just a few minutes
on the porch—"

"Unlike some other people, I finish what I start," she
retorted making reference to his training with Master
Grim, the blacksmith. Just as Prescott could apply himself with determination, he could just as easily resolve *not*
to do something. And once his determination was set, it
was intractable.

He leaned against his ebony cane, his eyes darkening.
"You know, you're about as much fun as a boil spearing."

"Ew." She made a face.

"I know." He grimaced. "It's on my mind since I attended one yesterday."

"Don't tell me they sell tickets to those things now?"

"I was the one holding the poor lady's hand. It really was—"

"Stop." She held up her hands. "I don't wish to know."

"I've got no one to spill my troubles to—"

She wedged her feet into the corner and grasped the chest. "Cease prattling and help me move this box."

"I cannot."

"Why not?"

"New breeches. I dare not dirty them, even for you, my dear."

"Do stop being such a Jack-a-dandy, Pres. You know I can't stand the façade."

After a moment, he shrugged. In the dim light she could see the transformation come upon him like a curtain dropping at the end of a performance. His shoulders squared. His face darkened. The look of frivolous disdain disappeared and his jaw set with its familiar determined line. His bearing shifted from indolent to more like a boxer's stance. That was the Prescott she'd grown up with, more ready for a brawl than a ball.

Catherine thought him more appealing in his true mien, but could understand how others might not see it so. Still, she was always astounded at how easy it was for Prescott to trade on his looks. Astounding, because he had been such an unattractive youth and was now considered quite the blade. His once carrot hair had darkened to a deep sable brown with only a hint of red. His pudgy, freckled face had thinned to a chiseled golden hue. His once fat lips now softened the angles of his face with lush sensuality. No one could have foretold how handsome a man Prescott was to become, least of all Catherine.

Prescott shook his head. "You know, Cat—"

"I do wish you'd stop calling me that."

"Certainly. I've noticed, Cat, you've grown quite Mrs. Nagel-ish of late."

Pressing her hand to her heart, she cried, "Why, Prescott, that's probably the nicest thing you've ever said to me."

"I didn't mean it as a compliment."

"I know, but I am choosing to take it as one. Mrs. Nagel is a saint to put up with all that she does."

"It's hard to love a saint."

"Is it easier to love a fraud?"

His face froze and for a moment she feared that she'd struck harder than she'd intended. Banter was one thing, injuring a friend, another.

Suddenly he laughed, a deep, resounding guffaw that practically shook the walls of the small room. "Oh, how I've missed you, Cat. The country air was not nearly as refreshing as seeing you." She was pleased he didn't drop his cultured diction. They'd worked on his elocution for years and it seemed quite natural to him now.

"I'm glad that I amuse you," she chided. "Now, please will you help me move this box?"

"Only for you, Cat," he replied, still smiling. Setting down his hat and cane, he moved to the other side of the trunk. "Allow me." With a hard shove, the trunk slipped loose, followed by a jarring bang of wood on wood.

"What the devil?"

Where the trunk had been, there was a long dark rectangle, about the size of an open newspaper, cut into the wall. On the side corner of the rectangle a board hung by a single bare nail, the other nails having fallen loose.

"A secret compartment in an orphanage closet?" Prescott scratched his auburn mane. "Jewels? Banknotes?"

Hope rose in her chest. The orphanage needed funds

badly. Could this be the answer to her prayers? "I wonder how long it's been there." She bit her lip. "And does Head-master Dunn know about it?"

"He would have said something, if he knew," Prescott insisted. "Did he?"

"Not a word. In fact, he had only wanted the front of the closet cleared out."

"That's our Cat, always the diligent worker," Prescott teased. "Ask for 'A,' get 'A to Z.'" Scratching his chin, he asked, "Could it be Festus's war booty, perhaps?"

Catherine grimaced, recalling stories of the vicious for-mer headmaster of Andersen Hall. "The sergeant major left a long time ago . . ."

"And in a frightful hurry . . ."

Anxious, she leaned forward, tugging at the loose board. It ripped free from its setting with surprising ease.

"Look, it's rotted through." He pointed to the wood. "It must have been the damp."

Tossing away the board, Catherine perched on her knees before the opening and peered into the gloom.

She felt a tug at her apron strings. "Hands off, Prescott."

The tugging stopped. "Spoilsport."

Prescott pushed his head beside hers. "Ugh. Smells like mold and rotted leaves, and it's clammy to boot. I pray you are not thinking of going in there."

She turned to him, chagrined. "The Prescott I grew up with would have jumped through that hole by now, with-out a care for the fusty air or the dirt on his breeches."

He squinted into the darkness. "The Prescott you knew was an atrocious little monster."

"I don't know that I like the changes that civilizing you has wrought. Where is your sense of adventure?"

"I leave that for the bedchamber, darling. If you'd like—"

"I'd sooner have my teeth extracted." Thrusting her head through the opening, she held her breath and tried to discern anything in the small space. *Dear Lord, please let there be something here to help the children*. The head-master had been trying to keep her from the truth, but she was no fool: The orphanage was perilously low on funds. The war was putting a strain on High Society's pockets, or so many patrons claimed.

"Ugh. It smells awful in here."

"Take this." A linen handkerchief was pushed into her palm.

"Thank you," she murmured, trying not to breathe the rank air too deeply. She pressed the musk-scented cloth to her nose, for once thankful for Prescott's generously applied perfume. After a moment, she leaned out. "It's dark as pitch in there. Will you hand me the light after I go in?"

"You are not going in there."

"I have to."

"There might be r-a-t-s . . ."

Catherine shuddered. She was terrified of them ever since a nasty encounter years before.

"I might consider going in myself," he offered seriously. "But I have an appointment this afternoon with a fair lady and I don't want to sully my clothing."

"No, just your reputation," she retorted.

"A reputation is not nearly as plaguesome as an empty belly," he replied smoothly. "Besides, since the woman I love does not return the favor, it's a good way for me to mend my shattered heart."

"You need a heart before it can be broken."

"And I was wondering why the men weren't lining up for the pleasure of your charms."

"Will you please just hand me the light once I'm inside?"

"Yes, dearie. But don't blame me when there is nothing in there but creepy crawly things."

Bunching her skirts, she took a deep breath and pushed her way through the small opening. The edges of the hole scraped against her sides as she slid through, her hands and knees landing on a creaky wooden floor layered with dust. Trepidation made her mouth dry and her heart pound. She tried not to think about bugs or spiders, and especially not the dreaded rats.

"Tsszz."

She jumped, her hair standing on end and her heart racing. Turning, she glared. "Blackguard."

He laughed. "It was too tempting."

Anger, she realized, had erased her fear and she was actually a little glad for his prank. "Hand me the candle."

She thrust the light into each corner of the space, trying not to breathe in the stifling air. Relief and disappointment swamped her. There were no rats, thank heavens, but no chests of treasure either. There was a plethora of spiderwebs . . . and a large rectangular hump in the corner. Stepping over, she pushed it with her finger. It was a satchel, with what seemed to be a large book. *Interesting*. Crouching down, she wiped off the dust and webs. Leather.

"What is it?" he asked.

"I think it's a book."

"Why would someone go to the bother of hiding a book in here?"

"An accident?" she ventured.

"Hand it over, let us have a look."

Lifting it up, she handed it to him through the opening, then passed him the candle. "I am coming out."

His face disappeared and so did much of the light. Holding her breath, Catherine climbed through the wooden opening, thankful to be out of there and back in the dusty closet. But where was Prescott? And what was he doing with the tome she'd found?

Chapter 5

"**P**res?" Catherine called, wondering to where he'd disappeared.

Dusting off her dress, she stepped into the corridor and looked in each direction. Then she saw the open window and recalled that this was one of his favorite childhood sneak-aways.

"Better light out here, Cat. Join me." Prescott lounged on the roof with his legs stretched out before him, regardless of the two-story drop below. Catherine envied his easy confidence. For her, going out on the ledge was a trial, one that Prescott understood better than most, since he had watched her fall from this very spot.

It had been in her very first year at Andersen Hall. She had been trailing behind a gaggle of older boys, anxious to share in some of their mischief. Marcus had been the leader on this particular outing (no wonder she had been so keen to follow). The lads had stolen gingerbread cookies from the kitchens, hiding them inside their woolen shirts. It had been chilly that day, but the sky was bright with autumn sun, so most of the children had been play-ing wage-war in the gardens below.

She had made it out the window and just two steps past its outer casing when her bad leg had slipped, driving her over the ledge. Her desperate fingers had grasped the edge barely in time. Her arms had shaken with the strain of hanging on and her legs felt weighted as they swung wildly beneath her in the thin air.

Her fall had knocked off some slates, alerting the chil-dren below. They'd rushed over, shrieking with terror. Catherine had been silent, her eyes tightly closed and her heart in her mouth, reliving her fall from the Caddyhorns' second-floor window less than a year before.

Suddenly hands had roughly gripped her wrists, yank-ing her up and over the ledge. She would never forget the darkly furious look on Marcus's handsome face or the scorn in his tone. "What the bloody hell were you think-ing? This is no place for a girl and a lame one at that! You're no cat."

She had been labeled for life. Her mortification had only grown when Headmaster Dunn had found out. Mar-cus had probably come to regret his rescue, since his punishment had greatly surpassed hers (but not her hu-miliation). Dunn saw Marcus as a leader who had abused his position and Marcus had paid dearly for that misadventure.

"Come on, Cat," Prescott called, ripping her mind back to the present. "Unless you're afraid . . ."

Prescott certainly knew how to pluck her strings. Even if she was terrified, she was loath to admit it.

"I thought you'd left me," she chided, lifting her bad leg and pushing it through the window opening. She maneu-vered carefully, using her hands as much as her legs, crawling like a monkey. Inelegant, but she did not falter. Her leg didn't ache so much on dry days like today.

Prescott watched her out of the corner of his eye, seemingly confident that she would not fall. The afternoon sun glistened on his thick, dark reddish mane.

"Look," he said, pointing to the volume. "The pages are parchment. The book's probably religious, but it doesn't look like anything I've ever seen in church." He closed it. "I'm hoping it's a collection of juicy bits of blackmail."

"If so, I'll burn it."

"And waste golden opportunities?"

"I will not exploit others' distress."

He handed it to her. The book weighed as much as Headmaster Dunn's Bible and overwhelmed her lap with its large, red, cloth bindings. It smelled of old leather, probably from the satchel it had been stored within.

"Dunn always says that books have souls," she murmured.

"Well, let's hope that this one has the devil's." At the look on her face, he cried, "I do have morals—"

"Yes, just very flexible ones." She studied him, trying to untangle his strange obsession with blackmail. "If other people are flawed, then you fare better by comparison?"

He shrugged, but did not meet her eye.

"We all have shortcomings, Pres. It's what makes us human."

"I prefer to be a god," he huffed. "Adonis, if you please."

Her lips lifted. "More like Pan, to me."

"Open the damned book."

She breached the volume and the bindings crackled with disuse. Bold black scratches marked the first page and she read, "Our doubts are traitors, and make us lose the good we oft might win, by fearing to attempt."

"Socrates?"

"Shakespeare's *Measure for Measure*," she replied distractedly, flipping to an inner page.

"A play? How boring. Why bother hiding such a tome?"

"I don't think it's a play at all," she murmured, scanning the page. "Look, this is about tying knots. Intricate ones."

Yawning into his hand, he pushed himself up onto his heels. "That's even worse than a play; it's manual labor." He stood, easily balanced on the tilted roof. "I'm appalled, actually, that someone thought enough of themselves to put such dry rot onto parchment."

Looking up, Catherine envied his easy grace. She had to keep herself from glancing down too frequently, or she'd topple. She squinted up at him and he graciously blocked the sunlight from her eyes.

"I'm off," Prescott declared, flicking dust off of his bright yellow coat. "And you see I was right about you." He waved his hands wide. "Even while having the benefit of all this beauty, you read a tiresome book. You'll never catch a man that way, Cat. Men like their women silly."

"And I like my men clever and modest. So I suppose that means I will have to do without."

He t'sked. "You have an exceedingly poor view of my kind, Cat."

"Growing up with the likes of you might have something to do with it."

"One day, Cat." He shook his head, exhaling noisily. "One day some poor sod is going to come along and show you the error of your ways." Tapping his finger to his chin, he added, "Or perhaps that poor sod might be me—"

"You've got the part about the poor sod right, Pres," she huffed. "But the rest is rubbish." She grazed her hand across the page, liking the feel of parchment under her fingertips. "I will never marry."

He was silent for so long, she looked up. He had an odd look on his face.

"What?"

He stared down at her a long moment, and she had the strange sense that he was about to say something important. Then he turned away and looked out over the lawn. "I miss wage-war."

"The battles?"

"The victory."

"I never really liked the game." She grimaced, recalling the times she'd bothered to play and had been the last picked for a troop. "It made me . . . tense. I always felt like something bad was going to happen."

"Like what?"

"Like I'd never be good enough. I'd always cause the troop to lose."

"That's why you hardly played?"

"Yes."

"You can't have any fun if you don't join the game, Cat," Prescott offered softly.

"I know. I know. But I never wanted the responsibility for a loss."

They were quiet a long moment, Prescott's old arguments hanging in the air between them. He'd always chided her for what he saw as her tendency to assume more responsibility than he considered healthy.

Prescott dusted off his hands. "Well, I need to rally or

I'll be late." Assuming his blithe tone once more, he added, "Promise me, Cat, you will at least try to do *something* amusing on this glorious day."

"Your definition and mine of amusing, Prescott, are worlds apart," she replied, turning the page and reading.

> *Lady Jamison is a fool. Spouting off to any who will listen about how she has so many jewels that she must keep a separate dresser for them. She's practically inviting trouble. And then to show off the brass key to the dresser she keeps around her neck? Who needs a key when a lock is no match for anyone who really wants to break inside?*

"Weren't the Jamisons one of the first families that was burgled by the Thief of Robinson Square?" Catherine asked Prescott as she scanned the page.

When she received no answer, she looked up. Prescott was gone. She must have been so engrossed not even to have heard him depart. Catherine pushed aside a stab of guilt at her ill manners. Though Prescott wouldn't take it to heart, she knew.

Turning back to the book, she flipped to the next page and read the bottom.

> *Luckily there's a trestle, handily placed along the west alleyway. It's far enough from any traffic to avoid examination and the sun will be late in casting it from shadow.*

Doubt slithered through her mind. No. It couldn't be . . .

A notation was scratched along the side of the page: *Information is the greatest weapon in any offensive!!*

She flipped the sheet.

The third Sunday is the propitious night as the housekeeper is off and her second sleeps late. That allows for more time to breach the lock if there's a snag.

Her heart began to pound as she quickly rifled through the pages.

Westerly. Garamond. Kendrick. The names popped out at her, glaring in their familiarity and the connection between them. Each family had been notoriously burgled by the Thief of Robinson Square. There had been whispers, she recalled, about how these families were particularly clutch-fisted when it came to charitable donations. About how they treated their servants poorly, despite living to decadent excess. Some had even hinted that the thievery was a reckoning, of sorts.

Then there was the matter of how the thief knew the exact locations of hidden valuables. Supposedly all of the Westerly servants had been sacked and quite a few from the other families as well. But the thief had never been caught. Apparently no one had even come close to unmasking the housebreaker.

But just as suddenly as the burglaries had begun, they'd ceased, relegating the Thief of Robinson Square to phantom amongst the score of London's legends.

Until today, perhaps?

Tracing her hand down the page, she reexamined the bindings.

It couldn't be the thief's diary, could it? And if it was, why was it hidden in a secret compartment at Andersen Hall? More importantly, how could they capitalize on this find? Could it somehow help the orphanage overcome its financial straits? Was there even a market for such a thing?

Catherine snorted. There was a market for anything in London these days.

Her eyes narrowed and she stared off into the distance, hashing through the possibilities. Were there any rewards outstanding for such information? Could they sell it to the highest bidder?

Doubts about exactly what she had in her lap plagued her. She wouldn't want to set up Andersen Hall or Headmaster Dunn for a mockery. This journal would have to be, without doubt, the genuine article.

A newspaper clipping slipped out. She read the headline. *"The Thief of Robinson Square Strikes Again."* Next to the title was a bold, black handwritten star.

Shocked, Catherine slammed the book closed.

"Oh, dear Lord in heaven," she breathed, her heart pounding, her mind racing. Still, it seemed too preposterous to believe.

Her eyes flew from right to left, ensuring that no one had seen. She knew that she was being overly fearful; she was on the rooftop for heaven's sake. Still, on the small chance that this was real . . .

A plan. She needed a plan.

First she'd hide the book, not let anyone notice her discovery. Yet. Then she would talk to Headmaster Dunn. He would know what to do. He always did.

Chapter 6

After slipping the book under her bed in her room, Catherine rushed down the hallway toward Head-master Dunn's study. Excitement swam in the pit of her belly. Was the tome *actually* written by the Thief of Robinson Square? Or simply the manifestation of some-one's obsession with the notorious thief who had the *ton* reeling shortly after the turn of the century? The fascinat-ing journal not only chronicled the Thief's exploits, but contained charts, maps and lists detailing robbing Lon-don's finest homes. It was almost a guidebook of how to burgle. Still, it was so far-fetched, her doubts lingered.

Catherine rushed into the headmaster's study, ready to proclaim her news. Her feet froze in their tracks as the words died on her lips.

A tall, broad-shouldered, raven-haired soldier stood staring out the front window, with his brawny back to her. His pristine crimson-and-gold coat seemed out of place in the dingy, book-riddled, paper-cluttered room around him. In fact, the soldier seemed so vibrant the room faded into the background, leaving only him, filling her gaze. Her heart began to canter and her mind went headily blank, sensations she had not experienced in seven long, drab years.

Catherine resisted the urge to grasp the door handle behind her for support; her knees had turned to jelly. Only one man on this earth had ever made her feel simultaneously silly, giddy and panicked simply by being in his presence: *Marcus*. What on earth was he doing back at Andersen Hall?

Distantly, she noticed that his raven hair was longer, now hedging his broad shoulders. He was taller than when she'd last seen him. Where she had grown an inch or two in the intervening years, remaining just below most men's collars, Marcus seemed to fill the room with his towering stature. Perhaps it was the white plume perched on his red-and-gold shako, but more likely it was that he stood at least a head and half taller than she.

He had filled out as well. His broad shoulders were a handspan wider, adding to the stirring "v" impression ending at his trim waist, emphasized to great effect by his striking crimson-and-gold uniform. He leaned with one crutch under his arm and seemed to be favoring his left leg. She couldn't help but notice how his muscular thighs were encased in tight white breeches and how a bandage wrapped his left leg. She distantly wondered at his injury.

Suddenly, he turned.

She was captured by his icy blue gaze, which, as it always had, seized the breath in her throat. She stood dumbly staring at her adolescent obsession, feeling once more like she was witless, and twelve years old.

"Good day," he ventured with a slight inclination of his head. His voice sounded deeper, with more of a rumble than she remembered, causing an odd quiver in her middle.

This was no lad, she realized, but a *man*. Yet, vestiges of his youthful appeal still remained: those piercing blue eyes, the black-winged brows, those lips that had spiced her dreams . . . She would recognize him amongst a thousand men.

He had broken his nose at some point since his departure, giving physicality to his devil-may-care mien. And with the stitches over his left eye and the crutch under his arm he appeared the essence of devastating pirate. The effect was further heightened by the calculating reserve clouding his gaze.

She knew that she should say *something*, but her mind was maddeningly vacant and her tongue thick with knots. Her heart seemed to slow and yet quicken under that penetrating blue gaze.

What would he think of how *she* had changed in seven years? No longer the willowy frail child, she was a woman of two-and-twenty who had filled out with muscle from earnest labor. Yet alone in front of her mirror, she could see the womanly curves just like her mother's.

Leaning on his crutch, Marcus slowly loped across the space separating them. Her heart thumped wildly and was lodged somewhere deep in her throat. She inched backwards, overwhelmed by the panic that had plagued her whenever he was near. Her back bumped up against the doorjamb; she was trapped by that searing blue gaze.

Stretching out his hand, he reached for her. A small voice in her head called out vague and yet frantic warnings, but she felt the unholy desire to let him touch her, and to give life to her youthful fantasies.

His palm grazed her cheek as he reached into her hair. Tingles danced over her skin where he touched, and they raced from there to her hairline. She shivered, and fought the heady yearning to close her eyes. As if she could, imprisoned by his sapphire gaze. Slowly he disengaged his hand, gently tugging something out of her hair.

Marcus looked into his broad, white-gloved palm. "Cobwebs." He looked up. "Don't they let you out?"

Catherine blinked, feeling as if she had been doused in icy pond water.

"Of course we do," Headmaster Dunn bellowed as he strode into the study from his adjacent private apartments, his outer coat and cane slung over his arm. "Someone else was supposed to clean out the closet, Catherine," he chided with a slight frown. "Well, there's naught to be done for it now. Have you finished yet?"

Her mouth opened, but she was so mortified no words would come. So she simply shook her head in the negative.

"Regardless," Dunn replied as he shrugged on his coat. "What I want, Catherine, is for you to lock that room. No entry by anyone. Nothing taken out from there. Do you understand?"

Dumbly miserable, she nodded.

"Thank you, Catherine. And please bring me the key immediately." He waved to his son. "You remember Marcus."

He said it as if it were a certainty, mortifying her further.

"Marcus, Catherine," the headmaster intoned, motioning to her. "Or rather, Miss Catherine Miller."

Catherine wished she could pretend nonchalance, but her cheeks were burning as she dipped in a slight curtsey.

"Catherine?" Marcus said her name so melodically it felt like molasses sliding down her spine. His blue eyes narrowed as he slowly nodded. "Cat? Right? The chit who fell from the roof?"

She wanted to sink through the floor and die in a shallow grave. In some respects, little *had* changed. He was the same sardonic Marcus who would just as soon mock her as speak to her. The last vestiges of her childhood fantasies evaporated into mist, and her heart ached to see them go.

"Unfortunate day, that was," Headmaster Dunn muttered, shooting his son a glare.

Pointedly ignoring his father, Marcus asked, "What are you still doing here?"

Her cheeks burned at his implication. *Shouldn't you have a real life by now?*

"Catherine is my second-in-command, so to speak," Dunn explained. "She helps me with the accounts, the business side of the orphanage. I don't know how I would get along without her." His voice trailed off.

She forced her desert-dry mouth to work. "Luckily, sir, you will never have to." She would never marry, never have a home of her own. Aside from the fact that no gentleman would want a spinster who'd lived in an orphanage, she had learned from the Caddyhorns the downfall of giving someone legal rights over her. She would never give anyone such power again.

At some point Jared *would* take his rightful place in Society, but she would be a pariah, an oddity who was gently bred but had no place in the *ton*. No, she would live and die at Andersen Hall, a decrepit old maid . . .

She realized that Dunn was staring at her derriere and she wondered if she was losing her mind.

The headmaster's brow puckered. "Are those leading strings tied to your apron?"

Whipping her hand around, she grabbed at ivory fabric. "I'm going to kill him," she muttered, praying that her cheeks were not as scarlet as they felt. She faced them again with as much dignity as she could muster. Amusement swam in each of their equally dark azure gazes. She lifted her chin. "Prescott loves his little tricks."

"Prescott?" Marcus scratched his chin. "The carrot-topped one with the freckles?"

Dunn nodded. "The very same."

"Are so many of the former charges still around?" Marcus asked, retrieving his other crutch from against the chair and resting both beneath his arms.

"Prescott only comes because of Catherine. He can't seem to keep away from her." Adjusting his lapels, Dunn added, "And Catherine enjoys the company, I'm sure."

She decided to ignore the implication that she had few friends.

Dunn sniffed. "I need you to be a good influence on him, Catherine. Help him find his calling to earn an honorable living—"

"Let's not get into that now, sir," she interjected. Even if she did agree with Dunn, it was none of Marcus's business. They did not need to display dirty linens before *outsiders*.

The realization jolted her. Marcus had been gone so long that she did feel at some level that he was not one of them. Not a complete stranger, but not an insider either. If she could interact with him as an acquaintance, suppress all of the disruptive feelings she'd had for him as a witless girl, then she could actually tolerate his presence. At least without making a complete fool of herself during his visit.

Her heart-wrenching embarrassment eased a bit. She was no longer that twelve-year-old ninny with her heart pinned to her sleeve. She needed to act like the intelligent adult she was, usually.

Marcus raised a brow, noting with cool approval, "She's protective."

"Like a mama bear with cubs." Dunn scratched his chin, startlingly like his son. "Which reminds me, Catherine, I want you to help Marcus get back in the saddle here at Andersen Hall. He needs to review the last three years' budgets, the expense ledgers. Everything." He turned to his son. "Catherine's really got an extraordinary gift with accounts." Facing Catherine once more, he added, "I want you to help Marcus in any way that he requires."

"But . . . why?" she asked, irritably shoving a strand of hair around her ear. She felt like she was reading a novel and had missed the chapter with the critical plot details.

"He's on the board of trustees now," the Headmaster explained. "Took Jensen's spot, may his worthy soul rest in peace. So he needs to be up to snuff on all of the workings here."

Catherine shook her head, her mind swirling. "When did this happen?"

"At the special vote of the board."

"Special vote . . ." she sputtered. "Since when . . . how long . . ."

Pulling his watch from his pocket, Dunn flicked it open and studied its face. "Marcus has served his country well in the King's army and now he's volunteered to serve equally as well at Andersen Hall. He's on leave because of his injuries and we have the benefit of his counsel."

Marcus was staying . . . seemingly indefinitely. She pushed aside her own qualms and instead focused on how illogical it all seemed. He'd always hated it here. The ill parting, his oath never to return . . . "But . . ."

"Well, hell hath frozen over," Mrs. Nagel declared from the open doorway.

"Ah, Mrs. Nagel," Dunn stated quickly, snapping the watch closed and shoving it back into his pocket. "Marcus has returned to the bosom of his family. Please welcome him home."

Catherine noted how Marcus cringed slightly at the word "bosom," or was it "family"? His face quickly became impassive once more. If she had not been looking directly at him, she might have missed his discomfiture. Something definitely was amiss.

"I never thought I'd see the day." Mrs. Nagel sniffed.

Dunn wrapped an arm about her small shoulders. "Marcus is a war hero, Mrs. Nagel. After all he's been through, he's seen the error of his ways in staying away for so long. He is here to make amends and help out Andersen Hall. We certainly could use his invaluable support."

Dunn shot his son a meaningful glance, and Marcus piped in, "I am so grateful, Mrs. Nagel, for the opportunity to serve Andersen Hall . . ."

The words reeled, Marcus then Dunn, and back again, weaving mollifying declarations about a brush with death, reform, grace and forgiveness into a web of whimsy.

To Catherine's chagrin, Mrs. Nagel was almost in tears by the end of the syrupy account. Well, Catherine was not so easily swayed. It all sounded too trite for the son who had angrily sworn never to return. Too smooth for the father who'd spent seven years in quiet mourning for his lost child. Something definitely was not being said here.

"When you have time, I have a few questions, sir," Catherine declared.

"I'm sure that you and Marcus would like to catch up," Dunn asserted. "But he only just arrived and he and I have much to discuss."

"Most assuredly," Marcus agreed. "Seven years' worth." Catherine couldn't believe that he said it without a trace of sarcasm in his tone.

She eyed the men warily, sensing a stratagem of some sort. But since when were Dunn and his son on the same side?

"If you will excuse us . . ." Dunn herded the women toward the exit. "I would like a word with my son."

Catherine opened her mouth, but Dunn interjected,

"I'm sure that you would love an opportunity to make yourself presentable, Catherine . . ."

Her cheeks burned, but before she could think of something witty to save face, the door closed behind her with a hard thud.

"You really should straighten up." Mrs. Nagel t'sked. "You look a fright. One might suppose that you had used your skirts to sweep the floors."

Gritting her teeth, Catherine dusted off her apron, then gave up, realizing that nothing was going to help.

"I'll have Betty pour you a bath," the matron suggested. Her gaze brightened. "And I'll ask Cook to bring young Marcus some spice cakes." The woman actually blushed. "I suppose I must stop thinking of him as young Marcus now. He is a man of the world. We must give thanks for his homecoming."

Catherine crossed her arms. "Don't you think it a bit odd that Marcus has returned all pleasant and smiles after such a frosty absence?"

Mrs. Nagel's lips puckered. "Give the man a chance, Catherine. He almost died serving his country. That changes a person."

"Enough to go from hating this institution to suddenly sitting on the board of trustees? The man didn't show one speck of interest in Andersen Hall for seven years and now he wishes to lend a hand? It makes no sense whatsoever!"

Mrs. Nagel scowled. "Don't be looking for bedbugs when you haven't even itched, Catherine. I know that you and Marcus had your disagreements as children, but you should not look for flaws simply because he did not return your affections."

Catherine started, appalled. "But this has nothing—"

"Go take your bath. And while in it, refresh your outlook."

Catherine gritted her teeth, realizing that she was not going to get anywhere with Mrs. Nagel. Some people only noticed what they wanted to see. "Yes, ma'am," she muttered, then headed toward the new rooms that Headmaster Dunn had recently assigned to her. There, at least, she would have some quiet and a chance to think. Headmaster Dunn had moved her quarters recently, another unusual move that had her wondering what was going on.

What could compel Headmaster Dunn to go behind her back and exclude her from orphanage affairs? Personal issues within the Dunn family were one matter, but when it came to Andersen Hall, the children, the board, her job . . . Well, it was just *wrong* to be so heavy-handed. And so unlike Uriah Dunn as to make her certain that there was much more to this little conspiracy than the father and son were professing.

Uriah Dunn always did everything in an honest, open fashion. Which meant that Marcus was clearly the instigator of this scheme. Marcus had to be at the center of it all. No, she did not like this new turn of events. Not one bit. And she was not about to let Marcus Dunn get away with it.

Chapter 7

$\mathbf{M}$arcus shifted on his crutch, suddenly uneasy at being alone with his father once more. They had barely exchanged two words when an uncomfortable Dunn had gone to retrieve his coat and Cat had rushed into the room. Now father and son stood face-to-face, as duelists do before a contest. Their rift yawned between them, a whopping purple elephant crowding them in the seemingly large office.

As an experienced officer who had faced countless dangers, it galled Marcus that seeing one old man would make his armpits sweat and his stomach churn. But he'd never given in to the desire to turn tail and run, despite shots flying, swords flashing and shrieking barrages. He was not about to do so now. So he stood firm under his father's scrutiny.

Dunn's penetrating blue gaze, the same that Marcus saw reflected in the mirror each morning, traveled from Marcus's stitched brow down to the crutches, to the leg he was favoring. Finally Dunn asked, "Is the injury real?"

Marcus shook his head in the negative.

"Well, you look fit," Dunn commented awkwardly.

"You, too." It was a lie and they both knew it. It was idiotic for Marcus to have expected his father to remain unchanged in seven years, yet somehow Marcus had. Age had not been overly kind to Uriah Dunn. He was still tall and imposing, with his feet planted wide as if he owned, and yet was part of, the earth. He still had a full head of thick wavy hair, but now it was almost completely steel gray, with none of the raven luster that had always marked Marcus and his father as kin. His face was ivory-pale and, as usual, clean-shaven, exposing wide laugh streaks around the mouth. Worry lines that Marcus did not recall marred his broad forehead.

"I hadn't heard back from Wellington." Pain flashed in his father's eyes, quickly veiled. "I, ah . . . didn't think that you were coming."

"I was . . . detained." Marcus did not bother to explain his incarceration or the deal he'd finally struck to save his friend Captain Luke Hayes's life.

"I am glad that you made it, although not the reason for your return." Dunn paused, then waved Marcus into a chair.

Setting his crutches beside him, Marcus eased into a hardwood-slatted seat, facing the door.

Instead of sitting behind his imposing desk, Dunn pushed a threadbare armchair directly before Marcus and sat. Marcus felt hemmed in, and did not like having anyone blocking his path to the exit, but he did not say so. Instead, he shifted his body sideways, allowing for mobility if he needed it. Similarly, that way he could avoid staring his father directly in the face.

"This is a good time for us to talk." Dunn began. "Most of the children are at chapel." He cleared his throat. "Now that I've had the chance to really think about our parting—"

Marcus stiffened. "You know why I'm here. It's best that we move forward . . . not waste time on . . . *ancient* history."

Dunn pursed his lips, obviously not well pleased. Still, he nodded, replying softly, "As you wish."

Marcus hid his surprise. His father was never one to acquiesce so easily. What was he scheming, an ambush of some kind? Marcus mentally shook himself. Dunn was not like the men he'd been facing these last seven years. His most devious plot was how to squeeze a few more pounds from Society for Andersen Hall. Still, to Marcus, Dunn posed a challenge that felt hazardous on a different level.

A knock resounded on the door. Dunn shot Marcus an apologetic glance. "Come."

Mrs. Nagel stepped inside carrying a tray with food, a pitcher and cups. "I have some of Cook's spice cakes for you. And some tea and milk," she explained, setting it on a side table.

"Thank you, Mrs. Nagel," Marcus stated, knowing he would sooner eat a soldier's boot at the moment; his stomach was so tied in knots.

Mrs. Nagel preened. "I've told everyone that you're here and they are just dying to see you." Raising a hand, she ticked off her fingers. "Cook, Old Bertram, Betty, even the gardener, Graves." Mrs. Nagel frowned. "Although he's retiring shortly."

Sighing, Dunn stood. "As I've told you before, Mrs. Nagel, rules are rules and he left me with little choice."

Marcus could see that some things never changed: His father was as intractable as ever.

The matron sighed. "Yes, well, here are some lovely refreshments for you—"

"Thank you, Mrs. Nagel," Dunn interjected, "but Marcus and I are headed to my club for a spot of luncheon." He patted his middle. "And we wouldn't wish to spoil our appetites."

Realizing that his father was trying to give them some privacy to discuss his mission, Marcus jumped to his feet, grabbing the crutches. "Yes, I'm primed for a leg of lamb. It's still a specialty of the house, is it not?"

"Like cutting through butter," Dunn agreed quickly. "I'm sure that the tutors would love the cakes, Mrs. Nagel."

"Oh." Disappointment flashed across her features. "I thought you might stay for a bit . . ."

Then Cat charged into the room. She had replaced her dirty apron with a similarly staid, albeit clean, one. Nonetheless her gown was a disgrace, a drab sackcloth, with the line showing baldly where she had dropped the hem.

The cobwebs were gone from her flaxen locks and her cheeks were shiny as if just washed. Her golden hairline was dark with wet and wisps of hair still spiked out of her loose bun like sticks of hay. She obviously had spared no time for a full bath or a glance in the mirror.

"I hope you didn't clean up on my account," he quipped.

Her porcelain cheeks reddened and tempests flashed in her smoky gray eyes, but she ignored him and turned to his father. "If I could have a word with you, sir?"

Why had he said that? Marcus asked himself. And why did it bother him so much that she would have such little care for her appearance? Perhaps because he was oddly drawn to her despite the hideous sack of a gown and the cobwebs. The attraction surprised him; he usually went for buxom brunettes, not willowy, flaxen-haired pixies.

Mrs. Nagel lifted the tray and left, sulking. "I'll tell Timmy to bring around the gig."

Marcus watched as Dunn and Cat moved into the hall. It seemed odd that they would show him the courtesy of allowing him to stay in his father's study. He realized that he needed to remember he was not a lad in his teens and should expect to be treated differently.

He bit back a groan. This mission was going to be a nuisance on so many different levels.

His eyes strayed to the girl, no, woman arguing with his father. He had to admire her gumption; few could go head-to-head with Uriah Dunn with the intensity that she displayed. Her gray eyes flashed icy fire at Marcus as she argued with the headmaster, obviously about him. How droll.

Was it his placement on the board of trustees that bothered her? Or the fact that his father had asked her to take Marcus under her wing? Although he had no intention of actually learning all of the things his father wanted him to, he rather liked the idea that she resented it. There might actually be some sport in this wretched circumstance yet. He bit back a chuckle. She was barely allowing his father, the mighty orator, to get a word in edgewise!

Had she always been this fiery? Memory surfaced of a waif with golden hair that stuck out like errant sticks from her thin braids. She'd been a timid thing, hanging about on the corners, her pink lips pinched. He'd really had little to do with her. He'd traveled with an older, more raucous crowd. She'd read a lot if he recalled correctly. And didn't play much with the other children. Her leg. She'd had a bum leg.

His eyes drifted to the discolored hem of her gown. With her graceful, even stance she didn't appear lame. In fact, she looked positively perfect. The hideous sack couldn't hide the bountiful swell of her breasts, the trim, bowed waist and the lush arc of her derriere. And he was enjoying watching it jiggle as she tapped an impatient foot. Her high, rounded rump had just the right measure of curve, perfect for filling his hands. Nothing brought his blood to boil like a curvaceous bottom undulating above him as he kneaded the smooth, soft flesh—

Aghast, Marcus coughed into his fist.

Cat and his father stopped arguing as their gazes fixed on him.

"I'm fine," he muttered with a slight smile. He waved. "Please, go on." Better that they were focused on each other than on him.

After a moment's hesitation, Cat turned back to Dunn and launched into another whispering tirade.

He'd been too bloody long without a woman, Marcus realized. He was starting to see nymphs where there were trolls. Well, not exactly a troll, more like a fishwife.

She was stabbing her finger in the air to make a point, for heaven's sake! His father was taking it quite well, listening patiently and trying valiantly to insert a remark here and there. Marcus wondered if he was used to her sharp tongue and those flashing eyes.

He couldn't quite tell their color, neither the darker agate gray nor pigeon-wing pale. They reminded him of tempests that traveled on the wind, darkening the clouds to swirls of iron, then lighting to vapor when the storm had passed.

When she was younger, her huge eyes had over-whelmed her pale, heart-shaped face, giving her a haunted look. Now the wide-set eyes were well balanced by wheat-colored winged brows above and lush, pink, bowed lips below. A small upturned nose was the only thing dainty about her compelling features. Especially when she was scowling like a disapproving matron.

He didn't know what he'd been thinking a moment before. Cat was a spinster, a bluestocking most likely, who'd rather stick her little nose in a ledger or argue about the price of bread than dance on a moonlit night. What other kind of woman would clean closets on a glorious day like today?

She was certainly nothing compared to Angelica, the raven-haired, dark-eyed beauty he'd left behind in Portugal. It was the abstinence, it had to be. And so long as he needed to maintain the appearance of his "injuries," bed sport was not an option. Typically, while occupied with a mission this would not have bothered him, and he wondered why it seemed more of a trial today.

"Enough, I said," Dunn bellowed, then blinked as if surprised that he'd raised his voice.

Cat crossed her arms, obviously not cowed. "But sir—"

"We are leaving." Dunn nodded to Marcus and grabbed his cane.

Cat's pink lips pinched and she glared, but kept her peace. Somehow he doubted that she would let the matter lie. Like any fishwife worth her salt, she could probably kick a dead topic to life at the drop of an innocent comment.

Grabbing his hat off the pedestal, Dunn set it on his head and headed out the door. Marcus followed close behind, not limping too badly on his crutches. He really was growing almost accustomed to the bloody things.

Catherine trailed him like a hound on the scent of a fox, only one kept on a tight leash.

Dunn hurried down the steps and climbed into the gig. It was an open black box with well-oiled springs and wide smooth wheels. Not nearly as fancy as others whipping about London, Marcus could see as he climbed in, but sturdy and well maintained. The breeze pressed against his face, carrying the familiar scents of horse, leather and oil.

"When will you be back, sir?" Cat called with obvious restraint, as Dunn accepted the reins from Timmy the stable lad.

"Not until late."

"Good day, Cat," Marcus called with a tilt of his shako. "I hope to see you again soon." He realized that it was true. Doubtless they would cross swords and he was looking forward to it. He almost groaned, knowing he was near bottom if he was seeking amusement from exchanging insults with a harpy.

Her eyes clouded dark to iron and a deepened scowl was her only response.

He really needed to find some entertainment while he was back in town.

Flicking the leathers, Dunn clicked his tongue and the horses sprang forward.

Marcus adjusted his crutches and settled into the seat as the familiar scenery rushed by, seemingly unchanged by the passage of time.

Columns of trees guarded the orphanage in squared formation, reminding Marcus of the battlefields where he'd rather be. Still, if one had to be in London, at least it was on a splendid day like today. The landscape was washed golden in the sun, the trees were heavy with emerald leaves and the fresh scent of pine filled the air.

As they approached Andersen Hall's wrought-iron gates, Marcus twisted around, oddly compelled. Cat still stood on the porch, her arms crossed, her shoulders hunched. Her very stance declared that she was ill pleased with his return.

Well, that made two of them.

Chapter 8

Leaving behind Andersen Hall's wrought-iron gates, Marcus resisted the urge to ask his father for the reins. Watching, he realized that Dunn was a competent driver, albeit on the slow side.

His father eased his grip on the leathers. The gig plowed onward, but at a leisurely pace. "I have to say, that didn't go *too* badly. Although," he added, "I'm not sure that Catherine is satisfied with our little performance."

"Do you always suffer her tongue so lightly?"

Dunn shot his son a censorious glance. "Don't give her any trouble, now, Marcus. She's a wonderful woman who's been through a lot."

"What child at Andersen Hall has not?"

Dunn grimaced. "Too true. But I know you, and you'll be tempted to stir up trouble where there's calm. So stop now before you even start."

"That's not very fair of you, is it? Judging me when I've been back in the country for a mere handful of days?"

Shifting in his seat, he sighed. "I suppose some things never change."

Marcus was pleased by the guilty scowl lighting his father's features.

"You're right," Dunn admitted, surprising Marcus. "I shouldn't have jumped to conclusions." He shrugged. "I suppose I'm a bit protective where Catherine is concerned."

Marcus bit back a comment that a father should be protective of his own son. He really had no desire to start up right where he and his father had last left off. They'd typically had difficulty finding a way to communicate besides arguing and it had always left Marcus feeling torn up on the inside. As if every insult he'd flung speared him just as well.

"Catherine's given up a lot for Andersen Hall." Dunn sighed. "I honestly don't know how I will get on without her."

"Why? Has she taken another position?"

His father's cheek's reddened.

"I certainly won't say anything, sir," Marcus assured. Not that it really mattered, he'd be leaving Andersen Hall soon enough when he'd completed his mission.

"Catherine . . . How shall I put this? Catherine is intended . . ."

"The poor fellow has best be deaf or have a strong constitution to put up with her sharp tongue."

"She's not betrothed . . ." Dunn's gaze grew thoughtful. "Although it's a wonder she's remained free this long. She's quite lovely."

Marcus examined the trees. "I hadn't noticed."

"No." Dunn sighed. "I suppose you wouldn't. You were never very good at seeing past people's outer trappings. Catherine does not care one whit for her appearance, I'm afraid."

Marcus decided to ignore the slight. His father didn't

know him half as well as he thought he did. But nothing Marcus could say would change his father's prejudices.

"Why was she so peevish, back there?"

Dunn grimaced. "She doesn't trust you."

Marcus's lips quirked, amused. "Really. Why not?"

"I suppose Catherine is . . ." Dunn shifted in the seat. "Protective as well."

"And she sees me as a threat. I wonder what could have led her to that assumption."

"I never said a word, Marcus."

"No, often you don't even have to. Your obvious displeasure is like a trumpet horn, it precedes you."

They rode along in strained silence.

Dunn peered at him from the corner of his eye. "I was thinking. Catherine is quite trustworthy, knows the ins and outs of Andersen Hall. Knows the trustees. It might be helpful for her to understand your true purpose."

Marcus straightened. "Don't tell me that you yield to that sharp-tongued lass?"

"Of course not." Dunn scowled.

"Good."

"But Catherine can get her nose bent if she smells something rotten. And she can be quite dogged."

"Are you saying she might cause me trouble if she's not satisfied with what she's being told?"

"I'm afraid so."

Marcus shrugged. "If she becomes a nuisance, I'll deal with it."

"What the blazes does that mean?" his father cried.

"No matter what you think of me"—Marcus hated the injury he heard in his voice—"I don't harm innocents."

Dunn's cheeks reddened. "I didn't believe that for a moment, Marcus. I simply . . . well, I didn't know what you meant."

Marcus ignored the old hurt of how poorly his father always judged him. They rode along in stilted silence.

Dunn shifted in his seat. His brow furrowed and his lips pinched as if he was fretting over something.

Marcus girded himself for another round.

After another few moments of shifting, Dunn peered at Marcus from the corner of his eye. "I . . . well, I was wondering how long you suppose you might be in England."

Marcus looked away. Once he'd accomplished his mission he'd be on the next swift boat headed to Portugal. Or better yet, Spain.

"I was hoping to take a visit to some of our cousins," Dunn added. "It's been a long time since you've seen Aunt Amanda or Uncle Phillip. Charles has a few babes of his own . . ."

Adjusting his stiff legs, Marcus offered, "Granted, it has been a long time, but I don't know that I have the luxury of an extended stay—"

"Aunt Tizzy just sent me a letter . . ." Dunn handed Marcus the reins and reached into his inner coat pocket.

Marcus clicked his tongue and encouraged the horses to a swift canter. His father frowned, but did not otherwise reproach him. Dunn scanned the missive and Marcus noticed that his father had to hold the paper with his hand outstretched very far to read it. Then he gave up and pulled out his gold-rimmed spectacles. Marcus shifted in his seat, not wanting to recognize his father as anything but indomitable.

"Here it is." Dunn read from the page, "Phillip seems even more forgetful of late, oftentimes becoming disoriented while walking about even in our own garden. He's recovered, but has not quite been himself since the fall. Then there's the issue of his wheezing. I do worry that he is not long for this world and don't know how I will cope without him." Dunn rested the paper on his knee. "It goes on with more along the same vein."

"If I recall, Uncle Phillip has always had one ailment or another . . ."

"Yes, but this sounds more serious. And I would hate for you not to see him before he goes."

Marcus sighed. "I haven't seen him in seven years. Will it truly make a difference now?"

"Family is important, Marcus."

The unspoken rebuke about their rift hung in the air between them. Dunn had never been very good at veiling his meaning.

His father sighed. "Someday you will learn to appreciate the importance of family."

"Let us first see how things progress in town with my mission," Marcus replied. "Thereafter, we can discuss Uncle Phillip."

Dunn shifted in the seat. "Yes, of course . . . thank you."

They rode along in silence, the tension now having eased a bit. As if Marcus had conceded something. He wondered if it was like that with most fathers and sons, a combative relationship of advances and retreats. He'd been around so few lads who'd had fathers while growing up that he really didn't know, but somehow he suspected that other fathers and sons knew how to communicate without verbal bloodletting. In truth, it did not matter. Marcus would only have to suffer through this reunion for a short time, then all would be back as it should be. Him, free in the field, his father shackled to his large brown desk. The thought of resurrecting the status quo somehow lifted Marcus's spirits.

The sun was well matched with a refreshing breeze that pressed against Marcus's cheeks and caused the white plume to whip about on his shako. He was enjoying the jaunt, despite the ache in his thigh at the bandages with every bump. Tam had insisted that they be tight enough so as to alter Marcus's stride and remind him of the ruse.

Marcus welcomed the sights and sounds of the city, only now realizing that he had missed London and its cast of characters. A man in an oversized, dowdy brown coat pushing bric-a-brac wares on a handcart. An old woman in a faded yellow hat with frayed fringe hawked flowers from a basket on her arm. An innkeeper swept the entry with a swift *whoosh, whoosh*, then stopped to chat with a passerby. The scent of cooked mutton filled the air, almost overcoming the odor of horse manure and refuse.

"Does London seem much changed to you?" Dunn asked, watching him.

Marcus realized that he'd been grinning and stopped. Stifling his exuberance, he answered gruffly, "A city is a city."

Dunn shrugged. "I always thought London was special. But then again, I have not traveled abroad as you have. I suppose I never had the urge to . . . escape."

Having no desire to discuss his abrupt departure seven years before, Marcus changed the subject. "I need to meet with the board members soon. I was thinking that a dinner party at your club might be a way to hoist the sails on my acquaintances. Get things moving along."

Dunn studied him a moment, then turned and waved to a stout woman with several bedraggled children hanging about her ample black skirts. Noting Marcus's stare, the littlest, a girl with toffee hair and freckles, stuck her tongue out at him.

"I will send word today. A dinner party is a good idea," Dunn admitted. "But I must confess, I am concerned."

"On which front?"

"That one of the members of the board, most of whom I consider dear friends, has fallen in with Napoleon . . . Well, it makes me question my own good judgment." His face looked pained. "I don't understand. These are good, earnest fellows. Righteous men—"

"Even righteous men make mistakes."

"True."

Did Dunn have any idea that Marcus was referring to him? Marcus doubted it. Dunn saw the world through stained spectacles.

"I simply wonder if I'm going to be able to look them in the eye in the same way," Dunn continued, his voice tinny with distress. "I would not want to endanger you because I have difficulty maintaining a façade."

"I have to agree, you were never much of a player."

"And for good reason!" Dunn stiffened as if affronted. "I pride myself in dealing with people in a direct, if politic, manner. I am no *actor.*" He said the word as if it was a disease.

"Acting might not be a much admired profession, but it does have its uses."

"The inquiries, I can understand." Dunn frowned. "Yet I wonder at your ability to lie and deceive so easily, Marcus."

Marcus felt his hackles rise. Simply to annoy his father, he clicked at the horses and they quickened their pace around a bend. "Unlike you, my superiors have never tried to make me into something I am not. Instead, they value me."

Clutching the side of the seat in a death grip, Dunn snapped, "I have always valued you, Marcus. I just never understood why you had to be so damnably Machiavellian."

The old nagging sensation in the pit of Marcus's stomach felt like shame. He hated it, and himself for feeling it. He was never who his father wanted him to be. Never up to snuff. Trying to keep a harness on his anger, Marcus bit out, "Contrasting to how you always treated me, Lord Wellington prizes my abilities. There might be times when my labors might be considered less than straightforward, but—"

"War is a dirty affair and no one within it comes out clean."

"That's not true! Men act with valor, honor—"

"War is a necessary evil. Yet evil it remains."

"And you are so without blame?" Marcus replied, feeling as frustrated and grieved as he had those torturous years before when his father had betrayed him. "Soldiers fight to protect their country, to save their families! You, on the other hand, were so busy rescuing strangers that you failed to salvage your own family!"

Dunn's hands fisted on his lap and he stared straight ahead. "You have no idea about what you speak—"

"Mother tried to pretend, but her grief was obvious to everyone but you," he cried, his voice rising as fury overtook him. "You were too lost to your causes—hardly a husband to her!"

"Patricia knew well and good the man she was marrying when she made her choice—"

"But what upset her the most," Marcus interrupted, hardly listening to his father's flimsy excuses, "was how you treated me!" The child within him wanted to kick up a jig for the joy of finally laying this indictment at his father's feet. "That you would treat others better than your own flesh and blood—"

"I never treated the children of Andersen Hall better than you. They'd simply been through so much. You had every advantage—"

"Except having a father who cared!" The anger surging through him felt good. Clean. Straightforward. Dunn wanted honesty from his son? Well, he was going to get it, in full measure. "I only thank heaven she wasn't around the last few years to see how you behaved toward me."

"I had to be hard on you. It was the only way to discipline the wildness out of you. I—"

"I will never forget those words the day you betrayed me." He shook his head as his hands clenched on the reins. " 'If only you could be as much of a son to me as Nicholas is.' "

Dunn flinched as if struck.

"How is your old favorite, Nick Redford, anyway?" Marcus scoffed. "Still the sycophant he always was?"

"You might be justified in your anger toward me," Dunn replied stiffly. His cheeks were splotched red with antagonism. "But Nick never did a thing to hurt you."

That his father would jump to Redford's defense so easily made his stomach churn.

"You might be surprised how much you and Nick have in common," his father continued. "He recently opened his own enquiry firm—"

"I'd sooner have Napoleon as a mess-mate," Marcus scoffed, fuming. He wanted to make the horses run faster, but the road had grown too congested with pedestrians. He was about to shout at them to move aside and make way for the carriage, but suddenly realized that he had lost track of where he'd been leading the mounts. He never lost his bearings!

Marcus mentally shook himself. He was known as cool in a fix, master of his passions. Resentment, rage, agonizing disappointment, these were emotions he could ill afford in his line of work. He needed to remain unruffled to get the job done. It could mean the difference between success and failure, life and death. And he was never one to countenance failure. The cost was too high.

Marcus realized that now, more than ever, he needed to keep his emotions under control. To be detached in his relationship with his father. And everyone else at Andersen Hall.

Despite the clatter of city noises, it seemed as if a bubble of tense silence encased the gig.

It took only a few minutes for Marcus to regain his bearings; it took many more for the final flames of his fury to dissipate.

Composed once more, Marcus steered the conversation back on track, "If you cannot present the appropriate façade, then stay away from the board. Send me to the gatherings that you would otherwise attend. I will come bearing your apologies."

His father seemed relieved to be discussing a new topic. "I suppose that's easy enough."

"We might suggest that the orphanage is undergoing a crisis of sorts that requires your steadfast attention. Finances being low would probably do."

"Not far from the truth," Dunn muttered.

"How so?"

Dunn shrugged. "Society's pinchfistedness. The war, bad investments and the like. It seems to go in waves, but we are definitely at a low ebb."

Marcus could not imagine anything critical threatening the orphanage. It seemed so immutable. "How serious?"

"Nothing I have not faced before." Dunn sighed, rubbing his eyes. "Your presence on the board might actually improve the situation. Everyone loves a war hero."

In his typical fashion, his father would utilize every resource to help his precious orphanage. Even his own son. With his emotions under control now, it hardly bothered Marcus. Hardly at all.

Chapter 9

The hairs on Catherine's neck stirred, as if a cool breeze had penetrated the small office. But that was preposterous, as there was no window in her tiny study. Distractedly, she rubbed her collar and patted the loose bun to make sure that her unruly hair remained in place. Then she went back to examining the high bill for tallow from last month's supply of candles.

Odd, yet the feeling remained. She frowned, puzzled. Her skin prickled, as if . . . *someone* were watching.

Slowly, she peered over her shoulder.

Marcus leaned on the doorpost languidly, as if it were the most comfortable chaise at White's.

Her heart leaped and then cantered. How long had he been standing there? Hastily, she jumped from her seat, crashing the chair backward onto the floor with a loud crack. She'd been watching every doorway for three days, wondering when she might encounter Marcus Dunn again. Every time one of the lads would announce a visitor, her heart would gallop and her palms would grow sweaty. Now that he was finally here, her mouth was dried to dust and all of the arguments she'd planned in her head evaporated into mist. Her mind was abysmally blank.

"Allow me." He loped forward on his crutches as she stood transfixed. He no longer wore his uniform, but an azurite blue coat that somehow managed to match perfectly his brilliant eyes.

With astounding grace for a wounded man, he leaned over on his crutches and lifted the chair with one bare hand, righting it. He pushed it against the wall to the left of the secretary and stepped near the desk. He was so close she could smell the cloves on his breath and the sandalwood pomade he used to sweep back his hair. It was a spicy, yet refreshing combination. She could even discern the new growth of whiskers on his clean-shaven face, ready to darken his chiseled cheeks within hours. His body's heat filled the tiny office, making her feel suddenly warm.

She wished to step back, to find her equilibrium once more. But that was not possible in the small space. So instead, she turned her back to him and adjusted the ledgers on the desk, barely moving them so as not to lose her place.

"Thank you," she mumbled, irritated that her voice was unusually shrill. "It was clumsy of me."

She was glaringly aware of her drab gray dress, staid chignon and dowdy apron. The idiotic thought of Headmaster Dunn's offer of new gowns flitted through her mind. It was another of his odd turns of late, one that she'd emphatically refused. But never had she felt so painfully aware of her aged apparel. At least there were no cobwebs in her hair, this time. Still, why did she even care?

"It happens to all of us," he murmured in that honey-and-steel voice.

She could not in good conscience stand with her back to the man, so after taking a steadying breath, she turned, unhurriedly, and clasped her hands before her.

He seemed in no hurry to speak, simply stood there watching her, with an infuriatingly amused glint in his eye. Although he had his father's broad brow, sharp cheekbones, strong jaw and aristocratic nose, the wide-set shape of his eyes and those smooth peach-colored lips had to have come from Mrs. Dunn, who had died before Catherine had come to Andersen Hall. Yet, Catherine had pored over the lady's portrait in the headmaster's study often enough to gather that Mrs. Uriah Dunn had been a pretty, if somber lady.

Marcus had never been somber. Fiery, devilishly stirring: That was Marcus Dunn as a lad. Always up to one mischief or another. The girls had adored him and his devil-may-care attitude. The lads had followed him about wishing they were he.

He still had that aura of excitement, but it had changed somehow. Now, there was an added sense of . . . *danger* about him. A hardness beneath the charm. Like he would play cards with you one moment and slit your throat the next.

Catherine blinked, appalled that she would think such a terrible thing about Uriah Dunn's son. No, he might be roguish and up to no good, but he would not harm her, not intentionally; at least some of Uriah Dunn's blood flowed in his veins.

With that comforting thought, Catherine lifted her chin. "How can I be of service to you?"

"Service to me?" he echoed, making the offer sound anything but innocent.

Her cheeks burned, and she decided that at least one of them needed to be frank. "You obviously want something. What is it?"

His brow lifted at her discourtesy. "I'm recently back in town. Can I not stop by to pay a visit to an old friend?"

The idiocy of the comment fueled her suspicions that all was not as Marcus was trying to make it appear. "You are very good at rewriting history," she charged, crossing her arms. "I wonder why. What are you up to, Marcus Dunn?"

He leaned back on his crutches. "Must I have a hidden purpose?"

"You show up after years of stalwart silence and suddenly wish to make amends? Don't forget, I knew you as a lad. I am not so easily played."

"Ahh. Old hurts still sting. So what was it? A frog in your pocket? A pine needle on your chair?"

Digging her nails into her arms, she fought to cool her mounting irritation. Oh, how she hated dealing with irascible males. They were always trying to deflect the blame to others. "I have no concern for the past. My thoughts bear only on today. I am speaking of your swift turnabout. It seems contrived, to say the least. Whatever your game, I will not be so easily duped."

His blue eyes glittered with calculation and . . . amusement.

Her fury swelled. "There's nothing droll about how you are manipulating your father. Lord help you if you hurt him."

His gaze hardened. "I would never injure my father." Somehow he seemed taller, broader, looming over her in the small room.

Resisting the urge to step back, she took a steadying

breath. "Then what are your intentions? The orphanage has little enough for you to steal—"

"I am no petty thief." His tone had edged to iron.

"Then what are you about?" She lifted a shoulder, defiant. "Because you are certainly not a man prayerful for forgiveness. You, Marcus Dunn, don't have a begging bone in your body."

The bastard smiled then. The wretched knave actually grinned. She wanted to throttle him.

"Seven years I've been gone, yet you find it so easy to mark me?" he asked, coolly amused.

"People don't change." Thinking of Prescott, she amended, "Except in extraordinary circumstances."

"And my confrontation with death is not one of those extraordinary circumstances?" Exasperatingly, the man seemed to be enjoying verbally sparring with her.

"I don't trust you," she declared, crossing her arms. "And leaving you free to wreak havoc on this worthy institution or hurt your father, even his feelings, is a negligence I will not endure."

"My, you're quick to play judge, jury and executioner."

"Lord help me, if you keep this up, I will contact every member of the board of trustees and see you exposed as the charlatan that you are."

"You have no cause."

"If enough questions are asked—"

"I'm on the board already, one of *them*. You wouldn't dare."

"Try me."

They stood silently, like pugilists waiting for the call to come to blows.

After a long moment, his dark brow relaxed, and he exhaled softly. "Very well then." He dropped backwards into her chair, setting his crutches beside him. "May I?" he asked, after the fact.

Stiffly she inclined her head. The man *was* injured, she was not about to deny him a little rest.

Removing his hat, he raked his fingers through his hair, sending a whiff of sandalwood pomade her way. He set his hat on the open ledger on the desk. The man undoubtedly knew how to make himself comfortable.

"Would you please close the door?" he asked.

She did not move. Being alone with him was bad enough, a closed door was inviting speculation.

"I cannot speak candidly to you if the world is to hear," he added.

Begrudgingly, she unwound her arms and stepped over to the entry. After taking a quick look down each end of the passage and seeing no one loitering, she closed the door with a thud. Her stomach churned and her cheeks felt overly warm at being closed in such small quarters with him, but she was not about to let anything stop her from securing the truth.

Taking a deep breath, she turned.

He lounged in her chair with his shiny black Hessians crossed at the ankles, making his eggshell-colored breeches cling to muscular thighs like cream on milk. A slight bulge showed where his bandages covered his wounded thigh and above that . . . She lifted her eyes from that unsettling view. She supposed his gilt-buttoned azurite blue coat was the latest cut, but Prescott would know better than she. Marcus wore it over a discreetly patterned waistcoat that looked to be silk and an intricately tied neckcloth of snowy linen.

The man did not have the right to be so wretchedly gorgeous, especially when she was such a frump. But her dress was paid for with honest wages. From where came the hefty coin for his fashionable ensemble?

No, she would not be deceived by his smooth veneer. He could have been Adonis for all she cared. He was up to no good and she would do whatever necessary to protect Uriah Dunn and Andersen Hall Orphanage.

"If you would?" Marcus waved to the small stool in the corner that she used when one of the children visited. A few of the lads called it the "chicken claw" for its scrawny three-legged foundation.

Catherine did not like that he was taking over her office, but she was willing to go along with him, for the moment. Lifting the stool, she positioned it as far from him as possible, near the exit.

Awkwardly, she sat. Trying to appear authoritative on a chicken-clawed stool was not an easy endeavor. So she clasped her hands tightly in her lap and set her back up against the wall, toes forward, ankles together but uncrossed.

Running his hand through his sable hair, Marcus let out a deep breath. "I cannot afford to have you running about stirring up trouble—"

She stiffened. "Is that a threat?"

His hand lowered quickly. "I do not harm females." Memory seemed to flash in his azure gaze. "Well, unless they have a knife at my back."

She had no idea to what he was referring, but declared, "If your intentions are foul, then I will run to the board, or the constable, as fast as my feet will take me, and will cause you no end of trouble."

He shifted forward, leaning an elbow on his uninjured knee. "Let me ask you this, Cat. Does your protective streak run just to my father and this institution? Or does it run deeper?"

"Deeper?"

"Are you patriotic, for example?"

The question took her by surprise. "I'm no anarchist, if that's what you mean."

"And Napoleon?"

"A powermonger."

"You don't approve of him?"

"The man lives for war, so he can amass land, prestige, power. He does not 'free' anyone except nations from their treasuries." Her eyes widened and her heart began to pound. "You don't work for Napoleon, do you?"

He stiffened as if offended. "I'd sooner slit my own throat."

Relief swept through her. "That, at least, is one point in your favor."

Marcus smiled. She was judging *him!* She really believed that she could trounce him if the need presented itself. Astounding. And inspiring. The little kitten had grown the heart of a lioness in seven short years. Her gaze was steady, her hands held firmly before her, giving the sense that she had nothing to fear. Her chin was lifted in an almost regal manner. She reminded him of a pixie version of Lady Justice.

Still, why was she so quick to conclude him immoral? Did she know his secret and why he left London seven years before? There were few who did and they would not utter a word for fear of the repercussions. "Do you hold anything against me, besides for returning unexpectedly after an extended and taciturn absence?"

"You left on bad terms with your father, the kindest of men. And oh, how he grieved. Then suddenly all is well. Something is rotten in the state of Denmark."

So she liked Shakespeare. Well so did he. "Pray you now, forget and forgive," Marcus quoted King Lear.

"This is real life, not a theatrical production. I want to

know what you're about and will settle for nothing less than the truth."

Distantly, he wondered if her skin was as silky as her voice. It did not matter, as he would never find out. "I will tell you the truth of my presence here, but only if you swear on . . ." He wondered what would be most precious to her. "Didn't you have a little brother?"

Fear flashed in her smoky gaze. So that was her weakness.

"If you swear on your brother's life, I will tell you what you need to know," he finished. He ventured her word alone would have been good enough, but he wanted to weigh her reaction.

Her chin lifted a notch. "I will make no such pledge. For you to even suggest it is perverse. Tell me what I ask, then I will decide if it is worthy of secrecy."

Good for her. He really was enjoying this little session more than he rightly should. "My father said that you were a sharp one. He left off the part about your mettle."

"Stop shilly-shallying and tell me the truth."

He leaned forward, meeting her frosty gray gaze. "I'm here to obtain money to fight Napoleon."

Her pink lips pinched in disbelief. "Obtain?"

"Not to steal it. But simply to gain some funding, some support needed for certain supplies necessary for the war."

"Why send you?" Doubt shimmered in her stormy gaze and one golden brow lifted. She'd never make it on Drury Lane with an expressive face like that. "There are plenty of influential officers. You have no connections."

"Not true," Marcus countered, enjoying how she challenged him. "I saved a certain nobleman's son and my appearance here in town is intended to invoke his gratitude. I can say no more of the circumstances as they are quite confidential."

She stared at him a long moment, then exhaled noisily, sending him a hint of minty breath. "All of that . . ." She waved her hands mockingly. "*Drivel* about patriotism, secrecy, Napoleon . . . And this is the best story you can come up with?" She rose, setting her hands on those luscious hips. "Whatever you're up to, Mr. Dunn, I will not let it stand."

Then she marched toward the door.

Chapter 10

⟨──❦──⟩

Impulsively, Marcus grabbed Cat's wrist before she could take one pace toward the exit. "Very well, I will tell you the truth."

She froze midstep, and looked down to where they joined, as if scandalized by his touch. "Unhand me!"

The skin beneath his fingers was so soft Marcus had to resist the urge to glide his thumb over the delicate flesh. "Stop being such a naysayer and I will tell you what you wish to know."

"Release me, at once!" She tugged at her hand, obviously assuming that he would comply. But his grip only tightened.

"I don't want to hurt you—" he offered.

"Then don't!"

"Lower your voice, you needn't alarm the children."

At that, her struggles ceased.

Her pink lips set into a line and those gray eyes flashed icy fire. "You have until the count of ten to unhand me or I will scream."

"Like a game?" Oh, how he loved a challenge.

"I don't play with overgrown bullies," she bit out.

This was more fun than he'd had in months. "Very well."

Her face relaxed.

"One," he murmured, grazing the pad of his thumb over the baby-soft skin of her wrist.

She gasped. Ah, so the lady was susceptible to distraction.

"Two." His finger dipped into her palm and circled languidly.

Her eyes widened and her mouth opened slightly as if seeking air. She stared at her hand as if stunned speechless.

"Three." He traced the veins leading back to her wrist, and felt her pulse hammering. Satisfaction rushed through him and he smiled.

"Four." Leaning forward he set his lips to her pulse and licked the silky flesh. Gently, he sucked, tasting salt and inhaling the delicate scent of lemons she carried.

Her breath hitched and her long lashes fluttered.

"Five."

Suddenly, Catherine whipped her wrist away, grasping it to her chest, feeling singed. She was quaking, she realized. From outrage . . . and from fear. How could he have that power? Her heart was racing, her cheeks flaming and her breath seemed difficult to catch. With one caress he'd caused an avalanche of heat from her cheeks to her hairline to her toes, to deep within her womb. She was appalled.

Was every woman so effortlessly toyed with? Or was her innocence an Achilles' heel? Or was he an extraordinarily talented seducer? She couldn't quite imagine any other man capable of such thing, but her inexperience made her unsure of herself.

When he'd caressed her, she'd had to fight the compulsion to close her eyes, to allow her thoughts to drift and let him have his way with her.

If she'd considered Marcus dangerous before, now she viewed him as lethal.

"Don't ever do that again." She hardly recognized her own voice it was so throaty. Stepping away, she hugged herself, shaken to the core.

"Do what?" he asked with a white, wicked smile, not even bothering to look innocent.

"Just don't." She wasn't going to play his game; she knew she'd lose. He was obviously a man of great experience and he clearly had no compunction about using his wiles for insidious ends.

Well, she would not be his instrument. She would not allow anyone such power over her. Catherine opened the door. "Get out."

The blackguard didn't even bother to stand. "We're not finished."

She shook her head, emphatic. "Yes, we are."

"Don't you want to know the truth about my return?"

She hesitated, dubious. Yet, somehow, she wanted to end this encounter without feeling so easily manipulated. Was that even possible with such a rogue?

"No more games," he asserted. "General's honor."

It was an old pledge from the childhood days of wage-war. Although Catherine hadn't played very often, she did understand the principle behind the assurance and did not think that he would breach it. Or would he? The man had no compunction about playing fast and loose with a woman he obviously had no interest in. Still, she'd gained nothing from this encounter and had given at every quarter. There had to be some way to save face.

Catherine lifted her chin. "Only if the door remains open."

"Fine. But come sit."

She hesitated, unsure of how to handle this wolfish man.

"It was unfair of me to try to intimidate you," he admitted. "I apologize."

Her eyes narrowed, she didn't trust one word he said. Not by a hair.

Pressing his hand to his chest, he offered, "You have to know how much that apology just pained me."

Well, perhaps a word or two.

Slowly, keeping a keen eye on the blackguard, she sat.

Relaxing back into the chair, Marcus adjusted his injured leg. She couldn't help the tinge of sympathy that tugged at her. But that did not mean that she would allow him to manipulate her again.

"My superior officer sent me," he began in a hushed, honeyed tone. She tried to ignore his false charm and concentrate on the facts beneath his words. "To save my hide."

"Why did he feel the need?"

He sighed. "I got myself into a bit of a fix."

Crossing her arms, she leaned back. "Now there's a surprise."

"My superior thought that I needed to get out of my regiment for a time. A break from the army altogether." His gaze hardened to blue frost. "It was not my choice."

"Then why comply?" She supposed that Marcus could squirm his way out of a pit of venomous snakes if he had to.

"I was made an offer that I found hard to refuse."

She tilted her head. "What was it?"

"Court-martial." The muscle in his clenched jaw worked. "And a few other choice punishments I'd rather not discuss in mixed company."

Oh, such a gentleman.

"I didn't want to come back." The anger in his gaze was

convincing, she had to admit. "In fact, I tried various means of changing my superior's mind."

"To no avail," she supplied.

"His view was fixed. And so was my fate."

"So you're here for . . . how long?"

He shrugged. "A month, mayhap two. Just until things . . . settle down."

"And then?"

"Back to my unit."

"In Spain?"

"Portugal, Spain, who knows. Wherever they decide I can best serve." The timbre of his voice was trying to communicate, "We are underlings in arms." It probably worked well for him.

"Then there's the matter of the money."

"The money?"

"What I told you before about collecting some funds was not a lie."

She raised a brow. "So you saved a man's life? And now the father is supposed to express his gratitude in blunt?"

"Let me simply say that a certain gentleman will be reaching deep into his pockets as evidence of his patriotism."

"Out of the goodness of his heart, I'm sure." Her tone was derisive.

"I can be very persuasive, when I want to be."

Slowly, she nodded. "So while you are here, serving on the board of trustees, you are simply . . ."

"Ingratiating myself into his circles."

"How politic of you." She pasted a false grin on her face. "I would have thought that you'd simply whip out your sword and hand him a quill and a bank draft."

"I only 'whip out my sword' when it pleases me."

Belatedly, realizing her tongue slip, she wanted to smash the wickedly amused look from his features.

"Besides, as I explained, I've time to cool my heels."

She inquired frostily, "So where are you staying during your visit to town?"

"Ah, so have you missed my presence at Andersen Hall already?"

She didn't deign an answer.

"At Weatherly's Boardinghouse, on Lamont Street. It's not the best quarters, mind you," he admitted. "But officers do get a special rate."

"Are we done?" she asked, reminded of how her peevish brother often spoke to her.

"Do I have your word that you will not tell anyone of my circumstances here?"

She was betting that he knew that she always kept her word. Headmaster Dunn had probably provided the intelligence in all innocence.

"Of course." She waved a hand. "I wouldn't spread the tale for all the tea in China."

He looked at her oddly as if he couldn't decide what to make of her comment. Then he nodded. "Thank you."

"My pleasure."

He smiled.

Her cheeks heated but she refused to look away.

"My father asked that you assist me with information regarding the orphanage. I would like to see the ledgers."

She felt herself bristle, but Headmaster Dunn *had* asked her and he was her employer. Even if he was completely blinded to his son's chicanery. "If you make an appointment—"

"Now would be fine." He stood, looming over her as he adjusted his crutch beneath his arm.

"I'm really quite busy."

"Aren't those the ledgers?" He pointed to the books open on her desk.

She gritted her teeth, unable to think of an excuse. Where was the harm, really? "The price of tallow intrigues you?" she inquired, standing. She hated that she had to crane her neck to meet his treacherous gaze.

He smiled, and it was so charming, she almost felt her lips try to respond in kind. So she frowned.

"Everything intrigues me," he murmured.

Could he coat it with any more hogwash if he tried?

"Fine." She waved to the books. "Enjoy yourself. But if you lose my page, I will be furious."

"But you're so even-tempered . . ."

She's never felt the urge to slap someone before but she was coming awfully close.

Stepping over, he removed his hat and lifted the book. He traced his large, nimble hand down the page of the open ledger, as if he could caress the information he wanted out of it. She felt violated for herself and her poor ledger.

She crossed her arms, staring daggers at his broad back.

"Where is the solicitation schedule?" he asked, not even bothering to look up.

"The what?"

He turned, a look of mockery on his wretchedly gorgeous features. "The list of all of the donors to Andersen Hall and what they've given."

"Oh, that." She gritted her teeth, wondering how he knew such an intimate detail of the workings of Andersen Hall.

"Please give it to me."

She stood, indecisive.

"Or must I ask my father like the boy whose nurse has refused to give him his milk?"

She didn't see that she had much choice. Headmaster Dunn had been quite adamant about cooperating with his son. He didn't want to hear any more of her theories about Marcus Dunn.

"Excuse me," she muttered.

Marcus watched as Cat stepped behind him and grasped his now vacant chair. She picked it up, then slammed it down with a loud thump next to the bookcase. She really was quite stiff-necked, a trait he appreciated only in himself, he mused.

He held out his hand for support, but the peevish chit ignored it. Stepping onto the seat and reaching for the highest shelf, she thumbed through the books. The gray fabric of her gown stretched taut over her firm breasts, completely eradicating the dreary effect of the high-necked, long-sleeved twill gown. It was a wholly artless motion, yet it couldn't have been done better by a seductress at Madame Foulard's House of Pleasure for the effect it had on him.

He swallowed, reminding himself that she was out of reach, figuratively, if not literally. He had not intended to tease her as he'd done before. It had not been well-done of him. But her challenges had been too tempting to ignore. And oh, to witness the shocked look on her face. To see the ice in her gaze thaw to flame. The woman was directing all of her passions into her arguments, instead of the bedchamber where they belonged. He could just imagine how fiery she could be between the covers. She had a natural sensuality that begged to be ignited. He could just see her with her silky blond hair splayed across a white pillow, her pink mouth open, inviting, her stormy gray eyes hooded as she cried out—

Blast if he wasn't going to have to do something about his randy thoughts. But he had few options. He'd lost his taste for pleasure houses long ago, when he'd won at cards and had paid for the entire night with a certain lass named Lucinda. Spending a whole night in a house of infamy might seem like heaven on earth to most men, but to Marcus, waking up in the morning and seeing the effect the night had had on the women had ended his brothel days forever. He'd stayed with the women all morning, listening to their stories, all the while noticing the bruises, the vacant looks, the suffering and despair. He'd never thought of the pleasure trade in the same light and would never partake again.

So relief from that quarter was not an option. And neither was Catherine Miller. He did not debauch innocents. Inwardly, he sighed, knowing it was for the better. It was not just her honor he was upholding by remaining aloof, but getting involved with a maiden would be a messy proposition. Cat, in particular, he suspected. And if there was one thing Marcus was good at, it was at keeping his life uncomplicated.

Seizing a thick volume, Cat turned in the chair, toppling slightly. Without thought, his arms reached for her, grasping her slim waist. Her small hand rested lightly on his shoulder, the other held the book.

"Oh," she breathed as her cheeks flushed a lovely shade of cherry. How he loved when she was discomfited. "I'm fine, really."

Everything at Andersen Hall smelled slightly earthy and damp. Except for the lemon-scented lady in his arms. Lemons, of all things. It was not perfume, but scented soap perhaps. He found himself partial to the clean, citrus scent, and wondered if there was anyone else in her life who appreciated it as well. A suitor, perhaps? But that was none of his affair.

She cleared her throat, looking anywhere but at him.

"Ah, thank you." Her voice was throaty with just a hint of unease. "But I'm fine."

"I won't bite," he assured, wanting to do exactly that. He had to fight his reluctance to release her. But after a moment, he stepped back and extended his hand.

She hesitated, then lifted her chin. Bully for her; she wasn't going to show him any weakness. Her fingers were warm and dainty in his palm as she stepped down, not meeting his eye.

"If that will be all?" she bit out, obviously unhappy with him and yet unable to do a thing about it.

"For now." He couldn't help himself.

She stepped toward the open door, seemingly desperate to escape him. "You can read everything here. Don't take anything from my office."

"I'm not a thief," he called out to her receding back.

"No, only a liar," she muttered under her breath.

He smiled, looking around the small office. It seemed so empty without her, but her lemony scent lingered like the smoke from a doused candle, still carrying the memory of heat and dancing flame.

Chapter 11

〜〜⁂〜〜

The next afternoon, Catherine stood in an alcove on Lamont Street diagonally across from a brown, wooden, four-storied structure with two large red-painted doors with gold frames. A crimson, white and gold sign swung over the doors on a spring breeze, declaring the establishment Weatherly's Boardinghouse—Marcus Dunn's temporary residence while in town.

In addition to being a rooming house, it apparently was a popular drinking establishment, as men in uniform had been coming and going for the last two hours. The officers seemed to travel in twos and threes, congenially slipping inside, then upon leaving, easily melting into the flow of the congested street. For all of the activity, Catherine's raven-haired scoundrel had yet to appear.

She adjusted the white oversized bonnet on her head, irritated that it hung so long over her ears. But it had been difficult to find a housemaid's dress that fit on such short notice, especially when everyone she knew who had one needed it for work. Luckily, a friend of one of the Andersen Hall staff had recently run off with an underbutler and had left her uniform behind.

The voluminous gray gown hung on her like a sack and she'd had to strap it up with a line of cord. Still, she doubted anyone would spare her a second glance. She would likely be judged a young servant with a clutchfisted employer who'd given her a used gown. Yet, she feared someone might notice that the young servant hovering about in an alcove had been there for hours, the epitome of idleness.

She'd already eaten the apple and hunk of cheese she'd brought along in her wool netted reticule, and the bag hung limply at her side. She wondered if Marcus Dunn would deign to appear before dinner or if she should use her coin for one of the meat pies they were selling down the lane. The scent of meat and pastry tugged at her middle like pincers.

Much of the pinched feeling was nerves, she knew. She had never been one for stealth, and spying on a dangerous man, one who already made her jumpy, was more than a bit nerve-wracking. But since Marcus wouldn't tell her the truth about why he was back, she was forced to figure it out on her own.

Ever since leaving the orphanage, her heart had been hammering and she couldn't seem to get enough moisture in her mouth. A meat pie might make her feel better . . . But what if she missed him? She'd already wasted a whole afternoon, and Headmaster Dunn would expect her back by dinner. He thought her on a trip to a circulating library and even though she often lost sight of the time while there, in good conscience she shouldn't be gone for so long.

But how well would she be able to conduct herself if she were starving?

Just as she was about to venture down the lane, Marcus exited the all-male establishment. She would have noticed the tall, broad, raven-haired rogue in a crowd of thousands, even without his bright crimson uniform and distinctive white plume.

"Finally," she muttered, but for all her bravado, her heart was in her throat and her pulse pounded in her ears. Imagining trailing Marcus was one thing, actually doing it was suddenly far chancier. She schooled her nerves to steady and studied her prey.

Standing in front of the boardinghouse, Marcus conferred with a lanky, red-uniformed man with a hat under his arm. The man's shiny bald head glistened in the afternoon sun. Catherine pressed the man's prominent hooked nose and weathered features into her memory, not knowing when she might need the intelligence.

Distantly she wondered why Marcus wore his uniform some days and discarded it on others. Likely to use it to influence his audience, she mused. She imagined him a slimy actor, pretending to be noble when he was anything but. Using his charm to disarm innocent young women, leading them down the path of depravity . . .

Her anger seethed. Oh, how often she'd mentally replayed those moments in her office, wishing that she'd slapped the supercilious smile off his face. Or stomped on his good foot and listened to him howl. The anger erased her fear, lending her the strength of purpose to follow Marcus wherever he went today.

The unknown man nodded patiently as Marcus spoke. The man must work for Marcus, she realized, and her heartbeat quickened even more. She hadn't counted on tracking two men, only one. That meant four eyes potentially discovering her, and the possibility of facing an unknown element. Her mind scrambled for how to deal with this turn of events, but just then, the man set his hat on his bald head and took off to the east. Marcus turned and loped along in the opposite direction, his crutches swinging easily before each stride.

Taking a steadying breath, Catherine adjusted her bonnet and tried to look nonchalant as she followed Marcus from across the thoroughfare. She hung back, ready to jump into the nearest alcove if he turned. But he moved blithely onward, as unaware of his surroundings as if he were on a stroll in a peaceful pasture.

She wished she could feel peaceful and wondered at her own disquiet. Was she so frightened of Marcus? Nervous at being discovered, yes, but not afraid of him. Somehow, she doubted that he would actually harm her. Debauch her, perhaps . . .

Her heart skipped a beat. She couldn't think of consequences, only of Headmaster Dunn, the orphanage and the children. Inhaling a deep breath, she tried to ignore the rank odor of refuse hanging over the street and focus on her quarry.

Marcus stopped to confer with a street urchin. Even from across the thoroughfare, his charm practically oozed for the world to see. The young lad was grinning a toothless smile as he readily accepted a coin from Marcus and scampered off. Marcus probably considered himself a philanthropist now.

Catherine's sense of unease intensified. Was it the boy? No, she didn't think so. Her instincts had saved her from more than one confrontation with her cousin, Stanford Caddyhorn, before she'd escaped her wretched aunt and uncle's house; since then she'd only grown to respect her intuition even more. Her eyes scanned the street, drifting over the muted gowns, white bonnets, brown caps and sundry faces. Horses' hooves clattered down the lane as a carriage rolled past.

Marcus moved off, loping along on his crutches, his white plume whipping on the spring breeze.

Catherine sped up, not to lose sight of him. That's when she saw the men.

Two burly ruffians dressed in brown clothing followed Marcus, their gazes intent, their movements less walking than stalking. They wore brown caps slung low over their eyes. An air of menace hung about them, evident from the determined looks on their features, the tight set of their shoulders and how their hands fisted at their sides.

Marcus stopped to chat with a shopkeeper and Catherine hung back, watching. The two men delayed their progress, pretending to examine a store window, a dressmaker's display, one with pink ruffles and bows. Catherine tasted cotton and realized that she was chewing on her thumb through her glove. What mischief had Marcus gotten himself into now?

A short, wiry fellow in a long black coat and sloppy black hat joined the two men, staring up at the same window display. He turned and quickly scanned the passersby. Catherine spun around and stepped over to a pastry stall, staring at the baked goods as if she were starved, but she couldn't eat now even if all the pastries were free.

After a moment, Catherine peered over her shoulder. The men had no eyes for her, only Marcus.

The short one spoke, then jerked his head toward Marcus. One of the taller men pulled a club from his pocket and showed it to the man.

They meant to assail him!

Catherine felt the sudden urge to do something. But

what? Marcus was the villain in this piece, wasn't he? If he was caught up in mischief, shouldn't he suffer the penalty of his actions? Still, he was Headmaster Dunn's son and if Marcus was hurt, or worse yet, killed, then Dunn would be devastated. And deep down, she knew, so would she. She might want to arrest Marcus's plans, but that didn't mean she wished him injury. Well, at least nothing permanent.

Reaching down, Catherine lifted a broken brick from the ground and slipped it into her reticule. The wool netting stretched heavily with its new contents. She felt like David readying his sling to face Goliath, but without his legendary confidence.

Marcus resumed his stroll and the men stalked him once more.

As Catherine trailed behind this powder keg situation, she wondered what was going to happen if the men attacked. Marcus seemed fit and strong, but he was injured. Moreover, it would be three against one. Somehow Catherine doubted that these men would fight fair. As if there was such a thing.

But they were on a busy street . . . doubtless these men wouldn't act so boldly. If people saw an army officer being attacked, they would rush to Marcus's aid, wouldn't they?

The short wiry fellow glanced over his shoulder, his dark piercing eyes fixing on her. It took every ounce of willpower for Catherine not to freeze in her tracks. She kept walking, her eyes set forward, her bad leg suddenly giving her more of a limp than she'd had in years. *I'm lame, no threat to you*, she cast the thoughts at the man. *I'm of no consequence.*

His gaze slipped past her and she almost sagged with relief.

Then the man's eyes lighted on another, just a few steps behind her. Pretending to fix her shoe, Catherine surreptitiously peered over her shoulder. Two beefy gray-clothed men stepped past her and trotted ahead, their gazes focused on the oblivious Marcus Dunn.

Five of them!

She had to warn him. No matter his offenses, she couldn't stand by.

Catherine stepped into the lane to cross the street, but her long hem snagged on her shoe. Impatiently she yanked it free. But when she looked up again, Marcus had vanished.

Her heart skipped a beat.

Where had he gone?

The three men stalking Marcus on his side of the street quickened their pace, then rushed into a narrow alleyway between two buildings. The two men on Catherine's side of the lane raced across and swept inside the same darkened passageway, disappearing into the shadows.

Marcus must have blindly given these men their chance!

Desperately Catherine searched the street for a constable, anyone. Then, upon seeing a foot soldier in his crimson uniform, she raced over and grabbed his arm. He looked down at her, his youthful face appalled.

"My friend is being attacked! Please help! He's an officer!"

The man's eyes filled with fear. Shoving her off, the soldier turned and dashed away into the crowd.

"Please, somebody, help!"

People veered away from her as if she were crazed, their eyes not meeting hers.

Terrified for what Marcus must be going through in the dark alleyway, Catherine rushed across the thoroughfare.

Horses' hooves stormed down upon her. She'd run directly into the path of a charging carriage!

Catherine raised her arms above her head and closed her eyes, certain death was upon her.

The driver screamed curses as he frantically steered the carriage's team to the left. Catherine stood frozen, her heart in her throat. The horses stampeded so close, Catherine could almost taste their sweat. But astoundingly, she was whole.

"What the bloody hell do you think yer doing charging into the street like that?" the driver shouted.

Catherine opened her eyes and lowered her arms, so shaken she could hardly breathe. She wasn't dead. The driver had saved her. But she had no time to thank him.

"Sorry!" Catherine sprinted toward the opening where the men had gone, hoping that the carriage driver would forgive her rudeness.

The sun did not penetrate the long, narrow passage, and within it the air was chilled. The odor of feces and rot and garbage assailed her as she rushed forward, trying not to think about where she was going or what she might do. Grunts and cries welcomed her from deep in the belly of the lane, so far from the busy street.

She turned a corner.

Two burly men circled Marcus, as he swung his crutch about like a weapon. Two men lay motionless on the grimy ground. The larger of the two men brandished a short silver knife in his hand, the other wielded a club. The man with the blade lunged at Marcus.

Marcus whipped the crutch down on the man's knife arm and flipped it back around for a thrust into the attacker's middle. The man grunted and slumped to the ground.

The other man stepped out of range of the crutch, seemingly having learned his ally's lesson.

Marcus was panting, as his hands clenched the crutch and he eyed his much larger opponent. Violence shimmered off him in waves along with an aura of . . . enjoyment. But that was absurd. The man couldn't actually be taking pleasure in this dangerous brawl. Doubt slithered through her mind. Had Marcus actually intended to trap his attackers? The quarry stalking the supposed hunters? Had he purposefully acted oblivious, all the while leading the men away from the bystanders?

Someone grabbed Catherine's bonnet and her hair within, wrenching her head backwards so roughly she was lifted off the ground. Pain shot through her head as she slammed up against a hard form. Something cold was pressed to her exposed neck.

"Stop or I'll kill the girl!" Gripping her hair so tightly she couldn't move, the man pushed a sharp blade to her throat. The *fifth* man, of course. Panic paralyzed her.

Marcus froze, his fiery gaze fixing on Catherine. Any amusement she'd thought she'd seen evaporated. His sea blue gaze was as hard as ice. His eyes narrowed. His upper lip curled. He seemed to grow before her eyes, looming with lethal intention.

"Drop it or I'll kill her!" the brute shouted so loudly in her ear that it rang.

Catherine wondered what Marcus would do, not knowing what to pray for. She didn't trust the man's word and doubted that Marcus did either. But she didn't want to die.

After a moment, Marcus held up his crutch in surrender, his shoulders sagging, his stance relaxing.

The man nearest Marcus straightened and snickered, as if the fight were finished.

He obviously did not know Marcus Dunn.

The knife at her throat lowered.

Catherine smashed her heel down on the wiry man's foot and whirled out from under his grasp just as Marcus hurled his crutch at the other burly man.

Behind her, her assailant screamed.

Catherine whipped around, and froze, stunned.

A knife protruded from her former captor's eye. Shrieking in tortured agony, the villain dropped to the ground, convulsing.

Involuntarily, Catherine stepped away, pressing up against the cold brick wall. She tore her eyes from the terrible sight and looked over at Marcus.

The iciness she saw in his gaze stopped her cold.

Behind Marcus, the burly, brown-clothed man slowly stood, a pistol raised in his hand.

"Behind you!" Catherine screamed, as she flung her bag straight at the attacker. With the broken brick lending it weight, the wool-netted reticule went hurling through the air. The missile slammed into the man's forehead with astounding accuracy.

The brute toppled backwards.

His pistol discharged in the air and a deafening blast rang out.

A noise cracked above Catherine's head.

She looked up.

Then all went black.

Chapter 12

Voices slithered into Catherine's consciousness, but she shoved them away. It hurt too much to hear, to think, even to breathe. Her head ached so badly she felt as if someone had hacked it through with a woodcutter's axe. With each pulsing of her heartbeat, her head exploded in shards of agony. She willed her body to still, her heartbeat to stop.

She gritted her teeth, fighting the nausea that roiled in her belly. It was worse than the throbbing. Inhaling deeply, she struggled for her equilibrium. There was nothing but the pain.

"—paid the keeper—"

"—don't leave the rooms—"

It was a man's gruff voice that sounded like trumpets roaring in her ears. *Quiet!*

"—the foolish chit saved my life."

That got her attention. Memory surfaced. Marcus. The brutes. The alleyway.

Girding herself, she opened her eyes. Golden candle-

light filled her vision so brightly it was like staring
straight at the blinding sun. She bit back a gasp from the
pain and closed her eyes.

"Did the message get to my father?" It was Marcus's
deep rumbling voice couched in a whisper.

"Yes, sir." The gruff man.

"And was he pacified?"

"Well enough for the present."

"Good."

Pushing away the pain, Catherine opened one eye,
barely a slit. She was in a bedroom, one she'd never seen
before. She lay in a black four-poster bed with a crimson
coverlet matching the long red drapes that were drawn,
shrouding the room in darkness. Brown wood paneling
covered the walls and the far white door was closed. A fire
burned in the white-manteled hearth, but Catherine turned
her eyes away, for the pain of the light.

Slowly, her eyes adjusted as she stared at shadows, then
she peered over to her left.

In the golden light of a candelabrum, Marcus stood before a mirror, his large hands clenching the tarnished
gilded frame. Her breath caught; he was practically naked
like some marble statue of a brazen Greek god.

She froze, careful not to make a sound. She felt like an
interloper, never dreaming that she'd have the opportunity
to glimpse the sight before her. Moreover, she didn't know
if she'd ever see anything so exquisite again.

Catherine soaked in the hard angles, sweeping planes
and flowing splendor of his beauty. His dark hair was
mussed, falling like a black curtain over his broad shoulders. His muscles were stretched taut as he gripped the
frame, obviously in pain. She wondered if those muscles
were as hard as they appeared. Would his skin be warm to

the touch? She swallowed, feeling something tighten deep inside her.

Her gaze hungrily devoured his buttery skin. The bulging corded muscles that rippled down his back in creamy waves. The canal running through the muscles, trailing downward to the thin, almost translucent scrap of white material that covered the twin globes of his muscular buttocks. The line of shadow between his buttocks could easily be seen through the shamefully thin fabric.

Involuntarily her lips parted, seeking more air.

She forced her gaze upward. A slash of blood marred the creamy skin of his side, dripping onto the white material. So he'd been cut in the tussle; it could have been so much worse. Vague lines and marks could barely be seen in the candlelight, indicating that this was not the first injury he'd suffered.

"Be quick about it, will you, Tam," Marcus's voice was a harsh whisper, but it seemed as loud as horses' hooves trampling in her ears.

The lanky hooked-nose fellow approached, a needle and thread in his sinewy hands. Catherine suddenly realized his intention and she swallowed, fighting a rush of nausea. But she was fascinated and couldn't tear her eyes away. Her heart began to hammer, pounding through her aching head.

Marcus's brawny legs were spread wide and his stance tense as his man set the needle to flesh. Marcus hissed, but made no other sound.

It took every ounce of Catherine's willpower to keep from retching.

The lanky man moved, blocking her view. She bit back a relieved sigh. Still, Catherine grieved to have lost the view. Although she'd never admit as much to a living soul, seeing Marcus Dunn's naked flesh was one of the most tit-illating experiences of her lifetime.

"Just need to knot it, sir," the man muttered. "There. You'll be right as rain, sir."

The man stepped aside. The creamy white flesh drew Catherine's eyes like a feline to milk. Marcus's injury was a mass of red just above the slope of his lower back . . . that swept into that tight round derriere.

Her gaze scanned those luscious buttocks, delighting in the landscape of his hard curves. Deep inside Catherine's womanly core, she felt a heat, a tightening, a yearning for something she'd never known she'd wanted before. It was unsettling, like an imbalance within her. One that ached with need.

"Thank you, Tam." Marcus turned.

Golden candlelight washed over his glorious torso, lighting his chest in intimate detail. Catherine bit her lip, entranced by the expanse of undulating muscle with a spattering of dark curls splayed across.

Catherine felt her nipples stiffen as if under the spell of Marcus's flesh. The tips pushed into the scratchy wool, making her yearn to shift restlessly beneath the blankets.

Dark fluff trailed from Marcus's chest down his trunk to that paltry shred of clothing covering his privates. A sudden ache swelled deep inside of Catherine as her eyes skated over that bulging white cloth. Her eyes drifted downward, to his powerful muscled thighs coated in a dark fuzz—

What?

Catherine's mouth dropped open, as the realization dawned on her. There wasn't a scratch on either of his strapping thighs! No bandage, no mar, no injury of any kind! Why, the lying—

"Knave!" she screamed, launching up from the bed.

Searing pain cleaved her head in two. She saw stars. Clasping her hands to her head, she tried to press her aching skull together, but the pain rolled on and on and on. Her stomach lurched and her vision blurred.

Hands compelled her sideways and held her shoulders while she vomited into a chamber pot. Her eyes stung as tears squeezed out the corners with every agonizing heave. Her face ached and her head exploded while she choked up everything she'd eaten in the last day until there was nothing left to give. Gasping for air as if she'd almost drowned, Catherine fell back onto the pillow, her eyes sealed. A layer of sweat coated her entire body and yet she was chilled.

Gentle hands set a cold, damp cloth on her forehead. She heard whimpering and realized that it was coming from her. She gritted her teeth and stopped the pitiful noise.

Another cold, damp cloth was laid on her chest, in the gap between her breasts, and another on the soles of her feet. Then two heavy woolen blankets were wrapped around her.

Miraculously, the pain eased.

It was such a relief Catherine wanted to weep. Distantly she realized that she was naked, but she couldn't think about that now. All she could focus on was the joy of the pain having been lessened.

Slowly the world came back into focus.

The mattress beside her sank with weight. The scent of sandalwood identified her "nurse". Fury and exhaustion warred within her. She wanted to kick him, shout at him, and at the same time she was too tired even to roll over.

"Feeling any better, Cat?" Marcus murmured softly.

She cracked open one eye and even that felt like a Herculean effort.

The candles had been extinguished, and the only light came from the dying embers of the fire. Marcus now wore a long burgundy dressing gown with golden cuffs and collar.

Catherine ignored the stab of disappointment that he'd dressed.

"You lied." Her voice was a rasp.

"Frequently. But with no ill intention."

"Every lie . . . is malicious."

He reached toward her and removed the now warm cloth. Dropping it into a bowl of water, he squeezed it and reset it on her forehead. It felt so good, she had to close her eyes.

"Rest now, Cat."

"You're . . . a . . ." She tried to think of something appropriately terrible but her mind was like pottage. ". . . knave."

Cat lost the fight and surrendered to the darkness.

"I'm glad to see you back to your old self," Marcus murmured, so relieved he felt weak. He was almost giddy that she'd regained consciousness so quickly and was feeling herself enough to chastise him.

If anything happened to Cat because of him . . .

Pushing away the dreadful thought, Marcus reached over and smoothed her velvety hair. When he'd imagined her golden tresses splayed on his pillow it was not with bloodied bandages wrapped around them. He had wanted her in his bed, but not like this. Never like this. Dark circles banked her eyes, and her porcelain skin was red and molten from her vomiting. Marcus traced his fingers lightly over her forehead, smoothing the lines. Her face relaxed even more. Her breathing evened with slumber, as small puffs escaped her pink bowed lips.

She'd grown the heart of a lioness in the years since he'd known her. Blossoming from timid wallflower to protective mother bear. Even going so far as to storm into a street fight . . . to accomplish what? Had she gone in to . . . *save him?* The idea was absurd.

Yes, she'd saved him, but it was instinct, pure and simple, it had to be. She didn't trust him, said so at every turn. She'd probably thought that he was mixed up with the men and had wanted to stop them. The notion of the righteous Cat storming into a conspiracy to stop it made much more sense. Yet, in the back of his mind, the prospect of Cat watching out for him lingered, and the thought was not displeasing.

Since his return, Marcus had seen how hard she worked for the orphanage, how much his father relied on her and how protective she was of everyone she loved. Deep down, he realized that he was a bit envious of the protectiveness his father elicited from Cat. He wouldn't mind someone caring after him with such dedication . . .

What was he saying?

He shifted uneasily on the bed. He was used to being on his own. A lone wolf hunting its prey. It was better that way, actually. Then he didn't have to watch out for someone else, didn't have to suffer an Achilles' heel. If he cared, then he was vulnerable. Alone, he avoided being exposed to manipulation or the threat of betrayal . . .

"You couldn't have known, sir," Tam muttered from over his shoulder.

Marcus started, almost having forgotten that the sergeant was there. Although he was bald as a doorknob, Marcus suspected that Tam was not much past thirty-five. It was hard to tell given his weathered skin with crinkles around his eyes, mouth and traversing his forehead in waves. He was tall, lanky and had a hooked nose so crooked some of the men called him "popper." But not when he was within earshot.

Tam was tough, having served in the ranks for as long as Marcus could remember, and moving up to become sergeant three years before. What Marcus liked about the man was that he was creative and had a mind of his own. He was not a sheep to be led to slaughter as sometimes happened to the ranks with certain of the ludicrous decisions of the officers. Tam chased the golden chalice of victory as steadfastly as any other, but did so while looking out for his men and his arse. That's why he was such a good man to have at one's back.

"An' her face was lost in that bloody bonnet, no wonder you didn't recognize her," Tam continued.

"Oh, I saw her, Tam," Marcus countered, recalling the glance he'd spared her. "But I dismissed her as a nonthreat. I should have suspected she'd do something, especially after our interview yesterday."

"Was she always this foolhardy?"

Slowly, Marcus shook his head. "I hadn't thought so, but perhaps I just didn't see it before. I might have misjudged her quietness as timidity, her small stature as weakness." He ran his hand through his hair. "I don't know . . ."

A knock banged on the door. Tam shot him a glance and stepped behind the doorframe. A club appeared in his hand.

Marcus stood, grabbing for his sword. He ignored the tinge he felt in his side and readied.

"Who is it?" he called.

"Your father."

Marcus would know that deep, disapproving tone anywhere. He nodded and Tam unlatched the door

With his typically economic movements, Uriah Dunn stepped inside. His face was somber as his eyes darted to the bed. His stern features hardened to granite.

Chapter 13

~~~

Girding himself for his father's harsh judgment, Marcus set his sword aside, careful not to place it anywhere near the sleeping Catherine. He motioned to Tam. After peering down each hallway, the good sergeant discreetly slipped outside and closed the bedroom door.

Marcus stepped behind him, set the latch and turned.

Dunn's penetrating blue gaze met Marcus's and it took all of Marcus's self-control not to look away. "Sir, I never intended—"

"Why did you have to drag Catherine into it?" Dunn barked.

"I didn't drag her into—"

"Then why is she lying there?" His father motioned to the bed where Cat lay. "With her head wrapped in blood-ied bandages?"

"She followed me—"

"You're a trained soldier, for heaven's sake! A spy!"

"Lower your voice!" Marcus growled.

Dunn's lips dipped into a disapproving scowl, but thankfully he stopped yelling.

Tossing his hat and cane onto the empty chair by the hearth, his father moved to stand by the bed.

"As I said in my message, she'll be fine." Marcus stepped to the other side, putting Catherine between them. "I took a gash, if it makes you feel any better."

Dunn's scowl deepened. "Of course it doesn't."

"Can you enlighten me as to why Cat was following me, in a costume, no less?"

"Costume?"

Marcus jerked his chin over to the gray-and-white pile of clothing in the far corner. "A servant's uniform, obviously not hers."

"Ah." Dunn scratched his grizzled chin. "I'd heard that a friend of the staff's had run off. But she was a portly woman. How did Cat get it to fit?"

"A line of cord. Do you know what she was planning?"

"Nay. I thought her at a circulating library."

"Which one?"

"I didn't ask. It's rare enough that she asks to go, I was just glad that she wanted to."

"And you didn't suspect anything?"

"Of course not." Dunn tilted his head. "Why are you interrogating me, Marcus? There is no fault in our quarter."

Marcus understood that "our" included Cat but not him. "I'm just trying to understand what madness inspired her to follow me as she did."

"I made it quite clear that I would not suffer any more of her arguments about you. Apparently she decided to take steps on her own."

Marcus shook his head. "Why is Cat so dead against me?"

"She probably fears you—"

"Bollocks." At the censorious look on his father's face, he added, "Pardon, but Cat doesn't seem afraid of much." He recalled how she fought the thugs in the alleyway and couldn't help the rush of admiration that surged through him. "The brassy chit saved my life."

"What?" Dunn grabbed the bedpost, as if his knees wouldn't hold him.

"Sir!" Marcus rushed over and caught his father in his arms.

"I'm all right," his father chided, gruffly. "Just taken off guard. I'm fine. Really."

Despite his protestations, Marcus eased his father into the armchair by the fire and poured him a brandy. Marcus did not like how his father's hand shook when he lifted the glass or the greenish pallor of his skin. Thankfully after a moment and a few sips of brandy, the color returned to his cheeks and some of the usual righteous fire banked his gaze.

After pouring a drink for himself, Marcus dragged another chair across from his father's and sat facing the door.

"Tell me what happened," Dunn commanded.

Marcus sipped his brandy. It was good tipple, but not nearly as fine as his usual fare. Since returning to London, Marcus had given up on his trading enterprise. His hands were full enough as it was. "I'd been marked—"

"Marked?"

"Someone was following me. I needed to find out who. So I walked alone down an empty alleyway—"

"Inviting trouble."

Marcus shrugged. "How else to expose a trap but by triggering the snare?"

"How many men were there?"

"Three," Marcus lied. No need to unsettle the man further.

Dunn grimaced. "A bit perilous, don't you think?"

"I've faced worse odds."

At the look of discomfort in his father's gaze, Marcus assured, "I'm well trained. They were amateurs. Ruffians."

"But you hadn't counted on Catherine."

Marcus blew out a breath of air. "No. She added a certain . . . *ambiguity* to the mix."

"But you're all right?" Dunn's gaze traveled over his torso.

Marcus motioned to his side. "Just a scratch."

Dunn straightened. "Why aren't you clothed, Marcus? You're alone in a bedchamber with an unmarried young lady and you don't even have the decency to dress. Have you no thought for Catherine's reputation?"

Marcus needed no further reassurance that his father was completely recovered from his little spell. "Do you want to learn what happened or not?"

"Of course I do," Dunn grumbled. "I just wish you'd consider some of the larger implications of your actions. I know that you said that Catherine shouldn't travel, but her reputation requires that you remove yourself at once and that she be cared for by women. I will send along two of the girls—"

Marcus shook his head. "This is a male-only establishment. They don't even allow maids. Tam and I were lucky to sneak her in here as it was. And that was only after wrapping her in my coat."

"But how, then, do you suggest . . . ?"

"I will take care of her and ensure that no one ever finds out that Cat was here."

"You? You're no nursemaid, Marcus."

"Who do you think took care of Mother those last months when you were off to your many meetings?"

"I know her fever lingered, but Mrs. Nagel—"

"Mrs. Nagel had to supervise the children; she couldn't give Mother the care she needed. Besides, when one is dying nothing compares to having your flesh and blood beside you."

Dunn blinked. His mouth opened, then closed. "I didn't know . . ."

Marcus bit back a retort; it was neither the time nor the place for opening old wounds. Moreover, he didn't have enough left in him this evening to tussle with his father.

His father's gaze met his, sincere. "I'm sorry, Marcus. I'd had no idea."

Marcus shrugged, but somehow he felt a bit better that his father now knew. Mayhap someday Uriah Dunn would take ownership of all the pain he'd caused by his absences. "If you don't mind, I'd rather not discuss it."

His father nodded. "Of course. So what happened at the ambush today?"

"I had a pistol at my back, in close range, and Cat tossed her reticule at the man."

Dunn lifted his brow. "Her reticule?"

"Yes, a flimsy netted thing, but she'd placed a broken brick inside."

"Ah. Like a sling." His father nodded admiringly. "Quick thinking."

"She's a smart woman, I'll grant you that." Marcus looked over at her on the bed. "Too smart for her own good, it seems. The bullet missed us both, but knocked down a brick from the building. It landed on her clever head."

Dunn scratched his ear. "So she must have known she was proceeding into trouble."

"That's the part I can't understand." Marcus straightened in the chair and leaned forward, careful not to stretch his injury. "I have to assume that she waited for me outside the boardinghouse and followed me." He shook his head, disbelieving. "But that means that she charged into that alleyway knowing full well that I was there with those men. What could she have been thinking?"

"Knowing Catherine and how suspicious she's been since your return, I'd say that she was trying to find out more about why you are here."

"Charging into an alley, alone, with five obvious ruffians and me? A bit brash, even for her, don't you think?"

"Not if she thought that you were in trouble. And I thought you said it was three men?"

"I didn't want to worry you," Marcus brushed aside. "And I can't believe that that slip of a girl planned to take on six men."

"Five. You're one of the good ones, remember?"

An unfamiliar hopefulness stirred in his chest, but he pushed it away. "I find it all too implausible to believe."

Dunn shrugged, sipping from his glass. "At the very least she would do it on my account."

"I don't understand."

"Undoubtedly. Catherine appreciates something you never have, Marcus." His father's eyes met his and something deep inside Marcus twisted. "I would be devastated if you were hurt. Or dead."

At this pronouncement, funereal silence filled the room.

Uncomfortable, Marcus tore his gaze away, staring at the fire.

Dunn leaned forward. "You are my lifeblood, Marcus. My flesh and blood. The thought of something untoward happening to you . . ."

Warning calls resounded in Marcus's head; he couldn't handle his father becoming sentimental. It was . . . too much.

"Well, nothing is going to happen to me." Marcus knew his tone shouldn't be so brusque, but he couldn't help himself. The next thing he knew his father would want to embrace him. Marcus almost shuddered, imagining it more awkward than one of General Quartermein's battle-field dinner parties. "I'm perfectly capable of taking care of myself."

"Catherine, obviously, did not think so." Dunn rubbed his hand over his eyes, appearing tired. His gaze moved to the bed and filled with guilt. "I suppose I should have tried to take precautions with Catherine. Given her more to do, distracted her somehow. But I've just been so wretchedly busy . . ."

Marcus's interest sparked. "But you haven't been with the board . . ."

"Nay, another matter." His father looked away. "A private matter of some sensitivity."

Marcus heard the reproach; Dunn would not share the details with his wayward son.

"Mayhap someday I will be able to tell you about it," Dunn added, making Marcus feel a bit better.

"I might have done a better job handling her, as well," Marcus admitted. Thinking back, he wondered if he'd have been better off telling her the truth about his reasons for returning to London. But the notion was so antithetical to his very existence, it hadn't really seemed an option. Still, he should have thought of something. "You were right in one regard, sir. Cat's dogged."

His father's features seemed to soften, like melting clay. "Cat's dogged?" He appeared to be trying not to smile. "Cat's dogged?"

Unbidden, Marcus's lips quirked. Scratching his cheek, he shook his head. "That was very bad."

Dunn nodded. "Almost as bad as the door is a-jar."

Marcus suddenly recalled arguing with his father for at least a half hour about the impossibility of a door being a jar. He'd been about six years of age, and even then, very determined. Dunn had patiently showed him the dictionary. Marcus had read the definition. Then he'd come back the next day and decorated his father's door.

"See?" Marcus had told his father, waving to his artwork. "*Now*, the door can be a jar." He'd painted a large white jam jar in the middle of his father's oversized study door.

Marcus recalled it so clearly, he could almost hear his father's booming laughter. It had been so glorious, an exquisite echoing sound that had reverberated deep in Marcus's soul. He'd almost forgotten that memory, until this moment.

Dunn sighed, smiling. "That was one lesson I will never forget."

"You'd said that I taught you that children have a logic all their own, often more rational than any adult's."

"Very true. And it has helped me enormously over the years."

"You kept that painting up for a long time," Marcus murmured, recalling the pride he'd felt every time he'd passed that decorated door.

"Until the paint was so scratched off you could hardly see it."

Marcus nodded, almost surprised by the sweetness of the memory. Their eyes met and for a moment, something connected between them. Marcus felt a sudden rush of affection for his father, but it was so foreign, so opposite to how he thought of his father, he shifted uncomfortably, looking away.

Cat groaned.

Marcus jumped from his chair and approached the bed. "I think that we're disturbing her."

Dunn rose. "It's time for me to take my leave, anyway. Without Catherine at the orphanage I will have my hands full."

Marcus hadn't realized. "I'm sorry about all of this, sir." He knew that he was apologizing for more than just inconveniencing his father, but he didn't want to examine that aspect too closely.

"Some things are out of our control, Marcus. In this instance, Catherine's determination." He stiffened. "I will have to tell the staff something; they will be curious about Catherine's sudden absence."

"Mayhap she is visiting a sick friend," Marcus supplied.

Dunn nodded. "That will do, I suppose." Setting his hat on his head, his father retrieved the cane. "Take good care of her, Marcus. She's a very special lady."

"I'm beginning to comprehend that, sir."

Chapter 14

〜᳒᳐᳐᳐᳐〜

Catherine awoke to the delectable scents of butter and honey. Her hollow stomach growled. The sound of feet treading on carpeted floor greeted her. She peeled open her eyes.

"I thought this might tempt you to join the living," Marcus offered smoothly while he set a tray with a mug and two steaming bowls onto the bedside table. He wore his raven hair tied back with a leather strap, yet it still hung past his broad shoulders.

Cathérine's cheeks flamed as she recalled every stirring curve and bulge of his glorious creamy flesh, and she was simultaneously relieved and disappointed that he was clothed. Yet, cobwebs of confusion made her memory a hazy spattering of images and she was having trouble distinguishing dream from reality.

Still, in the light of day—relatively speaking since the draperies were closed and the only light came from the candelabrum across the room—she felt improved. Yet, she couldn't help but notice the impropriety of his wearing only a simple white shirt and brown loose-fitting breeches in her presence. As if he assumed her beneath such consideration.

She bristled; it felt better being angry than embarrassed. "Where's the other man?" her tone was tart.

"Oh, Tam? He's out getting you something to wear."

Her eyes widened as her hands groped beneath the covers. She was bare as the day she was born!

"Don't look so appalled, Cat. I certainly didn't take advantage."

Because he wasn't tempted? Horrified and embarrassed she sputtered, "Where are my clothes?"

"You mean that dreadful uniform?"

She nodded and winced at the ache in her head. She raised her hand to her forehead and tentatively fingered wrapped bandages, wondering what had happened to her.

"My father took it back to Andersen Hall," Marcus explained.

Her mouth dropped open. "Headmaster Dunn was here?"

Lifting a spoon, he stirred the porridge. "Of course, he came to see for his own eyes that you were all right."

"And he left me here?" she shrieked. *Naked* and *alone with you*?

Marcus sat on the bed and Catherine had to lean her weight away to keep from rolling toward him. "You've taken a nasty knock to your head, Cat. It's not a good idea to move too much and my father recognized that fact."

"He really was here?" she asked skeptically.

"He left you a note." He raised a black-winged brow. "If, perchance, you didn't believe me."

Opening the drawer to the bedside table, he lifted out a scrap of foolscap and held it out to her. He waited patiently for her to accept the missive, so close she could smell his sandalwood pomade and his own spicy scent.

What a fix; to accept the note she had to reach out from under the covers! To ignore it, well where was the benefit in that?

Marcus's smile was amused as he unfolded the paper and held it up near her face. She tried to ignore the indignity of it all and scanned the paper. It was difficult to read in the dim light, but she would know that scratchy handwriting anywhere.

> *My dear Catherine,*
>
> *Thank heavens you are all right. I came by for myself to ensure that you are well and are receiving the best care possible under the circumstances.*
>
> *I know that you must be very confused, but Marcus will explain everything. Be sure to give him the opportunity.*
>
> *I pray for your speedy recovery.*
>
> *Yours truly,*
> *H. U. Dunn*

She scowled; Headmaster Dunn was assuming that she wouldn't give Marcus a chance to vindicate himself. Well, she'd already given him lots of opportunity and thus far it was *he*, not *she*, who'd failed.

"That doesn't explain much," she groused, wishing Headmaster Dunn wasn't so blind as far as his son was concerned. "Especially why he left me here."

"Do you believe that it's wise for you to ride in a bumpy carriage, or better yet, on a loping horse? Or would you rather walk the distance back to Andersen Hall?"

Just thinking about the options made her head swim.

And she felt so weak that breathing seemed a bit of an effort.

Marcus slipped the note back into the drawer. "Putting more information to paper is unwise, so Father hoped that I could be more persuasive this time."

Alarm bells sounded in her mind; she was naked, weak as a babe, trapped and alone with a man she couldn't tryst. *I mean trust!* she mentally corrected herself.

Marcus picked up a napkin from the tray and set it across her lap. "You haven't eaten in two days. Let us get your belly full so your ears can do their best work."

She blinked; he sounded more like a nursemaid than a blackguard. And the man intended to feed her himself? This was too bizarre. Perhaps that knock in the head was worse than she'd suspected and she was still unconscious. Under the blankets she pinched her thigh. She winced; it hurt like the dickens. Oh, dear heavens, this was real. She almost groaned from the ignominy of it all.

"Don't worry about your feebleness, Cat. I'm going to get you back on your feet again."

"Why you?" she couldn't disguise the panic in her voice.

"Would you prefer Tam?" Smiling, Marcus lifted the bowl from the tray. "Although he's quite good with a needle and thread, I thought you might prefer me." He was so close she could smell the mint on his breath and see the even white squares of his teeth as he smiled. How could he be so blasted blasé about this abysmal situation?

Needing to know more, she swallowed. "I'm in the boardinghouse, aren't I?" It was a male-only establishment. There weren't even any maids. She'd recalled thinking that it was a good idea not to have officers returning from war tempted with supposedly easy pickings.

Now it seemed like the worst of arrangements. "You brought me here from the alley?"

"Yes." The smile vanished from his features as he added seriously, "I'm glad you remember. I was a bit worried since head injuries can be tricky and you were out cold for a while. Your recovery should be fairly quick, I'd warrant."

Blast, he was sounding like a nursemaid again!

Desperately her eyes scanned the room, seeing nothing helpful. Perhaps she could take the sword leaning in the corner, slit her throat and end the misery now. She pushed aside the idiotic musing; she'd never been prone to dramatics; it was not the time to start.

If only Jared weren't off in Reigate. He would certainly be preferable to a hulking brute she hardly trusted.

"Now, let us sit up." Marcus reached for her, but aghast, she shrank backwards.

"Don't—" she sputtered.

"You haven't had any complaints about my care thus far," he teased.

"I was unconscious!"

He smiled. "Yes, and you were an excellent patient."

Not thwarted by her protests, Marcus slipped his hands under the covers and cupped her bare shoulders.

"Unhand me!" she screamed, but winced as the sound ripped into her head, making her see stars.

"You were unquestionably more cooperative when you were out cold," he muttered. Warm, long fingers eased under her shoulders and lifted her up to sit. Horrified, she struggled to cover herself, as he reached behind her and adjusted the pillows. Her skin flamed from her head to her toes and she was speechless, she was so horror-struck. She didn't dare meet his eyes.

Gently, he eased her back onto the pillow. "There. Isn't that more comfortable?"

She was too mortified to say a word.

Marcus lifted one of the steaming bowls and sat down on the bed beside her. Spooning out some porridge, he gently blew on it, sending the delectable odors of honey and cream wafting toward her. She swallowed, trying to ignore the pit of hunger in her belly.

The steam rising from the spoon soon dissipated and Marcus held the utensil out like an offering. "It was my mother's favorite recipe when she was ill . . ."

He'd *cooked* for her?

"Well?" he waited.

She supposed if he could be nonchalant about this bizarre circumstance, then so could she. "I can feed myself," she muttered, looking anywhere but at him.

"Excellent." He placed the warm bowl on her lap and held out the spoon.

Suddenly she realized that she'd have to expose her arm to eat. Lifting her chin, she decided that some things would have to be suffered to have a little dignity. Besides, the man had obviously seen it all already, and, gallingly, didn't seem remotely affected.

Carefully, Catherine wrapped the blanket deep into her side as she lifted out her arm. The cool air greeted her bare skin.

"Would you like me to light the fire?" he asked.

"No." She didn't want to stare at his curvaceous bottom as he bent over the hearth. It was hard enough regaining her equilibrium as it was.

The first bite of the porridge was like heaven on earth. Buttery, creamy grains slid down her throat so delectably she almost closed her eyes. Suddenly she realized that he was studying her, and chided, "Stop watching me."

Marcus shrugged and stood. "As you wish." He walked over to the closed red drapes and peeked out, allowing golden afternoon sunlight to spear across the emerald green carpet.

She tore her eyes away from his broad back and swallowed another bite. "How long have I been here?"

"Not very long."

"How long?"

He peered over his shoulder at her. "Two days."

Two days? The orphanage, the children!

"My father said not to worry; he would take care of Andersen Hall for the interim. He only asked that you please recover soon."

She didn't know whether to feel relieved or dispensable.

Marcus turned back to the window, staring out the glass. A casual observer might see his pose as relaxed, but she noticed how his eyes never stopped scanning the street below.

Surveying his profile, Catherine could easily see the bump on his nose where it had been broken, lending him a brutish air. Still, the golden sun kissed his chiseled cheeks and softened the strong angle of his jaw, making him devastatingly handsome. A man had no right to look that deuced gorgeous. She didn't want to know how weatherworn she must look.

Suddenly the memory of vomiting came back to her. That must have been Marcus holding her shoulders while she heaved. Oh, the indignity! But there was naught she could do for it now. So she pushed the memory from her mind and focused on the delectable porridge and on obtaining answers.

"What happened to me?"

He let the drapes drop and faced her. "A wild shot knocked a brick loose and you happened to be standing beneath it."

Ah, so that was the cannonball that had landed on her head.

"Who were those men?" she asked, licking her lips.

"That was what I was trying to find out when you came upon us."

Her spoon stopped midair. "So you purposefully led them into the alley?"

"Yes." His piercing blue gaze met hers. "I just wonder why you came after me."

Catherine looked down at the empty bowl, unwilling to explain herself. *Where had all the porridge gone?* Thankfully, Marcus had had the foresight to get two bowlsful. Catherine bit her lip hoping that the second helping wasn't for him.

Suddenly he stepped near and reached toward her. She started, shocked. Unruffled, he removed the empty bowl from her lap and replaced it with the full one. Her cheeks flamed once more and she chided herself not to be a skittish rabbit with him. The man could have molested her a thousand times over and obviously had not. But that still did not mean that she trusted him. And how did he always seem to know what she was thinking?

"You've a very expressive face," he explained, as if reading her thoughts. "Especially in the eyes."

She scowled, feeling at a disadvantage on so many different levels she wanted to scream.

"Also," he added, "I make it my business to read people."

"What business exactly is that, Marcus?" She waved her spoon, anger spiraling through her. "And while I'm asking, why are you so coiled up in lies? The sham with your leg. It's unconscionable leading others to believe that you are wounded."

"I catch spies." He approached the tray and lifted the mug. "Tea with milk and honey?"

She blinked, flabbergasted. *Spies?*

Grasping her hand in his large, warm fingers, he

slipped the mug into her palm. The heady vapors teased. Slowly, she sipped the tea, trying to sort out his comment. Another lie, perhaps? But for what end?

The Bohea was delicious; a better quality of leaf than she'd had in years. The orphanage purchased their tea leaves used. These obviously had not yet infused another's cup. It tasted positively decadent.

"Where does all of your money come from?" she asked suddenly.

"I have my officer's pay." At the look on her face, he added, "But to be frank, I'm enterprising. I find out what people want and deliver it. For a price."

"You mean spies?"

"No." He shook his head, emphatic. "That I do for my country. Oh, I take my wages, don't get me wrong, but there's no custom for me there."

"Who are you trying to catch?"

He turned and easily lifted the armchair from near the fire and set it beside the bed. Dropping into it, he crossed his long legs. "Someone in London."

She grimaced. "Obviously. If what you say is true."

His smooth lips lifted, amused. "You still don't believe me."

"Why should I? You've lied about everything since the day of your return." The tea was like liquid gold to her taste buds. She stifled a sigh of contentment.

"Even though my father clearly supports my efforts here in town?"

"Your father cannot see clearly where you are concerned," she replied dismissively.

"And they call me cynical," he muttered.

"That is, by far, one of the gentler terms I'd use for you."

Chapter 15

From the armchair next to the bed where Cat lay, Marcus studied the perplexing young woman as she sipped her tea. When he'd just placed the mug into her hand, he'd finally realized what her skin reminded him of: rose petals. And like a rose, Cat was silky soft but guarded by barbed thorns.

What had happened to her to make her so prickly? Why was she so suspicious of people's intentions? Andersen Hall was a decent place, far better than many other foundling homes he'd seen. So what had happened to her that had ensured that no one got too close to the lovely Catherine Miller?

Without understanding his own curiosity, Marcus had recently asked his father how Cat had come to Andersen Hall. According to Dunn, Cat and her brother had come to the orphanage claiming to have been orphaned when their parents had died in debtors' prison. Apparently, her parents had been tutors to fine families, hence, Cat and her brother's superior education and manners. Then her father had gotten into debt, so deep that nothing could get him out. He and his wife had been sent to prison while the children had stayed behind with a servant friend. Both parents had died of a fever while incarcerated. But that had been ten years ago; why was she still so bitter?

Well, she wasn't exactly bitter, Marcus corrected himself. Prickly, mistrustful, sharp, but not embittered. And so lovely he had to wonder why a man had not yet come along and swept her off her feet.

A wise man would have seen past the wayward haystick hair and wretched clothing. He would have found a way to silence that barbed tongue. Just the idea of giving Cat's tongue another occupation caused him to shift uncomfortably in his seat.

He'd been fighting his errant passion ever since he'd met Cat. Now that he was alone with her in his bedroom, naked, no less, the struggle had evolved into a full-blown war. But he'd be damned if he'd take advantage of a helpless innocent in his care.

Extending her milky white arm, Cat tried setting the empty mug on the table. *Stiff-necked lass.* If he focused on her mind and not her body, he might just win this skirmish yet.

Reaching forward, he removed the mug from her hand and placed it on the tray. Quickly, she slid her arm back beneath the covers.

During his visit, his father had suggested offering Cat the whole, uncomplicated truth to finally make her understand. Even though unusual, Marcus decided to give his father's advice a shot.

Sitting up, he rested his hands on the arms of the chair, as if to convey his open dealing. Over the years he'd learned that it was just as important how one appeared as what one said.

"My father suggested I be honest with you, as I have been with him," Marcus began. "Obviously he believes me. But then, again, Lord Wellington set the stage well—"

"The letters," she breathed, her eyes widening. Cat would definitely be a flop if she tried her hand at Drury Lane.

"So you knew about those." He shook his head. "My father assured me that no one saw those missives."

"I didn't read them," she replied defensively. "I simply figured out from whom they were sent."

She was a sharp tack, he had to admit. "Well, I am on a clandestine mission to catch a traitor to the Crown. Hence, the reason for my return."

Her smoky gray gaze was incredulous. "At an orphanage?"

"My question, exactly, when they gave me my orders."

Her lips pursed. "So you did not wish to come home?"

"No."

"But you came anyway."

"I had little choice."

"Because they ordered you to?" her tone was doubtful.

"They made me a proposal I could hardly refuse." He looked away, remembering Horace's proposition: Captain Luke Hayes's life in exchange for assuming the mission in London. His superiors knew him well enough to recognize that once he'd committed he would give it his all. But in negotiating Luke's release, Marcus had also demanded the return of the young captain's commission and a promise that Luke would never have to serve in the same regiment as that bastard Major Blackstone.

"What was the offer?" she asked, tilting her head. He liked how she cornered the facts and re-sorted them until she was satisfied. It was a refreshing change from some of the goosish women he'd known.

Cat's mind was worlds above his recent paramour's, he realized. But to give Angelica her due, he'd never been particularly interested in that aspect of a woman; it only complicated his existence.

"The offer," she prompted, pulling Marcus from his convoluted musings.

"What does it matter?" He looked away, adjusting his legs. "I had no choice."

Her pink bowed lips pinched into a stubborn line.

"All right," he admitted. "A friend was in a fix. It was the only way to get him out."

Her brow relaxed. "That's the first thing you've explained that truly fits your character."

"What do you know of my character?" he retorted. "We hardly knew each other years ago and I've been gone now for ages."

"Some characteristics are . . . immutable."

"What do you mean?"

"I remember Willy Limpkin."

Marcus remembered him, too. The sandy-haired, troubled lad had gotten caught stealing a neighbor's chickens. The penalty was twenty raps with a switch, and having to compensate the victim. Willy had taken this punishment in stride, but everyone had known that Willy could sooner write his name as put two pence together. The lad had never been quite right in the head.

"You gave him some tasks—" Cat said.

"The lad washed my shirt, for heaven's sake," Marcus interrupted, looking away. "It was nothing."

"You found a productive use for his time, and gave him the chance to pay his fine. Until the day he died he was proud to have made his own retribution. It was never charity."

"What's your point?"

"You have a certain code of honor when it comes to your comrades. Helping a friend in need is probably the only reason that you could give for your return that I would believe."

"I'm so glad you approve," he retorted dourly, yet deep inside he was pleased that she saw something redeeming in him.

"But I still don't understand why your mission would bring you to Andersen—" Alarm suddenly infused her features. "Is there any danger to the children?"

"No."

Her features softened with relief. She really was quite pretty, with those wide luminous eyes and that perky up-turned nose, and those bowed pink lips . . . He wondered if they'd taste sweet . . .

When she wasn't arguing, stabbing a finger to make a point or emphatically waving a spoon . . . These were good thoughts that drew him from his licentious musings.

"So why did you have to be placed on the board of trustees?" she asked.

"For the entry that I need."

"To get to whom?"

"That is one fact you do not need to know."

"Does your father know who it is?"

"He is taking my lead in this matter in all respects."

"Of course he would; he's not nearly devious enough to manage this affair."

He didn't know whether to be insulted or flattered. Still, it was nice that she finally believed him. It felt somewhat uplifting having her know his secret. She was bright, and surprisingly easy to talk to.

Worrying on that lower lip, she muttered, "On the board of trustees we have Hardgrave, Belton, Foxworthy, Renfrew, Griggs . . ."

Dunn had been right about Cat; she puzzled things until they fit. Not a healthy trait for a civilian. "Don't go there, Cat," he warned. "This is dangerous business, as you have regretfully learned firsthand."

"Most of the trustees contribute to the orphanage in a steady stream," she stated slowly, ignoring him. "It ebbs and flows, but usually remains somewhat constant once they are on the board." Her lips pursed. "Except for two. Mr. Griggs recently donated a large sum to the orphanage, more than three times his annual gift. Lord Renfrew, on the other hand, reduced his donation, by more than half."

Marcus knew this since he'd studied the lovely script of her neat account books.

"I'll lay odds it's Renfrew," she declared. "Griggs is too 'Hail to the King' and all that. Renfrew on the other hand is always jumping from one cause to the next. He believes that he knows best and that he needs to enlighten the rest of us. Did someone perhaps add kindling to his fire?"

He couldn't help but be impressed with how neatly she'd sized up the situation. Still . . . "This is no child's game of wage-war, Cat. It's certainly no place for a young woman."

Beneath the covers she crossed her arms. "I saved your life."

"I didn't need your help," he replied gruffly. "I was doing just fine on my own until you came along."

She shrugged. "Five men against one, and you were doing reasonably well—"

"Thank you for the endorsement."

"But the man had a pistol at your back and I dispatched the knave."

It was kind of nice having her calling someone else a knave rather than him. Still . . .

"Besides," she added. "If someone on the board of

trustees is exposed as a traitor, a threat to Britain . . . things will not go well for Andersen Hall."

"I did not choose to fight on this field—"

"Can't you just pack the traitor up and haul him off or something? Without anyone knowing what he's done?" she asked hopefully.

"My superiors were adamant; I must have clear and solid proof before I act overtly." He frowned. "I need to be circumspect in my enquiries until then. 'Kid glove treatment' is how they described it."

"No matter how you try to keep it quiet, if a traitor is found, Andersen Hall will be besmirched." Her face was tinged with anxiety.

"Andersen Hall has a strong foundation. It will survive."

"You cannot expect me to lie down and let those I love suffer." Her voice rose with conviction. "I will not let that happen again!"

"Again?"

Looking down at the covers, she did not meet his eye. "I cannot sit on the side if it is in my power to do something about it."

He decided to ignore her outburst. What he needed was her cooperation, and she obviously did not wish to discuss it. "Look, Cat. My father almost had an attack of the heart when he saw you injured." Marcus did not bother explaining how terrified he'd felt. "He's asked me to promise to keep you safe. I can't do that if you get the idea in your head that you need to get involved in a military operation."

"But I can help—"

"Doing what?" he asked gently.

"Headmaster Dunn says that I'm excellent with puzzles of any kind."

"This is far from a game, Cat—"

"Well . . . I can certainly find out more information if I

could attend one of the board meetings. I can be quite a credible actor, you know."

He laughed. He couldn't help it. A deep, rumbling boom escaped from his belly and it felt so wretchedly good he had to let another loose. And then another. He couldn't recall the last time he'd laughed so hard.

She scowled. "Well, I am. Headmaster Dunn says so, and so does Mrs. Nagel. And Dr. Winner—"

His laughter echoed in the intimate chamber.

"Well, I am," she grumbled. "Just, apparently, not with you."

Standing, he stepped over and lifted the tray. "I'm going to take this back to the kitchen. Is there anything else I could get for you while I'm about?"

She scowled at him.

His smile widened. "Oh, Cat, I'm sorry, but that's the first good laugh I've had in months. I thoroughly enjoyed it."

"Well, I'm glad that someone did. It's not nice to laugh at another's expense."

"No, of course not." He forced his lips down. "How can I make it up to you?"

She looked away, not meeting his eye. Obviously she wanted something.

"Please, Cat, let me know how I might make amends?"

"I'd really . . ." She bit her lip, looking so distressed he had to hide his grin.

"What? You can tell me."

"I'd really like a bath."

His lips fell.

"Is that possible?" She peeked up from beneath thick sooty lashes. Men would slay for a sweet glance like that.

"Your wish is my command," he murmured, not laughing any longer. It looked like the mêlée of his passions was about to launch a new offensive.

Chapter 16

◠◡◠◡◠

Trying not to think too much about what was to happen, Marcus examined his handiwork. Blankets, cloths, robe, soaps and small tub with water and pitcher. Nothing else came to mind.

Leaning over, he tossed another log on the blazing hearth. It would be cozy warm for hours. Facing the fire, he opened up the dark paneled screen to enclose the whole area near the fire, feeling Cat's gaze on his back from across the room.

He turned, facing her as she sat in an armchair in the far corner, a blanket wrapped around her lovely form so completely that nothing except her face showed.

"It's ready," he declared.

Cat rose. Her cheeks were high with color. "Thank you for going to such trouble."

"It's no trouble at all," he lied. The male-only establishment reserved bathing for a specified room near the kitchen. So that had proven unfeasible. The tricky part had been the tub. A large bathtub couldn't negotiate the long narrow staircase. A baby bather was the best he could do.

Procuring ladies' soaps and a robe had been the easiest part. Marcus didn't bother to mention how much he'd enjoyed going through all of the soaps and picking just the right scent he thought Cat would like.

Cat moved closer, but the blanket was so tight, she had to walk in quaint tilting mincing steps.

"I'll be in the corner." He pointed to her recently vacated chair. "If you need me."

Approaching the dark, reddish violet screen, she turned. "I know that you should be here in case I need help," Cat murmured. "But this is . . . strange."

"Do you want me to leave?"

She looked down at the floor. "When I just got up from the seat, my head was swimming."

"And now?" he asked, concerned.

"Better. It's just frustrating, the light-headedness comes and goes."

"It's only been a couple of days, Cat," he replied gently. "Give it some time."

She grimaced. "I'm not a very good patient, I'm afraid. I hate being sick and have little patience for it."

"One thing I've learned from the war is that if I'm not whole, then I can't do my best work. So I try to give my body the time to heal whenever possible."

"You're right," she murmured. "Are you certain you don't mind staying?"

"Not at all. I have some reading to catch up on."

Her hand grazed the dark panel. "This is a beautiful silk screen. Not quite violet, not quite red . . ."

"I can't recall the color the proprietor told me it was. I just asked for the darkest one they had."

She swallowed. "I owe you a lot of money, Marcus—"

"This is the Crown's business, Cat. It won't cost me a farthing," he lied. "Go take your bath."

Stepping away, Marcus grabbed one of the Andersen Hall ledgers from the table and sat in the big armchair. It was still warm from when Cat had sat. Keeping his eyes glued to the pages, he called, "Do you have everything that you need?"

"Yes. I love this soap. Orange blossom, isn't it?"

He smiled to himself. "I'm glad you like it. I couldn't find lemon but thought it might do." Keeping his eyes from straying across the room was more difficult than he'd imagined.

"I love it."

So did he. The heady sweet scent wafted all over the chamber and he wondered if anything had ever smelled so divine. He crossed his legs, keeping his eyes averted from that screen.

December Contributions, he read. *Column One.*

The sounds of trickling water and the fire crackling interrupted his thoughts.

Marcus pulled his shirt collar, feeling suddenly very warm.

The water splashed and a female exhalation of happiness teased his ears. All thoughts of donations slipped from his mind. The urge to peek was so great, Marcus forced his eyes closed. Perhaps a snooze was in order.

Leaning back, he adjusted his legs, getting comfortable for a nap. In the field Marcus could sleep in almost any circumstances. He certainly should have no trouble in a warm room, a comfortable chair and a safe venue.

The sounds of liquid sloshing in the tub caressed his ears. The scent of orange blossoms teased. In his mind's eye, he imagined the water coating her soft skin. He suddenly wished he could be that liquid. Or better yet that he could lick it off Cat's naked flesh.

Marcus swallowed. He needed to keep a better rein on his licentious thoughts. She was an injured lady in his care; he knew better than to behave like a randy schoolboy.

"Ow!"

His eyes flew open as he sat up. "What's wrong?"

"Nothing, I just bumped my elbow."

"Have a—" the words died on his lips. The golden glow from the hearth cast a shadow on the screen, outlining Cat's glorious silhouette in intimate detail.

Marcus's mouth dropped open; he suddenly felt bereft of air.

In all his years, Marcus couldn't have imagined setting up, so innocently and yet so effectively, a virtual feast for his senses.

Marcus swallowed, his heart beginning to pound in his ears.

If he were a true gentleman, he'd leave the room. But how could he do so without letting her know why? Moreover, he couldn't in good conscience leave a damsel in distress, could he?

He should look down at the ledger, avert his eyes . . .

But for his life, he couldn't tear his gaze away. Cat's shadow gracefully played across the violet red panel, drawing his gaze like a starved man to bread. Those sloping shoulders, sweeping curves, round, pert breasts and lush globular derriere were enough to make his shaft rise up and stand at attention. It was so stiff it almost hurt.

"This is strange," Cat called out.

"What?" his voice cracked. He prayed she didn't notice. He couldn't let Cat know, not in a million years, what delicious torture she was inflicting. She'd die from mortification and never let his perverted soul near her again.

"Me, bathing with you in the room."

"Is there anything that I can do to alleviate your discomfort?" Did that sound as dissolute as he thought?

"You've been only the gentleman, Marcus."

If you only knew.

"I suppose I'm just being silly. But still, I feel deuced awkward."

The water splashed. She turned and in perfect silhouette, he watched, mesmerized, as she glided the cloth over those pert, round breasts.

His mouth dried to dust. He was a knave, a rogue, a blackguard of the first order!

"Will you talk to me?" she asked. "Maybe it won't feel so . . . strange."

He scrambled for something ordinary to say. "It's 'King's purple', I believe."

"What?"

"The screen color."

Devil take it! Now she'd know that he was gawking at the panel! "Not that I'm looking," he added quickly. "Do you need any more soap?"

Her movements stilled. "Are you all right?"

"What makes you ask?"

"You sound out of breath."

He coughed into his fist. "I'm fine. Just a little something caught in my throat." Thankfully she began her ministrations once more. That lucky cloth rolled over Cat's breasts and down to her belly.

Marcus began to sweat. But he was sure to keep his mouth closed this time and not make a sound.

Her hands strayed down to her middle, making circular rotations around her abdomen.

Marcus's shaft was so hard it pressed up against his breeches in excruciating pleasure.

Lifting her foot, Cat set it on the rim of the tub and began rubbing the cloth over her leg. In silhouette, Marcus could see every delicious curve of her calf, her knee, her thigh and that fantastic juncture between her legs. Oh, the way her luscious rump hitched in the air . . .

It took every ounce of Marcus's self-control not to tear down that screen and ravage her on the floor. But she would have hated him forever and he would've hated himself for it, too. So he silently witnessed the luscious agony of Cat bathing herself in a wholly artless erotic display, knowing that he'd never be able to touch her. He was a bastard in so many ways; but he didn't debauch innocents.

Suddenly she straightened. "Are you still there?" A hint of nervousness laced her sweet voice.

"I'm sorry I couldn't get a larger tub," he said, scrambling to think of *something* to say. "But the officers usually use the bathing room."

"It's not an issue." Leaning back down, the cloth swept over her calf. "Thank you for taking the trouble to find this for me."

No, thank you.

The cloth traveled up her knee to her thigh, slowly heading toward that incredible juncture between her thighs.

Marcus tugged at his collar. *This room is hotter than Hades and it's about to get a lot hotter.*

Three raps sounded at the door with double pauses between. Marcus didn't know whether to curse or thank the heavens.

Behind the screen Cat grabbed for the robe. "Ow."

"What's wrong?" he called.

"Just my head." Her voice had dropped to a whisper. "Who do you think it is?"

"It's only Tam." Adjusting his breeches, Marcus stepped over to the door. "What is it?"

"Sorry to bother you, sir," the good sergeant replied through the door. "But there's something I need to discuss with you."

Marcus called over his shoulder, careful not to look back. "I'll be but a moment, Cat."

"Certainly," she called.

Marcus's hand settled on the knob. Opening that door and leaving that room was turning out to be harder than he'd imagined.

"I'll be right outside," he delayed.

"Take your time."

Well, there was naught to be done for it. Taking a deep breath, he turned the knob.

Chapter 17

⟨~∽◦∽~⟩

The cool air in the hallway was not nearly as stimulating as the orange blossom scent inside Marcus's bedchamber. And the sight of the hook-nosed sergeant certainly no comparison to visions of Cat in silhouetted splendor.

"Tam," Marcus greeted with a nod.

"Sir."

"Don't say a word," Marcus advised, yanking on his collar.

"About what, sir?" Tam's eyes were fixed on the doorframe above.

"Good. What news?"

"I found one of the blokes from the alleyway. He was in a tavern sulking in his gin."

"Which tavern?"

"Tipton's."

Marcus felt his hackles rise. "Joe Tipton owns that tavern and he holds me in ill regard." Marcus did not bother explaining Joe's involvement in his misadventure with his father seven years before. "Did the two of them seem connected in any way?"

"Nay. The bloke hovered in a corner as if waiting for someone. The host hardly took notice of him. No one showed. Then the man went home to a place on Chadwick Lane."

"He lives alone?"

Tam smiled. "Oh, yes, and the rent's paid through the end of the month, so he ain't going anywhere any time soon. I have a man keeping an eye on the place, but I wanted to let you know."

"I will conduct that interview, Tam."

"Certainly, sir. You're the one they call 'The Wolf,' not me."

"The Wolf?"

"You're either sniffing something out or chewing someone up." Tam's voice carried a hint of pride, but Marcus didn't know if he liked the moniker. Well, better The Wolf than so many of the other labels tossed about camp.

"Here's the address." Tam handed him a scrap of foolscap.

"I'll be leaving in about half an hour. Get yourself something to eat. Then I want you up here at the end of this hall. No one comes, no one goes. I'll tell Cat to tap three times if she needs anything."

"Yes, sir."

"And set someone to watch Tipton's Tavern. Joe's been one to keep a few games running on the side and he has no love for me."

"Yes, sir." Tam spun on his heel and headed down the dark, narrow passageway toward the stairs.

Marcus turned back to the wooden door, wondering what Cat might be doing inside.

Taking a deep breath, Marcus knocked on the door and

let himself in. The heady odor of orange blossoms greeted his return. He could barely contain his disappointment as his gaze traveled to the now folded screen, with the cloths and soap piled neatly beside it.

Cat sat in the big armchair at the opposite corner of the room with her feet tucked daintily beneath her. Marcus couldn't see a scrap of skin beyond her fingertips and face as she was bundled up in a voluminous, peach silk robe. Her wet hair was covered with a floppy white bonnet with a peach-colored ribbon slotted through. With her shiny, cherry-tinged cheeks and pink-bowed lips she looked positively delectable.

Marcus felt like the Big Bad Wolf stalking Little Red Riding Hood and chided himself to behave. Pasting what he hoped was a harmless smile on his face, he asked, "Feeling better?"

"Worlds. Thank you." Her golden brow was furrowed and she was nibbling on that adorable pink bottom lip.

"Do you need me to change your bandages?"

"I did it myself."

He pushed away the feeling that his nursing was no longer needed. "Is something troubling you?"

She looked up, her smoky gray gaze locking with his. "This whole traitor business. The attack on you, the fact that Lord Renfrew is involved in something nefarious that could implicate all of us—"

"I never said it was Lord Renfrew."

"You didn't have to. I know the board members well enough and Lord Renfrew has been acting oddly now for quite some time."

"Oddly?"

"In all the time I could remember, Renfrew has never hired a single one of Andersen Hall's former charges.

Even though he's got sizable households and considerable loss of staff from what I hear."

"That's unusual?"

"Most trustees go out of their way to give the Andersen Hall charges a position when they get the opportunity. But not Renfrew. He gave money, loaned his name to the institution and sat on the board." She shrugged a dainty shoulder. "I suppose he thought it was enough."

"But that's changed?" Marcus pulled a chair opposite to hers and sat. Not only was she easy on the eyes, but she might just give him some helpful information for his investigation.

Propping her elbow on the arm of the chair, she rested her chin in her hand. The sleeve of her robe drooped giving him a glimpse of pink wrist. "About six months ago, Renfrew came to Andersen Hall for a visit."

Marcus shifted his gaze to her face. "For what purpose?"

"He wanted our help in retaining fifty young, strong men to help with a building project."

"What kind of project?"

"He didn't specify."

"Did he say where this project was?"

"He said at his estate in Peterborough."

"He said? You didn't believe him?"

"My friend Katie received a letter from her brother, one of the men that Renfrew hired. But it was sent from Dover, not Peterborough."

This was interesting intelligence, indeed. "Could the brother have taken off? Or been reposted?"

"No. In his letter he indicated that he was still with the other men."

Marcus leaned forward. "Did he say what the building project was?"

"No." She exhaled loudly. "All he talked about was how bad the food was and complained about the long hours. Still, it indicates that Renfrew lied."

Marcus rubbed his eyes. "Or that he changed his mind."

"So it's not helpful at all?" Her tone was disappointed.

"Actually, you've given me something to chew on."

"So you'll follow up on it?"

Marcus's mind raced through the implications of confirming his target to Cat and having her know some of his plans. After considering the possibilities, he decided that there was little harm. "I will."

"How will you prove it, if Renfrew is up to something?"

"Well, first I have to know the man."

"Have you had any luck?"

"Being on the board, at meetings, at the club, I've been able to establish a place in his circles. It's been . . . enlightening." He didn't bother explaining how much he'd learned since his return to London about the complicated Lord Renfrew. The skeletons in his closet, the rash idealism and raw ambition that drove him. Marcus knew every piece of property the man owned down to the last brick and every bank account to the last draft. Marcus knew when he shaved, what he ate, how he spent his funds, whom he bedded.

More importantly, Marcus knew whom Renfrew trusted. It had been a productive investigation so far, yet Marcus was still without the proof he needed to nail the bastard. Without doubt, however, he'd have it soon. He always got his man.

Suddenly Cat looked up. "How long does it typically take to unravel a plot? Or is timing even predictable?"

"The whole business is unpredictable . . ."

"But in this instance?"

"I would venture no more than a few months. Probably less."

"And then you'll go back to Portugal?"

"Spain, most likely."

She tilted her head. "Do you like what you do, Marcus?"

He started, surprised by the question. "I suppose, I've never considered it . . ." He shrugged. "I gain satisfaction in a job well-done."

"Sounds like my bookkeeping." Lifting her chin from her palm, she waved a hand. Marcus tried not to be enthralled by her every action. "I don't love doing it," she explained. "But it's important work. So I try to do my best to see it done reasonably well."

"Mayhap we're not so different in that respect," he answered slowly. "I don't enjoy it, per se."

Her brow furrowed. "The soldiering or the killing?"

"Both," he replied, impressed that she understood the distinction. Faces he would have preferred to have forgotten filtered through his mind.

"Bringing people to justice, helping my country . . . it's all well and good. But some men actually take pleasure in the killing . . . I do not."

"But you are good at it." It was a statement, not a question.

"Yes."

"Why did you go to war, Marcus?" she asked, her gray gaze assessing.

Marcus was not about to explain how going into the military had helped him escape prosecution seven years ago. Moreover, how it had gotten him away from his irate father.

Looking away, he spoke lightly, "I've always been up for an adventure. War is as grand an adventure as they come."

"But seven years of it?"

"The longer you're in it, the more it feels like home," he lied, trying not to think about how much he hated it sometimes. But it had become a way of life and he'd found ways to make it bearable, even pleasant at times. He'd been around long enough to learn how things worked and how to make them work for him. Besides, where else would he go?

"Why did you depart London in such a hurry seven years ago, Marcus?"

He shrugged. "It was past time for me to leave. My father and I weren't ever going to get along. It was best for all."

"I can't agree. Since your return I've seen a marked difference in your father."

"Really?"

Lifting a shoulder, she bit that lovely lower lip. "He's been away a lot, granted, with you."

He didn't bother correcting her; instead, he wondered what that personal matter was that had his father so engaged.

"But when I've seen him," she added, "your father has been more contented than he's been in years."

"Hmmm." Marcus could think of nothing more to say.

"And although I'm not happy about the reason for your return . . ." A lovely shade of cherry blossomed on her shiny cheeks. "I'm glad you're back."

Marcus wasn't going to lie and tell her he was happy about having to return to London and face his past. But by the same token, he couldn't in good conscience say that it was as terrible as he'd feared.

They faced each other silently, awkward awareness filling the small chamber.

"I suppose I should be off . . ." he murmured.

She swallowed. "Where are you going?"

"To speak to one of the men from our little encounter the other day."

"Is Tam going with you?" Was that a hint of concern in her voice? Something deep inside of him warmed.

"Tam is staying here. He'll be down the hall if you need him. Knock three times if you need anything. He will do the same."

"Three knocks, all right."

"Well, then . . ." He stood, feeling reluctant to leave.

She licked her lips, an innocent enough gesture, yet not to his licentious mind. Slowly, she rose from the chair. It was astounding how petite she seemed, barely coming up to his collar, when she had such a resilient personality. "I suppose I will see you soon?"

"I should be back in a few hours. Call for Tam if you need anything."

Reaching out, she clasped his hand. Her fingers were soft in his grasp. He suddenly wondered at how his callused hands must feel to her.

"Godspeed," she murmured.

Without thought, he leaned forward, pressing his lips to her smooth forehead. The scents of soap and orange blossoms overcame him. "Get some sleep, Cat."

Then he left quickly, before he did something he knew he'd regret.

Chapter 18

~⟲⟳~

Cat heard Marcus's loping gait coming down the hallway to her office at Andersen Hall and self-consciously tucked a stray hair in her bonnet and adjusted her starched apron. Although she no longer wore a bandage, she'd gotten a larger cap to help avoid headaches and her wayward hair was always spilling out.

It had been two whole days since he'd brought her back to the orphanage and she'd been waiting with bated breath for his return. During the course of the four days of his nursing her back to health, she'd come to relish seeing his handsome face. She'd enjoyed listening to his rumbling voice and watching him move about the chamber in that smooth, graceful prowl she'd come to appreciate.

Since he'd left her at Andersen Hall she'd missed seeing him so much that she'd felt like a prisoner denied sunlight.

And now the imaginary window had just burst open, letting in the spring breeze. Quickly, she stood, bumping her chair back into the wall with a thud.

"Tossing furniture around again?" he teased, reminding

her of his prior visit to her office. His deep voice rumbled, sending a thrill rocketing through her middle.

"Hello, Marcus," she murmured, as her traitorous cheeks heated.

"How's your head?" His penetrating blue gaze swept over her features, as if seeking reassurance. His concern almost melted her heart.

He'd been the most considerate man in Britain while caring for her and she'd needed every ounce of self-control to keep from fantasizing about the man every waking moment.

Marcus was not of her world, she knew. He was like a shining comet blazing through her black sky. But soon he would be gone and she would be back to her gloomy, lack-luster existence. But she hoped to have some lovely memories of their friendship once he'd left. She only prayed that day didn't come too soon.

"Fine," she replied, soaking him in. Today he used his crutches, once more the epitome of wounded soldier. His fine azurite coat with ivory buttons perfectly matched his brilliant eyes and she couldn't help the tingle in her belly every time his gaze met hers. His eyes were like magnets, drawing her near . . .

But she had to resist. If he had an inkling of how she felt, it would be too mortifying, too awful to bear! He had been very careful to keep his distance during their time together. Being a good friend and companion to her but never giving any indication that he was interested in her in any other capacity. He almost certainly thought her a green chit. Too naïve for his worldly tastes. He probably had a different lover in every port. . . .

Jealousy flashed though her, and she lowered her gaze, afraid he might see. Marcus was a free spirit, a ship floating on the untamed sea. She refused to have him think of her as a barnacle clinging to his side. Remembering how he'd dealt with the chits growing up, she recognized that if he knew how she felt, he'd probably do his utmost to keep her at arm's length. Something she couldn't endure.

"You look well, Cat," Marcus intoned, pulling his hat from his head and running a hand through his loose hair.

She wondered how soft it might feel between her fingers. Inwardly she sighed, realizing she would never know. "Thanks to you."

"You are an excellent patient."

She smiled. "I had a good nurse."

Recalling his tending, she marveled again at how easy it had been for her to lower her defenses with this man. Once she'd decided he was telling the truth, of course. She'd never been one to relax her guard around others. And no wonder, after her experiences with her cousin Stanford Caddyhorn.

Stanford used to jump out at her from behind corners and doors and grab her in places no decent person would touch. He'd even hid in her wardrobe once, scaring her half to death. Her screams had brought the servants running and the little monster had played it off as an innocent prank. Not amusing to the girl he was trying to molest. Even today, she still checked under her bed, in the closets and behind curtains before undressing every night. Sometimes she even shot up from bed in the middle of the night to recheck the closets, behind the curtains and under the bed, because she could not sleep without knowing for certain that no one lay in wait.

Yet somehow, Marcus Dunn had managed to breach all of that wariness, and in only a few days. Amazing.

"You seem much improved," he remarked, bringing her mind back to reality. "Perhaps you were correct about being ready to go home."

"I didn't want to be a burden on you—"

"Never a burden, Cat." He smiled and she felt the heat all the way down to her toes. All thoughts of the Caddy-horns slipped from her mind.

"A bit heavy," he added. "But never a burden."

She couldn't help but grin, recalling being carried down those narrow stairs in a traveling trunk. "No one noticed our little subterfuge did they? I mean, no one has said anything?"

"Weatherly's Boardinghouse remains as it always was: a bastion of male exclusivity."

"Good. Although, I'm sorry that I ruined your traveling trunk."

"I can still use it."

"With holes?"

He shrugged. "It was a neat trick to get you air, if I do say so myself. Well worth the effort."

She smiled shyly. "I'm glad you think so. But I still intend to purchase you a new trunk. Before you leave, that is . . ." Biting her lip, she looked away. He was so good at reading her and she feared he might see how much she dreaded the thought.

They stood awkwardly in the small office, the prospect of his parting hanging over them.

Catherine couldn't help but notice how Marcus's dove gray breeches showed off his muscular physique in excruciatingly gorgeous detail. She'd never noticed men's legs before, but ever since she'd caught a glimpse of those moon-pale thighs lightly grazed with dark fuzz . . .

Catherine coughed into her hand, looking anywhere but at him. Searching for *something* to say, she whispered, "Have you had any luck with your investigation? Any news?"

He nodded slowly, as if pulled from thought. "The fellows who attacked us in the alleyway led us to a gent named Lernout."

"Is he connected to Renfrew?"

"We have no indication so far, but I have yet to interview the man. Tam is searching him out as we speak."

A nervous fear fluttered in her belly, but she forced herself to have faith in Marcus's abilities. "So you still believe that your façade is secure?"

"I must move forward under that assumption." He scratched his chin. "I'm curious about that letter you mentioned. The one from your friend's brother posted from Dover. Often the most mundane facts can prove insightful. May I have a look at it?"

"I gave it to your father, in case he saw you before I did." Catherine had considered using the letter as a reason to seek Marcus out. But she'd been too embarrassed that he might see it as the flimsy excuse that it was. "He's in his office. I can go get it for you . . ."

"How about we go together?" He turned, extending his arm. Then he frowned. "Blast, with these crutches, I can't . . ." Shrugging he showed a lopsided grin and waved a hand. "If you would lead the way, Cat?"

"Yes, of course."

Wretchedly conscious of any limp she might have, Catherine led Marcus down the hallway. She sensed his presence like a fiery summer wind pressing against her back, stirring the hair on her skin. His magnetism was a heady mix of male appeal, her not-forgotten adolescent yearnings, and her long-standing loneliness, she was sure. But since her convalescence, that attraction had combusted into a yearning so heated it kept her from sleeping at night. And from doing much of anything else, it seemed.

She could hardly focus on the accounts, on the children . . . Her mind would drift off and it was starting to affect her job. Even Mrs. Nagel had commented on her distractedness.

Headmaster Dunn had been the only one who'd known that she had not been visiting a sick friend but had been recovering herself. He was the only one thus far who'd held his tongue about her preoccupation. But, since her return, he would stare at her for long moments, his gaze thoughtful. Oh, how she hoped he didn't know she was infatuated with his son! She prayed no one ever found out or she would never hear the end of it.

Still, for the disturbance Marcus's presence wrought in her life, having him around felt *stunningly* good. She felt all atwitter, hot and nervous, excited to be in his company. The problem was, how could she behave normally in his presence? How could she not make a total fool of herself over a man who probably didn't think of her as anything more than a lowly spinster secretary? A secretary short on looks and long on the shelf, she recalled her brother's scathing assessment.

"I wonder, Cat," Marcus murmured, "why you've never married."

Her foot missed a step and she grabbed the wall for balance.

He stopped close behind her, reaching out to grasp her arm. "Are you all right?"

Her cheeks blazed and she pretended to look at her shoe. "My toe caught."

"Sorry, that was a bit personal, wasn't it?"

She shrugged, feeling his heat through her gown where his hand held her arm. "I don't know that we can get any more personal than we've been."

"Oh, you'd be surprised," he murmured, his smooth voice veiled with meaning.

She swallowed, hard. For her life, she couldn't meet his eye. He must be speaking generally, right? He couldn't mean *with her*? No, it was not possible; and she wasn't going to make a fool of herself thinking otherwise.

"You must be what? Three-and-twenty?" Marcus asked. "Why have you never tied the knot?"

Catherine blinked, bristling. "I'm *two*-and-twenty, for your information." Straightening, she stepped away. "And I have not married because I never wanted to." She didn't bother mentioning that no one had ever tossed the handkerchief her way.

"I thought every woman lived for the exercise of bringing a man up to scratch?"

She stiffened. "Well, I'm not every woman." She couldn't explain how the Caddyhorns had taught her that any institution that gave someone legal authority over her was out of the question.

"That, Catherine Miller, is obvious."

He smiled, and she couldn't help but feel mollified. He did consider her special. How, she did not know, but at the moment, it didn't matter.

"Why are you so dead set against it?" he asked.

"Marriage for a man is all well and good," she supplied. "He gets all of the power. For the woman who becomes his property, it's more like servitude."

"Ouch. And I thought that *I* was cynical about the parson's mousetrap." He scratched his ear. "But if it's as onerous as you say, why do so many women do it?"

"Habit?"

He laughed, a deep booming timbre that reverberated within her. "You're an original, Cat. I'll grant you that."

Catherine tilted her head, unable to help herself. "Why did you ask about marriage, Marcus?" *Why do you care?*

"I don't know." He shrugged, looking away. "I suppose

we've spent a lot of time together and I can't understand why a woman like you has remained unattached for so long."

"Woman like me?"

"You're too lovely—"

A yowl escaped from her mouth. She quickly covered her lips.

"What?" he asked, a look of irritation flashing across his handsome features.

"Had you said that I was smart or a good conversationalist, then that might have made sense." Gesturing to her gown, she laughed. "But lovely? Now I know you're teasing me."

He shook his head. "And women call me obtuse . . ."

"Someone called you obtuse?" she asked, surprised. Marcus was one of the swiftest men she'd ever met. It was one of the things she found most attractive about him. That, and those dreamy eyes, strong shoulders . . .

"Seriously, Cat. Why do you walk about in drab gowns and scrappy shoes? I would hope that my father isn't keeping you under wraps so that some man doesn't sweep you off your feet and leave him alone with his accounts and ledgers."

Her cheeks flamed with embarrassment for her attire, and pleasure at his compliment, ludicrous though it was. She looked away. "No one is going to sweep me off my feet, Marcus. Don't be ridiculous."

"I wonder," he murmured. "Has anyone truly tried?"

At the hint of challenge in his voice, she looked up. Those brilliant eyes fixed on her, so close she could discern his black irises within the sea of blue. She felt imprisoned by his gaze, so intent it seemed to smolder with azure fire. Her heart began to pound and a sudden rush of heat swamped her face.

"Why, that's . . ." Her brain struggled to find the words. "Laughable . . ."

"I don't jest when it comes to these things." His voice was like honeyed wine: sweetness cloaking the fiery tang of spirit. "And you should have a better understanding of your charms. Lest you draw attentions you might not want . . ."

Wanting was all she seemed to be feeling at the moment. Her breath grew heavy and her mind seemed to muddle. Heat blanketed her body, loosening something warm and wonderful in her middle. It felt so good, she bathed in his proximity like a buttercup bows toward the sun. Leaning toward him, seeking . . .

Those gorgeous peach lips that she had dreamed about in her youth opened provocatively. "You really are—"

Suddenly a muted *thud* could be heard from down the hallway.

Catherine blinked, reality yanking her away from the fantasy of her lifetime. "Wh-what was that?"

Listening, Marcus stiffened like a twine stretching taut to steel. His eyes narrowed and his lips thinned with concentration. Something crashed, followed by a yell.

"Stay here!" he shouted, tossing aside his crutches and tearing past her down the corridor.

Lifting her skirts, Catherine sped down the hallway after Marcus. The sound had emanated from Headmaster Dunn's office. Had something fallen? A bookcase tipping over, perhaps? Images of a child trapped added fuel to her flying feet.

Wheeling around the corner, she tore into the headmaster's office. The sight before her was a nightmare beyond her imaginings.

Chapter 19

～～◯◯◯◯～～

Catherine pressed her hand to her opened mouth, shocked at the scene in Headmaster Dunn's office. Furniture was scattered, books askew and Marcus wrestled on the floor with a swarthy, soot-haired man.

The men grunted and huffed as they battled with their fists. A bloodied knife was clutched fiercely in the attacker's hand, his wrist held at bay in Marcus's taut grip. The assailant was a burly brute with meaty fists, a huge back and bulging muscles protruding below his filthy rolled-up shirtsleeves. His garments were smeared in blood and the odor of unwashed male radiated from him.

The ruffian rolled on top of Marcus, pinning him to the floor. Marcus was the smaller, leaner of the two and seemed to be struggling with his bandaged leg.

"Help!" Catherine screamed over her shoulder, praying that someone would hear. "We need help in the headmaster's office! Mr. Jones! Bertram! Come quickly!"

Catherine grabbed an umbrella from the stand by the door and whacked it over the lout's head. The man snarled, trying simultaneously to swat at her with one hand and stab Marcus with the other. Every time that meaty arm swung in her direction, she recoiled, then dove back in for another crack at him. *Thwack!* The umbrella splintered on the man's head, breaking into pieces. Catherine tossed the broken handle at the man's back and it bounced off uselessly. She grabbed a new umbrella and lunged forward for another whack. The man swatted at her and she jumped away.

Suddenly Marcus hoisted the attacker in the air with his leg, flipping the burly man backwards over Marcus's shoulders. The assailant crashed onto his back with a reverberating thud as a *whoosh* of air gusted out of his lungs. The knife clattered into a corner. The assailant lay still, seemingly as shocked as Catherine was by the maneuver.

Panting, Marcus bounded up and pinned the ruffian's chest with his good knee, setting his hands on the man's shoulders, pressing him to the floor. His panting echoed in the suddenly quiet chamber. The silence after the storm.

A muted groan emanated from behind the great brown desk, chilling Catherine to the bone.

Headmaster Dunn!

Catherine sprinted behind the massive desk and found her beloved mentor lying in a pool of his own blood. *Oh, my God.*

"How bad?" Marcus cried, as the attacker began thrashing about once more.

She blinked, roused from her shock. Crouching, she pressed her hand to Dunn's face, panicked. "I-I don't know! He's as white as a sheet! And there's so much blood!" So much blood . . .

The metallic odor assaulted her . . . she covered her mouth, as if to hold back her horror. Dunn looked so helpless, completely unmoving.

"Press down on the wounds to stem the bleeding!" Marcus shouted.

His orders whipped her shocked mind into action. She needed to find the wounds and stop the bleeding. Yanking open Dunn's woolen coat, she tore open his once ivory shirt and tried to make sense of the damage.

A dark hole surged red on the milky-pale skin. "There's a wound on his upper left shoulder!" she shouted. Thank God he was still warm; it fueled hope. The partially opened shirt was soaked crimson near his belly. It was difficult to undo the linen, it was so soaked with blood. But fear lent her hands strength. She yanked hard, exposing his wide, pale stomach. "Another on his lower left side, below his belly. I-I think that's all."

"Bear down on both but put the most force on the stomach wound!"

She pressed her hands to each of the gashes, using her stronger right hand on the lower one. Blood seeped through her right fingers, no matter how hard she tried to stem the flow. "I can't stop the bleeding from the stomach wound!"

Sounds of struggle came from across the room, but she couldn't see anything from behind the desk.

"Use cloth!" came Marcus's shout, followed by a grunt.

With her right hand she pressed the wound and with the other, she untied her apron. She cursed her sticky, fumbling fingers, but soon the strings came loose. Removing the apron and bunching it, she held it against the gash, pressing down hard while trying not to hurt him. She replaced her left hand on the shoulder wound and began to pray.

Many boot steps clambered into the room, but Catherine was too intent on Dunn to even look up. "Someone fetch Dr. Winner!" she cried.

Benjamin Bourke's head appeared above the desk. The twelve-year-old boy's eyes widened and his tea-skinned face drained of color. Distantly she worried about a young lad witnessing such horror, but she couldn't think about that now. "Fetch the doctor immediately!" she cried, desperation making her voice shrill.

Quickly Benjamin ran from the chamber.

Cursing and grunts came from across the room.

Suddenly Marcus was beside her. He pulled her hands away and studied the wounds. His features were grim.

"It's bad, isn't it?" Her voice caught.

Placing her now blood-soaked apron back on the gashes, he ordered, "Get some bandages. And some water. I'll take care of him. Go!"

His commands gave her hope and quickly she stood.

As Catherine raced out the door, she stole a glance at the blackguard. Kirby Jones and Jack O'Malley had apparently arrived at her calls and essentially sat on the soot-haired ruffian while he thrashed about on the floor. With his bruised face, thick red lips curled into a bloodied snarl, his unkempt black whiskers and bruised deep-pocketed dark eyes, the man was positively terrifying. Reassuringly, the brute's hands were bound together with a leather cord and that cord was strapped to the leg of a heavy armchair.

Thank heavens Marcus excelled at what he did. And if there was any man who could save Headmaster Dunn, it was he.

Pushing all thoughts of death and dying aside, Catherine rushed out the door intent on finding bandages and water. And quickly.

"I'm so sorry, Marcus," Cat's words were threaded with grief.

Sitting on the top step of the veranda, Marcus didn't bother to turn. He could feel her behind him, staring at him, judging him. He'd been a worthless sod as a son and when his father had needed him the most, he'd botched it once more. Well, he'd have no further opportunity to let his father down. Death was his final failure.

"Dr. Winner . . . Dr. Winner said that you did everything possible. That because of your battlefield experience, you probably gave . . . your father"—her voice cracked—"more of a chance than even he could've." She sat beside him on the step and gently grasped his limp hand in hers. Her touch warmed, but little could breach the coldness that draped him. He knew that he should squeeze her hand, give her some sort of reassurance; she was grieving, too. But for his life, he could hardly move; he was exhausted down to his soul.

"Is there anything that I can do for you, Marcus?" Cat asked quietly.

Her flaxen hair was wild about her face like bits of straw, reminding him of when she was a girl. But instead of a rosy bloom on her cheeks, they were smeared with blood. Her gray gown was soaked in crimson and even her shoes looked as if they'd been dropped in a bucket of blood. No longer did she smell of delicate fresh citrus. Instead the metallic, cloying odor of death surrounded her.

The stench of mortality was all too familiar to Marcus. In war, Marcus tried to detach himself from the reality of death as much as possible, allowing him to survive and do what was necessary. But when the loss was so close, so personal, the boundaries wouldn't rise. He couldn't escape the finality of it all. Or the grief.

Marcus felt a piercing ache deep in his chest, but strangely, it was his mother's face that shimmered before his vision, not his father's. It was his mother's brown eyes brimming with sadness, as she laid a frail hand on his cheek and said a final farewell. Sorrow sliced through him so keenly he found it hard to breathe.

His mother had been the one person whom he could count on. The one individual who'd loved him completely. Who'd given her love freely, wholly and without condition. She'd never judged him. She had embraced his multitude of flaws as simply amusing parts of her beloved child. Even though it had been twelve years, he felt her loss like a cavernous hole in his heart where an icy wind whistled through.

When she'd died, Marcus's grief had been excruciating. He'd run off to the forest every day so no one could see him weep. Alone in the dark coppice, only the creatures of the wood heard his howls.

And the adults had left him to his grief. Yet a part of him hadn't wanted to be alone. He'd been sixteen, and even though he'd wanted to be treated like a man, deep inside he'd felt like a child, alone and afraid and aching for his lost mother.

His friends had been the ones to help him break out from the grief. He clearly recalled his seventeenth birthday. He'd taken off to the woods once again. Alone with his sorrow, he'd thought about the cake his mother would have made for him and the candles she would have hand-dipped especially for the occasion. But in the midst of his melancholy, his cronies had arrived bearing a box tied with twine. In it, they'd said, was a gift worthy of the adventuresome Marcus Dunn. They, obviously, wanted their old friend back, not the morose loner he'd become.

Curious, and more than a bit relieved at the interruption of his bereavement, Marcus had opened the box. Inside had been a bottle of gin, a map and a young lady's cotton chemise. His chum Kenny Lane had explained that Marcus's charge for his birthday adventure was to drink the gin (with his friends of course) then to follow the map and find the owner of that cotton chemise. It had been a birthday celebration that Marcus would never forget, thanks to the kind of cheer that only seventeen-year-old boys and a willing Delores Tafton could bring.

Remembering it now, Marcus almost smiled, but his lips seemed leaden and his heart not quite able to muster the cheer. He was older now, and knew that no bottle of gin or roll in the hay was going to make this pain disappear.

His next birthday had been not nearly as memorable, he recalled, but it had been easier to face without his mother. Each birthday even more so after that. Year after year had separated him from his mother's death, and eventually the sorrow had dulled to a blunt ache. On the rare occasions when Marcus would consider his lack of grief, he felt guilty for his callousness. But there was naught he could do for it. Moreover, he was too busy to overassess his feelings. There were studies to be learned, games to be played and friends to laugh with. As his arguments with his father had grown more acrimonious, his mother's memory had taken on a sweet, hazy quality. Gone was the bitter tang of anguish.

Now grief crashed upon him like a wave battering a seashell against the reef. He was drowning in salty tears, unable to surface from the pain enough to breathe. His chest hurt, his eyes stung and he felt frozen in a silent agony of the soul.

A soft hand caressed his face. He looked up. Cat sat beside him, wiping away his tears. He hated the pity he saw in her gaze. Hated how weak he must seem. A grown man crying for his lost mother who'd died twelve years before. Deep down, he recognized that losing his father had rekindled his grief for his mother. Just as with her final illness, he had felt impotent, like a failure because he couldn't do more to stop the fever from burning the life out of her. But now, truly, it was his fault. He'd been in the house as a murderer attacked his father, and he'd been so wrapped up with Cat, he'd not heard . . . had not acted in time . . . It had been within his power to save his father. And he'd failed.

He didn't know what to do with the pain, the grief, the guilt, so he pushed the emotions aside and rose, standing out of Cat's reach. He wiped his eyes. "I have to go."

"Where?" She stood. Her gray gaze was soft with concern and her features creased with worry.

He looked away, unable to meet her eyes. "I need . . . I just . . ." He swallowed. "I need to go sit with my father." The words were out before he'd even considered them. He knew that there was no more he could do to help his father, that the Uriah Dunn he'd known was no longer in that empty shell. Yet, he needed to do it. He couldn't quite understand why, but it was imperative.

"Of course." Cat nodded slowly. "I'll make sure no one disturbs you."

"Thanks." He swallowed. "And if you could get me some towels and water . . . I'd like to . . . cleanse him."

"Of course."

As they turned toward the orphanage door, she spoke softly. "I have a friend who told me something interesting once."

"Hmmm," he murmured, following her inside.

"She said that in her tradition, to sit with a . . . lost loved one . . . is a way to honor that person. That to clean the . . ." She swallowed. ". . . body is a sacred endeavor." Stopping, she turned around. Biting on her lower lip, she shrugged, not meeting his eye. "Somehow, I know . . . that your father . . . he loved you *so* well . . . he would be pleased that you would do him this honor. It would mean a lot to him."

Quickly, she spun on her heel and kept walking as if afraid she'd overstepped her bounds.

He stood dumbly, watching her go as the backs of his eyes burned with unshed tears. Cat's compassion moved him. It gave him a strange warm feeling deep inside his chest that thawed some of the bitter grief. Somehow, he didn't feel so dreadfully . . . ill-judged, useless . . . misunderstood . . . unwanted . . .

His feelings were in a scramble, but one true belief shone though: he had someone on his side. His father was dead, murdered. His mother long buried. But in this dark, cruel world, there was a flicker of warmth, a welcoming smile and a woman that truly cared about him.

Chapter 20

Catherine had left Marcus to his father, checking in on him now and again. Poor Marcus. It pained her to see how devastated he was. He blamed himself, she knew, when there was no fault in his quarter. In fact, if Marcus hadn't arrived, Catherine didn't want to think about the damage that the murderer might have inflicted on the children. Knowing Headmaster Dunn, he would have been glad it was only he who had suffered. He'd always put others before himself.

Rubbing her eyes, Catherine choked back her tears. Lord, how she missed him. It was like a stone barrier protecting her from the outside world had suddenly disappeared, and it was up to her to brave the elements alone. For herself and the children. She felt the enormity of her responsibility like a weight on her soul.

But the bitter wind seemed somewhat tempered by having Marcus near. He gave her grief a focus, and allowed her to feel not so wretchedly alone in this sorrow.

He'd stayed with his father all through the night, until

the undertaker had removed Headmaster Dunn that morning. Then Marcus had disappeared, to where she did not know. She worried for him and wished he'd return soon.

With Marcus gone, Catherine had been left to face the grieving children and the staff. They'd expected her to be a pillar of strength when all she'd wanted to do was melt into a useless puddle of tears.

Finally, she couldn't take it anymore. She'd closeted herself in Headmaster Dunn's study, closing the doors. Yet the stench of blood was even now too potent for her hollow stomach and she had no choice but to open the windows for air. So she could not escape the muted sobs of the children outside as their strict schedule was thrown into chaos by the headmaster's sudden death.

The main house was too silent; absent were the sounds of chattering voices, playful laughter and slamming doors that usually pervaded the halls.

Thank heavens Jared isn't here. It's a blessing he doesn't have to face Dunn's murder. But her mind reared away from the excruciating reality. She couldn't grasp it, it was so bizarre.

On her knees, she worked in a daze, knowing she had to keep moving or she would shatter. Hands belonging to someone else collected the precious books from where they lay scattered around the hardwood floor of Dunn's office. Catherine was ghostly cold; moving, functioning, but not feeling anything. She couldn't; it was too much for her fragile composure.

Bucket, soapy water, rags. Catherine tried to think of anything else she might need, but her mind was clouded in a thick fog. Such a mess. Such a nasty mess. Headmaster Dunn would hate for his office to be so unclean. To be cluttered with books, papers and keepsakes was one thing, but he always abhorred filth.

She labored as if in a dream, talking herself through each step. Chairs righted and set aside. Books cleared and placed out of the way. Can't get any water on Dunn's prized collection. What would happen to these precious books without their guardian? The children . . . Her mind reared away from any thoughts of the future, clouding into a daze of solitary purpose: to cleanse this room of the taint of carnage.

Next, scrub the floor.

Standing before the last stack of books, she turned and studied the dark stain splayed behind the desk. It was almost the color of Cook's molasses pudding. An odd shade for someone's lifeblood. A shudder ran through her; perhaps she was not so detached after all.

She turned away, examining the furniture. To clean the stained floor, the desk had to be moved.

Leaning forward, Catherine pushed with all of her might, making sure that her good leg took the brunt of the effort. The bulky desk budged barely a finger's width. She tried again. Her arms quaked, her heart was pounding with the effort and her feet scrambled for purchase. The desk barely moved a half a finger's width more.

"Here," a deep voice pronounced. "Let me help you."

Blinking, she straightened, shocked by Nicholas Redford's sudden appearance. She had not heard the door click open, yet there he was and the entry yawning wide open. She shouldn't have been so surprised to see Headmaster Dunn's protégé, but everything seemed so illogical to her these days.

Redford placed his large, gloveless hands on the side of the desk and set his broad shoulder to the corner. He was a tall man with a wide forehead fringed with thick black brows that matched his black, collar-length hair. He had sharp cheekbones, shadowed by scruff, a jagged nose, wide lips and a hint of cleft chin. The faint scent of almonds he wore always reminded Catherine of honey cookies.

Redford was the most celebrated orphan to come from the orphanage. With hard work, dedication, and a razor-sharp intellect, he had worked his way up to being a Bow Street Runner, and was now the respected owner of a new enquiry firm. Dunn could not have been more proud if Redford was his own son, and Redford returned the fondness. Of course Redford would come when he'd heard the awful news . . .

"Well?" he asked, waiting crouched with his shoulder set to the desk.

Wordlessly, she positioned her palms above his, planted her feet and readied.

"Heave!" he called.

The massive desk skid across the chamber with a mighty groan. It slid so quickly, Catherine would have fallen but Redford caught her in a firm grip about the waist.

Steadying her, he looked down, his dark brown eyes searching her gaze. "Are you all right?"

"I'm fine." She stepped out of his embrace, looking away, unable to meet his eyes. She didn't want him here, didn't want to talk to anyone. She just wanted to be alone to clean the room.

"Can you tell me what happened?" His voice was gentle, but she sensed the powerful emotions he held in check.

Crossing her arms, she hugged herself, not wanting to discuss it. Still, Catherine reminded herself that Redford had never turned his back on the place that had given him his start. He was always available to help out at Andersen Hall when needed, whether it was lending his muscle when they rebuilt the orphanage's dairy or helping the children find suitable positions upon leaving the home. He was a good man who loved Dunn well. She owed him the truth.

"Headmaster Dunn . . ." She felt like she was talking through a mouth full of liniment, it seemed so difficult to speak. ". . . was attacked . . . Marcus . . . Marcus fought the man . . . stopped him . . . but we were too late for Headmaster Dunn." Her shoulders sagged with defeat. "We were too late . . ."

He said nothing for a long time. She stood miserable, having no desire to breach the silence.

The muffled sounds of sobbing could be heard through the open door as well as the scuffle of many feet on planked floors.

"Do we know why?" he asked gruffly, his voice steeped in anger kept under taut control.

She shrugged. "The man had . . ." Her eyes burned, but she pushed away the pain, unwilling to surrender to it just yet. "He had the headmaster's watch . . ." What a waste, for a wretched ornament! Her anger seethed and she pushed the heels of her hands into her eyes so hard she saw stars. "He mentioned a strongbox . . . The fool . . . If only . . . if only . . . he hadn't believed . . ." She quaked, feeling as if she was going to splinter with the pain.

Strong hands gripped her shoulders and squeezed. "The bastard will pay," Redford's voice was infused with quiet fury. "If I have to do it with my bare hands, he will die for this."

"That which cannot be saved *must* be avenged," a gruff voice murmured from the threshold.

Catherine looked up, blinking away the white haze that plagued her eyes. She almost hadn't recognized Marcus's voice; it was so rough with strain and emotion.

Marcus's bruised eye had yellowed to a greenish blue and his lip was still puffy, but the swelling had diminished. He'd changed clothes at some point, but still, he looked as if he'd hardly cared while he'd dressed. His ivory cravat was so loose it fairly hung down the front of his unbuttoned green coat. The striped waistcoat underneath was slightly askew. Although his white breeches were clean, his brown boots were scuffed, and he leaned heavily on his crutches.

She marveled at how he could think of his ruse for his mission at a time like this. Yet she knew that Headmaster Dunn would have wanted him to stay the course, even at a time like this.

Redford released her and turned. His hands were balled into fists and his russet eyes flashed fire.

"Dunn." His tone was curt as he noticeably did not use Marcus's rank.

"Redford."

Neither man moved to shake hands or express any welcome to the other. The air practically crackled with tension.

"I'd heard you were back," Redford bit out.

Marcus turned to her, pointedly ignoring the other man. "I've sent for my belongings."

Redford's eyes narrowed. "Why?"

Catherine shook her head, trying to clear it. "Belongings?"

"You're going to need some help around here. My . . ." His voice faltered, then his features hardened to stone. "My father would have wanted me to stay."

"Since when do you give a bloody damn about what your father wants?" Redford charged, stepping forward menacingly. "He posted to you for years and never got one blasted response. He waited for any word from you, feared you for dead—"

"My relationship with my father is none of your bloody business," Marcus's tone was brittle. "Nor is where I choose to reside."

"It is when it implicates Andersen Hall," Redford retorted. "You turned your back on this institution and everyone in it seven years ago. Don't think that you can just prance back in and all is well."

"My father didn't object to my return," Marcus interrupted, his gaze colder than winter.

"Of course he didn't, the man's a saint! But that doesn't make you worthy of forgiveness."

"You bloody toady! You didn't have a father of your own so decided mine would do!"

Their arguments had cleared the mists in Catherine's mind to clarity, allowing the sorrow to leak through. It was so heavy it felt like a rail parked across her shoulders. "Stop it!" she cried, raising her hands. "I can't take it!"

The men seemed to become mindful of her presence. Still, they eyed each other with wariness that bespoke old animosity.

Redford shifted his shoulders. "If I believe that there is a true change of heart, mind and *deed*, then perhaps . . ."

"Who the hell are you to judge me?" Marcus's tone was harsh.

Moving over to the desk, Catherine leaned heavily, besieged by their animosity and by her sorrow. The emotions hammered at her, making her feel battered.

Marcus stepped forward. "You, Mr. Redford, weren't the one laying his life on the line for King and Country the last seven years—"

"Donning a uniform does not make you honorable," Redford retorted.

"Neither does taking up a tipstaff and—"

"I can't take it," her voice was barely a whisper. "It's simply . . . too much . . ."

"He started," Marcus insisted, wagging a finger. "I was merely trying to do the right thing—"

Redford snorted, crossing his arms. "There's a first time for everything."

Sudden anger swept through her like a flash fire, dispelling the despair. "Will both of you please grow up!"

Redford turned to her. "Now see here—"

"Really, Cat." Marcus scowled, then winced at the pain from his bloodied lip. "You cannot speak to us as if we were children."

"Then stop acting like them!" She stepped forward, the urges to weep and scream warring within her so profoundly she shook. "If not for my sake, then at least for the sake of Headmaster Dunn, please, find some way to get along."

Redford was frowning, pensive. Marcus was studying her as if she was a heretofore unknown specimen.

"I understand that you are both dreadfully upset. It's a terrible . . ." her voice faltered. "Terrible day. Emotions run high . . . But still, if we don't pull together, we will rend apart." Pressing her hands together she pleaded, "Even if you don't mean it, you two need to put on a brave face and stand shoulder to shoulder. For the sake of staff, the board, the children . . . There is so much more at risk here than your childhood rancor."

The men exchanged a glum glance of truce. The tension in the room eased a notch.

She pointed to the blood-soaked floor. "Better that you take your animosity and direct it at the true culprit here."

The men's gazes traveled to the floor, and she could see their grief, even as each man tried to mask it. Distantly she wondered if these men were at odds because they were so alike. But she was too exhausted to truly care. She simply wanted them to behave.

"You're right," Redford acknowledged, squaring his shoulders. "Now is not the time or the place." The anger simmering in his dark eyes seemed to promise that that day would come.

"I didn't mean to upset you, Cat," Marcus murmured, looking away.

Quiet descended in the chamber, broken only by the muted sobs drifting through the window, mixed with bird-song and the rustling leaves.

After a moment Redford turned to Marcus. "There was only one assailant?"

"No one came to the bugger's rescue," Marcus replied, leaning forward on his crutches. "But the lads searched the grounds just in case. And I had them patrol last night."

She pressed her hand to her chest, alarmed. "Alone?"

"In groups of four with explicit orders to send for help if anything or anyone was about," Marcus added sooth-ingly. "They encountered no one."

Redford scratched his chin, his cocoa brown eyes sharp with speculation. "Was anything else found on the thief?" Redford seemed to have slipped into his Bow Street Run-ner role. Probably as a way to deal with this catastrophe.

"Just the watch."

Redford nodded slowly. "So you believe that robbery was the motive?"

"He mentioned a strongbox," Marcus replied, his face suddenly hardening. "But I haven't yet had a real crack at the knave. When I do . . ."

A shiver slid up Catherine's spine. She could hardly imagine what he meant, and she didn't wish to know. In her heart, she just wanted it undone.

"John Newman is the warden at Newgate Prison," Redford stated, straightening as if coming to a decision. "Only he can grant permission for prisoners to be questioned."

Marcus's eyes glinted with contained violence. "I'm sure he will find it within his heart to permit me such privilege."

Redford nodded. After a long moment, he adjusted his hat on his head. "John Newman and I are old friends. I will visit him this afternoon and make the arrangements for an interview." He paused, meeting Marcus's gaze. "If that suits you?"

"That would be most . . . helpful," Marcus acknowledged, with a nod.

"Good day then." Redford tipped his hat to Catherine and moved toward the door.

Marcus shifted aside, saying, "Redford?"

Redford stopped.

"If I could ask a boon of you?"

The investigator's face darkened, but he nodded as if he was prepared to listen.

"If you see Joe Tipton, do me a favor, and don't tell him I'm back."

"And if he already knows?"

"Just give him as little information as possible." He shrugged. "With everything going on here . . ." His eyes drifted to the bloodstained floor. "I'm not quite ready to face some of my past . . . misadventures."

Redford scowled. "You're still a selfish bastard—"

"The man's father just died in his arms," Catherine cried. "Giving him some peace for a few days is not too much to ask."

Looking away, the investigator grunted, not indicating a negative or positive response. Suddenly he looked up. "Miss Miller says that you trounced the bastard." He sniffed. "Before he could do worse."

Marcus shrugged.

"Well, for that alone, I'm glad you were here."

"I didn't do it for you, Redford."

"No. But I'm glad just the same." Turning, Nick Redford was gone.

Chapter 21

"**N**icholas Redford is a good man," Catherine stated, closing the door behind the investigator. "You should try to get along. No matter your feelings, your father loved him well."

"Too well," Marcus muttered. "Better than his own son."

"Don't be ridiculous. It's like comparing air and water."

"Don't you mean oil and water?"

"No," she replied, trying to be patient. "We need both water and air to live yet they are totally distinctive."

"Aren't you a well of wisdom, today?" he scoffed, setting aside his crutches and dropping into the chair.

It seemed that Marcus was covering his sorrow with belligerence. Catherine felt for his pain, but wished he would find another channel for his grief.

"Sorry," he muttered, running a hand through his hair. He looked out the window. "I can't seem to rein in my temper today."

Her feelings softened. "It's been a difficult time . . ."

"Yes, well, for all of us, I suppose. So I don't need to be a complete cur." He shrugged looking away. "I'm just so . . . angry."

"A man murdered your father, Marcus. Headmaster Dunn wasn't even my flesh and blood and I want to kick up a riot."

His penetrating blue gaze fixed on her. "Really? You seem so calm."

She shook her head. "If it makes you feel any better, I want to kill the blackguard that did this. But at the moment, the only thing within my power is to pick up the broken pieces." She shook her head. "I'm not like you and Nick Redford. I don't have the chance to make things right. I don't have the skills to take matters into my own hands. If I did . . ." Then so much would be different. Mayhap the Caddyhorns wouldn't be such a thorn in her side. Mayhap she wouldn't feel the festering wound burning inside of her every time she saw mention of her wretched relations in the papers. The houses, the jewels, the riches that should have been Jared's.

"Thanks, by the way," Marcus murmured.

"For what?"

"Defending me to Redford."

"I was chastising both of you, if you recall," she replied gently.

"Still." His sapphire eyes met hers, sincerity and pain burning within. "You spoke up for me. Thank you." He said it with a weighty tone that made it sound like she'd done much more than she had.

Her heart went out to him that he would count such a little thing as so important. Hadn't others stood beside him? What had happened to make him feel so terribly alone? Or had he always felt this way, but she'd assumed otherwise?

Thinking back, for as long as she'd known him, he'd been the center of a boisterous crowd. The lads had all wanted to hover in his shadow and the girls had begged for his attentions. She'd always assumed that where she sat, on the edge of the crowd, was the loneliest place to be. Could it be that Marcus had felt isolated as well, despite the company? Catherine had always presumed that when one was accepted, one was connected. But she began to wonder.

"My father's been busy recently," Marcus said suddenly, pulling Catherine from her thoughts. "With a personal matter. Do you know what it was?"

"I thought he was with you and the board."

Marcus shook his head. "No. He left that to me. So you have no idea?"

"None whatsoever."

His gaze darkened, reckoning gleaming in those sea blue depths. "I cannot assume that this was a random act of violence against my father."

A chill slithered down her spine.

"My guess is that he's a hired hand." Marcus's voice lowered. "The question is: Who is directing that hand?"

A wave of nausea swept over her as his implications sank in. She didn't know which was worse: Headmaster Dunn's death being an arbitrary act of violence or premeditated murder.

"Are you all right?" Jumping up from the seat, he reached out and squeezed her arm. His grip was firm and reassuring, giving her the strength she needed to weather the queasiness. His sandalwood pomade seemed to help a little as well, combating the metallic tang of blood.

"I can't believe what you're saying," she whispered. "It's madness."

His face was grim. "It's my world, Cat. Which is why I didn't want you anywhere near it."

"So you think perhaps that . . ." She mouthed, *Renfrew*. ". . . is behind this?"

"I cannot assume otherwise. And I must hasten my plans before anyone else is hurt."

"Hasten?"

"I don't mean to sound callous, but at least my father's death will force the trustees to meet more frequently." Shaking his head, he seemed surprised. "I suppose I do have a lot of my father in me."

She blinked. "Of course you do. Why do you say it like that?"

"When my father had his eye on the target, he used every means of achieving it. I, apparently, am willing to do the same."

"He would be proud of you, Marcus, for not wavering. He would have wanted you to go on . . ."

"I *have* to go on, Cat. I need to know if that bastard is behind my father's murder."

"If *he* is responsible for this . . . then how, how can you even bear to be in his presence?"

"To extinguish something, one must get close to it. . . ." The muscle in his jaw worked, and his face hardened to marble. "And I will sit down for tea with Napoleon himself if it will avenge my father."

The backs of her eyes burned with unshed tears for Marcus, his controlled grief and his path. She saw no joy at the end of his journey, only more death, betrayal . . .

Her lower lip quivered. "I don't know how you can stand it all, Marcus . . . The world you live in is so . . . awful . . ."

Leaning forward and pulling her close, Marcus murmured, "It's not really as bad as all that. I do good work for His Majesty."

She pressed her face into the hollow at his shoulder and the rough wool of his coat scratched her cheek. Pain seared her heart and she wanted to fall into his brawny chest and sob her heart out. Only her concern for how hard this must be for him held her back, but barely. "But at what cost?" She sniffed. "This has got to wear on one's soul."

"My soul is just fine." His hand smoothed her hair. "But it's nice to know that someone is worried about it wearing a little, instead of it burning in a fiery hell of damnation . . ."

"That's not funny, Marcus," she cried, anxiously. "All of this death and betrayal . . . How can you take it?"

She felt his chest rise and fall in a sigh. "We all have our crosses to bear, Cat. Besides, I don't hear you complaining about the children, the orphanage, the work you do. You're so strong, thank heavens."

"I'm not strong," she muttered into his chest, feeling pitiful. "I'm just a secretary."

"On the contrary, you are the anchor that's going to help this place weather the storm. The children are depending on you. Andersen Hall is depending on you."

Catherine felt his words like manacles gripping her body and locking into place. Giving in to sorrow was a luxury she never could afford. Part of her resented the inability simply to experience her grief, but mostly, she was resigned.

Since her twelfth year she'd had to be responsible for herself and her brother, always doing what needed to be done regardless of what she wanted. Her lips tightened. If she'd had her wish she would have had a normal youth, dance lessons, shopping expeditions, candy crèmes, a coming-out ball. She pushed aside her self-pity. She might not have it easy, but, oh, it could have been so much worse.

She needed to follow Marcus's example. He was grieving so badly, her heart ached for him. Yet he forced himself to move forward, stay the course and keep his priorities in the forefront of his mind. She was more than a little awed by his fortitude.

"What . . . what happens now?" she asked, pulling herself together.

"I cannot bring my father back," Marcus replied. "But I will do everything in my power to see justice done."

Justice was Headmaster Dunn's most sought-after goal. To Catherine, it suddenly outshone all others. Looking up, she implored, "I want to help you, Marcus. I want to do my part."

His gaze softened. "That is quite honorable of you, Cat. But you know that that's not possible."

"But, I can do many things. I want to help you . . ."

"You will have your hands full here, I'm sure," he replied, looking out the window.

The leaves rustled in the trees and Cat realized that the children must have gone to dine, for all was quiet. The poor children . . . Andersen Hall would never be the same. Everything was so terribly altered by this tragedy. She felt so impotent, so terribly afraid for the future.

"I want to do *more*," she beseeched. "There must be something I can do." At the dubious look on his face, she added, "I saved your life, don't forget."

"And it almost cost you your own." He shook his head. "No, Cat. This is no business for you."

"But—"

"Come on, Cat. Remember what we're talking about.

This is dangerous work. You're not cut out for such endeavors." He looked down at her and, despite the patience she saw in his gaze, she could not help but be reminded of years before when he had hauled her up from the roof. Pain slashed through her; she was lame, unfit in his eyes. Why did the thought upset her so much?

He sighed. "Don't look so injured, Cat," he soothed. "This is simply a charge better suited to . . . well, me. It's what I do. And I couldn't do my job if I was distracted with worry for you."

Pushing out of his arms, she stepped back, covering her hurt with anger. "If you will excuse me, I have work to do." She waved to the bloodstained floor. "Something suited to my talents."

"Come now, Cat, that's not fair . . ."

"Leave me alone, Marcus." The ferocity in her voice frightened even her. "I want to be alone."

He studied her a long moment, then shook his head. "I know you're grief-stricken, Cat. But don't let your reasoning become clouded. You're a rational girl. Once you think about it, you will see that I'm right." He waited for her to say something, but she pressed her lips together, knowing that she would sooner bite her tongue than placate him.

Frowning, he swiveled on his crutches and headed for the door. "I'll be back later."

She slammed the door closed behind him, uncaring that the thud shook the walls. She just barely restrained herself from kicking it. Instead, leaning against the hard wood, she hugged herself as pain, anger, grief and frustration raged within her.

Marcus didn't see her as whole; she'd always be an invalid in his eyes. Weak, powerless, in need of protection. She loathed the idea that he viewed her as needy. But deep down, she had to recognize that part of her humiliation stemmed from the fact that she secretly wanted him to see her as a woman. A whole, flesh-and-blood woman. But he couldn't. To him, she would always be the lame chit who'd fallen from the roof.

Why was she so intent on driving herself mad with idiotic girlish dreams? Why couldn't she accept her lot and live with it, as Jared had suggested?

She shouldn't be angry with Marcus. He was just trying to protect her. He was an honorable man, facing terrible things. He had more to worry about than her welfare. And, yet, he was concerned for her well-being. She should be touched by his thoughtfulness, not angry that he wouldn't let her hurl herself into danger.

His protectiveness was somewhat nice, she had to admit grudgingly. When he was near, she felt safer than she had in years. But who would protect her once he was gone?

She would be alone at Andersen Hall, no Headmaster Dunn to lean on, no Marcus to brighten her day.

The weeping burst upon her like a storm. Lowering herself to the floor, Catherine pulled the bucket toward her and lifted out the rag. But she was so exhausted, she couldn't move. She simply sat there on her knees, sobbing, bemoaning the things that would never be and the woman she would never become.

Chapter 22

~~~~~∽◯◯∽~~~~~

Late that night, in the darkness, Marcus prowled the halls of the orphanage, unable to quench the physical need to *move*. Turning the corner, he banged into the wall, only then realizing how foxed he truly was. He'd found Graves's cache in the gardener's hut. And hadn't stopped swigging until the pain had numbed.

Numbed, but never truly receded.

His father was dead. He repeated the phrase over and over in his mind to bring the fact home to him. It was too hard to believe. Dunn was almost a mythological figure: powerful, indomitable, and all-knowing, if absolutely maddening. For him to be gone was like irreparably tearing the composition of the world. Everything seemed . . . out of balance.

The shadows in the silent hallway seemed to nip at his heels, so he kept moving, his hand dragging along the walls with a quiet *whoosh*.

There were so many things Marcus wished he had had the chance to say to his father. So many words he longed

195

to hear. So much anger, still, at his father's betrayal seven years ago. And the guilt, that terrible guilt. He'd let his father down in so many ways . . .

He had no parents; he was an orphan truly, not just by inclination. He was like the others at Andersen Hall, even though he'd always considered himself so very different. Now the only family he had was the army. A depressing thought. He knew he should embrace his isolation as if it were a beloved companion. For it would be his attendant for eternity. Constant, enduring and never to let him down. But somehow, the notion didn't help.

Marcus eased himself down another corridor. His mission was the only thing keeping him sane, he realized. The possibility of meting out justice and assuaging some of this anger. Doubts circled him like a scavenger bird eyed corpses. Was his mission the reason his father was murdered? He prayed it wasn't so, yet by the same token, hoped that Renfrew was responsible. So Marcus could tear his heart out.

Marcus walked blindly, sensing where he was and what was around him without truly soaking it in. The dormitory was up the stairs. The library down the next hall. His father's office at the other end of the building.

A sound whispered down the hallway, seeping through his sodden brain. Someone was treading softly, trying not to be discovered. Images of the blackguard attacking his father flashed in his mind. He'd seen hundreds like him and they usually traveled in packs. Slowly, his lips curled back into a feral smile. Oh, he hoped they'd come back for more. He'd give them something to chew on. The Wolf was hungry and it was time to hunt.

Marcus's heart began to pound, energy swamped his limbs. His head was still not clear, but his body knew exactly what to do. He hung back, pressed against the hard wall in shadow, waiting for the man's advance around the bend. Marcus snapped his arm out, grabbing for purchase and whipping the rascal around.

The delicate scent of lemons somehow seeped into his consciousness. *Cat.* Desperately he yanked backwards, trying to negate his maneuver, but a knee suddenly smashed between his legs with such ferocity, he saw stars.

The next thing Marcus knew, he was flat on his back on the floor, clutching his groin with both hands. Pained seared from between his legs to every extremity and he couldn't breathe. His stomach roiled as nausea overtook him.

"Oh my God! Marcus!" Cat cried. Her small hands touched his shoulders. "I thought you were an intruder! Are you all right?"

He gritted his teeth against the agony, waiting for it to fade as all pain did.

"Is there anything I can do?" she asked, concern marring her voice.

Mutely he shook his head.

She waited, silently, thank heavens. He didn't think he could stand a prattling female at the moment.

The nausea slowly passed and the throbbing in his groin eased from excruciating to acute. He waited until his breath no longer came in short gasps. "What the hell were you doing skulking about?" he bit out.

"I wasn't skulking . . . And I could ask you the same question." At his silent reproach, she added, "I was checking on the children."

"At four o'clock in the morning?"

"I couldn't sleep." She looked down, her flaxen hair the only radiance in the darkness. "Seeing them calms me. I'm so upset about your father . . ."

Where was a drink when you needed one? He didn't

want to talk about his father's murder. Didn't want to think about the sorrow.

He realized that she had not removed her hands from his shirt. Her touch warmed him, the only thing to do so on this cold night, he realized.

"You smell like . . ." Even in the shadows he could discern her grimace. "Oh, that Mr. Graves—"

"I knew where to find his cache," Marcus defended.

She sighed. "I suppose we all have our ways of coping." Gently, she slid her warm hands underneath his shoulders. "Can you stand?"

He wasn't nearly as jug-bitten as she presumed him to be, but he kind of liked how she was coddling him. He couldn't recall the last time someone had bothered. Slowly, he leaned forward, making sure not to appear too clearheaded.

Wrapping her small arm around his waist, she helped him to stand. She felt so bloody good; it took every last shred of decency in him not to kiss her right then and there.

"You're staying in the guesthouse?" she asked.

"Yes."

Exhaling loudly, she hugged him close. "Lean on me, then." Her tone was resigned. "I'll get you to bed."

He tried to ignore the rush of heat he felt at her ingenuous words. *She's an innocent. Too good for the likes of a cad like you,* he chided himself.

With her willowy arms wrapped about his waist and his arm draped across her shoulder, she led him down the hall.

He liked the feel of her cotton robe beneath his fingers and the way she let out a breathy sigh every time they turned a corner. He tried to ignore the hunger growing inside him as her soft breasts pushed into his midsection.

As they headed out the back door, Marcus leaned over, smelling her hair. He'd have never guessed how enticing the scent of lemons could be. Then orange blossoms came to mind. And the incredible scene of Cat washing her naked body by the firelight . . .

He tilted his body slightly sideways, anxious for her not to discover his stiff rod. He didn't want to frighten the girl. Or maybe he should. Tell her to run from him . . . screaming.

The fresh air helped a little as they exited a side doorway.

Marcus knew he should give up on playing the needy drunkard, but she felt so bloody good, he realized his principles had deserted him. And where was the harm? Lurid thoughts weren't crimes in and of themselves.

With every step down the path, her robe brushed against his thighs. It was a delicious agony, over all too soon as the guesthouse drew near.

Slowly, they climbed the steps together, hips pressed close. He had to bite back a groan. *There's no port for you here, sailor*, he told himself. But still, he was loath to let her go.

No candles were lit and the parlor was cloaked in shadows.

Their feet squeaked on the wooden floor as they entered the bedroom. He felt her tense. "You shouldn't be here," he muttered, suddenly finding his scruples.

"No one will know." Her voice was breathless. Was it simply from the walk, or was she likewise affected by their intimate embrace?

Gently, she helped him lie on the bed and flipped the coverlet over him. "Oh, your boots—"

"Don't bother. I've slept in them before."

Hands on hips, she stared down at him. He wished he could see her face, but it was cast in shadow.

Finally, she mumbled, "I suppose I'd better go, then."

"Good, idea," he murmured, more to himself than to her. *Run away as fast as you can.* But part of him dreaded the moment the door would close behind her, leaving him once again abandoned to his crushing grief. He felt once more like the lad of sixteen who'd been left to suffer a parent's death alone.

Still, his selfishness galled even him. He couldn't ask Cat to stay, it went beyond the pale. Besides, he couldn't be responsible for his actions tonight. A cold jug was the only companion he could hope for.

"On your way out," Marcus implored, "can you bring me the flagon on the table?"

Silently, she turned and went into the parlor.

Something crashed.

He sat up. "Are you all right?"

"I'm fine. Fine."

She returned with an earthen jug and handed it to him.

"Thanks." Uncorking it, he took a long, hard swallow. The fiery liquid burned the whole way down. He exhaled loudly, feeling the heat rush through his guts. Not nearly as warming as flesh-and-blood companionship, but it was all he had.

He looked up, surprised to see her still standing there.

"You know," she murmured, "I thought, after everything . . . I would collapse exhausted, but . . ."

"You can find no peace this night." He inhaled deeply. "I know exactly how you feel."

"Does that . . ." She seemed to be motioning to the jug. "Does it help?"

"Not really, but it's all I've got."

"Don't say that, Marcus," she murmured. "It's not true."

He swallowed. "You should go—"

"I-I don't want to."

Charged silence filled the shadow-cloaked room.

Finally, ignoring the warning calls in his head, Marcus held out the jug. "Want to try?"

Slowly, she reached for the handle. Their fingers brushed and thrills shot up his hand. Cat gasped.

Now he had no doubt she felt it, too.

She sounded breathless and he felt like he could sense the rise and fall of her soft breasts. Marcus swallowed, knowing he was sinking into dark waters but not wanting to swim away just the same.

Lifting the jug to her lips, she took a long, deep swallow, and came up coughing and sputtering.

"Are you all right?" He jumped up, patting her on the back.

"Dear heavens!" She pressed her hand to her breast, wheezing. "That's strong."

"Little sips, Cat. Little sips."

Nodding, she licked her lips and took another swig. She exhaled loudly. "It tastes like one of Nurse Jane's cures."

Slowly, she sank down onto the bed and set the jug in her lap.

Marcus knew that he shouldn't, but he sat down beside her. They hadn't done anything *truly* wrong. And it was a difficult time for her. Where was the harm in giving her an ear to listen, a shoulder to cry on . . .

She took another sip and quivered. "God, this is dreadful."

"It's not as bad if you have something to eat. But I'm sorry, I don't have anything for you."

"Wait." With her free hand, she reached into her dressing gown pocket and pulled something out. "How's this?" She tucked what felt like a small, hard pebble into his hand.

"It's a mint drop," she explained as she placed one in her mouth. "Little Evie thought I looked sad and gave them to me to cheer me up."

Marcus stared down at the tiny candy he could hardly see in the darkness, remembering how precious confections had been when he was a child. For a little girl to give up her sweet for Cat . . .

Inexplicable sadness overwhelmed him. Discomfited, he cleared his throat, and murmured, "Have you ever heard the story about the origins of mint?"

"No," she replied, taking another sip. "Ah, much better."

She handed him the jug, and he helped himself, trying not to think about how her pink lips had just pressed to that round opening.

The spirits slid down his throat, and his muscles relaxed. "Well," he began. "Mints, like licorice, have been around forever."

"I don't like licorice very much," she interjected, leaning against him. "Only in small doses." Her body fit neatly alongside his, all warm and soft and lemony-smelling . . .

"The name mint comes from a Greek myth involving Hades," he rushed, trying not to think of how good she felt.

"The god of the underworld."

"Yes." He took another swig. "As the story goes, Hades was in love with a nymph named Minthe."

"I thought that Hades was supposed to have been married?"

"To Persephone. Who was not very happy with Hades' dalliance. So she changed Minthe into an herb."

She rolled her head into his shoulder. "Let me guess, mint."

He shifted. Devil take it, she smelled heavenly. "Yes."

Reaching over, she took the jug.

"Slow down, Cat. This stuff catches up with you."

Nodding, she handed it back and he set it on the bedside stand. "I remember reading somewhere," she offered, "about ancient Greeks planting mint leaves near graves. Was it to remind Hades of what he had done?"

"Yes, and to mask the smell of death, I'm sure."

Why did he have to say that? She didn't need to be reminded!

Silence enveloped them, broken only by the sounds of the night.

"It's all right," she mumbled. He felt her shrug. "What's . . . done's . . . done . . ." Her voice took on a singsong lilt. "Is done . . ."

He did warn her, right? She's a grown woman and he did warn her . . .

"Oh, what a terrible pun," she intoned. "Done is Dunn, and pun." Slowly, she drifted backwards, lying down on the bed. "Oh that's really bad . . ."

Before he knew it, he was lying down beside her. "It's almost as bad as 'Cat's dogged.'"

"Cat's dogged!" she squealed, covering her mouth. "That's funny! Who said that?"

"I did." Sadness overcame him as he recalled the conversation with his father. He remembered the sense of connection, of breaching old wounds. Now Marcus would've given his right arm for his father's embrace. Sudden tears flooded his eyes.

"I'm so sorry, Marcus." She sniffed. "I'm so sorry. I loved him, too."

Reflexively, he reached out and she curled into his arms, pressing her nose into his neck. Her shoulders quaked and her tears dripped down his collar. He closed his eyes, letting his silent tears converge with hers.

Holding her, sharing his sorrow, made it better somehow, sweetness interlacing with the bitter pain.

After a time, she pulled back slightly, her face so close to his, their noses could almost touch and he could almost taste her minty breath.

She sniffed. "Every time I think about it . . . The attack. The blood. My heart . . . my heart pounds . . . so fast and . . . and I feel so afraid . . ."

"There's no need to be afraid . . . I'm here," he murmured, smoothing her velvety hair. "I won't let anything bad happen to you."

Cat shuddered and pressed her nose deep into his shoulder, wrapping her arms about his chest, seeking solace. She seemed so lost, so lonely. He recognized her anguish, knowing it all too well himself.

"It is like my mind races but goes nowhere." Her voice quivered with a hint of panic. "I feel like I ought to be doing something but have no idea what. I want to help you, the children, Mrs. Nagel. But I don't know what I'm supposed to do. I can't seem to sit still . . . But feel like I'm going nowhere."

"Shhh," he soothed. "You don't have anything to do or anywhere to be. You're fine."

She hugged him close. "I'm so glad I ran into you. I just . . . didn't want to be alone tonight."

"I'm here, Cat. I'm here."

"I'm so . . . glad . . . Marcus."

After a few minutes, he felt her limbs relax. Her breathing steadied as she lay in his arms, so trusting, so innocent. She let out a sweet, breathy sigh.

Marcus had known many women in his time, but few had ever asked for or given such comfort. Excitement, play, release, yes. But nothing like this . . . sense of . . . affinity. He realized that as he soothed her, he felt his own frayed nerves settle. He caressed her hair, like skimming his hands over a running brook, it was so smooth. Her lithe body fit neatly into his, pressing into his chest and along his limbs. Darkness cloaked them in a cocoon of intimacy that he prayed would not be breached any time soon. It had been so long since he'd felt such comfort.

Thoughts of his mother came to mind. In the peace of the shadows, he allowed some of the grief to wash through his heart. Like water streams over a jagged rock making it smooth, he experienced the ache, but along with it the sweetness of the memories. It was somehow easier to face the grief with Cat in his arms.

Slowly, thoughts of his father seeped into his mind. Marcus suddenly recalled the day his father had taught him how to ride. Walking the mare wasn't so bad. That was fun, actually, to feel a sense of control over such a great beast. But he'd gotten a bit ahead of himself and had kicked the horse's side, sending them off on a wild, bumpy ride that had knocked Marcus on his bottom.

"Learn your lesson and get right back on and do it better," his father had commented coolly. There had been no censure in his tone, no look of reproach in his deep blue gaze. Marcus had dusted off his breeches and gotten right back on.

He'd learned his father's lesson well that day, as he did so many others. How to read, how to decipher a map, how to tie trick knots. These were some of the invaluable skills that Marcus carried with him every day, unthinkingly falling back on the instruction that his father had imparted. His father's mark would forever be upon him.

Marcus recalled sitting beside his father in his parents' spacious bed, reading the big heavy Bible together. He could almost smell the musty parchment and see the closely typed lettering. Marcus could almost feel his father's long legs stretched out beside his smaller ones. Marcus had loved the story of Moses going up the mountain. Together he and his father had read those passages over and over so that Marcus almost knew them by heart.

Hugging Cat's warm body to his, Marcus closed his eyes and let the memories sweep over him. For the first time in as long as he could remember, he welcomed the darkness.

Chapter 23

Lightness seeped in through Marcus's closed eyelids. Birds chirped a merry tune, the trees rustled and the air smelled pleasantly of pine, dew and . . . lemons? Something agreeably warm blanketed his right side, assuaging the brisk morning breeze.

Marcus tried to peel the cobwebs from his foggy mind. Rarely did he fall into such a deep slumber, always remaining one quarter awake as to be on the ready for any nasty surprises. For some reason last night he had succumbed much more deeply than usual and he was having difficulty rousing. Morpheus enticed him back into slumber with promises of sweet dreams and gentle rest, but he knew that on a certain level something was not as it should be. And it was something he should know about citrus fruit.

Marcus opened one eye. He was used to waking up with aches and pains and in strange places, but nothing could have prepared him for waking on a bed with lovely Cat Miller nestled in his arms. It took him a moment to realize where he was and recall the events of the night before.

Cat snuggled in his arms, her nose pressed into his neck, her arm draped languidly across his chest. Dear lord, her knee was pressed up against his groin, soliciting the *exact opposite reaction* from last night when she'd felled him.

His manhood was swollen, hard and throbbing, demanding release. His body had a mind of its own and it made no distinction as to whether the woman in his arms was fair game or not. And she was most decidedly *not*, given her innocence. All his body knew, nonetheless, was that she felt good up against him and that it wanted her.

He schooled himself not to act like a beast, and to behave like the gentleman that she deserved him to be. But then she shifted in her sleep and her hand skated down to his stomach. His rod leaped in response and the blood in his veins flamed with desire. It took every ounce of self-control not to move an inch as he reined in his insistent passion. *Devil take it; she feels good.* Too good for a man who needed to keep his hands off her.

It was barely dawn, the sun's fragile golden rays scarcely setting the trees aglow outside. There was still some time before the whole orphanage awoke and Marcus wanted to be careful that no one came upon them. He did not want to think of the implications for Cat if someone saw them together. A man's indiscretions were usually easily forgiven, a lady's, rarely. Even in the friendly orphanage, few would understand the platonic beauty of sharing their grief. He wouldn't have appreciated it, he realized, had he not experienced it himself.

Slowly, Marcus edged away, gently trying to slide out from under Cat. One inch, then two. She groaned, shifting restlessly. He froze, waiting for her to settle back to sleep. She could use the rest, he told himself, it was best not to wake her. Dark circles still banked her eyes, he noticed. Not to mention that he didn't want her to wake and witness his embarrassingly aroused state.

Her pink-bowed lips were parted slightly as she let out a dainty snore. Her brow was smooth and relaxed and her eyelids so translucent he could discern the tiny veins lining them. She really was remarkably lovely.

"Oh," she murmured, her brow furrowing as she leaned up on one elbow. Her golden hair speared around her head like a spiky halo, and her porcelain skin was flushed pink. She blinked groggily and rubbed her eyes. "Must have fallen asleep . . ."

"Yes, well, ah . . . I believe that we should get up before anyone starts looking for you. You never know when someone will come—" He didn't actually just use that word, did he?

Catherine rubbed her muddled head, muttering, "No one will come looking for me. Not today. There's early-morning chapel, and that's when I usually do my accounts. It's the best time for quiet." She yawned, trying to unscramble her jumbled thoughts. Then she remembered. The guesthouse. The spirits. Marcus's bedchamber.

Catherine blinked, suddenly fully awake, and from tip to toe aware of the lithe body lying beneath her. She lay sprawled across Marcus, adhering to his hard muscle like a layer of crème upon pudding. It felt astoundingly pleasurable, yet . . . unsettling, too. His body radiated an agreeable warmth, particularly in the brisk morning air of the open window. And yet, that warmth seemed to elicit an extravagant amount of heat from her roused body.

She was overly warm, and although having slept, she felt astonishingly . . . restless. Her breasts were mashed against Marcus's chest, giving her an unusual sense of agitation. Her legs were parted with his thigh pressed in the most outrageous, yet utterly enticing manner between them. She felt the unholy urge to answer some sort of call, but she did not quite understand who or what was invoking her. All she knew was that being with Marcus felt really good and she wanted more of it.

"If you would . . ." He shifted beneath her to rise, using his foot for leverage and inadvertently pushing his thigh deeper into the crevice between her thighs.

Heavens! She almost swooned with the heady pleasure surging through her.

He suddenly froze. Did he recognize or understand what was happening to her? She didn't know whether to be appalled or ask him about it.

"Cat," he urged, his rumbling voice making her belly tickle in the most beguiling manner. "We really can't stay here."

She might not understand what was happening. But the last thing in the world she wanted to do at that moment was to separate from this enthralling man.

"Does your head hurt?" she rushed, quickly, laying her palms across his chest and burying her chin atop them, as if she wanted to meet his eye to confer.

He blinked. "No, actually."

"Mine doesn't either. Isn't it supposed to?"

"It depends on how much one imbibes."

Now what? "You don't smell of spirits any longer," she noted. "Do I?"

His brow furrowed as he leaned forward and sniffed. "No, only lemons." He tilted his head back and his raven hair fell like a black fan over the burgundy coverlet. He stared up at the ceiling. "Why . . . why aren't you using the orange blossom soap I gave you?"

Because I'm saving it for when you're gone. She could easily envision the lonely nights when she would unwrap the sweet-scented soap and inhale the memories of her short time with Marcus Dunn.

But a cold lump of cleanser would not keep her warm on a dark night. Nor would the remembrance of a brush of his fingers or a hug when she wept. The memories seemed so insignificant, so unequal to the lonely future yawning wide before her. She wanted more, she realized. Much more to remember, much more to cherish, much more to *know*.

She wanted to live before she died. And Marcus Dunn was the only man who could make that happen.

"If we move quickly, then no one has to know you were here," he said, laying his hands on her shoulders. He rose to sit up, bending from the waist.

Catherine didn't want to go, and she didn't want him to either. But she didn't know how to stop it from happening. So she simply refused to budge. And found herself suddenly facing Marcus's very full lap.

Dear Lord in heaven! His manhood was as stiff as a pike!

Her gaze flew up. From the look in his eyes, *he knew* that *she knew* and he didn't know *what* to do.

Her heart began to pound and heat flooded her cheeks. He found her desirable! Perhaps even a tiny bit as much as she desired him!

Cat swallowed, knowing that if she did not do something, Marcus would do the gentlemanly thing and remove himself from her presence—the very last thing in the world that she wanted him to do. She needed to act, and quickly, or her opportunity would be lost. Possibly forever. But what to do?

Her heart raced and her mouth was dry as dust but she garnered her courage. Cat reached her arms up, grasping Marcus firmly around the neck and pulled herself up against him, sliding up his chest.

He swallowed, raising a black-winged brow. His gaze shimmered with passion so intense, she felt caught up in those sea blue depths. The current sucked her deeper, into an eddy so strong she felt swept away. Her mind clouded, her breath grew heavy, and her blood began to pulse slow, deep and rhythmic. Her suddenly dry lips parted and she licked them, wanting to quench the thirst that only he seemed able to satisfy. Through it all, he did not reach for her, did not move to kiss her as she so desperately wanted.

The tension within her built until she couldn't take it any longer. "Can you kiss me, Marcus? Is your lip well enough?" she breathed, not knowing from where her courage came. All she knew was that if he didn't touch her soon, she would expire.

After an agonizing half second, he muttered, "My lip is fine." His mouth descended upon hers, crushing her lips with the most exquisite sweet pleasure she'd ever experienced in her two-and-twenty years of life. Her body melted with the heat searing from his kiss to every extremity and back again. He tasted faintly of mint and musk and better than Cook's chocolate crèmes.

He urged her mouth open, and boldly his tongue touched hers. Thrills rocketed from her mouth straight to her womanhood. She writhed against him, the restlessness making her flame. His tongue played deliciously with hers, guiding her, testing her, intoxicating her so that she felt the unholy desire to swoon. But she wouldn't dare miss this!

Her palms moved, greedy for the touch of his skin. Pushing aside his linen shirt, her hands grazed his broad chest. Smooth skin over hard muscle.

His hands cupped her shoulders, and slowly cascaded down her back to the slope of her derrière with the most enticing caress. Her hips bucked and the area between her thighs surged with excruciating heat.

He released her lips, only to set his hot open mouth to her neck beneath her ear. Her head swam, as her body gave in to the heat, his caresses, and his scent, filling her with a need she instinctively understood.

"Stop me, Cat," he begged as his breath whispered along her neck. "Tell me to stop and I will."

"Don't . . ." She shuddered.

His hands froze and he pulled back seeking her gaze.

Pressing her palms to his cheeks, she yanked his mouth back to hers. "*Don't stop*, is what I was saying."

She kissed him and felt his smile beneath her lips, wondering if she was doing it correctly and only half-caring since it felt so good.

Rolling on top of her, he settled between her thighs. But instead of joining her expectant lips, he set his mouth to the hard nub of her breast, nibbling it through the thin fabric of her robe. She shuddered as insistent desire surged through her. Never had she wanted anything more in her life as she wanted to be touched by this man.

As if answering her silent prayers, Marcus's hand slid downward to her belly, her hips, and with excruciating tardiness to the aching core of need between her thighs.

Through the gown, his palm pressed against the dampness of her womanhood. She wanted to die from it, it felt so heavenly. Involuntarily, her hips bucked, pressing into him, telling him without words how much she wanted him. His heavy breath was her only indication that he understood. Until, with his other hand, Marcus reached for the hem of her gown and lifted it.

Elated, and slightly terrified, Cat unconsciously rolled her thighs together as the cool morning air skated across her bare skin, up her calves, her thighs, and finally, to the hot core between her legs. She swallowed, nervous, as his fingers followed that same path, eliciting excited bumps along her virgin skin. Garnering her courage, she bent one knee, opening herself up in the most intimate way to his touch.

His hand grazed up the tiny hairs on her thigh.

Her breath caught.

She swallowed, then slowly parted her thighs even more. She wanted to leave him with no doubt as to her desire.

Nimble fingers slipped into the warm, damp folds of her womanhood, toying within.

She gasped as lightning rocketed through her womanly core. Heat gushed. Her heart danced. Her breath came in rushing pants as her body quivered. She closed her eyes. Her hips began to undulate to a magical rhythm that Marcus played. She groaned, lost to the sensation, caught in the vortex of an amazing inferno, her womanhood at its center, pulsing with desire.

She felt Marcus's mouth press hot and damp against the cloth at her breast as his fingers stroked between her thighs.

She moaned, biting her fist to keep from crying out.

His fingers lunged partway inside her core. Her breath caught, her back arched, her hands gripped the coverlet. Her womanhood was slick, wet, hot and throbbing with need. With agonizing leisure, he withdrew, only to thrust inside again and again and again. But only partway. She wanted *more*, wanted him deeper inside, but instead he pulled his fingers out, to play with the hard nub of her womanhood. She gasped, as pleasure rocketed through her. His pace quickened, rubbing, teasing, toying with her most sensitive essence. She was lost, battered by an onslaught of sensation that threatened to overwhelm her.

She couldn't take any more, but would die if he stopped. Her heart hammered in a crescendo, her breath locked in her throat.

His mouth found hers, urging, sucking, demanding. Taking her higher, carrying her up, up, up . . .

Hot pleasure surged through her in undulating waves, sending her flying to an exquisite place she'd never known existed. He captured her cries in his mouth, holding her tightly as she flew.

Chapter 24

Slowly, the world came back into focus for Catherine. She was breathing again, she realized. But her heart was still hammering against her ribs like a bird trying to escape from its cage.

Marcus had removed his lips from hers and his hand from her womanhood. Disappointment shot through her, but it was overwhelmed by a sense of *awe*.

Dazed, she opened her eyes. Lying beside her on the bed, Marcus was watching her with hooded eyes. Desire still banked his gaze, sapphire coals blazing *for her*. Inside she thrilled, still amazed by the glory of it all.

She reached for him, and he came to her, his lips locking down on hers with fierce, searing kisses. His hips rocked, pressing his manhood deep against her heat, but not inside. The thin fabric of his breeches could not contain the evidence of his unyielding desire. It rubbed against her sensitive flesh, sending small waves of pleasure surging through her, reminding her of the crashing pleasure she'd experienced just moments before.

His lips moved to her neck just below her ear as he murmured, "My adorable feline, how I enjoy stroking you." His words caused a delicate clenching deep inside her core. "Will you do the same for me?" he asked throatily. He waited, his breath drifting across the fine hairs on her neck.

Hesitant, yet curious, Catherine let her fingers explore the muscular arc of his shoulder. Slowly, her hand skimmed down his broad back to the enticing slope above his buttocks. She licked her lips; somehow touching him there brought a sudden rush of heat deep inside her womb.

She smiled with the pleasure of exploring his beautiful body. Her hand continued down, over his tight, round buttocks, back to his hip, to the seam where their bodies joined.

His breathing was coming in rapid pants and she felt his heart hammering against her chest where he lay on top of her. She wanted to touch him as he had touched her, but she could not reach.

As if understanding, Marcus reared up. Grasping her hand, he lay backwards and, although slightly nervous at this new experience, she followed readily, lying beside him. Slowly, she swept her hand over the large bulge in his breeches, amazed by its solidity and its heat.

"Let me make it easier for you." The rasp in his voice betrayed his tension as he rose, then quickly whipped off his breeches and smalls.

Cat had seen young boys when they'd bathed, but nothing could have prepared her for Marcus's long, engorged shaft, thick around as one of Mr. Graves's prized cucumbers. It stood at attention from a mass of black curls between muscular white thighs lightly grazed in a sheen of dark hair.

For a moment, panic sliced through Catherine, but she

pushed it aside. She was a woman of two-and-twenty, if she didn't do this now, she never would. A giggle escaped from her lips.

"What?" he asked, breathlessly.

"I was deciding to 'take the bull by the horns.'"

"I've never heard it called that," he bit out. "But taking it sounds fine with me."

She reached for him. The tips of her fingers caressed the head of his shaft. "It moved!" she cried, yanking her hand back.

"That's a good thing," he replied gruffly, guiding her hand back to the tip of his manhood. "I like it when you touch me, Cat. Do you?"

"Yes," she breathed, amazed. The velvety skin over warm, pulsing muscle really was quite stimulating. His member felt good under her fingertips; so good, in fact, that soon she was toying with it, touching it all over to see how it felt. It seemed alive as it pulsed and jumped and heated, reacting to her touch. Enthralled, she grasped him in both of her hands and squeezing, rubbed up and down.

"Are you enjoying yourself?" he asked, amusement coloring his tense tone.

"Actually, this is . . . fascinating."

"Not so hard, Cat," Marcus murmured gently, resting his fingers across hers but not stopping her.

"Oh, sorry," she replied. "How's this?" she asked, trying a little trick that she used while kneading piecrust.

"Oh, my God," he gasped, his face contorting.

"Should I stop?" She froze.

"No!"

So she repeated the maneuver, adjusting her technique, enjoying the feel of him under her fingers and being amazed by his reactions. His breath came in short gasps, his every muscle braced as if waiting for violence and his hands locked at his sides in tight fists. His whole body tensed to iron. Marcus panted. His hips bucked. He groaned, and the shaft beneath her fingers throbbed with sudden intensity. His back arched, just as he grabbed his smalls and held them over his groin. Catherine drew back, not knowing what to do.

After a moment, his body relaxed and he let out a long breath. She wondered if he'd experienced what she had just moments before, but she was too shy to ask. How could she explain what had happened to her, anyway?

Gently Marcus wiped his smalls across his shaft. "My God, Cat. You'd think you had practice the way you did that."

"I have."

His head whipped up. "What?"

"Baking," she replied lightly, enjoying how his face quickly relaxed. "I like helping Cook with the dough. Pies, pastries and the like. Then I'm one of the first to enjoy the fruits of my labor." Her cheeks heated and she could not help the smile that teased her lips as the taste of his kisses still lingered. She laid her head on his shoulder and sighed. "But today's treat was a much better reward."

"For me as well, Cat." Kissing the crown of her head, he wrapped his arm about her shoulders. "You really are an extraordinary woman, Cat."

"I hope that's a good thing," she murmured, enjoying listening to his steady heartbeat. He smelled so good; earthy beneath his spicy scent and the hint of sandalwood.

"A very good thing," he replied, his fingers gently grazing her shoulder.

Snuggling closer, she relished this intimate time.

Marcus kissed her head. "We need to get up, Cat. Before anyone misses you."

"No one shall miss me." But she sighed as she said it,

knowing that he was right. Some things were too good to last.

"I'm as loath to rise as you, and thankfully, not because my head aches from overimbibing." Slowly, he sat up, stretching his strapping arms above his head. His muscles bulged under pale, smooth skin. Involuntarily, she licked her lips. Lord, he was a masterpiece to behold. And for a short time, he'd been hers. All hers.

Reaching over, he grabbed his shirt and shrugged it on.

Sighing, she rose. This had been too fantastic to last and duty beckoned to her with its shackles too heavy to ignore.

She inhaled deeply, amazed at how . . . buoyant she felt after everything, and so little sleep. Despite her insistent responsibilities, she still wanted just a few more precious moments with Marcus.

She ventured, "I must admit, what we did, well, that was not exactly how I envisioned coupling would be."

"Well," he replied gently as he pulled on his breeches, "what we just did was not exactly coupling, Cat."

She started. "What?"

"Well, for all intents and purposes, you are still an innocent."

"How can that be after . . . ?"

"I did not breach your maidenhead. What we did was more like a . . ." He waved his hand as if searching for the right word. "First or second course to a meal."

"You mean there are more . . . servings?" she asked, feeling very green and unsettled. *And after that, what on earth could be dessert?*

He nodded as he stood. "The main course, so to speak."

"But why didn't we . . . ?"

Stepping over to the dresser, he dipped his hands in the basin and splashed water on his face. "What we did . . .

well, I needed to be certain that you would not become with child."

With child.

"Oh," she breathed, as something inside her twisted with an ache she'd always known was there but had never wanted to recognize. No marriage meant no children for Catherine. Being around the babies at Andersen Hall had secretly fueled Catherine's desire for a child of her own. But that was obviously not meant to be. *Servitude to a husband*, she reminded herself, was intolerable.

She shifted to another less excruciating hurt. "Do you do . . . the other courses with other women?"

He ceased wiping his face with the towel. In the mirror, his reflection frowned. "I don't want to talk about other women, Cat. It's irrelevant." Wiping his hands on the towel, he turned.

"Not to me, it isn't," she retorted, suddenly knowing that he probably made it all the way to dessert with those other women.

"Don't look so furious, Cat." Dropping the cloth, he stepped near. "It's not about my not wanting to do more, but I need to be realistic. I'm going to be heading back to the Peninsula shortly. I can't leave you behind with child. I wouldn't do that to you."

"That's very considerate of you," she muttered, feeling cross. "You could have simply given me a crust of bread and called it a meal."

"It was not my intention to touch you at all," he replied seriously, lifting her chin with his finger. His blue gaze was gentle, yet still held the dark tinge of his passion. "But I couldn't help myself. You really are extraordinarily beguiling." His smooth lips grazed hers. "I don't know how you've escaped other men for as long as you have."

Perhaps because only Marcus seemed to awaken this amazing desire in her. The thought of him disappearing from her life again made her heart sink. Pulling away, she crossed her arms. "So you intend to go back to the war?"

"Of course," he replied, stepping back. "You knew that."

She nodded dumbly. Yes, he had said it all along, but that was before his father was murdered. And before Marcus had touched her. Somehow, she felt as if her world had irreversibly shifted by their intimacy, yet he, obviously, was not similarly affected. She needed to stop being so naïve, she chided herself.

Pasting a bland look on her face, she asked coolly, "How long, do you think, until you leave?"

"That depends upon my investigation."

"Did . . . did you learn anything helpful from the man who killed your father?"

He scowled. "His name is Conrad Furks. Ever heard of him before?"

Mutely, she shook her head.

"The bloody knave was useless. He swears never to have heard of Renfrew . . . still, the bastard was probably lying through his teeth . . ." Looking up, he suddenly asked, "Have you ever seen Renfew with an exotic cane, by any chance?"

"What kind of cane?"

"Ivory and black-tipped. In the shape of an eagle's head."

Her heart skipped a beat.

"You're as white as a sheet, Cat," Marcus cried, alarmed. Grabbing her arm, he asked, "So you've seen it."

Yes, she'd seen something like it, but it had been over ten years before. Her uncle, Dickey Caddyhorn, had loved that blasted accoutrement more than his own children.

He'd claimed it was a gift from his benefactor, the Earl of Yardley, just before the man had passed away. More likely, Dickey had purloined the thing while the body was barely cold and everyone was too grieved to notice. But it couldn't be the same cane. That was impossible.

"Furks claimed that a hooded man with such a black and white-tipped cane hired him to kill my father," Marcus explained, excitement infusing his voice. "If you can link Renfrew to the cane, it's not much, but it's a connection I can work with."

No, the Caddyhorns couldn't know about her and Jared or they would have swooped down and claimed guardianship. There was no connection. Catherine blinked, realizing that Marcus was expecting answers. "Uh, no, I've never seen Lord Renfrew with anything like that."

"Oh." He released her, obviously disappointed. "Then what upset you?"

"I was just remembering," she evaded. "All the blood . . ."

He took her hands in his, explaining gently, "The memories will fade, Cat. They might jump back at you at the oddest moments . . . but for the most part, they will go away."

"Is that what happens to you, with the war?"

He nodded. "After a while you learn to close your mind to it." Marcus squeezed her hands. "Look, Cat. Before you go back inside, I just wanted you to know that I never intended for . . ." He waved to the bed. "This to happen. I respect you. I still do." He bit his lip, his sapphire gaze earnest. "I just . . . well, I don't want you to feel uncomfortable around me. I would hate that, Cat."

"I wouldn't like that either," she replied truthfully.

"Then we're still friends?"

Friends? After that heart-stopping, world-spinning flight

to the stars? Quickly she looked down so he couldn't read the disappointment in her eyes. What had she expected? Him on bended knee with a ring in his hand?

She couldn't afford to get distracted by girlish fantasy. Her only hope was to enjoy the precious moments she had with Marcus until they were lost forever.

Looking up, Catherine pasted a smile on her wooden lips. "Of course we're still friends." She tried to ignore the relief flashing across Marcus's features. "Always."

Chapter 25

❧❧❧

"**M**iss Miller! Miss Miller!"

Catherine awoke with a start and realized that she was not on a ship rocking to the sway of the waves with Marcus at the wheel, but in her drab office reading accounts. Or at least she was supposed to be, until she'd apparently fallen asleep sitting up.

"Taking a snooze, eh?" Gardener Graves intoned from the threshold, his shoddy cap in his hands before him. His fingers gnawed at the already threadbare rim. He always carried his vocation with him in every aspect of his person: from his earth-stained fingers, to his craggy tea-colored skin from years of exposure to all weathers, to his grass-stained breeches, to his mud-crusted shoes.

"Uh, I suppose I must have," she murmured, wiping a drip of saliva from the corner of her mouth.

"Accounts would put me down, too." He chuckled. "But for good."

Rubbing her eyes, she asked, "Ah, what can I do for you?"

"Just wanting to let ya know that I weeded the vegetable garden."

An outsized cucumber suddenly flashed in Catherine's mind. Her cheeks warmed and she coughed into her fist, scrambling for composure. She had tried not thinking about Marcus all day, yet often unbidden reminders popped into her mind at the oddest times.

"And," Graves added with a shrug, "just wanted to thank ya again, fer giving me me job back."

"As we discussed, with everything so . . . upset, it's a good idea to keep things on as even a keel as possible." Catherine knew the man was contrite and furthermore, she couldn't face having a stranger around. For all of his faults, Gardener Graves loved Andersen Hall well.

Whipping a dirty cloth from his pocket, he pressed it across his eyes. "Well, I thank ya just the same." Then he was gone.

Catherine stared down at the ledger once more, wondering if she should go get a cup of tea.

"Miss Miller," Mr. Gillis intoned, standing in the threshold.

She stood and curtseyed, pasting a smile on her face. Her little office was so busy it was starting to feel like the town square on market day. "Mr. Gillis."

The gray-haired attorney was a handspan taller than she, but Catherine was used to looking up when dealing with most men. Especially tall, brawny gorgeous ones. She wondered what Marcus was doing this afternoon while she withered away in her tiny office.

"I came as fast as I could when I heard the dreadful news," the attorney murmured, pushing his gold-rimmed spectacles up his nose with one hand as he gripped his papers' case to his chest with the other. He always seemed a bit disheveled, giving him an air of confusion. But Headmaster Dunn had once told Catherine that Gillis was too busy in his brain to focus on material things such as properly knotting his cravat.

Clutching his case to his chest, he stepped forward. "I'm beside myself with Headmaster Dunn's murder, Miss Miller. Positively beside myself."

"Thank you for coming, sir. It is a terrible, terrible day for us all."

"Cat," a familiar voice rumbled from the doorway.

"Marcus!" Again, it was as if a window had opened in her airless office. The never-ending foot traffic, the dreary details, the depressing calls all melted away, leaving only golden sunbeams shining through.

Marcus stood on the threshold, resplendent in his navy blue coat with shiny brass buttons lined in military rows, crisp white breeches only marred by the thick bandage. His crutch hardly diminished his imposing stature as he towered over the diminutive attorney.

Conscious of Mr. Gillis standing beside her, Catherine tried to act composed when she was thrilling inside. "Mr. Gillis, Major Marcus Dunn."

Marcus tilted his hat to the attorney. "It's been a long time, Mr. Gillis." Catherine was surprised at the distaste darkening his handsome features. His black-winged brows were knitted, his sensual mouth pressed tight and his nostrils flaring.

"Marcus." Gillis hugged his satchel to his chest like a shield.

"It's *Major* Dunn now." Ice encased Marcus's tone. "State your business and begone, we haven't much use for back-alley scribblers today."

Catherine blinked at the insult, wondering what was going on between these men. The tension was thicker than a midnight fog in winter.

"I'd have thought the army would have whipped the insolence out of you by now," Gillis huffed.

"No, only my patience to deal with cockroaches like you."

Gillis's lips pinched. "If it weren't for your father . . ." Suddenly the man blinked rapidly and closed his mouth. Rubbing his hand over his forehead, the attorney sniffed. "He was probably delighted beyond reason to see you again. It's what he wanted most . . . More than anything . . . The blasted sentimentalist."

For an instant, the anger on Marcus's face cracked, exposing a searing grief that tore at Catherine's heart. Then his features fixed once more. Except for his azure eyes being shiny, he looked hard as granite.

Gillis seemed oblivious to Marcus's pain. Scowling, the attorney reached into his satchel and removed an oblong box. "I brought your father's will."

Marcus stiffened.

Gillis slapped the box onto Marcus's chest. "I thought you might want to read it, if you give enough of a damn about your father's last wishes on this earth."

Marcus clasped the package to his chest, the skin of his hand dark on the ivory box.

Gillis faced her. "And I will return later, Miss Miller, to discuss another matter with you. When we can speak privately. Good day." He tipped his hat and shuffled out the door.

Wordlessly, she and Marcus stared at the box in Marcus's arms. Reaching out, Catherine squeezed his hand.

He did not meet her eye. "Gillis . . . a long time ago, Gillis did not do right by me." He looked down. "I'm not one to forgive easily."

"He could have been kinder, as well." She didn't know

what else to say to this man who was wracked by so much pain.

"How are you holding up, Cat?"

That he could think of her when he was so obviously hurting melted her heart. "As well as can be expected, I suppose," she answered truthfully. "It's been a long day."

Marcus cleared his throat. "Cook happened to mention that you hadn't eaten much today. I thought . . . you might like a respite."

"That would be lovely," she replied quietly, amazed that he could think of her hunger when he was facing so much.

"I hope that you don't mind," Marcus added. "I had a small meal set out in the guest quarters. I thought you could benefit from some time away from the main house."

"Oh." Inside, she thrilled. To be alone again with Marcus. She wanted to dance a jig.

But she reminded herself that her behavior had to set an example at Andersen Hall. To go to Marcus's quarters alone was exceedingly improper. It was daylight, there were no spirits to add as an excuse. Her duties pressed upon her like creeling stones.

But then again, as secretary she might have matters of importance to discuss with a member of the board of trustees. Especially during such an unsettling time. And Marcus had been so considerate; it would be exceedingly rude to turn him down.

She nodded. "That would be wonderful. Thank you."

As they exited into the bright sunshine, Catherine blinked, suddenly realizing that she had been closeted in her office for most of the afternoon. She inhaled deeply, glad for the opportunity to loosen the knots of anxiety sewn in her shoulders all day. She'd been too tense to eat;

the last thing she truly enjoyed was the mint candy she and Marcus had shared last night.

The thought stirred a heat deep in her middle, but she tried to ignore the memory and not assume anything from Marcus's invitation. They were friends. Friends broke bread together now and again, didn't they? He was probably trying to reestablish their relationship; to ensure that there were no misunderstandings.

Still, excitement surged through her, simply to be in his presence. It had been a difficult day, and being with him made everything somehow seem more bearable.

She inhaled a deep breath, trying to enjoy the moment. Birds twittered overhead, leaves shimmered on a spring wind that carried the scent of pine and the trees gave pockets of shadows every few feet, making the air warmer and cooler with every few steps down the path to the guesthouse. As Marcus loped along beside her, his off stride with the crutch clattered a nice rhythm on the pebbled trail.

The golden rays glistened on his dark hair, making it look like shiny black silk. She resisted the urge to reach up and liberate the raven curl that had snaked under his collar. Even after this morning, she had no right.

"I confess," Marcus stated slowly, as they traveled along the path, "I struggled with myself over whether or not to stay away from you today."

She blinked, her heart sinking. "Why would you want to do that?"

"It's one thing to say that we are friends, but after last night . . ." He shrugged.

"We are friends, Marcus. And nothing really has changed," she lied.

"I'm glad to hear it."

Stepping along, Catherine tried not to be disappointed

that he didn't want more. But then again, where could it lead? He was an honorable gentleman and she never wanted him to feel duty-bound to marry her, something she would never allow, anyway. So, friendship was the best she could hope for, she told herself. She should be happy for what they'd shared.

"It was very thoughtful of you to have a meal prepared for me," she ventured. "I know how busy you must be . . ."

"Oh, it was not out of consideration for you, Cat. I just wanted to see you again." Marcus smiled a wide, white smile. "And you know what a selfish bastard I can be."

Some of the tension inside of her loosened, and, smiling, she shook her head. "Rumor and innuendo."

"My reputation precedes me!" he cried, feigning shock.

"You and your reputation do not have much in common, Marcus Dunn. And it's your own fault."

"Why do you say that?"

"Sometimes, you invite discredit." Abruptly she recognized that this was something that bothered her about Marcus. Catherine peered at him sideways hoping that she had not insulted him with her frank reproach.

"How do I invite discredit?" he asked, seemingly interested.

Raising a shoulder, she explained, "You assume that you are going to be condemned, so you start off in a very defensive manner—"

Abruptly, he stopped. "And this is what you think of me? A man who does not have a civil tongue?"

She squinted up at him in the bright sunshine, having to crane her neck to look up at him. "No, of course not. You get along quite amiably with me, now that you trust me anyway. But seeing you with Mr. Gillis, Nick Redford—"

"You think I trust you?" His dark brows were furrowed and his azure eyes seemed to be puzzling something out.

"Don't you?" Catherine blinked, surprised that this was the source of his perplexity. "Even a little bit?" As she stood waiting for an answer, she realized that she was holding her breath, and schooled herself not to act like an infatuated adolescent. It didn't matter if he trusted her. Did it?

He seemed to consider the idea for a moment. Then, placing the ivory box under his arm, he held up his hand, fingers wide. "I can count on this hand the people whom I would consider trustworthy, Cat."

She felt her lips droop. "Oh."

He shook his head, as if surprised. "Yet, somehow, you have managed to be among them."

She couldn't help her pleased smile. "I feel honored, Major Dunn, to be in such small company."

"Watch out, Cat." He wagged a finger teasingly. "You may yet redeem mankind in my eyes."

"I'm not a man," she huffed playfully, crossing her arms.

"That, I noticed." Turning, Marcus motioned to the four short stairs leading up to the guest quarters. "After you, my fair lady?"

Catherine started, not having realized that they had arrived.

Now that the prospect of going inside was upon her, Catherine hesitated. Yes, her new mantra was to enjoy the moments with Marcus, but still, he was bringing out all sorts of strange feelings in her, making her long for things she'd never considered to be part of her spinster existence. To be with him, alone, in his quarters went beyond the pale, even if no one bothered to condemn her. The question was: Would she eventually condemn herself?

Marcus stood, watching her, the epitome of patience. Somehow he seemed to sense that this was a big step for her. Was it likewise a test to see if she trusted him enough to enter? Her mind raced madly from one possibility to the next, with one clear imperative: She wanted to go inside. She wanted to be with Marcus. She wanted to experience some of the excitement that overcame her when he was near. For all of her concerns about propriety and temptation, Catherine longed for the thrills that only Marcus seemed to bring.

Taking a deep breath, Catherine grabbed the wooden railing and climbed the stairs. She tried not to focus on the enormity of the course she was taking.

Chapter 26

❧⟡❧

Catherine stood in the parlor of the guesthouse suddenly uneasy. She was tempting the fates, she knew. She couldn't profess innocence when she had consciously gone off alone with the man who'd so recently taken her to the heights of pleasure.

After setting the box and his crutches in a chair, Marcus rushed over to open the salon's windows. "Sorry, I like to keep things locked up while I'm out."

The room smelled of timber and the faint scent of sandalwood. Would she forever dream of that clean, woody scent whenever she experienced desire? Or would the aroma remind her of a lover lost? Or perhaps a lover gained? Marcus was not yet gone . . .

Dear Lord in heaven, she was turning positively maudlin over this man! Would Marcus ever go through these mental gyrations over hair pomade? Involuntarily she giggled, feeling a bit giddy.

"What's funny?" he asked, motioning to where a white-cloth-covered tray sat on the table.

Coughing into her hand, she shrugged. "Ah . . . your pomade. I like it. Sandalwood, right?"

"And that's amusing?"

"Yes." Even Marcus's pomade excited her in some manner or other, making the remainder of her pale existence seem even more colorless for its contrast. She could hardly consider the day he returned to the Peninsula, leaving her behind in her drab life to wrestle with the myriad of issues facing Andersen Hall. It was enough to make one want to turn tail and run.

"Come," Marcus urged. "Sit. You look as if the weight of the world is resting on your small shoulders." Yanking off the cloth, he described, "Fresh rolls. Cheese. Dates. Apples. And my special dish, saved only for a favored few."

Catherine peered uncertainly at the brown mush piled high in the bowl. "I'm not one for experimenting . . ."

"It's good, I promise." He sat on the sofa. It suddenly seemed very short. They would inevitably have to sit side by side.

"What's in it?" Nervous, she leaned close and sniffed. "Cinnamon?"

"Stop delaying and try it."

Catherine sank onto the sofa, trying to ignore how closely Marcus's thigh rested near hers. When had this sofa last been restuffed? It seemed somewhat lumpy. The floral fabric at least did not appear tattered, except for a small spot near the right wooden leg.

Peeking sideways, she could see the edge of the burgundy coverlet on the bed through the half-open door. The bed had been made, the events of this morning now a memory. She dragged her eyes from the adjacent bedchamber, trying not to be reminded of the pleasures she'd experienced just hours before.

Tearing off a piece of roll, Marcus spooned some of the brown concoction onto the bread and held it out for her.

"Uh, thank you," she murmured.

Their fingers brushed, sending tingles racing up her arm. Flustered, she almost dropped the food, but he gently cupped her hand in his. She swallowed, feeling completely out of sorts.

"Taste it," he urged, removing his hand. She tried not to show her disappointment at losing his touch.

Lifting the food, she sniffed. "Definitely cinnamon." Lord, she hoped she wasn't prattling. She took a nibble, tasting apple and cinnamon.

"That's the most trifling bite I've ever seen in my life," he declared. "Eat it."

The mush was surprisingly tasty. She took a bigger bite. The chunky concoction rolled across her tongue, at once honey-sweet, but with a nutty, smoky tang. "It's delicious." She ate another nibble, then another, finding the food irresistible. "You must tell me what this is."

He shrugged, obviously pleased. "I will have to kill you if I do."

"Then I will die happy." She met his smile with one of her own, feeling some of the tension ease out of her. Marcus really was quite charming company.

Spooning some of the brown mush onto a small piece of roll, he swallowed it whole, grinning as if in heaven. At that moment he looked like the youth she'd known, handsome, playful and well pleased with himself.

"I taste apple," she murmured, swallowing another bite. "And walnuts. Honey. Cinnamon. Very sweet. But there's something else. Something smoky I cannot identify."

"Mashed dates. And my secret ingredient, a splash of Scotch whiskey."

"How did you come up with this?" she asked, taking a

slice of hard cheese and slipping it into her mouth. The creamy, nutty cheese was a wonderful counter to the smoky-sweet taste. She followed it with a sip of beer and closed her eyes. "I think that I might actually swoon," she murmured, licking her lips.

When he did not answer, she opened her eyes, only to find him staring at her lips. Self-conscious, she raised her hand to her chin. "What? Do I have food on my mouth?"

Slowly, he leaned forward, his muscled thigh pressing up against hers. Carefully he traced his long finger across her upper lip, searing her skin with his touch.

Her breath caught. The fine hairs on her neck and arms lifted, causing sensitive tingles all over her skin.

"Froth," he whispered, looking down at his hand. Languidly, like a cat, he licked his finger.

Catherine's mouth dropped open, as she stared at that lithe finger, dumbfounded by the sudden heat rolling from her toes up to the tip of her hairline and back again. Marcus smiled; a slow, sensual lifting of smooth, delectable lips. Something inside her belly twisted, but it was hunger of a different category.

Her gaze locked with his. Those azure eyes smoldered with desire, drawing her toward him like beacons on a fog-drenched night. He wanted her. He knew it, and was not shy about letting her know it. Now every muscle in her body knew it, too, especially the moist juncture between her thighs.

Her heart began to pound and her breath grew heavy. The amazing heat grazing across her skin tingled, as if recalling his touch and yearning for it once more. She found herself leaning toward him, wanting him with a hunger that eclipsed any longing she'd ever experienced before.

"Friendship is a nebulous term, don't you think, Cat?" he murmured. Edging closer, he lifted her finger and dipped it into the warm mug of beer. She shivered, but not with cold.

"How can one define it?" His voice was a deep rumble that reverberated down her spine. "Respect, consideration, companionship . . . *intimacy*."

Lifting her finger, Marcus licked the pad. Her mouth opened, as she gasped in a heavy breath. Hot tension enveloped her muscles, wound tight and yearning for release.

"Ay, there's the rub. *Intimacy*. How much is *too much*?" He placed her finger into his mouth, fingertip flat on his tongue. He sucked. Her head swam. She suddenly found it hard to breathe. He was watching her, but she was having difficulty focusing. Her lids were so heavy, they insisted on closing. Her world became a dark vortex of heat—his hot, wet mouth and the heady brush of his tongue across her fingertip.

Unexpectedly, he removed her hand. Disappointment shafted through her. She opened her eyes, trying to catch her breath and her scattered senses.

"Is that too much, Cat?" he asked, watching her carefully. "You tell me."

"I . . . I've never quite . . . had a friendship like this . . ." she managed to breathe, trying to grasp a thought and hold it.

"How much intimacy do you want, Cat?" he murmured, his gaze hooded, his movements languid. "How close do you wish to get?"

She swallowed, nervous but ready to jump off that precipice and fly. She wanted these memories to last a lifetime. "Close. Very, very close."

His nostrils flared. "I like tasting you, Cat. I hope you don't mind if I sample some more." Before she could answer, he placed her thumb in his mouth, deep inside the warm, wet womb. She thought she might expire. Heat swamped the hub between her thighs. The muscles inside her womanhood clenched. His tongue unhurriedly swept across the pad of her thumb. Her womanly core convulsed, reminding her of the joyous rapture of that morning.

Her mouth grew moist, and she licked her lips, wanting to savor him as he was savoring her.

He leaned forward, his breath drifting across her cheek on a whiskey-cinnamon breeze. "You want a taste?" he murmured, placing her finger inside her own mouth. Surprised by the move, she sucked, sampling her flesh.

As he watched her, his eyes darkened to almost black. His nostrils flared and his olive skin flushed slightly red. She could feel the heat rolling off him in waves. His excitement ignited a matching flash in hers. Releasing her hand, she seized him, pulling him close.

Catherine kissed Marcus as if he was the fountain of youth and she on her last dying breath. Opening her mouth, she plunged her tongue inside with a lack of inhibition that shocked her, but she was beyond caring. All she wanted was his taste, his feel and the salvation of his touch.

He tasted smoky, sweet, enticing, intoxicating.

Wrapping her hands around his neck, she leaned backwards, taking him with her. He let out a low groan, reverberating in her mouth.

Positioning himself deep between her open legs, he blanketed her with his heat, making her feel at once secure and desired.

Her tongue danced with his as her pelvis rocked to some rhythm answered by the force of his shaft pressing against her hot, wet core through their clothing. His hard manhood drove her wild with the need to be filled.

His hands were everywhere, touching, kneading, tickling. "Blast these buttons," he murmured, fumbling with the fastenings down her back. Shifting around for better purchase, his bootheel knocked the platter, sending dates, apples and beer flying.

"Bloody hell," he swore, sitting up.

Her stomach sank; he wasn't going to give up that easily, was he?

"I have a better idea," he declared, sliding one hand beneath her knees and the other beneath her shoulders. With amazing ease, he hoisted her off the couch.

Planting a quick kiss on top of her head, he headed toward the bedroom door. Elation rocketed through her as he carried her in his arms. Kicking the door open wider with his boot, he dropped her unceremoniously on the bed. Immediately he covered her with his broad frame and showered hot, openmouthed kisses on her partially exposed neck. Rolling her onto her stomach, he straddled her, unfastening each button with an ease that left her feeling a bit discomfited.

"You're very good at that," she muttered, toying with a stray thread on the burgundy coverlet.

"I'm a quick shot as well, Cat." Leaning forward, he kissed her ear. "Agile fingers are a necessity in my profession," he whispered. "It doesn't mean I'm a rake."

"You're certainly more experienced than I," she mumbled.

Rising higher on his knees, he rolled her over and eased off of her, lying beside her on the long bed. Bending an elbow, he rested his head in his hand, looking down at her. His handsome face was somber. "Listen, Cat. I'm not proud of myself. Chasing after an innocent is probably one of the lowest—"

She frowned. "You're not chasing—"

"Hey, I'm certainly not keeping my hands off you, like I should," he huffed, raking a hand through his raven hair. "I just want you so badly."

"I don't want you to keep your hands off me," she cried.

"That's part of the problem, Cat." He exhaled loudly.

She scowled, wishing that she had never opened her mouth in the first instance. So what if he'd been with other women? He was no monk, and never claimed to be. Did she always have to ruin everything?

Gently, he coiled her hair around her ear, murmuring almost to himself, "I've never faced such temptation before. Your innocence . . . but your passion . . ."

"I have never felt this before either, Marcus" she insisted. "And I don't want it to go away."

"But it has to." He sighed. "Once I leave . . ." He sat up. "Hell, this is one mistake I'm not going to make—"

She grabbed his hand and squeezed, pulling him toward her. "How can you be such a selfish bastard?"

"What?"

"I feel like I'm drowning, Marcus . . ." Releasing him, she sat up, her hands clenching and unclenching in her lap. "Drowning with no land in sight."

Moving to sit beside her, he grasped her hand. "I know that this is a difficult time, Cat. But I don't want you to do something that you'll regret."

Better to have regrets than never to have lived!

He shrugged. "Someday you'll wish to marry and—"

"I wasn't lying before when I said that I never wish to wed," she interrupted. "It's not something that I will ever want."

"But maybe someday you'll feel differently."

"There is no someday for me, Marcus." She shook her head, emphatic. "I never wish to marry. Nor do I wish to contemplate the future." She looked up. "I can't worry about tomorrow. Today is all I have."

Interlocking his fingers with hers, he studied their hands a long moment. Then he looked up. "This is really what you want?"

She nodded.

"For today, then." Leaning forward beside her, Marcus's lips met Catherine's in a long, lingering kiss. His hands stroked down her arm, grazing her hip. The embers of her desire reignited, not the frenzy of before, but a passion that smoldered between them.

Raking her fingers through his hair, she indulged her senses, savoring the silk under her fingertips and the sandalwood scent. Her hand explored his broad shoulders, feeling the hard muscles under his woolen coat. She loved the feel of the fine hairs at the base of his neck.

Slowly, he peeled her gown off her shoulder, and only then, did she realize that her buttons were mostly undone. Somehow he'd also managed to shift aside her chemise. The air was cool on her shoulder, soon warmed by his playful lips. He nibbled along her collarbone, slowly drawing the garments lower and lower, until they slipped off her other shoulder and hovered around her waist.

Shyness swept over her and she reached to cover her breasts. But he gently pulled her hands away, kissing each palm with a reverence that awed her. Then he eased her onto her back and with an amazingly light touch, peeled all her clothing off her body.

Smiling, he tossed it to the floor.

Catherine was completely nude in the glaring brightness of day, utterly exposed for his perusal. Discomfited, she rolled her bad leg underneath her good one.

"Beautiful," Marcus murmured, then set his lips to the underside of her breast. His hands gently glided down the downy skin of her bad leg, drawing it out, caressing it with a worshipful touch. "All of you is beautiful," he murmured, his breath caressing the sensitive skin of her breast.

All thought of discomfiture vanished.

Those magical lips licked and kissed and nibbled their way around to the raised bud, drawing it in so deeply into his mouth she gasped with pleasure. Her back arched, her hips jerked and she clutched his shoulders for support.

He was relentless in his attention to each nipple, going from one to the other. Fingers caressed her skin, trailing down to her belly, her hip and soon to the source of her agitation.

She closed her eyes. Long fingers stroked the tight curls between her thighs, urging her legs wider. Agile fingers slipped between the wet folds of her flesh. She cried out, her heart pounding so hard she thought it might burst through her chest.

"So wet," he murmured, his face agonizingly near her hip. Moist kisses trailed down her belly and she clenched up, suddenly nervous at his intimate proximity to her core.

"Shh," he whispered, gently rubbing the hard nub between her thighs. Her muscles convulsed and relaxed, wallowing in heated moisture.

Suddenly his mouth pressed against the hard nub of her womanhood. A silent cry caught in her throat. She clenched the coverlet in her fists.

His tongue played over her. She saw stars. She inhaled sharply, desperate for air. His mouth and fingers tormented her with devastating pleasure. She was whimpering, clutching the coverlet for her life. Her legs were locked tense, her body arched like a bow.

He took her higher and higher toward that amazing . . .

Heat swamped her. Her muscles convulsed, again, and again, battering her with shattering release. She was lost.

Catherine's mind slowly rejoined her body. Her heart still pounded, her lungs almost ached, as she lay limply in his arms. At some point Marcus had lain beside her and wrapped his arms around her shoulders. Gently, he kissed her neck, just below her ear.

She felt so good with Marcus, so safe. As if no one could hurt her when he was near. Ridiculous, actually, but comforting, just the same.

Slowly, she reached down, intent on giving him a share of the pleasure she'd just enjoyed.

"Shh," he murmured in her ear, sending a delicious ripple of air over her neck. "Relax, there's no rush."

Sighing, she smiled. This had not been a mistake. She was never going to regret this moment for the rest of her life. Her only hope was to make it last as long as possible.

He lay beside her fully clothed, gently twining her hair in his fingers. Despite the hard manhood pressing against her naked thigh, he toyed with her hair indolently, as if, indeed, he were in no hurry.

"Marcus?" she asked, her voice still weak.

"Hmmm," he murmured, splaying soft kisses near her ear.

"Are we going to get to dessert?"

His lips froze. "Dessert?"

"Yes. You said that what we did before was like the first or second course in a meal—"

"What you're going to get," Marcus replied, slipping his arms beneath her and tossing her over, "is a sound thrashing." With his palm, lightly he swatted her naked bottom.

"Stop that!" she squealed, rolling over and scooting back on the bed.

On his knees, he stalked closer to her. "Don't ever tell a man who's just given you the 'lover's kiss' that you want more."

Lover's kiss. Just the sound of it heated her womanly

core. "What if I want to give you a 'lover's kiss'?" she asked.

His breath hitched. His eyes smoldered with naked desire and she couldn't miss the large bulge straining against his breeches.

Elation and a sense of power surged through her. She smiled, feeling wicked. "What if I want to be the one flying you to the stars?"

"To the stars?" his voice was a hoarse whisper.

"Flying." She reached for him. "Let me show you."

Chapter 27

❦❦**A**h, here you are, Cat," Prescott cried, stepping over the threshold to the porch. "I've been looking all over for you."

Catherine looked up, trying to hide her disappointment that it was not a different handsome man come to visit. She hadn't seen Marcus all day and every moment that passed seemed like torture until she saw him again. It had gotten that bad, she realized, and in only four days. Her entire existence was centered on when she would see him and how she would be able to slip away to be with him. It kept her sane while going through Headmaster Dunn's funeral, through the agonizing conferences with the committees of the board of trustees, through the endless staff meetings.

Leaning over, Prescott bussed her on the cheek, his musk perfume wafting around her like a bouquet. She liked the aroma, but found herself comparing it to a refreshing woody scent she'd come to savor.

"I would have come sooner, but I was at a friend's

house near Bath and had not heard the news," Prescott explained.

Dropping onto the chaise beside her, he adjusted his bottle green coat and stretched his long legs before him. His snowy white breeches were so tight, Catherine could see the outline of his muscled thighs and quickly looked down at the embroidery in her lap.

She was unused to noticing such things in men and somehow felt unfaithful even to do so in all innocence. She wondered if men, Marcus in particular, felt any similar disloyalty when around other females. She could not think of Marcus and other women! She had to remember that she had no claim on him and that their time together was fleeting.

"I can't quite believe Dunn's gone," Prescott avowed, tossing his hat, cane and gloves aside. He ran his hand through his wavy ginger hair, brushing it out of his green eyes.

"I was wondering why I did not see you at the funeral," she murmured, watching the sky darken. The air smelled damp and an agitated wind shook in the trees. A storm was brewing.

"Hell, I'm gone hardly a week and the world tips on its end. Dear Dunn and Lady Langham both murdered in the same week. It's wont to make one wonder if there's not an epidemic afoot."

"Lady Langham?" she asked, diverted.

"Don't you read the broadsheets?"

"No, actually, I can hardly keep up with the goings-on here, it's too much to follow the rest of the world's. So what happened to Lady Langham?"

"Lord Beaumont killed her. A lovers' tiff supposedly."

"How horrible!"

"Yes. Well, the man will surely swing, if the papers are

to be believed." He sighed. "And how are you holding up, Cat?" His voice was threaded with concern.

"Fine." She shrugged, focusing on a missed stitch. "Busy." Tossing aside the embroidery, she gave up. She hardly had the concentration to tie her shoes these days.

"Poor Cat, running around trying to take care of everyone." Wrapping an arm across her shoulder, he patted her arm. "Have you had a good cry yet, darling?"

"Leave me alone, Pres," she chided, but she did not push him away. For all of his tough talk, he loved Dunn well and must be sorely grieving.

"No, you were never one for a good bawl. Stiff upper lip and such, our Cat." He sniffed. "Enormously good eulogiums for the old bugger, I heard."

She smiled sadly. "Dunn would have enjoyed them. Especially when Vicar Kranz spoke. The man was up and down in under ten minutes. A record."

"Perhaps the old dog was enjoying it from up there." Prescott motioned to the leaden sky. Looking down, he toyed with one of the shiny brass buttons on his coat. "Did Marcus Dunn, perchance, speak at the funeral?"

Word certainly traveled fast. She tried not to blush but her traitorous cheeks betrayed her. "Yes."

"What did the dastard have to say?"

"He's not a dastard."

"Leopards don't change their spots."

"You did."

He huffed. "I grew up."

"They why couldn't he?"

"You actually believe the drivel about him being a war hero?"

"He is a hero."

Removing his arm, he straightened. "Oh, dear Lord in heaven, you've fallen for him!"

"Don't be ludicrous." She turned away, hoping not to give anything more away. Just because she enjoyed Marcus's company did not mean that she'd fallen for him. Simply because she melted in his arms and quivered at his touch didn't warrant a full-scale affair of the heart. It couldn't, because she couldn't afford it to.

"He's playing you for a fool, Cat. Can't you see it?" His hand clenched and unclenched on his thigh. "The man hardly knew you existed growing up. I can understand why now he's all of a sudden discovered you. But the man has the staying power of a pail of milk. He'll sour soon enough. Until then he'll lie to you to get whatever he wants. He's lying—"

"What makes you think that he's lying?"

"Because *all* men do!"

She stared at him, shocked. "Would you lie to bed me?"

Silence engulfed the porch. Lightning flashed, a moment later followed by a rumble of thunder.

"Would you lie to me, Pres?" she insisted, leaning forward.

"The thought never occurred to me," he muttered, looking away.

"But if you wanted to bed me, would you lie?"

"Who says I don't want to bed you?" His emerald gaze fixed on her and he raised a brow.

Catherine scowled at him. "I'm being serious."

"So is he," Marcus declared from the threshold, leaning forward on his crutch so that it looked more like a weapon than a support.

Prescott jumped from his seat so quickly, his cane clattered to the wooden floor.

Catherine stood, her heart doing that special dance whenever Marcus was near. Her heart beat a little faster yet seemed slower, as an intoxicating lightness flushed through her body. She swallowed as the familiar sense of being flustered overcame her.

Inhaling a deep breath, she watched the men, experiencing an inexplicable sense of guilt. But that was ridiculous.

Gripping her hands in her skirts, she felt the need to explain. "Prescott wants me about as much as he wants Mrs. Nagel. This is a purely theoretical discussion."

"She's a mighty attractive old biddy," Prescott murmured, under his breath.

"Be nice," Catherine ordered to her old friend. "Marcus, you remember Prescott Devane? Prescott, you remember Marcus Dunn."

The men eyed each other and Catherine almost imagined them to be like stallions gnashing their teeth at a challenger. Marcus was the taller, brawnier of the two. He looked devastatingly handsome in his chocolate brown coat with ivory buttons, ivory breeches and tall brown leather boots. His shiny raven hair was pulled back in a leather thong and the scent of sandalwood pomade teased her senses.

Prescott, although shorter, still looked as if he would give Marcus his due in a contest. Slender, muscular and lithe, there was a toughness to Prescott derived from lessons learned young and not forgotten. Even wearing the trappings of Society, underneath it all he was still the rough-and-tumble orphan, ready to pick a fight with the biggest lad around. His green eyes blazed with a ferocity that would cow lesser men. Marcus, it seemed, was not one of them.

"I believe that the lady asked you a question, *Pres*," Marcus drawled seemingly nonchalant, but tension showed on his darkly handsome features. "Would you lie?"

Prescott shrugged. "To bed Cat? Of course I would." He glared. "Any man would."

"Not I." Marcus smiled, looking like the cat who'd licked the cream. "I wouldn't and I needn't."

Catherine decided to ignore the implication that she was easy quarry. "Now—"

"You will," Prescott declared. "At some point or another you'll deceive her, disappoint her. And what then? You'll be off to the next battle. What about Cat? What about her then?"

Marcus's smile drifted to a frown.

Catherine shifted from one foot to the other. Prescott's assessment was a little too close for comfort.

Catherine decided that this conversation had gone too far into unsettling territory. "Pres was just telling me about the murder of a noblewoman . . ."

"Murder seems rampant these days," Prescott drawled, his green eyes flashing with meaning.

"So is hanging." Scrutinizing Prescott, Marcus suddenly murmured, almost to himself, "You look different."

"What in the blazes does that mean?" Prescott demanded, his fists clenching.

"You've changed."

"I'm no longer a runt to be kicked around by the bigger boys, if that's what you mean—"

"Now wait a minute. I never—"

"You, Jimmy D., Kenny Lane, you're all one and the same."

"That's not fair, Prescott," Catherine chided. "You know as well as any of us that one person's misdeeds do not carry over to others."

"They do by association."

Marcus adjusted the sleeves of the chocolate brown

coat. It was an elegant cut that emphasized his muscular frame. "It was an innocent comment, Prescott. Never mind it." Facing her, Marcus asked, "Cat, if I could steal you away for a moment . . . ?"

"A moment?" Prescott asked, sarcasm lacing his tone.

"Certainly," Catherine replied. Feeling guilty about leaving Prescott when he had been searching her out, she turned to him, adding, "I will be back shortly. Will you wait on me?"

"For a lifetime, darling."

Marcus's frown deepened to a scowl.

"Catherine," a familiar voice called.

Catherine turned. Jared stood in the threshold, his face pale as putty, his features bleak.

"Jared!" She rushed to her brother, encircling him in her embrace. He was a few inches taller than she, but soon he would likely tower over her. For the moment, the fourteen-year-old clung to her, his lanky arms wrapped tight, quaking in her arms.

"So you know," she muttered, referring to Headmaster Dunn.

She could sense Marcus's and Prescott's departure as they discreetly left down the stairs to the garden. Considerate men.

Jared sobbed, hugging her close. He smelled as if he hadn't taken a bath in days. Peering down, she could see that his clothes were filthy. Anxiety coiled through her.

"I didn't find out . . . until I got back . . ." His voice was hoarse with grief.

She pulled away to peer into his eyes. That familiar Coleridge gray gaze was filled with misery. Her anxiety escalated to fear, but she moderated her tone, knowing that Jared was already distraught.

"Sit down, Jared." She gently pulled him to sit on the sofa. "Let us talk."

They sat side by side, clutching hands.

Jared's handsome face was a mess; snot ran down his nose, dirt smeared his cheek. His sandy-colored hair, a few shades darker than her own, was matted with filth. Catherine took out a linen and handed it to him. "Take a deep breath. Collect yourself, Jared. Do you want something to eat?"

Mutely, he shook his head.

After a few moments, he looked up, his gaze resigned. "They're going to arrest me, Catherine. I'll probably hang."

Chapter 28

Catherine tried not to panic. "Tell me everything, Jared," she directed her brother. "To the last detail."

Jared shook his head. "Headmaster Dunn was my last hope."

"Start at the beginning, Jared," she urged, ignoring the impulse to shake the facts out of him. "Please."

He swallowed. "Thomas Winston invited me to join him in a game—"

"Who's Thomas Winston?"

He blinked. "Oh, yeah. Um, Sir John Winston and his wife and son came to visit the Hartzes."

The Hartzes were the family that Jared and his tutor, Peter Leonard, had gone to assist, Catherine recalled. "How old is he?"

"Eighteen."

Her heart hardened. Good enough to know better. "What happened?"

Wiping his hand across his eyes, he muttered, "Well, I was a real buzzard, Catherine. A cat's-paw of the first order—"

"Just tell me what happened," she ground out.

"They set me up for a fall and I didn't see it coming. Oh, looking back I can see it all. But I was so blasted happy to be included in the fun. And then the winning. It had felt so good and it was more money than I'd ever laid my hands on—"

"Line up the facts, Jared," she directed, clenching her hands in her skirts. "One, two, three." It was an old game between them, and Catherine prayed it would finally set him straight.

"One, Thomas Winston invited me to join the game with his valet, Linnows, and two of the underbutlers, Kent and Gregg. Two, I won for a while, and then lost the lot. Three, Thomas Winston loaned me the blunt to keep playing." His lip curled in disgust. "He said that I couldn't win back my money if I didn't have something to play with."

Her heart sank. "How much do you owe him?"

"Twenty-nine pounds, seventeen shillings, eleven pence."

"Oh, my Lord." She covered her mouth. It was more than a year's salary for her. As it was, everything she made went toward Jared's tutor and expenses beyond what was provided for by Andersen Hall. She hardly had a pound to her name. "What were you thinking, Jared?" she whispered.

"They assured me that if I couldn't pay it back, they'd help me out. Then they told me that there was a way to extinguish the whole debt."

The sinking feeling in her middle dropped down to her toes. "How?"

"They said it was a game. Just for fun. That I could borrow Sir John Winston's pocket watch—"

"Borrow?" She swallowed.

"Thomas assured me that he'd return it. But when I

gave it to them, they laughed and Linnows put it in his own pocket and wouldn't give it back." His lower lip quivered. "They said that if I told anyone, they'd honestly swear that they'd seen it in my hands."

"Where was your tutor, Mr. Leonard, during all of this?"

One shoulder lifted into a shrug. "He and Lady Winston's companion . . ."

Catherine swallowed as her mind scrambled for what to do. Her mouth was dry as sand and she realized that she was terrified. She willed herself to calm her racing heart.

"Headmaster Dunn . . ." A fat wet tear slid down his dirty cheek. "I can't believe he's dead. He's more of a father to me than . . ." Sobs shuddered through him.

Sighing, she hugged him close. "You can't feel guilty about it, Jared. Father is gone, and Headmaster Dunn was the worthiest replacement you could hope for. He was the best of all men."

"I thought Headmaster Dunn could lend me the money . . . Talk to the authorities . . ." He wailed. "But he's dead . . . And I was so selfish . . . It's just too awful . . ."

Hugging him, she let him cry. What were they going to do?

From where would they get almost thirty pounds? And what to do about the stolen watch? She bit her lip so hard it hurt. Now that he'd run away, he'd be suspected of misdeeds. No one would believe the word of a penniless orphan. They were in the jakes for sure.

"He was well and truly fleeced," Marcus agreed. "It's a common enough sham."

"I'm wondering how Jared couldn't have known!" Cat cried as she paced from one end of the parlor in the guesthouse to the other. Her hands clenched in her swirling gray skirts as she swept around for another turn. Her cheeks were high with color and her pink lips set in a firm, displeased line. He could almost see the tempest swirling in those stormy gray eyes. Marcus recalled thinking of her as a pixie version of Lady Justice. But now that he knew her, he couldn't imagine thinking of her in such staid terms. At that moment, she reminded him of a storm goddess, ready to toss down lightning bolts and smite her enemies to save those she loved. She was as passionate in her loyalty as she was in her love play, an enthralling combination.

"I want to kill the vultures." She shook her fists. "Give them their twenty-nine pounds, seventeen shillings, eleven pence and show them what to do with it."

Marcus suddenly recalled how Cat had hammered at Furks with the umbrella handle. How when Marcus had grabbed her in the hallway she'd smashed him in the groin. She was no kitten, she was a lioness ready to attack when those she loved were threatened. He somehow knew that she would help him if he ever needed it. The thought pleased him.

"What do you think, Marcus?"

He blinked, bringing his attention back to the matter at hand. "If only he hadn't run away." Marcus scratched his chin. "Now for certain they've set the stage for his guilt."

"What was he thinking?" she cried. "Or mayhap he wasn't thinking. He was so caught up in being with his chums—"

"He's fourteen years old, Cat. It's what lads do. I don't know that he could have recognized the swindle. Especially since these knaves were older and seem experienced in the game."

She halted before him, hands on hips, breasts heaving. She was magnificent. "At fourteen years old, would you have fallen for such a trick?"

Marcus tore his mind away from her beauty to answer truthfully, "I don't know. I was a bit more skeptical, I suppose. But that doesn't mean, under the right circumstances, that I wouldn't have fallen victim just the same."

She dropped onto the sofa in a huff. "I don't know what to do, Marcus. I haven't the money to pay the swindlers, not that they deserve it. I don't have the watch to return to Sir John Winston. And heaven only knows what's going on in Reigate. The constable could be coming here for Jared at this very moment."

"When was the last time you asked anyone for help, Cat?" he murmured gently as he sat down beside her and grasped her small hands in his. The scent of orange blossoms teased.

Marcus could see Cat's reluctance in the stiff set of her shoulders; the tense way she clutched her hands in his and in how she wouldn't look him in the eye. "I . . . I'm not asking you to bail me out, Marcus . . ."

"It's Jared who's in trouble," he corrected.

She shook her head. "Jared is the only family I have. If anything happens to him . . ." She frowned, staring down. "He's all I have."

Marcus was surprised at the disappointment shafting through him that she didn't consider him her own. But that was ridiculous. They had no permanent obligations to one another and that was how he liked it. Wasn't it? He reminded himself that he needed to be pragmatic; if everything went as planned, he'd be leaving soon for the Peninsula. Somehow the thought was not as reassuring as it once was. He pushed aside the discomfiting reflections.

"I will find this Linnows fellow and Thomas Winston and get the watch back," Marcus stated. "After I have a little chat with these gents, I doubt that they'll be harboring any grudges for their loan."

"This is not your problem, Marcus—"

"What are friends for?" Somehow the moniker seemed so . . . inadequate. "Let us be honest, Cat. We're more than friends. It's the least I could do for you. And it's no trouble, since it's on my way back to London."

Her brow furrowed. "Back to London?"

Releasing her hand, he stood and stepped over to the window. Outside, the sky boiled with impending storm. The clouds were leaden, the air dank with moisture. Thunder boomed in the distance. "I'm off this afternoon. It's why I came to see you before. I wanted to say good-bye."

Catherine felt as if she'd taken a pugilist's blow to her middle. She had felt so relieved to be able to share her troubles with Marcus. Had so appreciated his considerate ear. His kind offer was more than she could have expected. But now, she couldn't help but feel abandoned. "You're leaving?"

"Lord Renfrew's heading for Dover this afternoon. Tam and I will follow behind and learn once and for all what's going on there."

Inhaling a deep breath, she tried not to let her anxiety show. "Just you and Tam? Can't you take a few more men with you?" *Like a hundred?*

"Don't worry, Cat. We'll be fine. The letter you shared with me and my enquiries have given me more information than I could have hoped for in such circumstances."

"Such circumstances?"

"The snare. Everything points to Dover. I'll have my evidence . . ."

"What about the 'kid glove' treatment your superiors insisted upon?"

His lips curled. "I've been too docile. I feel like a bloody politician. Now it's time for some action."

Catherine would never describe Marcus as docile.

Fierce, wolfish and with a wild beauty that stole her breath, but never docile.

"Renfrew is guilty. Soon I'll have the evidence to prove it. And," he continued, his face hardening to granite, "I will find out if Renfrew is behind my father's murder."

Catherine swallowed. "And then you'll return to the Peninsula."

He looked out the window, his face closed and impassive. "Of course."

How could he find it so easy to leave me? she wondered. Then she reminded herself that Marcus was like a ship sailing on the open sea. He probably felt little for her except a passing fancy. But to her he would always be the man of her dreams. Even if they were never meant to come true.

"I want you to know, Marcus," Catherine began slowly, "how much I value our . . . friendship. How, no matter what happens, I will always be cheering for you to succeed."

His gaze met hers, and her breath caught at the tenderness she saw in those sea blue depths. "I feel the same, Cat. Very much the same."

It felt so much like a final "good-bye" that her heart wrenched in her chest. "Will you be coming back to Andersen Hall again . . . before you're off for good?"

"Yes. I still haven't read my father's will. I haven't been up to it, just yet. And well . . ." He shrugged. "I feel like I have a few loose ends to tie up here."

She wondered if she was one of those loose ends. How did he usually break it off with his paramours? A gift? A long, heady round of lovemaking through the night? Although the thought was appealing, her heart was heavy.

"I confess, when I agreed to sit on the board of trustees it was simply to cloak my activities," Marcus added. "But now that I've had a chance to serve, I am beginning to appreciate the importance of what you do. When a child comes here, the deck is stacked against him, but you try to give him a new hand. An opportunity to succeed." He shook his head, as if chagrined. "I suppose I simply didn't grasp it as a child. The importance of the work that you do."

"It's your father's vision that guides us, Marcus." Catherine felt tears burning the back of her eyes. Lord how she missed that wonderful man. "He crafted the path, we simply follow his plan." She prayed that Dunn's vision didn't disappear now that he was gone. It would be a travesty.

"My father . . ." His voice cracked and his face was filled with contained anguish. His gaze met hers, soulful and awed. "My father was a good man."

"The best." She smiled, wiping a tear.

"I'm coming to appreciate that. Too bad, it's after he's gone."

She rose from the sofa and took his large hand in hers. She loved the feel of his calluses, knowing he'd worked hard in earning them. "You are a good man, too, Marcus. He was so very proud of you."

Shrugging, he didn't meet her eyes. "I don't know, Cat. The work you do here, well, it's more than I've ever done for anyone."

"That's not true, Marcus. You safeguard our country and protect us from people who would do us wrong."

"Sometimes I wonder." He sighed heavily, running a hand through his hair. She hated the torment she saw in his gaze. "I do so much damage in the name of good, Cat."

"There's nothing to wonder about, Marcus. If you have any doubts, just think of how you are going to arrest Renfrew's nefarious activities and safeguard our beloved country. You will ensure that he will never hurt anyone else." She squeezed his hand. "What you do is imperative. And there are very few who are able to do it. I wish I could be half the hero you are."

His lips lifted slightly and some of the anguish in his gaze eased. "I've been called many things, Cat, but a hero?"

"You are to me."

"Perhaps it's time for a pair of spectacles," he teased.

She grimaced, dramatically. "My vision has been a bit blurry lately . . ."

He chuckled. She was glad for the lightness lifting his brilliant gaze. "You are one in a million, Cat." He leaned forward. "May I have a kiss good-bye? For good luck?"

Catherine felt that charming smile all the way down to her toes and could not stop her lips from lifting. He'd grown so dear to her in such a short span, she wondered if she'd ever experience anything as magical as her time with Marcus Dunn.

"You mean the mighty Marcus Dunn needs luck?" She raised a brow.

"Only the kind you offer."

Their lips met and it was as if a harmonious timbre chimed in her mind. She felt as if there was a bond connecting them, one that shimmered with the intensity of their attraction and the caring budding between them. But her heart ached that it could never bloom full flower. He was a comet blazing through the sky, and she the earthbound mortal witnessing his glory.

With seeming reluctance, Marcus released her. Clenching his hands to his sides, he stepped away. "I suppose you'll be spending some time with Prescott while I'm gone."

"Prescott?" she murmured, trying to memorize his

handsome features for the long days and lonely nights to come. His bruises had healed, although his eye still had the faint tinge of yellow if you knew to look for it. She loved the dark iris of his eyes, making his gaze beam like brilliant sapphires. Those, along with his dark looks and sensual lips were enough to steal her breath away.

"He's turned out quite well." Marcus frowned, studying his hands. "He's . . . handsome."

She blinked, diverted. "What . . . ?"

"It's not that I notice these things much," he declared. "But the contrast is so great from when he was young. He had all of those freckles and the pudgy lips. And that carroty head of hair. Well, he looks much improved. And he does seem taken with you . . . It's just a bit . . . of a . . . surprise."

"A handsome man being interested in me is surprising?"

"No, of course not. It's just that he's attractive enough for even me to notice. And he's always hanging about, I hear. And even Dr. Winner—" He shrugged, looking away. "Never mind. I don't know what I'm saying."

Was he jealous? Inside she thrilled. But that wasn't very nice of her, was it?

Leaning forward, he brushed his lips over hers. "One more kiss. I suppose I do feel like you bring me luck."

Quickly, she wrapped her arms around his neck and showed him, with her mouth and her body pressed close, her longing for him to be safe.

"Have a care, Marcus," she murmured in his ear. Then swiftly she unwound her arms and slipped out the door. She hated good-byes, she realized, especially when they felt like corkscrews twisting inside her heart.

A heavy raindrop spattered onto her nose, then another onto her eyelash. Unmindful of the rain, she headed back toward the house, her heart heavy, her litany of fears a yard longer. She wondered if there would ever be a time when it didn't feel as if the world was spinning out of control.

She wished that there was something to do. Some way to take fate into her hands and wield it like Marcus did. He took chances, fought villains and made a mark on the world. Mayhap one day so might she. Fantasy, Jared had called it, but it was all she had.

Chapter 29

❦

○○○

Catherine was lost in a gloomy mist the rest of the afternoon. It must be the weather, she tried to convince herself. It had been pouring ceaselessly since Marcus had gone. She'd watched Marcus depart with Tam and was so sad and so fearful for the monumental endeavor he undertook, she felt like a powerless wretch.

"Two gentleman's 'ere to see the headmaster," young Elias called from the threshold of her office.

Shaking off her reverie, she stood. "Who are they?"

"Sir John Winston and 'is son Mr. Thomas Winston."

Catherine's stomach twisted. She swallowed. "Well done, Elias. You announced them correctly." Her mind raced for how to proceed. What would Headmaster Dunn do?

Hear them out. Then apply reason. And charm. But Catherine had never been particularly good at "charming." She prayed to the heavens to invoke Headmaster Dunn's spirit for the reason and Marcus's for the charm. Lord help her, she was in trouble. But this was for Jared.

265

Nervously she tucked her hair into her bonnet, praying she could make a good impression. "Did you offer them refreshment?"

"Yes, Miss Miller. Jest like ya taught me. But they jest wanted to speak with the man in charge. I set them up in Headmaster Dunn's office and came right 'ere."

"Well done, Elias. Thank you."

Girding herself for battle, Cat went to greet their visitors.

"So as you can see, Sir John," Catherine finished breathlessly. "The business with the watch was a game. It was always meant to be returned." Lifting her lips into a wooden smile that she prayed would be seen as charming, she added, "As a father, you can appreciate the impetuousness of a fourteen-year-old boy."

"Hmmm." Sir John Winston scratched his chin. Nodding sagely, his blond ringlets flopped about his shiny, pinkish face. A hint of gray in his coiled hair hinted he must be about forty-five years of age. He had somewhat kind eyes and a bemused air, in contrast to his son, whose pale blue eyes gleamed with malicious satisfaction.

Sir John turned to his son who leaned against the window frame, the epitome of ennui. "What do you say, Thomas?"

Thomas Winston had the same blond ringlets and shiny pink-tinged face as his father, except where the senior Winston was corpulent, the son had a few years left before his waist expanded to his father's girth. And where the father seemed kind, the eighteen-year-old Mr. Winston was a snake.

"If he returns the watch and pays the debt, then mayhap all can be forgiven," the younger Winston drawled.

Catherine bit back a retort and instead turned to Sir

John. "As I explained, the watch was left in Reigate, in your son's valet's possession—"

"The last I saw it," Thomas countered, with a curl to his upper lip, "it was in your brother's hand. And I will explain it thus to any constable—"

Sir John held up his hand. "I know we must follow the law, Thomas, but let us not forget the many tangles you pulled me into when you were this lad's age." His eyes strayed around dear Headmaster Dunn's study. "Moreover, this lad is unfortunate, and we must take that into consideration."

Catherine took her first easy breath in the last half hour.

Thomas scowled like a petulant child. "You always taught me that debts are to be repaid."

Sir John smiled, showing uneven yellowed teeth. Probably from cigars, Catherine surmised. He wore the odors of stale tobacco and fleur de rose perfume like a bouquet. "That I did, that I did."

Turning to Catherine, he held his white-gloved hands out wide. "As you said, Miss Miller, your brother is a bit young and doesn't have town polish. Yet last I knew it, right from wrong were basic concepts that even a simpleton could understand. The boy must return the watch and repay the debt."

Catherine swallowed as panic sliced through her. She hoped that the sweat under her arms did not show through her woolen gown. "But it's quite a sum of money for us."

Sir John brushed his hands together as if there was something dirty about discussing finances. Still, he turned to his son, and asked, "How much was the debt, Thomas?"

"Fifty pounds."

Catherine's mouth dropped open. Thomas glared, practically daring her to call him a liar.

"Are you quite certain of that sum?" she bit out. "It seems, so . . . exact."

"Absolutely, *Miss* Miller," Thomas drawled. His gaze raked over her breasts down to her waist and below, making her feel violated.

"And the watch," Sir John added. "Mustn't forget about my watch. It never quite kept the time, but still, it's the point of the thing. Let us say, twenty pounds. That's beyond fair, Miss Miller."

Might as well make it a thousand, for all the money Catherine had to give them. "Sir," Catherine began, but her mouth was dry as dust. She coughed into her hand. "I don't have that kind of money."

Shaking his head, Sir John sighed. "Then it will be out of my hands." He turned to his son. "Come along, Thomas. Our business here is done."

Thomas stiffened. "But they haven't paid."

"You can't expect people such as these to have the funds readily available. It takes time." Turning, he smiled a yellowed grin at Catherine. "You have seven days, Miss Miller. Then I go to the authorities."

After they'd departed, Catherine dropped her hands into her face and groaned. *If only Marcus were here.*

Catherine looked up, amazed by how much she'd grown to rely on his counsel in such a short time. *"When was the last time you asked anyone for help, Cat?"* he'd asked. Would she have accepted the money if he'd offered it? Shockingly, she might have. But Marcus wasn't there. Prescott would give it to her if he had it, which she knew he didn't. He'd just broken it off with his latest "lady friend." And there was no other source for the funds. What was she going to do? If she had anything of value she'd pawn it.

Suddenly the leather-bound journal she'd found in the

dusty closet flashed in her mind. It could still be valueless but it was worth the effort to find out. But who could help her discern its value?

"Thank you for seeing me, Mr. Gillis," Catherine offered as she sat down in the attorney's musty office. Papers were piled high on every available surface, from the big brown desk, to the tatty, striped sofa, to the wooden table and chair by the blazing fire. Catherine once more reminded herself of what Headmaster Dunn had said about Mr. Gillis. His mind was too full to worry over such trifles like neatness and fashion. And he had served Andersen Hall well for years. She hoped he would have some recommendation regarding the journal. He might point her in the direction of someone who could assess its value, if any. If not, mayhap he had some advice on how to proceed with the Winstons.

"As always it is a pleasure to see you, Miss Miller," Mr. Gillis declared, pushing his gold-rimmed spectacles up the bridge of his nose. "I apologize for the mess, but my office was recently burgled."

"Burgled?" Her eyes widened.

"Yes." He scowled. "Nothing of value, thankfully, was taken. But they made an absolute mess of my files."

"I'm so sorry, sir," she replied. "I had no idea. I wouldn't have called upon you had I known."

"Oh, it's no bother, Miss Miller. In fact, the reportage, thank heavens, was with me at home. So it's safe and sound."

Reportage? She opened her mouth.

"As Headmaster Dunn's secretary, I'm sure you were involved, but still, it's a big undertaking and I don't know if you'll wish to continue fighting Baron Coleridge's title petition," Gillis ventured. "Will you tell me, by the by?"

Catherine felt the blood drain from her face. "What?"

"Who he is." His sharp brown gaze was assessing.

She licked her dry lips.

"Headmaster Dunn did not impart that intelligence to me," he continued. "But I would dearly like to know. Would you care to enlighten me?"

Slowly, she shook her head.

He nodded. "That is your prerogative, I suppose, as it was dear Dunn's. Are you going to continue his efforts of stopping the title claim?"

"I'm not certain," she replied, feeling as if she'd stepped into a nightmare.

"Then you'd better have the reportage, so you can determine for yourself the best course. These folks have a list of indiscretions a mile long. If you do decide to proceed, I don't envision having much difficulty." Moving around the desk, he lifted up his brown satchel and leafed through the papers inside. "The only problem you might have is in making the contacts. I can help you there if you wish."

"Thank you, Mr. Gillis," was all she could think of to say.

"Ah, here it is."

Catherine accepted the papers as if in a dream. Across the top was scrawled in bold black lettering: CADDYHORN.

Catherine felt faint. If she hadn't been sitting down, she would have dropped straight to the floor.

"Headmaster Dunn was handling this matter on his own, but he wanted me to have the record. In case anything . . ." Scratching his head, he mussed his unkempt gray hair even more. ". . . happened to him." A strange look entered his eye.

"Surely he hadn't believed that the Caddyhorns would stoop so low as to try to harm him?"

He looked up. "Are you all right, Miss Miller? You face is white as a sheet."

"I'm fine," she murmured, looking down to hide her distress.

"Mr. Gillis," a young shiny-cheeked clerk called from the open doorway. "Mrs. Lattimer's man of affairs is here to see you for his three o'clock appointment."

Mr. Gillis started. "Ahh, yes of course." Still distracted, the attorney waved a hand. "I'm sorry, Miss Miller, but I have a standing appointment. If you would care to wait in my sitting room, I should be done in about three-quarters of an hour. Please stay, we can talk then."

Blindly she stood, amazed that her knees could still hold her. Slowly she made it out of the office, but instead of stopping in Mr. Gillis's sitting room, she floated out the exterior door.

"Miss Miller!" the attorney cried behind her. But she was lost in a daze.

The cane. Ivory and black-tipped. In the shape of an eagle's head, Marcus had said. The one that belonged to the man who had hired Headmaster Dunn's killer.

It was too much of a coincidence. Deep in her heart, Catherine *knew* it had to be true. If the Caddyhorns had found out that Headmaster Dunn was challenging their title petition they would have had no compunction about having him killed. Distantly she wondered why the Caddyhorns' vicious man-of-affairs, Mr. Kruger, hadn't been the one to hire the thug. Conrad Furks, Marcus had called him. Mayhap Kruger was dead. Alas, the heavens couldn't be that kind.

Catherine would never forget the terror when she and Jared had desperately jumped down from the second-story window the night before they were to be sent to Bethlehem Lunatic Asylum, better known as Bedlam. She'd overheard Kruger's idea to lock them away and declare them insane. Then it would be only a matter of a few greased palms before the title was Dickey Caddyhorn's. As it was, the money was there for the taking since Dickey was their legal guardian.

The bushes had saved Jared when he'd fallen, Catherine remembered. She hadn't been so lucky. Her drop had ended on a ledge and her leg had bent wrong and broken.

She could still almost see the nauseating stars she'd seen with every dragging step she'd taken, could almost experience the excruciating knives piercing her limb. She'd never forget the torturous journey towing her little brother through the blustering snow. The agony of climbing up the ladder to a neighbor's barn's loft where they'd taken refuge for the remainder of the night. Only to have to scurry away in the morning as the Caddyhorns' man-of-affairs, the wretched Mr. Kruger, questioned the barn's owners about the children's whereabouts.

That was when Catherine had almost lost hope that they would escape with their lives. Kruger was a tenacious hound, even more unscrupulous than his employers. In an act of desperation, Catherine had placed her cherished brooch and Jared's ring, both Coleridge heirlooms, on the riverbank and had laid tracks leading into the churning dark waters. Then, she'd taken her lilac cloak and soaked it in the glacial river, and with icy-numb fingers had lodged it beneath a submerged rock.

She'd foresworn her name that freezing morning; she was no longer Catherine Coleridge, but Catherine Miller. She went from being daughter of an honorable baron to being a destitute orphan whose parents had died in debtors' prison. At least that's the story she'd told Headmaster Dunn when they'd finally found their way to Andersen Hall.

Tears streamed down her cheeks as she recalled how Dunn had offered them shelter, food and care for her leg.

In all of the years since, he had never once challenged their version of who they were and how they'd come to such desperate straits.

He must have known! she realized. He'd started acting differently toward her, had offered her new gowns, had moved her to a new room . . . right after her nasty argument with Jared over Mr. Graves's drink! He must have been in the chapel. He must have overheard. He knew. Uriah Dunn, the man who'd helped her for so many years, had known her precious secret and had kept it hidden even from his own attorney.

He'd secretly been opposing the Caddyhorns' title petition. He was fighting for the children who were too afraid to fight for themselves. And it had cost him his life.

At the bottom of the musty stairwell, Catherine broke down on her knees. Sobs wracked her as she clutched her satchel to her chest, rocking to and fro. Aching pain deep inside her chest pinched so badly, she fought for breath.

The Caddyhorns had killed her beloved headmaster. It was her fault. If it weren't for her and Jared, Dunn might yet be alive. Grief, guilt and anger swirled inside her heart, leaching her soul to black.

Vengeance. She wanted to taste it; needed to exact it. The Caddyhorns were long overdue for a reckoning.

If only she were like Marcus, seizing the initiative, staking a claim for what was right. If only she had the means . . .

Means . . . Dear Lord in heaven. For all of her thoughts of settling scores, she had but seven days to pay the Winstons or Jared would be arrested. It wouldn't matter who had the title then, Jared couldn't claim it from a prison cell, or worse yet, from a gallows.

If the Caddyhorns hadn't stolen our inheritance, the money wouldn't be an issue, she thought bitterly. They'd taken so much, murdered, stolen, swindled at every opportunity. *They should have a taste of their own medicine, she mused. Let them be the victims for once.*

But the possibility of the Caddyhorns' facing justice was so remote, she bowed her head in defeat. Her chin bumped into something hard in her satchel. Then she remembered. The journal. The Thief of Robinson Square.

The idea flashed in Catherine's mind like lightning. Bright, intense and magnetic enough to draw her to it like a beggar to the flash of silver. It was so well timed she felt like it had to have been providence. The journal had been sent down from the heavens to save her.

There was one way to find out if the book was on the up and up. One chance to determine if she had it within her to seize the day. One means of securing the money she needed quickly to save her brother.

Could she dare? Would it be possible?

"Our doubts are traitors, and make us lose the good we oft might win, by fearing to attempt," she quoted the journal in the echoing stairwell.

The journal had also said that intelligence was the key. Catherine recalled every detail of the house where the Caddyhorns resided since it had once been her own family's London residence. As of ten years ago, she'd known which room each member of the Caddyhorn family slept in as she clearly recalled the heartbreaking day when they'd infested her childhood home.

Catherine would never forget her impotent outrage when Lady Frederica had taken her mother's precious jewels, especially the pieces that Catherine had known were intended for her. "They're a woman's ornaments, not a child's," Lady Frederica had said with disdain. Catherine had known at that moment that Lady Frederica never intended for her mother's precious pearls ever to rest on her own daughter's neck.

Lady Caddyhorn had always slept with her treasures under her pillow. Catherine would bet good money that she still did. But it would be easy enough to find out. Lady Caddyhorn was far from subtle and she always had a household of disgruntled servants. And servants talked, especially when they were ill-treated by their employers.

So Catherine had intelligence, a good portion of it, and only needed it to be verified. Then it would be up to the journal to walk her through the rest. She just prayed that the book was as good as it appeared.

Her life—and Jared's—were depending on it.

Chapter 30

Marcus kicked his heels, spurring the borrowed stallion onward, feeling the great mount's muscles bunching and stretching beneath him.

Beside him, Tam followed suit. He bounced around on the chestnut mare as a banner flops on a frantic wind. He was going to be sore as hell in the morning, but the good sergeant was keeping a stiff upper lip tonight and Marcus was glad for his staunch spirit. The lanky man hunched over the horse's mane, his lean features creased in deep concentration, as if he held on for his life.

Marcus wondered if offering to let Tam slow and come later was not a bad idea. But he didn't want to injure the man's pride. Better a man's pride than his bollocks, Marcus recognized. "There's a village coming up around the bend," Marcus cried over the wind. "Why don't you stay over while I go ahead? I still have to stop in Reigate. You can easily catch up with me in London."

"Nay, sir," he puffed. "I'm right as rain and it's by your side where I'll stay."

Marcus grunted, the man was going to be bedridden more than likely, but Tam knew his own endurance better than anyone else. And Marcus appreciated the show of support. It had been a rough week and Tam's assistance had been invaluable.

Renfrew was dead. His confessions heard and memorized. The evidence laying out his guilt was at that very moment being carried by messenger to Lord Wellington. The stage where Renfrew had been setting his scheme had been burned to the ground in a heap of ash.

It had been a fool's design, destined for failure from the start. But even in failure, it had caused enough damage to have been a tragedy. This was one mission that had left Marcus with a sour taste in his mouth for the devilry that man could lay on his brother.

In the same spirit as when siege layers of old would catapult diseased carcasses over a wall, Renfrew was trying to find a way to infect the British army. The problem was, he couldn't find a disease suitably injurious that didn't cripple every carrier he tried to have transport it.

Stupid, irresponsible, knave. Renfrew hadn't seemed particularly disturbed by the fact that his efforts had cost the lives of countless men and women in the remote area near Dover where he'd been hatching his schemes.

The only thing to have upset the blackguard was when Marcus had accused him of killing his father. The man had been virtually affronted. Marcus hadn't believed a word of his protestations. He had to have been behind his father's murder. It had to be Marcus's fault, albeit indirectly.

Marcus cursed the scoundrel and wished a pox on all of his comrades in arms. But those men would be tasting Wellington's wrath soon enough. Each name had been carefully logged with their activities and locations. They'd all be dead within the week.

Marcus spit on the side of the road. A nasty business. He couldn't wait to see Cat and be reminded again that there was sweetness and good in this world. He hadn't slept a decent night since he'd left her and he could use that sense of hopefulness that she seemed to infuse in him. Oh, how he'd missed her. He urged his mount onward into the wind.

Darkness was descending on the road, but it was a well-traveled path and the horse's eyes were sharper than his. The moon scarcely hid behind a nearby ridge and was beginning to give additional illumination. The clatter of his stallion's hooves and those of Tam's mare filled his ear with welcoming rhythm as Marcus settled in for a long ride. The scent of chimney smoke reached him and lights suddenly appeared as they made it around a bend.

"Are we going to change horses, sir?" Tam enquired, adjusting his hat that kept slipping into his eyes. The back of his bald head shone in the pale moonlight.

"At this pace, we're going to have to. I can't abide exhausting a good mount." Even if every instinct in him was urging him toward London as if the city itself was burning. He couldn't quite explain the feeling driving him onward, the need to get back once more to where he should be. "But these horses are hardy," Marcus added. "And have more leg in them. So we can wait a bit."

"If you hadn't noticed, I'm not much for riding, sir," Tam ventured, grabbing for his hat. "Sorry to be holding you back."

"There's nothing to apologize for, Tam. You're a foot soldier, not cavalry. And I thank my lucky stars for it." Marcus gently tightened his grip on the reins and eased the horse's stride. The pace wouldn't save much time in getting to the village and Tam seemed so stoically miserable. "We'll walk into the village from here. I feel the need to get to London posthaste. But that doesn't mean that I have to wound my best sergeant in the process."

"I'm your only sergeant, sir," Tam remarked, but in the light of the moon, relief flashed across Tam's craggy features.

"But the best one I could hope for."

Tam yanked his reins and the mare's pace slowed to a trot, sending the sergeant bouncing. The mare was puffing almost as loudly as her rider, her breath misting in the night. "Andersen Hall is going to look mighty welcoming to me," he muttered, as the pace eased. The mare's tail swooshed behind him. "I'm sure you can't wait to get home."

"Andersen Hall is not my—" Marcus stopped himself, realizing that the feeling thrumming through him might actually be a sense of belonging. Yet, it did not relate to Andersen Hall, but to the lovely lady he'd left behind.

When Marcus was with Catherine he felt almost light-hearted, reminding him of the sensations he'd felt after he'd been promoted two summers past. In celebration, he'd had a few beers and had fallen asleep in the shade of a lovely palm on a sandy white beach. He'd felt good about himself then. He was a winner. A man worth reckoning.

He felt that way when he was with Cat—successful, and worthy of it. Moreover, she made him feel as if she'd always be on his side. That with her, betrayal was simply not an option. The idea was a bit astounding to Marcus, given he lived in a world where treachery was as common as a cold. She gave him a sense of hope, he realized, that he'd thought lost long ago.

Tam coughed into his hand, then spit. "I'd be rushing back to Miss Miller, too, if she was mine."

Mine. Marcus did feel possessive about Cat. But he had no claim on her. In fact, miracle of all miracles, for all of their fantastic love play, never once did he breach her innocence. It had been a mighty struggle, but at least on that front, he'd won. And it had made him an exceedingly inventive lover. Marcus had been as impressed with himself as he'd been with the pleasure that could be gotten if one used one's imagination.

Cat hadn't been very appreciative about not getting to "dessert," though. Marcus shifted in the saddle, feeling the familiar pull in his loins whenever he thought about bedding Cat. Obviously she had no idea how hard it had been on him. She was passionate enough to tempt even the most chaste priest. Reason had won out, however. He didn't need a babe complicating his life any more than she did. Especially since neither one of them wanted to marry . . .

"It's tough being away from your girl," Tam commented, matter-of-factly. "I don't envy you when you have to say good-bye for good. Soon enough we'll be back to the Peninsula."

Marcus adjusted his coat and frowned, finding the notion unpleasant.

Perhaps when the war was over . . .

That seemed so distant; he almost could not imagine it. Would she wait for him? He knew it was utterly selfish to demand that she suspend her life until his return. Knew that he had no rights over her. And so much could happen in the interim. He might die, she might . . . His mind reared away from thoughts of anything untoward happening to his precious Cat.

"Unless, o' course," Tam commented, swatting at a gnat, "she comes with us. Dr. Wicket could certainly use the help. Having a compassionate hand like hers to hold would certainly make me want to heal quicker."

"She'd never leave the children," Marcus murmured,

watching the lights from the houses grow closer. *Unless Andersen Hall closes its doors*. Then it might be a blessing for her to get away. But they would have to marry . . .

Surprisingly, the thought of wedding Cat did not repulse him, as it usually did when he considered the shackles of marriage. But then he was reminded of his reasons for avoiding the parson's mousetrap. "I couldn't do that to her."

"Do what to her?"

"Marry her. It would be unfair."

"I've heard it called many a thing . . ."

"My father was always off working for his causes," Marcus explained. "Leaving me and my mum behind. I couldn't do that to Cat. I'm a selfish bastard, but that's a bit much even for me."

"Fighting Napoleon's an honorable charge—"

"So were my father's causes, but it's abandonment, no matter the reason. It's not fair to her, nor would it be just to our children." *Our children*. An uncomfortable chasm yawned open in his chest.

"She'll make a good mum," Tam reflected.

"The perfect mother," he murmured, trying to decipher the strange emptiness swirling in his middle.

"She'll bring some gent up to snuff, I'm sure. With 'er fine manners an' education."

"She's not interested in marriage," Marcus replied distractedly.

Tam snorted. "There's not a woman alive who doesn't want to leg-shackle a man."

"I wouldn't be so sure," Marcus countered, recalling the adamancy in her tone.

"Rubbish. I've seen 'em like her before. They may talk about independence, but in the end they'll fall. Usually for the man with the most perseverance."

"Perseverance?"

"You know, the ones who hang about. They wait until the moment's right, then they make their move."

Prescott Devane's handsome face suddenly flashed in Marcus's mind. Jealousy sliced through him more keenly than a glacial wind.

Tam sniffed. "The best time to nail 'er, on my opinion, is when she's lonely. Or someone's just left her. Then the bloke provides that shoulder to cry on and it's downhill from there. Easy pickings."

Marcus felt the sudden urge to kick his horse and tear into London. He'd kill Devane if he laid a bloody hand on his woman!

"It's not such a terrible end, though," Tam commented. "They both get what they want in the long run."

Marcus schooled himself to calm. "I do want Cat to be happy," he murmured to himself. *But not with another man.* But it was more than jealousy that moved him. She couldn't leave him to live a solitary existence. A lone wolf, traveling in a pack of thousands, isolated, without a home, dying alone . . .

The ache in his heart appalled him.

But what to do for it?

His intentions were noble in not wanting to marry her and abandon her. Right?

Yet, wasn't it selfishness personified *not* to marry her? Yes, he'd sworn never to do to a wife and child what his father had done to him and his mother. But who said that he had to abandon his wife? Who said that he couldn't learn from his father's mistakes and have a better care with his own family? His reasons for not wanting to marry suddenly seemed insubstantial for the first time in his adult life.

As far as children went, he thought that he might make a reasonably decent father. If he could follow his father's positive lead and not make his father's mistakes, he might be quite good, in fact.

But what kind of husband could he be? That was a bit trickier. He knew that he was self-centered. Used to having his way and being free from commitment. Could he make that sacred vow to a woman and stay with her "until death do us part"? Astoundingly, for the first time ever, Marcus could imagine the possibility.

Mayhap because never before have I met a woman who could entice me to stay by her side. The revelation almost knocked him from his horse.

His mind reeled. The world seemed to shift and bend before his eyes as realization dawned. Cat meant more to him than any woman he'd ever known. But what did that signify? He was too cynical to believe in love; it was a fantasy crafted by poets and balladeers. And even if it were true, the idea of Marcus Dunn falling victim to such drivel was preposterous. Or was it?

For the first time in his life, Marcus truly wondered. Was the delight that he felt every time he laid eyes on her love? Was the sense of connection he experienced whenever their fingers brushed or he held her hand or they kissed, was that love? Was the feeling of belonging that drove him toward London like a hound to its pack love? Was the joy she brought every time he witnessed her smile or heard her tinkling laugh love?

As he rode toward Reigate in the darkness of the night, strange thoughts and feelings swirled inside of him, until Marcus felt like he couldn't tell his arse from his elbow. All he knew for certain was that he wanted her. All to himself. The selfish bastard that he was. Now, he just had to figure out a way to keep her.

Chapter 31

❦❦

"**O**h, my God, Prescott," Catherine exclaimed as she raced into Headmaster Dunn's chamber where Prescott rested in the bed. "I came as soon as I heard."

Prescott sat up in the bed with pillows stuffed behind him. They had cut away the fancy sleeves of his purple coat and ivory, ruffled shirt, and rolled back the garment, exposing pale wrists leading to stark white bindings. A yellow tinge colored the bandage, which, along with the bitter, slightly noxious scent, indicated that Dr. Winner had applied his mixture of calendula flowers and olive oil.

"Where were you?" Prescott cried.

She couldn't tell him that she was out digging up information on the Caddyhorn household. Any more than she could tell him about her meeting with Joe Tipton, owner of Tipton's Tavern. A long time ago Headmaster Dunn had told Catherine that Joe had served prison time a few years back for pawning stolen goods. The two had had a strained relationship, but a strong acquaintance nonetheless. Catherine had used the measure of that acquaintance to ask Joe Tipton a favor, to pawn one item of jewelry that she intended to procure tonight from the Caddyhorns. She aimed to choose something of just enough value to pay off the Winstons, something that was not easily identifiable as the Caddyhorns'.

To her immense relief, Joe Tipton had readily agreed. Then astoundingly he had offered to help her unload much more than one item if she so wished. From their conversation Catherine surmised that Joe Tipton was quite active in the "commerce of goods" as he'd called it and didn't worry overmuch about the origins of such property. It was amazing what one learned if one asked the right people. Simply amazing.

"Well?" Prescott demanded.

Catherine blinked. "I'm so sorry I wasn't here, Pres. But I'm here now."

"I shouldn't have snapped at you, Cat," Prescott muttered, staring down at his lap where his bandaged hands rested. "My hands just hurt so badly it makes me feel raw, and angry and, well, to be frank . . . crabby as hell."

She smiled, sympathetically. "Well, you can be as crabby as you like with me. What are friends for?"

"Thanks, Cat."

She hated the pain she saw in his sea-green eyes.

"Mrs. Nagel told me what happened. You're a hero, Prescott. I-I can't imagine . . ." She rubbed her eyes, as anxiety roiled in her middle. "Your quick thinking saved Evie. Thank you, Prescott. Thank you."

"I'm just glad I was there."

"Me too, and that you and Evie are safe."

Catherine felt haunted by what might have been if Prescott had not decided to go to the kitchen for an apple. Evie had hidden in the kitchen until everyone had gone.

Then she'd climbed up on a stool to get at Cook's freshly baked cookies. Prescott hadn't seen the stool tip over, but had come in right after Evie had fallen into the fire. He'd raced over and pounded out the flames as they'd eaten away at Evie's clothing.

Catherine sent off a prayer that he'd come in time to save Evie from the worst of the damage. She sent up a second prayer of thanks that Prescott had been wearing his gloves. The damage could have been so much worse. So much worse.

But what could be done for them now, beside caring and healing? Catherine felt so helpless; she wished she could do more. The thought snaked into her mind: If she had money she could pay Dr. Winner for his care, she could buy Prescott new clothing . . . She couldn't think about tonight, couldn't consider anything past the dawn.

Hearing Dr. Winner's familiar shuffle, Catherine turned to the entry. "How is Evie?" she asked anxiously.

The good doctor sighed, scratching the tuft of brown hair ringing his receding hairline. His kind brown eyes were worried and his loose lips had slipped into a grim line. "Burns are a nasty business. Hurt like the devil. But Prescott got to her early. Stopped the fire from doing its worst. She's young, she should heal well enough." He nodded to Prescott sitting on the bed. "You really did her a service."

"Prescott is a hero," Catherine agreed. Stepping toward him, she rubbed his shoulder. The muscles beneath her hands were wound hard into knots. She could tell that he was in pain and trying not to show it.

"I'll be able to mine this one for many a mile," Prescott jested. "Nothing draws a woman like a noble deed."

"That's my Prescott," Catherine teased, relieved that he still had his sense of humor. "Milking it for all it's worth."

Prescott turned to Dr. Winner and jerked his chin at Catherine rubbing his shoulder. "See, it's working already."

Bending over, Catherine hugged him close. "You don't need to catch on fire to get a hug from me, Prescott."

Pressing his nose into her hair, he sighed, "Oh, the lengths I'll go to for a little feel . . ."

On a normal day she would have punched him in the arm for such talk. Today, she simply held him tighter.

"Oh what a day, what a day," Mrs. Nagel cried, shuffling into the room. The stout, gray-clothed matron kept wringing her hands in her white apron as if wishing to do more to help. It pained her terribly when one of her charges was hurt, as was evidenced by the usually impeccable woman's attire. Her gray gown was wrinkled as if it had been trampled, and her snowy white cap was askew.

Mrs. Nagel's gaze traveled the chamber, growing shiny with held back tears. "If only Headmaster Dunn were here . . ." No one had used the room in the short time since Dunn's death, but it had been the natural place to bring Prescott from the kitchens. The dormitory would not do and they wanted somewhere where the poor man could lie down.

Catherine swallowed, her throat constricting. "He's with us," she murmured. "Always. He was watching out for us today. Things could have been so much worse. So much worse."

"And how are you feeling, Prescott?" Dr. Winner's eyes narrowed as he studied his patient.

Prescott shrugged. "I'm all right. Not half as bad as Evie."

"You're going to need to rest," Winner advised.

Prescott leaned forward. "I thought I might go visit Evie—"

"You will do no such thing!" Mrs. Nagel declared. "It

took me almost an hour to get her to sleep. I'll not have you interrupting her nap."

"Lie back, Pres," Catherine urged, pushing gently but firmly on his shoulder. "You need your rest as well. You must heal."

Reclining against the pillows, he awkwardly adjusted his bandaged hands. "I don't know that that's going to be possible."

"You do as you're told, Prescott Devane," Mrs. Nagel ordered. She sniffed, pulling a linen from her pocket and wiping her nose. "What a terrible day. Two children hurt . . ."

"I'm not a child," Prescott muttered, but he was obviously touched.

"In my mind you're still the snot-nosed brat who used to hide under my skirts," she huffed. Her gaze clouded. "I just can't understand why Cook wasn't in the kitchen this morning."

"It's not her fault," Catherine soothed. "It's no one's. How was Cook to know that Evie was hiding in the kitchen? Cook had no reason not to go to the garden for more herbs."

Mrs. Nagel's hands twisted in her apron. "Evie should have known better than to try to reach the cookies. It's a rule. She knows better than to break the rules—"

"Well, she's paying for that mistake," Dr. Winner interrupted. "And she likely will be doing so for a long time to come. Burns are some of the most painful injuries I've ever treated."

Catherine noticed the crease between Prescott's sable brows and the grimace on his face. The poor man must be in agony. "I'm just so glad you were wearing your gloves," she stated, shuddering.

"Yes. Lucky break there," Winner concurred. "You

likely won't even scar. The blistering will hurt like the dickens, but after a few weeks you should be fine."

"Did you give him any laudanum?" Mrs. Nagel asked, stepping to the other side of the bed and laying her hand on Prescott's brow. Not many women could get away with that maneuver, Catherine opined.

"Not yet," the doctor replied. "He's refused it thus far."

The stout matron scowled. "Well, give him some. He must sleep. Or he will not heal."

"I won't," Prescott countered. "I don't need it."

Mrs. Nagel pressed her hand on the edge of the mattress and Prescott tilted. Inhaling sharply, his face turned white as chalk. "Don't need it, my boot."

"You're going to take it, Pres," Catherine declared. "If I have to pour it down your throat myself."

Prescott leaned up on his elbows. "Will you stay with me, Cat?"

Staring into those vulnerable green eyes, she wondered if she could put off the burglary set for tonight. But opportunely for her plans, it was the housekeeper's day off and she could certainly use all the providence she could get. According to the Thief's book, changes in household staff always provided a few additional precious moments. And Sir John Winston's deadline was drawing near.

"I'll stay as long as you need me," she murmured. If he remained awake and needed her, she would view it as a sign not to do the burglary tonight. If he fell asleep easily, then . . . the game was on.

Catherine stepped aside while Dr. Winner reached into his black bag and pulled out a decanter. Yanking off the stopper, he held it out to Prescott, who eyed the bottle longingly, obviously in pain.

Dr. Winner held the decanter to his lips and Prescott swallowed it in one gulp. He grimaced. "Ugh."

"You'll be glad for it in a little bit." Winner nodded, putting away the decanter and taking out another. He set it on the bedside table. "If you wake in the night—" Realizing Prescott's incapacity, he continued, "Call out. I'll be next door and will give it to you."

"Cat's going to stay," he murmured.

"Well, I'll be here just the same," the good doctor replied.

"I will set up a pallet, Doctor," Mrs. Nagel nodded approvingly. "Thank you for remaining."

Winner shrugged. "I want to be near, in case Evie needs me." The pair stepped out of the chamber, speaking in hushed tones.

Prescott's eyes fluttered closed as he was obviously exhausted.

"Sleep, Pres." Catherine planted a kiss on his forehead. Sighing, she pulled over the chair where they'd tossed Prescott's breeches. Lifting the soot-covered white garment, Catherine marveled at how flimsy it seemed compared to her heavy gown.

Suddenly the thought flashed in her mind; how was she supposed to climb a trestle and crawl around a rooftop with long skirts? Lifting the breeches, she examined them. Could she dare?

"How is he?" Jared stepped beside her, resting his hand on the back of her chair.

With her heart hammering, Catherine quickly dropped the breeches to the floor.

"I'm fine," Prescott muttered opening one eye. "Better than you. I heard you lost your shirt . . ."

Jared's pale cheeks tinged pink and he bowed his sandy-colored head. "My stupidity knows no bounds."

"You're just a little green." Prescott closed his eye and

sighed. "We all were once. All you need is a bit of schooling in the finer art of cheating—"

"Now wait a minute!" Catherine cried.

Prescott licked his lips. "To spot it and avoid it, Cat. Not to do it. Although with the cads he was dealing with it might not have been a bad idea."

"We have to pay it back even though the bastard lied about how much I owed him," Jared groused, his Coleridge gray eyes seething with indignation. "It makes me so angry, I'd like to rip Thomas Winston's forked tongue right from his mouth."

Catherine couldn't imagine how furious Jared would be if he knew that Sir John Winston had only given them seven days to pay the debt.

"It's like stealing," her brother growled. "It's just not fair."

Catherine had to resist the urge to push his pale hair from his eyes. "It's your word against his, Jared."

"Yes, I know." Clenching his fists, he scowled. "Impoverished orphan against well-connected aristocrat. If I came from a noble family, if I had a title, maybe he wouldn't have been so quick to make me his mark!"

Catherine's eyes widened; what was Jared saying?

"Yes, at the other side," Prescott muttered, his eyes closed, his face relaxing. "The better side . . . the world is at your doorstep." His mouth hung open and he unleashed a loud snore.

"The advantages of being nobility are innumerable, Jared," Catherine whispered. "But I won't lie to you; they still might have fleeced you just the same."

"It's just, well . . ." He shrugged his lanky fourteen-year-old shoulders. "I'm beginning to appreciate the extra latitude given to nobility."

"Whether it's deserved or not," Catherine added, crossing her arms. "There are many commoners who are more honorable than ten Thomas Winstons. Some might be born to a higher class but nobility comes from deed and word." Watching Prescott to make sure that he was asleep, Catherine added, "What I want for you, Jared, is the opportunity. That's what the title and money can supply. It's up to you to make the most of yourself from there."

Jared grimaced. "You sound like Headmaster Dunn."

Pressing her fist to her mouth, it took every ounce of self-control for Catherine not to blurt out the fact that Headmaster Dunn had died trying to protect his title. She didn't want Jared to do anything rash, but deep down she knew it was time for Jared to know the truth. Or at least some of it.

Quietly, she stood and closed the door. Motioning for Jared to join her in the far corner, she whispered, "There's something you need to know."

With his eyes wary, he moved next to her, his hands clenched in the pockets of his brown wool coat. "What?"

She swallowed, realizing that she was almost as rusty at sharing secrets as she was at asking for help. Mayhap it was time she exercised both faculties. "Headmaster Dunn knew about us."

"What?" he shrieked.

"Lower your voice."

Closing his mouth, his brow furrowed. "How?"

"He must have heard us arguing—"

"When?"

There were so many arguments to choose from, it seemed. "That night by the chapel . . ."

"But why didn't he say anything?"

"In his own way, he did. He moved me to new rooms—"

"Headmaster Dunn told me that he wanted me to go to the Hartzes' so that I could be exposed to how fine families conducted themselves. To see the workings of a noble household. He said that he wanted me to learn how to act when I move about in Society . . ." his voice trailed off.

"We thought he meant for when you worked in a noble household. He really meant for when you were the *master* of a household."

Understanding lit up his familiar gray gaze as he nodded. "He knew."

"Yes." Her brother was quick. Inhaling deeply, she dropped the next revelation, "And he was fighting the Caddyhorns for your title."

He gaped.

"He did not tell anyone about you," she reassured, resting a hand on his arm. Leave it to dear Headmaster Dunn to find a way to help them without exposing them. "He was digging up misdeeds on the Caddyhorns and had a list of influential people with whom he shared the intelligence." The list had made her gawk. Among the many members of the House of Lords had been the Lord Chancellor himself, Lord Eldon.

"I doubt that they will take your title," she asserted. The question was: When he came of age, would he?

Jared's face was contorted with grief. She hated that what she was saying hurt him, but he needed to know how much Headmaster Dunn had sacrificed for them. The rare, beloved man.

Her throat constricted as she struggled against the tears. "He was fighting for us, Jared. And . . ." She couldn't bring herself to say the awful truth, stating instead, "He was fighting our battle. But now he's gone and it's up to us. He clearly wanted us to take our rightful place when the time came. Both of us."

Jared hung his head. His long, sandy hair fell before his face and she wished she could see his features. Staring down at his shoes, Jared stood quietly for a long while and she let him be. This was a lot to digest, especially for a lad of fourteen.

When he finally looked up, there was new determination lighting his gray gaze. "He will not have fought in vain, Catherine. I swear, on everything that I hold dear, I will make certain that his efforts were not in vain."

A tear slid down her cheek.

"That your efforts, Catherine . . ." His voice caught. "That everything you've done for me . . . that I can someday make you proud of me."

Unwinding her arms, she pulled him close. "I am proud of you, Jared." Her vision blurred as the tears poured out her eyes. "And what I've done for you, I did for myself, too. We're in this together, remember."

His shoulders shook as her little brother clung to her. She didn't know who was holding on tighter. Together they cried, sharing the one thing that they would have forever: each other.

Chapter 32

❦

*S*omehow stealing into one of London's most noted *residences should be more daunting*, Catherine thought while scaling the moonlit trestle carefully, hand over hand, foot alternating foot. *And it certainly should not be this utterly . . . exhilarating.* The vitality of each measured movement, the brisk air of the predawn, the electrifying possibility of the hangman's noose if caught . . . It was a surprisingly intoxicating brew, almost as heady as Gardener Graves's home-brewed spirits.

Thoughts of Marcus brought fresh anxiety, and involuntarily, her climb slowed. Was he safe? Would he return to her whole and well?

Dear Lord in heaven, she had a job to do, one that did not allow for distraction! Catherine pushed all thoughts of Marcus from her mind.

Eagerness and elation thrilled through her as the roof's ledge inched closer into view. She felt like a lioness on the hunt, a predator driven by primal hunger. These feelings were so wholly unfamiliar to her that she felt as if she were someone else—a stranger, the antithesis of herself. This stranger had never known gut-twisting fear, had never been besieged by gnawing feelings of powerlessness, had never cowered from her enemies. This stranger had not failed in her one true charge—protecting her brother and his legacy. She was whole, powerful, and most significantly, not crippled. This stranger was perfect. And she was about to execute a burglary of historic consequence, personally and publicly.

Oh, what she would have given to have the boys who'd grown up with her at the orphanage see her now. She would have loved to make them eat their taunting words. "Cow-hearted cat," they had called her when she was young, for her timidity and her inelegant gait.

Well, tonight she was the master thief, crafty as a fox, nimble as a panther. *Nimble? Catherine Miller?*

Catherine gingerly flexed her foot as she inserted it into the next square in the trestle. Amazingly, her bad leg did not hinder her. In fact . . . it was almost as if in assuming her new guise, her old injury had magically disappeared. Did the pungent tang of vengeance overwhelm any ache?

Whatever the cause, it seemed that her reserved disposition and ungainly gait were discarded behind the vine-covered wall of the Caddyhorns' garden. Thank the heavens.

Or perhaps it was the unfettered breeches. No wonder men were so free-spirited; they had great liberty of movement. Just the feel of rough wool on her bottom gave her the oddest sense of . . . exhilaration. And it invariably brought her thoughts around to Marcus . . .

What would he think of her efforts tonight? She could never tell him, she realized. He was so protective. Part of her liked how he cosseted her, the other part resented the gorgeous oaf's heavy-handedness. The fact that he'd been so protective as to defend her maidenhead made her want to scream. It also had been a fantastic challenge, trying to tempt the man away from his noble intentions . . .

Oh, how she missed him since he'd been gone. Nothing felt the same as when he was near. He was like sunshine after the rain . . .

The shriek of a cat ruptured the stillness of the fashionable neighborhood, ripping her from her wayward thoughts. Her heart skipped a beat and she stopped her ascent. Would the servants rouse? She held her breath, waiting to see what axe might befall her.

This is madness! a small voice cried in her head. *Who do you think you're fooling? You are no master thief. You are cow-hearted Cat and you will be until the day you die. Turn around and pretend that this never happened. If you leave now, no one will be the wiser for your foolishness . . .*

Marcus . . . Marcus would be livid if he knew . . . Jared . . .

Jared needed her help. If she wavered, if she didn't pay off the Winstons, then everything she'd worked for, every step she'd made since she was twelve years old would have been for naught. Headmaster Dunn would have died for nothing.

These thoughts fueled the fire of vengeance already blazing through her blood.

That which cannot be saved must be avenged.

Slowly Catherine reached for the next rung. With her eyes fixed on the roof's ledge, she resumed her climb once more. She had been such a fool when she had last faced the Caddyhorn clan. Reacting with shock and outrage to fourteen-year-old, pudgy-faced Stanford Caddyhorn's lurid propositions and inappropriate fondling. He was her cousin—and *no one* was supposed to touch her like that!

Running to Lady Frederica Caddyhorn for help against her dreadful son had been the ultimate act of naïveté. Instead of handling the problem, Lady Frederica had told Catherine that she was deluded and quite possibly around the bend. Her dear Stannie could not possibly be interested in such a reedy waif as her.

Lady Frederica and her husband had then decided that Catherine needed to be locked in her rooms so as not to "contaminate" Stanford with her delusions. It had been Kruger's inspired plan to imprison Catherine and her brother in Bedlam.

The haunting memories of betrayal, impotence and fear suffused Catherine's straining muscles with strength. Envisioning how she and her brother might have ended up at the hands of their "charitable" relations made her blood boil.

She'd waited ten long years, hiding out like a frightened mouse too afraid of her own shadow. She was finished being the victim. Done allowing her enemies to get off scot-free. It was time to be decisive. To be brave. To take destiny into her own hands. Tonight, as she executed her burglary, she would have her chance for revenge and the opportunity to do some good. Inwardly she saluted the spirit of the Thief of Robinson Square.

Just as the book had directed, the garden gate was left open for easy escape. It had been simple enough to learn the servants' schedules from the footman Catherine had befriended. It had been a bit trickier getting him to confirm that Lady Frederica Caddyhorn still slept every night in her second-floor bedroom lying atop a cache of jewels. Still, the man had thought his tales of the Caddyhorn household would win him her favors. If he only knew . . .

I'm climbing a three-story building! The realization shrieked in her mind. Mayhap she truly was around the bend, but if so, she'd been sent there by the Caddyhorn clan.

Vengeance beckoned, with its heady spices too tempting to ignore.

Only about twenty more rungs until the top. The fragrant scent of roses wafted up from below. Her hands and feet heartily ate the distance to the rooftop, its ledge illuminated by the silvery moon. Cresting the trestle and rolling onto the roof, Catherine progressed across the upper edge of a row of tiles, eyes fixed on the chimney joint. It was the perfect fastening for a rope, just as the journal had described. All lingering reservations about the journal dissipated in the face of the accuracy of the particulars. The chimney joint was precisely where it was supposed to be, Lady Frederica would be where she was expected, and it was time for settling old scores. This night old ghosts would walk London's rooftops and claim their reckoning.

Slipping the rope through the joint and knotting it exactly how she'd memorized it from the thief's pages, Catherine slowly slid backwards over the roof edge, landing awkwardly on balled feet onto a small terrace one story below. She stood motionless for a long moment as her leg pinched, then recovered. She ignored the slight ache. Wrapping another rope around the leg of the iron balustrade, she climbed over the rail and, holding on to the hemp, leaped to the lower veranda beneath.

There was little time. Dawn was moments away; its glow barely lighting the sky, its mellow rays on the verge of peeking out from under London's rooftops. Many men were serving His Majesty in the war against Napoleon, but there were still plenty about the city streets to call alarm at the sight of a person scaling the home of one of Society's notable families. If the Caddyhorns even *knew* of her existence, all would be lost. Jared . . . She would return his clothing and he would never be the wiser. If he ever found out . . . she couldn't let that happen.

Gently pushing open the doors, Catherine slipped her finger upward through the crack as she eased the doors backwards, just like the journal had described. The latch slipped free. She was almost giddy with relief.

Brushing past the long draperies, she stole into the darkened chamber. The cloying scents of fleur-de-rose and camphor filled the air. Four strides to the bed and there was Lady Frederica, snoring to a three-pattern beat.

Catherine stood over the woman who could have been a savior to two grieving children and instead had become their affliction. Catherine was so angry, so infused with nervous tension, that her hands quaked.

The whole of London must hear my clamoring heartbeat!

She schooled herself to calm. Now was the opportunity she'd been anticipating for ten long years. It was not the time to dither.

With her heart cantering, Catherine slipped an eager hand underneath the feathered pillow, hunting for the promised cache.

The lady snorted.

Catherine froze, breath arrested. Every dream, every whisper of hope could be shattered in this speck of a moment.

Time seemed to condense. The world distilled into darkness, camphor, and the large immobile lump on bed.

She will wake! I am dead. I have failed my brother. I have failed them all. Marcus!

The whole lot depended on Lady Frederica's next move.

Rolling over, the corpulent lady resumed her snoring once more.

A small puff sounded as Catherine resumed breathing.

This was truly madness! But could she turn back now? If she failed again . . . Failure was not an option. Jared's life depended on her staying the course, keeping her aim sure.

She felt the mantle of responsibility as if it were a sodden cloak on her small shoulders. She felt the overwhelming urge to crumble and flee.

Marcus would never flee. Marcus would have swept in, executed the job and have been done by now. Thought of the dear, capable man who fought wars for King and Country inspired her back to stiffen. Thinking of how hard he was working against a murderous traitor infused her limbs with energy. He was a hero, and for a moment, she would be like him, doing what she must to save the day.

With a renewed sense of purpose, Catherine searched under the pillow. Her fingers locked onto a soft velvet pouch with rock-hard contents. Yanked gently, the heavy pouch slipped free from the pillows. Blessedly, Lady Frederica did not move.

With a quiet surge of triumph, Catherine pocketed the weighty purse and slid a "calling card" under the pillow where the cache had been. Quickly, she turned and slipped out the terrace door just as the first rays of dawn lit the overcast sky.

Surprisingly the journey was much easier on the way back than going, even with the climb back to the rooftop to retrieve her ropes. Probably because of the rush of success charging through her. Still, the added weight of the jewels unbalanced Catherine more than she would have thought. Her bad leg slipped a time or two as she descended the trestle, causing her breath to catch and her heart to skip to a staccato beat the whole way down.

But she moved on, relentlessly driven by fear that now that she'd actually done the job, she might yet get caught with the stolen jewels on her person.

Relatching the garden gate behind her, Catherine silently raced toward the abandoned stable where she'd left her mount. Her leg ached like the dickens from doing more exertion than she was used to, but she was not about to slow down.

She'd succeeded! The thought added wings to her bootheels and she was inside the barn before she knew it.

Knickers whinnied at seeing her, still lazily munching from the bag of oats she'd left. His brownish yellow coat almost melted into the stable's dusky background, yet the stripe down his nose glowed like a beacon drawing her approach. He was tied within a stall that hadn't seen an occupant for a few seasons past. The place was covered in dust and smelled of old manure. A rat scurried past. Catherine jumped aside, intent on her mount. A few fragile rays of light peeked in from the loft window and it was past time she was on her way.

After shoving the cache of jewels into the leather saddlebag, Catherine changed from Jared's clothing into a pale gray gown. Her breath was coming in short pants and her chest burned with exertion. She stole a quick swallow of water from her pack to ease her parched throat and then led Knickers out of the barn into the pale light of morning.

It looked to be a glorious day.

Chapter 33

❧~⌒◯◯⌒~❧

For the first time in as long as he could remember, Marcus was thankful to be passing through Andersen Hall's wrought-iron gates. He urged his mount to slow to a walk and directed the mare toward the stables. He was exhausted to the core. After the euphoria of success had worn off, the usual wretchedness that he felt after a mission had set in.

The questioning of his actions. The damage he'd had to inflict. The men he'd had to kill. Not that Renfrew had deserved anything less. But it was as if his evil had somehow rubbed off on Marcus, leaching his soul to black.

On the long silent stretches of the dark ride back, Marcus had had too much time to think, too much opportunity to see the faces and feel the darkness of what he did.

He was getting too old for these wretched missions, he realized. He needed to see Cat and feel redeemed. Her sweetness was the balm his soul required. Her loyalty the air he needed to breathe freely once more.

Golden rays of light stretched long over the green lawn

rolling before the army of trees guarding the orphanage. Cat would be up shortly, if she wasn't already, Marcus noted as he dismounted.

Timmy, the stable lad, stepped out of the barn. "Blast it's like Tattersall's on auction day," he muttered. His dusty brown cap had slipped into his eyes and he shoved it back onto his sandy crown.

Marcus handed over the reins. "An extra ration of oats for Polly. And brush her down well. She did me great service."

"Good morning, Major." The lad's scrawny shoulders were hunched and his chin stuck out, like he had a bone to pick with someone. "Glad you're finally back." There was a certain satisfaction in Timmy's tone. "Oh, I can't wait to see Devane's face now that yer here."

Marcus froze in his tracks. He turned.

Timmy had led the mare into the barn.

Marcus strode inside, blinking his eyes quickly to adjust to the light. Usually the scent of hay and manure made him feel at home, now all he experienced was a sudden nausea in his hollow belly. "What the hell are you talking about, Timmy?"

Timmy grunted, hauling a bucket over to Polly's stall. "Blast, it's aint right, if ya ask me."

"What's not right?" Marcus asked, schooling his impatience to cool. The lad would tell him, he just wanted his drama. Well, Marcus would give him thirty seconds. Mentally he ticked off the time as he eyed the mounts in the row of stalls. His father had always been a horse enthusiast and had often asked donors to contribute in horseflesh to maintain Andersen Hall's stable. Not one of the horses would be deemed acceptable by polite Society as a "park hack", yet it was a modest, if respectable stable.

"Women tearin' off in the middle of the night," Timmy declared. Keeping his eyes trained on the brush as he swept the mare's flank, his surly expression deepened into a full-blown scowl.

Marcus's heart skipped a beat. "Who?" he asked, but he already knew the answer.

The lad busied himself at the mare's shoulder, keeping his eyes averted. "Miss Miller." Timmy glowered. The pace of the brushing accelerated. "And I'd bet a good saddle it's that blasted Devane's fault."

Jealousy flashed through him like whipcord. Marcus ground his teeth. "Prescott Devane?"

"Yeah. The bugger thinks 'e's better 'an us. With 'is fancy coats and full a pretension—"

Trying to keep his tone level, Marcus interrupted, "Is Miss Miller all right? What did Devane do?"

"'Er 'ead's in the clouds is all. Carryin' men's clothes around—"

"His clothes?" Marcus shook his head, his anxiety soaring. "What the hell's been going on here?"

"Devilry!" Timmy declared, attacking the horse's withers with the brush. The mare nickered and stepped sideways. The lad laid his hand on her neck and she relaxed. Timmy resumed brushing. "The 'eadmaster's barely cold an' 'e's movin' into the man's bed. The man's bed for lawd's sake!"

Anger swept over him like a brush fire. "Prescott Devane moved into my father's rooms?"

"They say 'e's a hero. But it's the oldest trick in the book." Timmy stepped around the mare, stabbing the brush in the air to enunciate each point. "The chits get all a' swoon when a man acts all gel'nt—"

"You mean gallant?"

"Yeah. The ol' knight in shining armor trick. Works every time." He spit into the hay. "Although I'd a thought Miss Miller was smarter than that." Tossing the brush into a bucket, Timmy reached for a comb. "I'll bet 'e's even faking the injuries. That's the second oldest trick in the book; the ol' nurse ploy. Plays on a woman's sympathies. Take a fine woman like Miss Miller, and between the hero maneuver and the nursing ruse, she's lost fer good."

Marcus's heart was pounding through his chest so hard it hurt. Blood roared in his ears. He didn't recall leaving the stable or even walking the path to the main house. He simply found himself standing before his father's wood-paneled door, the same door where years before he'd painted the white jar.

"Dear Lord, your hands are like magic." It was Devane's voice. "I never thought such a little thing could feel so heavenly, Cat."

Marcus saw red. He punched the door open and it bounded against the wall with a crash.

Cat turned, her eyes wide with surprise. "Marcus!"

She stood beside the bed where Devane sat on the edge. The bed was unmade. His clothes were strewn on the floor.

"Hey!" Devane cried as if Marcus was the trespasser.

Marcus's eyes flew to Devane's drawers, which hung short to the calves. The sight of his naked feet sent the last vestiges of Marcus's restraint over the edge. Stomping over, he grabbed the intruder by the collar of his dandified purple coat, yanked him into the air and tossed him onto the floor.

Devane landed on his bandaged hands and howled like a wounded dog. But then Devane rolled over and scooted away, defter than Marcus would have expected for a *supposedly* injured man.

Grabbing Marcus's arm, Cat cried, "Stop it, Marcus!"

That she would defend this scum ripped something fragile inside of him. Tossing her off, Cat rebounded off the bed and he couldn't help himself; he was thankful that she wasn't hurt.

He was the one in pain. His heart burned with a scorching ache that made him feel razed by its devastation. His eyes burned, his mouth tasted of bile. If he weren't so bloody mad, he'd be sick.

Dr. Winner tore into the chamber. "What the hell is going on?"

Mrs. Nagel rushed to Devane's side, screaming, "What's the matter with you?" She threw her arms around the quaking sod. "Can't you see that he's hurt?"

Cat stood before Marcus, blocking his path to Devane.

"Move aside," Marcus growled.

Instead of budging, Cat jumped up and threw her arms around his neck, hanging on for dear life as if she could stop him. She was so brave, his little lioness. But she was not *his*. No longer his. Betrayed. Again, betrayed.

"Stop and look at me, Marcus," she begged, her voice muffled by his coat. She hung on him, her arms around his neck, her legs dangling beneath her. She was rushing to Devane's rescue, trying to protect her lover. Fighting their enemy. He stood frozen, feeling suddenly cold. Terribly cold. He didn't care any longer. He couldn't; it hurt too much.

"Look at me, Marcus." Cat placed a palm to his cheek, drawing his gaze down to hers as she sank onto her tiptoes. "Please. Look in my eye."

Those luminous gray eyes. He'd never quite identified the color. Smoky. Nay. Slate? Storm? Cold, icy, tempest? No. He was seeing things. For all of her unfaithfulness, she was never cold, not his fiery, passionate Cat.

But not his. Never to be his. He was winter, dark, lonely winter, filled with black frost. She was golden-haired, citrus-scented spring, teasing him with her proximity, but never to be his.

"It's all right, Marcus," she soothed. "I'm here."

But it was not all right. It would never be. Not really. He welcomed the coldness, draping the loneliness around him like a chilly shroud that could shield him from the pain. Numbness was better than feeling this . . . agony. It buffeted him, making his knees weak. But as he did when on duty, he locked his legs, braced his muscles and leaned into the assault, closing himself off from the pain.

"What the hell is wrong with him?" Winner exclaimed as he and Mrs. Nagel helped Devane to stand.

"Why did he attack poor Prescott?" Mrs. Nagel cried.

Everyone was against him, Marcus realized. Just as they had been before. He was alone. The Wolf, Tam had called him. Perhaps his sergeant had been right. Mayhap he was destined to travel alone. Die a lonely, bitter man.

"Prescott, can you stand?" Cat asked over her shoulder.

"Yes."

"Help him outside," Cat directed the other two. "Then close the door."

"Cat—" Prescott argued.

Mrs. Nagel scowled. "Now see here, Catherine—"

"Just go! He won't hurt me."

"How can you—?"

"Just leave!"

The threesome shuffled out, shooting Marcus glares as they went with obvious reluctance.

Marcus was so numb he hardly even cared.

"Close the door," Cat ordered.

It shut with a reverberating thud.

Her heart was thumping against his chest, he realized. Fast, warm. But it could not penetrate his chill. He wondered if he'd ever be warm again.

Slowly, her arms drifted downward as she released him, dropped to the floor and stepped away. Watching him with a wary eye, she moved sideways, never turning her back to him. After everything they'd shared, how could she believe that he'd intentionally harm her?

Reaching the armchair, she leaned over and lifted the footrest from the floor. She turned and walked over, placing it before the tips of his boots. She was so close that her silky hair grazed his fingertips. Unthinking, his fingers flexed as if to reach for the golden tresses, but instead he clenched his hand into a fist.

Then, she stood on the footrest, using it like a stool.

Those beautiful gray eyes were level with his. Her pert nose was barely inches from his own and those delicious pink-bowed lips were so close he could smell the mint on her breath. It reminded him of a magical morning only a short time ago. Through the frost, his heart pinched.

A line marred her lovely brow and her lips were pressed tightly in a troubled frown. She exhaled loudly, her breath washed over him in a minty breeze.

"How's Tam?" she asked, surprising him. "Is he all right?"

"He'll need to ice his bollocks," popped out of his mouth of its own volition.

Her lips lifted slightly and the crease between her brows eased. "Other than his . . . privates, how is he?"

He shrugged. "Fine."

"And Renfrew?"

"Dead." That's how Marcus felt. Cold, lifeless, the blood having drained out of him, leaving nothing left but an empty corpse.

"He was guilty?"

"Very."

"I'm so sorry, Marcus." Sadness filled her gaze. Gently, she grazed a hand over his cheek. "It must have been awful for you, Marcus. I'm so sorry you had to deal with that."

Despite himself, something inside him stirred. She understood. He ignored the impulse to press his cheek into her palm.

"How do you feel?" she asked softly.

He swallowed, wondering why they were even having this conversation. "Bleak."

Shaking her head, she sighed. Reaching up, she brushed a lock of hair from his brow. He wondered where his hat had gone.

"So soft," she murmured. "When I was little, I used to wonder if it was as soft as it looked. It is."

Her fingers soothed his brow, gently gliding over his temples.

He swallowed, not wanting it to feel so good. Not wanting to feel anything.

"Do you know," she murmured, "while we were growing up I used to jump and hide whenever you came near?"

Gentle fingers combed through his hair, raising tingles along his scalp.

"You terrified me."

"I wouldn't hurt you," he rasped.

"Oh, I wasn't afraid that you'd hurt me." Her gaze tempered, but her fingers never stopped traveling, caressing, soothing all over his face, feeling so lovely that he wanted to close his eyes. But he didn't. He wanted to look her in the eye when she broke the news to him. He wanted to remember her every expression when she ended it. She would be kind, he knew, it was her nature. And he would memorize her features and her tone and how she acted the day she crushed his heart into a thousand pieces of rubble.

"I was afraid of how you made me feel." Fingers traced his jaw, oblivious to his unseen pain.

He swallowed. "And how was that?"

Her brow furrowed, and her eyes drifted up to the left. Her fingers ceased moving and a shaft of disappointment knifed through him. "Flustered. Nervous. Like I had ants crawling under my skin and inside my middle."

"Ants?" That didn't sound good.

Her eyes met his, smoldering, intense. "And warm." Enchanting fingers grazed his features as she spoke. "It would start with my cheeks." Her hand drifted over the fuzz covering his cheek. "Then move up to my hair." She grazed his brow. "My whole head would heat up as if I'd moved too close to a hot stove." Her pink lips bowed into a dreamy smile. "That's what you were to me, Marcus. A fire. Blazing, dangerous . . . exciting . . ." Her eyes locked with his and his heart skipped a beat. "But not anymore."

He braced himself. Now she would tell him that the flames had petered out. How she was fond enough of him, but that the fire was gone. She had a new love. A new man who made her flame. Devane now drew her passion.

"It's different, now," she murmured, her voice husky. "Because the fire burns from deep within me. Hotter, more intense." Her hand drifted down his collar to his chest and slipped through the opening of his coat to his shirt. He could feel her hand pressing against his heartbeat as if holding it in her palm. "It never goes out," she continued. "Just smolders, flames, blazes hot, then smolders again. It's with me, always. Like you are always with me."

He blinked, confused. This didn't sound like a typical "go our separate ways" speech. Granted, Cat had never done this before, but still, it was a pretty straightforward business . . .

The hand beneath his coat gently slid up and down in the hollow of his pectorals, feeling so reassuring, he didn't quite know what to make of it.

"And"—her lips drew near, teasing him with her minty breath—"it's no longer just my cheeks that burn for you."

A fragile flicker of hope kindled deep inside of him. But no, she'd given her heart to Devane. He didn't want it, didn't want her. Not anymore. There's no going back after betrayal . . . No way to mend that breach . . .

Gently she nibbled along his jaw, his neck and his ear-lobe. "I no longer jump away like a frightened rabbit," she whispered, her breath teasing inside his ear. "I want you and I'm not scared of it, Marcus. I'm no longer afraid of how you make me feel."

Hope suddenly blazed higher, tempting him to believe. Despite himself, he asked, "But Devane—"

"I don't want Prescott." She bit his lower lip between sharp teeth and released it, declaring, "I want to dance in *your* flames."

The ice encasing his heart cracked. "But I saw him—"

"There is no one but you, Marcus. You are the only man in the world for me and there can be no other."

The fissure in his chest erupted and he began to thaw. He wanted to believe, oh how he wanted to believe.

"I would never betray you, Marcus." Her velvety cheek brushed his. "I am still untouched by any man. And quite anxious for you to remedy that situation."

Her words caused the most incredible feeling of full-ness in his chest.

Her lips claimed his—open, wet, *possessive*. He opened his mouth with an eagerness born from despair. *I'm not a lone wolf,* he thought. *I have my mate.* Her tongue glided, played, enticed, drawing him in as a bee is drawn to sweet nectar. Her fingers splayed across his chest, warm and en-thralling. She was spring, melting the wintry frost frozen inside of him over so many years. She'd given hope rebirth, when he'd thought he'd lost it forever.

Pulling slightly away, Cat wrapped her arms around his neck and hugged him close. "I'm so glad you came back to me, Marcus," she murmured. "I'm so glad you're home."

Chapter 34

❦❦❦

"I'm coming in," came a call from behind the door. The entry opened and Dr. Winner stood in the threshold. His loose lips were rounded into an "O" and his brown brows almost reached his receding hairline.

Catherine tried to pull back from Marcus's embrace, but he held on, keeping her close. She peered over Marcus's shoulder and cleared her throat. "Uh, hello, Dr. Winner." Her cheeks burned, but she wasn't half as embarrassed as she knew she should have been. She was an unmarried woman kissing a man, obviously not her husband . . .

The thought brought an ache to her heart, but she pushed it away. Today. He was hers for today. She couldn't think of tomorrow.

"I need the laudanum for Evie." Winner scooted past them and retrieved the bottle from the bedside stand.

Catherine knew for a fact that the good doctor had three more bottles in the other room. She appreciated Winner's concern, but wished that everyone wouldn't judge Marcus so harshly. If only they knew how much horror he had to

313

face. If only they could see how sweet he truly was.

"Evie?" Marcus blinked. "What's wrong with Evie?"

Dr. Winner waved a hand. "You tell him, Catherine." Then he exited the room, considerately closing the door behind him.

Concern flashed in the sea blue depths of Marcus's gaze. "What happened to Evie?"

Catherine sighed. Marcus was back to himself, and it was time, she supposed, for her to get back to reality as well. "There was an accident. Evie was playing in the kitchen. Her gown caught fire."

"How bad?" his voice cracked.

Recalling the frightful red marks and Evie's cries, she shuddered. "Dr. Winner says that it will be a difficult recovery, but that she should be all right. It could've been so much worse." She shook her head. "So much worse. Prescott stamped out the flames with his hands. Thank heavens he was wearing gloves."

Marcus's face fell as realization dawned on him. He released her and sank onto the bed in a daze. "Dear Lord, I threw him to the floor." He groaned, covering his eyes with his hands.

Gently she stroked his black hair. "You weren't yourself—"

"I almost hate myself for asking, but I have to know. What were you two doing when I came in?"

"I was scratching his back. With his hands bandaged, he can't scratch his itches."

"Oh." He dropped his hands, self-loathing filling his gaze. He shook his head. "I'm a fool. There's no excuse for behavior like that. I owe a round of apologies." He shook his head. "To Devane. And Winner. And oh, dear Lord, Mrs. Nagel. They must think I'm a monster . . ."

Catherine sat down beside him. "Marcus," she started,

trying to keep her tone mild and nonjudgmental, "why did you attack Prescott?"

He took her hand, pressing it between his palms. "I thought you'd left me for him. When I heard that he'd moved into my father's room and was sleeping in my father's bed—"

"Who told you?"

"Timmy."

She shook her head. "Blast, how that lad likes to kick up the dirt and see what sticks."

"He said the oddest things about you and Devane's clothing . . ."

Her cheeks heated and she realized that Timmy's flair for the inflammatory was almost a talent. He'd seen her holding Jared's clothing wound around the satchel of jewels.

She wasn't ready to talk about her nocturnal activities. Marcus was too raw and in many respects, so was she. She couldn't believe she was actually considering spilling everything to him.

"So you have no feelings for Devane?" Marcus asked, vulnerability lacing his tone.

She blinked, refocusing on Marcus. "Prescott is my dear friend. But he and I . . ." She shook her head. "We don't fit."

Knowing it might lead to his own downfall, he garnered his courage, and voiced his fear, "I believe that he loves you."

She thought about it a long moment. "I don't think that he does. We're like . . . chums." She shrugged. "Don't misunderstand me, I love him, but we're better off as friends, is the only way I can put it."

"I need a word with you when you come up for air, Cat," Prescott demanded from behind the closed door.

So Winner had told Prescott about her kissing Marcus.

Why did she suddenly feel guilty? Because, she realized, even if she understood that Prescott didn't love her, he was very fond of her still and might be hurt, if only a little.

Marcus glanced from the door back to her. "You still believe he doesn't love you?"

"He's just worried about me, I'm sure. We watch out for each other." Brushing aside his raven hair, she kissed his cheek, loving the scent of sandalwood. Sighing, she rose, sorry for her reconciliation with Marcus to end.

Marcus stood. "I owe him a monumental apology. And my thanks, for Evie, for taking care of you . . . He's a good man."

"Don't look so surprised. People do grow up."

He nodded. "Leopards do change their spots sometimes."

They shared a secret smile. Something tender fluttered in Catherine's chest, then it spread over her, like a blanket, warming her to her bones.

Marcus leaned over and kissed her gently. "One more for good luck." Then he walked over to the door.

Taking a deep breath, he opened it.

Prescott stood in the threshold, his golden-hued face molten red. It looked as if his bandages were fresh and thank the heavens he didn't look too much the worse for wear. The ferocity she saw in his gaze reminded her of the angry child he'd been, and worry suddenly sprouted in her middle.

Marcus opened his hands in supplication. "I'm so sorry for how I treated you, Devane. I was under a gross misimpression. But that's no excuse."

Prescott started, as if surprised. Then his eyes narrowed. "Afraid I'll call you out?"

"There's no need, Devane. It was my fault entirely. I apologize."

Prescott's lips pressed into a stubborn line that Catherine knew well. "And if I don't accept it?"

Fearful, Catherine stepped over and gently grabbed his arm. "You must be feeling terrible. Let me help you to the bed."

"I don't want to go to bed," Prescott growled, "I want to rip his bloody head off."

Catherine shot Marcus a meaningful glance. "Why don't you go look in on Evie. I want a word with Prescott."

"You're sure?"

"Absolutely. I'll see you later." With an inward sigh, she watched Marcus turn and walk out the door. The man had no right to be that gorgeous.

Gently she eased Prescott into the armchair by the window. Then she lifted the footstool that had brought her so close to Marcus and carried it over to Prescott's chair.

While she turned and grabbed a blanket, Prescott placed his bare feet on the stool. She laid the blanket across his lap and pulled up a chair facing him.

He watched her every move, like a hawk does its prey. "Do you love him?"

"Yes." She was surprised by her lack of hesitancy.

"It's not some lingering infatuation from when you were a child?"

She shook her head. "No. This is real."

He swallowed, turning to stare out the window. "How can you be so sure?"

Exhaling loudly, she shook her head. "I just know."

"Will you marry him?"

"I can't leave Andersen Hall, especially when things are so unstable. And I can't leave my brother."

"I didn't ask that, Cat. I asked if you would marry him." His green gaze met hers. "You've always sworn that you'd never wed. Servitude you'd called it." He jerked his chin toward where Marcus had gone. "What about him?"

"He's going back. I can't leave." She shrugged with a

helpless smile, trying to ignore the ache in her heart. "It's not an option."

"So what will you do?"

She sighed. "Love him until he leaves."

Prescott pursed his lips, looking out the window. The cries of children playing wage-war could be heard outside. "Cat?"

"Yes?"

"I have a confession to make." His gaze met hers and the strain she saw in it tore her heart. "If the roles had been reversed. If it had been me coming in and finding you with him . . . Well, I wouldn't have stopped at tossing me to the floor." He grimaced. "I was milking it, I'll admit it." A glimmer of mirth entered his green eyes. "The old nursing sympathy ploy works almost as good as the knight in shining armor tactic."

She smiled, so glad to see the tension in him ease. "You always have one trick or another up your sleeve, Prescott Devane."

"Yes, well, someone has to keep things interesting around here."

Oh, if only he knew how very interesting things had been . . .

"You haven't insulted me in days." He sighed. "I wonder that this love business isn't dulling your sharp tongue."

"Don't fret, honey." Standing, she patted his shoulder. "I will always have an insult handy just for you, Prescott."

"Thank heavens, I was worried."

They shared a smile. Seeing how his eyes were red-rimmed and drooping and how the crease was back between his brows, she gently tucked the blanket. "You look dreadful."

"I wasn't begging for one now, Cat." His voice was thin with pain.

"No, really, you look wretched. Try to get some sleep."

"You just want to rush to your lover," he muttered.

She grimaced, her cheeks heating. "Guilty as charged."

Prescott tried to keep his voice light, "Oh, go on. I just hope he knows what a lucky bastard he is. If not, I might just have to kill him."

With a dreamy smile on her face, Cat planted a kiss on his temple. "I'll be back to look in on you soon."

"Not too quickly, I hope," he muttered.

Marcus had never wanted anybody this much in his entire lifetime. Cat had come to him at the guesthouse as she had before, but she was different this time. Oh, she had her usual double dose of passion that, as a rule, had him bounding eagerly like a hound after a bone. But this time, something had altered for her, and hence, for him as well.

Gone was the hesitation of a naïve woman exploring her passion. Cat was truly the lioness, aggressive in taking the lead and demanding her pleasure. Nothing in all of his years could match the effect of Cat's alteration on him. She made him feel so desired, so electrifyingly *wanted*, *needed* and *loved*, that he felt like a true Adonis.

And like any true god, he was panting after the mortal woman who had him begging on his knees for her.

He was breathless, his body throbbing, his skin afire with desire for this one woman who made him burn. Catherine Miller was the most beautiful creature on the face of the earth and touching her, kissing her, and listening to how she whispered his name was making Marcus happier than he'd ever thought he could be.

She lay stretched out naked before him, her arms entwined above her head in a golden halo of tresses. Her gray eyes were hooded, her pert nose glossy with sweat and her rosy lips open and swollen from his kisses. Her back was arched, emphasizing the roundness of her exquisite breasts and the curve of her luscious waist and derriere. Her porcelain skin was rosy with heat, enhanced by the play of golden sunlight washing in from the open window. She took his breath away. She was a masterpiece; but only his to savor.

"You are so beautiful," he murmured, bending forward on hands and knees to plant kisses along her bare collarbone. "My little lioness . . ."

She smiled, a slow, wicked grin that caused his rod to jump in anticipation.

"Me-ow," she purred, leaning up and licking his nipple.

Her tongue traced the hard nub, going around and around in electrifying circles. Then she took it whole into her mouth and suckled. He felt his groan all the way down to his shaft.

"Marcus," she moaned and it rippled through her tongue to his nipple.

He closed his eyes, wallowing in the desire pulsing through him. "God, I've missed you." It was a guttural cry.

Her hands traced his lower back, grazing over his bottom. With both hands, she grabbed his buttocks and squeezed.

"I love how you feel," she murmured, releasing him and gliding her hands up to his shoulders.

His mouth claimed hers and she tasted sweet, intoxicating, divine. He adored her, he realized, and couldn't get enough of her.

Wrapping her legs around his waist, she rocked her hips, propelling him toward that sacred crevice between her thighs. He pulled up, desperately fighting the urge to drive himself deep into her hot core.

"I want you inside of me, Marcus," she breathed. "Filling me."

"But . . ."

She pushed him aside and rolled on top of him, strad-dling his waist. "I'm not asking you, Marcus. I'm telling you." Lifting her hips, she arched her back and guided his shaft to the opening of her womanhood.

Her velvet heat tormented the head of his rod, making it stiffen even more with desire. He'd never been this hard in his life.

He knew that he should stop her, but for some reason he couldn't remember why.

Slowly she sank downward, sheathing him partway. It took every ounce of his self-control not to buck, not to ram himself full inside of her and mark her as his.

Sweat lined her upper lip and her body was taut with tension. She eased down with excruciating slowness.

He felt it, then. The tightness. The barrier that proved that she'd never been touched by any man, save for him. For all of her assertiveness, she was an innocent. His in-nocent. Guilt washed over him. He should be protecting her, especially from an undeserving cad like himself.

She wouldn't leave Andersen Hall; he understood her sense of duty and admired her for it. What would happen when he returned to the Peninsula? What would happen if she became with child? His child . . .

Was there a way? Cat was his, as clearly as if she were crafted by the gods just for him. If they could only just—

Her inner muscles clenched, driving all thoughts of the future from his mind. She plunged downward with a harsh gasp, sheathing him within her so wholly he saw stars. She felt fantastic, embracing him with her molten heat. No woman had ever felt better.

Cat dropped forward, her hair falling in golden waves. She was breathing hard, her arms quaking.

"Are you all right?" he cried, terrified that he'd torn her in some irreparable way. It shouldn't feel that bloody fantastic for him. He bit his lip, desperate not to move for fear that he would harm her further. He was a monster, a beast—

"Fine," she gasped. Shaking the hair away from her face, she sat up, clenching him so tightly within her he thought he might expire. She swallowed. "It's so much . . ."

It might just kill him, but he had to offer, "Do you want to stop?"

"Just give me a moment."

She stirred above him, and groaned. He felt the ripple from the head of his manhood to every part of his body.

"It hurts?" he bit out.

She shook her head, her golden hair shimmering in the light. "No," she breathed. "It feels, really . . ." Slowly, she shifted again. ". . . *really* good."

Her hips undulated.

His body thrummed, as if she were the musician and he her perfectly harmonious instrument. It felt so bloody sweet, he had to fight the desperate urge to close his eyes. But he wanted to see her face, appreciate her pleasure.

She smiled, moving this way, then that. He marveled at her obvious delight. She was like a child in a candy shop, hesitant at first, then relaxing and taking her fill.

Her pace quickened.

Her smile faded. Her brow locked with concentration. Her eyes closed, her mouth opened. Her golden hair whipped about her face as she rode him, spearing him deeper and deeper inside of her with every thrust. Her breasts bounced to her rhythm and he reached for them, grasping the soft mounds and teasing the hard, rosy nubs.

Her breath came fast as she placed her hands flat on his chest. "Am I doing this right?"

"Oh, yes."

"But you're watching me."

"You're exquisite," he breathed. "I want to see your beautiful face when you take your pleasure." *For the first time*. But it wouldn't be her last . . .

"But I don't want you watching me. I want you . . ." She ground her hips, rolling them back then forward, an excruciatingly delicious gyration. Pleasure rocketed straight through his shaft, making him gasp from it.

"Dear God!"

". . . Riding the wind with me."

"Don't stop," he choked out, clenching her waist.

He couldn't see her expression, his eyes were rammed shut. But she got the message. She gyrated her hips with that fantastic forward-and-back motion that made him want to scream, if he'd had any breath left in him.

A red haze swept over him where he only knew the heat, the raw animal tension, the yearning drive propelling him to that demanded release. So close, so damned close.

Blindly, he reached forward, finding the tight bud at the juncture of her thighs.

He heard a strangled cry. Her hot inner muscles clenched wildly, taking him over the edge, milking him. Lifting his hips, he pounded into her, pouring his seed, with a harsh grunt. His world collapsed into itself.

Cat fell atop him, their sweaty bodies slipping together in a vapor of musky passion. He could hardly breathe, simply gasped over and over, struggling for air. For sanity.

His arms were like deadweights as he wrapped them around her and cuddled close. He'd never felt this way before, he realized sleepily. He felt . . . home.

Chapter 35

Marcus woke to the sounds of boot steps clomping on wood. Years of training had him out of the bed and reaching for his uniform before he'd even woken. But his uniform wasn't where it was supposed to be on the edge of the bed.

He blinked, trying to stir the cobwebs from his mind. His clothes were strewn on the floor of the outer salon where Cat had ripped them off of his eager body. Cat. She was gone.

He almost wished that he hadn't insisted she leave for propriety's sake. She was probably at the main house seeing to Evie or Devane or handling the myriad issues he admired her for.

Deep voices filtered in through the wooden walls. He could count three, no four men outside. The outer door opened, then closed. They were in the salon.

He thanked his lucky stars that Cat was not here, as he grabbed the sheet and wrapped it about his waist. The last thing in the world she needed was to get caught in bed with him. He distantly recognized that the idea of a scandal that might force her to wed him held some appeal. But it would take more than a scandal to win Catherine's hand.

Wrapped only in a bedsheet, Marcus reached for his sword. Unsheathing it, he positioned himself a few paces directly before the threshold.

Tam opened the door.

Marcus let out a breath, relieved. He lowered his weapon. "Glad to see you, Tam."

"You as well, sir." The trusty sergeant had a pained expression on his face. From the look in his eyes, Marcus knew trouble was afoot.

"Who's outside?"

Closing the door, Tam approached and lowered his voice. "There's three men wantin' a word with you."

Resheathing his sword, Marcus dropped the sheet. "Hand me my boots."

"Uniform might be in order for this instance, if ya don't mind me saying so, sir."

Setting the sword within hand's stretch on the dresser, Marcus opened the wardrobe and reached for his white breeches. "Where's Cat?"

"Up at the main house."

"Did she see the men?"

"No, Timmy, the stable lad, sent them here first."

Score one for Timmy.

"The leader is a gent calling himself a Solicitor General," Tam explained as he helped Marcus into his shirt. "The other two are Bow Street Runners."

"They like to be called police constables or officers."

"I know." Tam walked over to the wardrobe and removed Marcus's crimson shako. He fluffed the white plume, and adjusted the gold adornment. "What's a Solicitor General, anyway?"

Marcus grabbed his crimson-and-gold coat and shrugged it on his shoulders. Oddly, Marcus felt somewhat uneasy putting it on. Probably because he hadn't worn it in a while, he dismissed. "He's a Law Officer of the Crown."

"What does that mean?"

"Nonmilitary. He's the Crown's legal representative on matters involving public welfare. In the courts, providing legal advice, questions or authority and the like."

"Ugh, a *lawyer*."

"They do make the world a wordy place," Marcus muttered, fastening the final brass buttons of his coat. "By the by, how are you feeling?"

"Like I've been trampled by that blasted mount instead of riding it." Tam handed him his sword. "But I've been worse."

"And you'll be better." Marcus secured his weapon and checked the knife in his boot. Wondering what an Officer of the Crown would want with him, he asked, "What's this Solicitor General's name?"

"Dagwood."

Something inside of Marcus hardened. "So he's not a magistrate anymore . . ."

"You know him?"

"I haven't seen him in a long time." About seven years. The last encounter involving Dagwood had gone dreadfully. Marcus had been so overwrought by his father's betrayal he could hardly stand.

But Marcus no longer felt like that enraged twenty-one-year-old. He was a man, well regarded, and . . . he suddenly realized, well loved. Catherine's kisses still felt as if they were upon him, marking him. He could almost hear her loving whispers still in his ear. The scent of their sweet lovemaking hovered all around him.

For the first time in as long as he could remember, Marcus didn't feel like the rug was about to be pulled out from under him. He felt good. He felt whole. Not even Dagwood could bother him now.

"Let us greet our guests, shall we?" He smiled, feeling better than he had in years.

"Magistrate Dagwood!" Marcus cried as he opened the door and stepped into the salon. He was relieved to see that trusty Tam had removed Marcus's strewn clothing. There was no evidence of the incredible seduction that had taken place only a few short hours before.

Dagwood lounged with his cane near the sofa, behind him the police officers were positioned near the closed door. Each Bow Street Runner wore street clothes with the requisite tipstaff hanging from his hip. One was wheat-haired, the other carrot-topped, close to the color Prescott's used to be. The men's hands rested easily at their sides and their faces were composed, as if they did not anticipate trouble. Marcus wondered what Dagwood had told them, then dismissed the thought. Dagwood was too self-preserving to share his secrets.

"It's Solicitor General, now, Dunn," Dagwood drawled with obvious irritation. Except for the streaks of silver at his temples, the attorney didn't appear much older than he'd been seven years before. Much of his hair remained jet-black, cut short in the Greek style, and his pallid face bore few of the telling lines of age. Still, some things never changed. Dagwood's eyes were still like black coals of burning ambition. The man had probably chewed his way to the top.

Marcus smiled. If the man gave him trouble, Marcus would give him something to chew on. Dagwood was a sheep to his wolf. "To what do we owe this unexpected pleasure?"

"You know why I'm here."

Marcus scratched his ear, commenting. "No, but I'm sure that you'll enlighten me soon enough." He waved to the sofa. "If you would?"

The attorney sat, making a production of adjusting his elegantly designed coat. It looked to be a Weston cut, dark blue with gilt buttons, with a pale cream waistcoat underneath topped by an enormous beige neckcloth and pointed collar. His black cane and hat appeared upper-notch as well.

"You've done well for yourself, Dagwood." Marcus positioned himself across from the man in a hard-backed wooden chair.

"By appearances you would seem to have done the same, *Major*." The attorney peered through his quizzing glass. "But I know better."

"How's that?"

Dagwood jerked his chin. "What happened to your injury? Last I saw you, you were practically an invalid. Now suddenly you are fit and whole. A contrivance, perhaps?"

"You saw me?"

"On Bond Street."

"And you didn't stop to acknowledge me?" Marcus pressed his hand to his heart. "I am wounded."

Dagwood scowled. "So what happened to your leg?"

"Luckily for me, I'm a quick healer."

Through the quizzing glass Dagwood gave Marcus a long, hard stare.

Marcus wondered if that actually worked to intimidate people. He realized that he no longer had the patience he once did for such games. Now, he had a woman to woo. "It's kind of you to visit, Dagwood. But I am a bit late for an appointment . . ." Marcus stood, indicating dismissal.

Dagwood dropped the monocle. "I'm not finished with you!"

"Then perhaps you would do me the courtesy of getting started." His tone was meant to be terse.

The attorney frowned. This interview was obviously not going as he had expected. "I am no longer a simple magistrate, Dunn. Try not to forget that my office supplies me with a certain amount of influence that can be exercised in many different ways."

Marcus didn't know to what exactly the man was referring, but he schooled himself to be careful. A Solicitor General could cause Andersen Hall unnecessary grief, and he did not want Cat or the children to have to pay for his insolence. Still, a man could only take so much.

"I simply do not wish to waste any more of your valuable time than I have to." Marcus leveled his tone. "So if you would simply get to the point of your visit, we would both be better served."

Dagwood blinked, staring at Marcus as if he were a conundrum. Seemingly less certain of himself, he turned to the police officers. "If you men would wait outside?"

"Yes, sir."

Marcus nodded to Tam. The sergeant followed the men out and closed the door.

The attorney adjusted his coat and rearranged his legs before him, obviously priming himself for a verbal sparring.

Marcus tried to contain his inner groan.

"I hear Lord Wellington's behind you." Dagwood sounded impressed.

"What do you want, Dagwood?"

His dark eyes gleamed with satisfaction. "How do you think your General Wellesley is going to feel when he hears that you've been arrested?"

Marcus smiled. "That depends, I suppose, on the charge."

"Burglary, of course."

"Is your career in such straits that you need to dig up old ghosts?" Marcus scoffed, removing his shako and setting it on his knee. He ran his gloved hand through his hair; the scent of lemons mixed with the heady odor of Cat's lovemaking was still upon him. Lord, he missed her already.

"Ghosts as old as last night?" Dagwood raised a brow.

Marcus scowled, annoyed. "What the blazes are you talking about?"

"Last night the Thief of Robinson Square burgled a fine home making off with, well, you know exactly what was stolen as"—he leaned forward dramatically—"you are the thief!"

"Did you come here expecting me to drop on my knees and confess?" Marcus shook his head, disbelieving. "Was that your grand plan?"

Dagwood's face flushed pink.

"It had to be, for, undoubtedly, you have no evidence against me." He shifted, uneasily recalling his father's betrayal. "You didn't seven years ago either. All you had was my father's word."

"I would have found the evidence—"

"And my father would have told your dirty secret to the world." Marcus had to marvel at his father's ingenuity. He did inform on his own son, but likewise found a way to save him from prosecution. For the first time, Marcus could truly appreciate his father's ingenuity. "But all of this is water under the bridge—"

"It's not; you broke your vow. We had a deal—"

"Which I have honored. Whatever you are talking about is not my doing."

"But the evidence!" Dagwood defended, his face blotching red. "The feather calling card, the unseen entry—"

"Everyone in London knew that modus operandi."

"But you're back in town."

"I was in Dover. Then Reigate. At Lord Hartz's estate." Marcus suddenly wondered why Cat hadn't asked about his visit with the Hartzes. She was probably as overwhelmed as he by the events surrounding his return.

Dagwood leaned back, seemingly less sure. "When did you come back?"

"Just this morning."

"You could have arrived early enough—"

"There are countless witnesses who can attest to my whereabouts at the inns where I took refreshments and changed horses." Marcus stretched his arms above his head; he was still sore from the hard ride and the deliciously hard riding done to him. "Sorry to disappoint, Dagwood. But you will actually have to catch the thief this time."

"But—"

Marcus dropped his arms. "There are no 'buts,' Dagwood. I didn't do it. More importantly, if you try to pin it on me, you will have to explain to the world why you let me go seven years ago."

Dagwood looked as if he'd swallowed a sour grape. "But if it's not you, then who?"

"I don't know and I don't really care." Marcus realized that that wasn't quite true. It irked his pride that someone had the gall to try to attach a crime to him, even if it was to his former nom de guerre.

Dagwood's face fell into a mask of defeat. At least he was smart enough to believe the truth when it was spelled out for him. The attorney shook his head, muttering to himself, "First Beaumont, now this . . ."

"Beaumont?" Marcus asked, curious at the man's sudden droop.

"I got the wrong man," Dagwood confessed, sighing. "I couldn't truly be blamed; the evidence was all there . . ." He shook his head. "They set the stage well, but I should have seen it. I should have dug further . . ." He scratched his head. "It wasn't even a case that I would normally assume . . . I was just so certain. So—"

"Bloody ambitious?" Marcus supplied.

Dagwood scowled, then shrugged, his face relaxing. "One does not become Solicitor General by resting on one's laurels." He exhaled noisily. "If I didn't know better, I'd think that someone was out to undermine me."

Marcus shrugged. "It's possible, I suppose."

"I'm full of myself, Dunn." Dagwood raised a brow. "But that does not mean that I imagine that the world revolves around me."

Marcus hid his surprise. Dagwood wasn't quite as contemptible as Marcus remembered him. But then again, Marcus had changed quite a bit himself in seven years.

"You're here on a mission, aren't you?" Dagwood suddenly asked.

Marcus didn't bother to reply.

"I could see how a sharp blade like Lord Wellington would use a man of your . . . unique talents."

Marcus straightened, warning calls sounding off in his head. "Don't get any ideas, Dagwood . . ."

Dagwood leaned forward, resting his elbows on his knees. "The Thief of Robinson Square is your persona. Doesn't it bother you, just a pinch, that someone else is trying to blame you for his crimes?"

Marcus had to hand it to the man; he knew how to pull the puppet strings. But Marcus was not dancing.

Dagwood slapped his knee. "Of course it does. Can't you just see the news accounts? 'Thief of Robinson Square Strikes Again.' Lord only knows what else they will try to blame you for."

Marcus shifted, uneasy. "I really am quite occupied . . ."

"The next thing you know," Dagwood continued, "you'll be responsible for Napoleon's next coup! And the thieves will get away, clean as a whistle, because of your inaction. Unless . . ." He scratched his chin, eyeing Marcus as if he were a shiny new sword all his own. "You help catch the thief usurping your name. Lord Wellington would certainly be willing to grant the Solicitor General a few days of your time if I explained how badly your skills are needed."

Marcus almost smiled. The man was good. And the offer was more tempting than he would ever have supposed. This would certainly provide a nice excuse for an extended stay in London with Cat before returning to duty. *Returning to the Peninsula.* The thought left him cold.

Leaving London meant leaving Cat. How far was he willing to go for her hand? He needed some time to canvass his efforts and figure out his campaign. Dagwood might just buy it for him.

"Just a few days," Marcus acquiesced, his tone terse. Dagwood didn't need to know that he was doing him any favors.

"Excellent!" Dagwood slapped his knee. "Who better to catch a thief than the master thief?"

"Yes," Marcus muttered, wondering what he'd just signed up for. "Who better?"

Chapter 36

Marcus and Dagwood went directly to the scene of the crime, the residence of Mr. Dickey and Lady Frederica Caddyhorn. Marcus had never met the couple, but from the Mayfair address and elegant furnishings, could tell that they were not without means.

He and Dagwood waited in the portrait gallery as a manservant droned on about the prestigious family lineage. The servant wore his brown-and-gold uniform like a badge of honor, obviously impressed with his employers and their imposing lineage. Marcus suspected that the oratory was par for the course for him.

"In sum, charitable to a fault was honorable Lady Margaret." The manservant's nasally voice echoed in the long rectangular gallery, as he motioned to the picture overhead. In it, the dark-haired, gray-eyed lady looked almost as bored as Marcus felt.

Inhaling dramatically, the servant moved toward the next picture on the wall. By Marcus's accounting that made seven portraits thus far.

"Where the hell are they?" Marcus muttered under his breath for Dagwood's ears only. "You'd think that they would want to meet with the men investigating their burglary. You are the bloody Solicitor General, for heaven's sake."

Dagwood's face was the mask of patience as the manservant stood beneath the next portrait waiting for them. "The position of Solicitor General is bestowed, Dunn. Don't forget, I am still a commoner." He coughed into his gloved hand. "Some in polite Society believe that it is due course to have others wait upon their convenience." He grimaced. "But, I must admit, this is a bit over the top."

As they drew near, the rotund servant waved a meaty gloved hand up at the picture. "This is the late Baron Coleridge."

Marcus glanced up at the portrait. A dark-haired, slate-eyed gentleman in a hunter green coat with gilded buttons stared back at him. The deceased baron had a handsome enough face, with a robust nose, firm mouth and dimpled chin. Bored, Marcus's eyes shifted back to the droning servant.

The man sniffed. "He was the brother to Mr. Caddyhorn."

Marcus's eyes drifted back to the portrait. There was something familiar about the man's countenance.

"A terrible carriage accident befell him—"

Something nagged at Marcus's memory. He had never met the late baron, he was sure. Could the man have been one of his father's donor's? The man had never served on the board of trustees of Andersen Hall, of that Marcus was certain. Marcus yanked on the thought like a seamstress pulls at an errant thread, but it would not unravel. "Was he the only victim?" Marcus stepped closer, trying to decipher what was niggling at him. The man vaguely looked like Cat's brother. But many people had gray eyes and dimpled chins.

"Nay. His wife died of injuries the next day."

Marcus looked around. "Where is her portrait?"

The manservant coughed into his white-gloved hand. "She is relegated to the east vestibule." He waved to his right. "Around the corner and down the far passage, if you wish to view it." The man didn't appear interested in making the journey.

Dagwood glared at the opposite doorway, as if staring at it might summon the absent Caddyhorns. Over his shoulder, he asked vaguely, "Why? Was she a commoner?"

"Her lineage was good enough, but her father was in *trade*." The man said the word as if it were a disease.

"Were there any children?" Marcus pressed, a strange idea swirling into his mind. But many people were distant relatives in London. Resemblances were commonplace.

"Wait a moment." Dagwood turned to the manservant, his face suddenly interested. "I heard something about Mr. Caddyhorn seeking his brother's title. Why is a petition required?"

"A tragedy . . ." From the man's tone it was obviously an oft-told story. "Baron Coleridge's young son drowned—"

Marcus felt an inward disappointment somehow. But nay, it had been a far-fetched thought anyway. "Was he the only child?"

"No."

"What happened to the other?"

The stout manservant's face tinged pink. "Well, there was a girl, older than the lad. But she's dead, too."

Marcus shot Dagwood a look, raising his brow. A foul wind hovered around the Caddyhorns, it seemed. "How did she die?"

"She drowned." The manservant's face contorted, as if he suddenly realized how odd it sounded.

"Two children drowned?" Dagwood's tone had taken on a prosecutorial edge.

Marcus gladly stepped aside and let Dagwood do the questioning.

"How? When?" the Solicitor General asked.

"Together." The manservant swallowed. "I wasn't in service then, I simply heard the tales . . ."

Dagwood stepped closer, raising his quizzing glass to his eye and glaring at the man. Marcus had to give Dagwood credit; the manservant practically quaked. "What tales?"

Sweat popped out on the manservant's brow, and he glanced at the empty doorway as if to beckon help. "Well, the children, they ran away . . ."

"When?"

"About fifteen years ago or so." He mopped his brow with his gloved hand. "Or maybe it was thirteen. I don't know, for certain."

"What time of year?" Marcus asked, trying to determine the weight of the motivation for their flight.

"Around Christmastide."

"In the dead of winter . . ." Marcus murmured. "Something had to compel them not to return, you'd think . . ."

"Well, the girl was mad." The manservant yanked at the stiff collar of his uniform. "Crazy as a loon, they said. Dragging off her young brother in the winter's night."

"Crazy," Marcus muttered, recalling the faces of the children at Andersen Hall. "Or desperate."

"So what happened to them?" Dagwood demanded.

"Their tracks led to a riverbank. They were never found."

Marcus looked up. "No bodies?"

"Nay. Some say they were eaten by wolves."

Could it be? It was so far-fetched . . .

Dagwood shot Marcus a skeptical look. Then he turned to the servant. "It's been many years, why the need for the petition for the title to pass?"

The manservant shifted from foot to foot, his face miserable.

"I can find out well enough from fifty different sources," Dagwood chided. "No one has to know it was you who told."

"Lady Huntington."

Dagwood nodded. "Ahh,"

"Ahh, what?" Marcus asked.

"Lady Huntington is notoriously stubborn and her husband is an influential member of the House of Lords. If she chooses to impede someone, she is willing to labor to do it."

"Why should she care?"

"She is a distant relative of my employers." The manservant coughed into his fist. "And she was very close with the late Baron Coleridge's wife."

"The one whose portrait is relegated to the east vestibule?" Marcus enquired.

"One and the same."

"So she took issue with how Lady Coleridge was treated by your employers during her lifetime and does not wish to see them profit by her death," Marcus concluded.

"That's the sum of it. Lady Huntington is not exactly a favorite in this household," the servant supplied in modulated tones.

"There you are!" a deep voice cried from the entryway.

Marcus turned.

Clutching his satchel to his chest, Mr. Gillis practically

stampeded toward them with a wiry gold-and-brown-uniformed servant struggling to keep up from behind. Gillis halted before them, his black shoes scuffing the shiny hardwood floor. "Don't say a word, Marcus!" he wheezed. "Not a word!"

Dagwood turned to both servants. "If you would excuse us?"

The servants couldn't seem to escape fast enough.

"Calm down before you get an attack of the heart, Gillis," Marcus chided.

And Marcus was not jesting. The pudgy man was panting and huffing, his plump face shiny with sweat and his clothes looked as if they'd been trampled, they were so wrinkled and askew.

Dagwood frowned, obviously not happy to see the second man in London to know his secrets. "There is no need for dramatics, Mr. Gillis, Dunn is not under arrest."

Still huffing, Mr. Gillis adjusted his gold-rimmed spectacles on his bulbous nose. "He's not?"

Dagwood turned to Marcus. "I'm going for a walk to see if I can't 'happen upon' our hosts. I will leave it to you to explain." He strolled off in the opposite direction from that the servants had taken.

Gillis looked up, craning his head. "Truly? You are not under arrest?"

"I appreciate your rush to my defense, Gillis. But I do wish you'd have more faith." He lifted a shoulder. "Truth be told, I am giving Dagwood a bit of assistance."

The attorney's mouth opened, then closed. His lids fluttered behind his spectacles, his gaze disbelieving.

Marcus scowled. "I would not breach my vow, Gillis. I have not assumed the mantle of the Thief of Robinson Square for seven years."

"But, I thought . . ." He scratched his mussed graying

hair. "I heard it was the Caddyhorns burgled and that the feather was left, your calling card, so to speak. And well, I thought it had to be you."

Marcus straightened, recalling that elusive sense of familiarity and his far-fetched notion. "Am I supposed to be acquainted with them?"

"You mean you don't know about . . . ?" His voice drifted off, making Marcus want to grab him and shake the end of the sentence out of him.

Instead, he gritted his teeth. "Please enlighten me, Mr. Gillis."

"I assumed that Miss Miller must have told you . . ." the attorney muttered, his head wobbling.

Marcus's insides suddenly went cold. "What would Cat have told me?"

Gillis looked up. His eyes were watery and he bit his lip as if on the verge of tears. "I miss your father. So much . . ." Still clutching his case, he removed his spectacles and rubbed his eyes. "If they had anything to do with it . . ."

"Please tell me what you're talking about, Mr. Gillis," Marcus urged.

Replacing his spectacles, the attorney sniffed, composed once more. "Your father was challenging the Caddyhorns' petition for the title. He asked me to keep the reportage . . . in case." His voice caught. "If anything happened to him."

Marcus started, stunned. Renfrew's protests reared in his mind. If Renfrew hadn't hired his father's killer . . .

Gillis continued, "I knew that your father had given you your journal, so I presumed you'd taken up your old persona—"

"My journal?" Marcus stepped backwards, feeling like he'd taken a blow. "My father burned it."

"But it was in the—" Gillis sighed. "You haven't read the will."

Looking away, Marcus bit out, "I haven't . . . been able to face it."

"Many relatives are loath to read a dear one's will," Gillis's tone was matter-of-fact. "For fear of what it might say or to have to acknowledge the death . . . It's a common enough reaction." He shook his head. "But if you aren't the thief, then who is?"

Marcus met the man's eyes. "What did the will say, Mr. Gillis?"

"The document is a fairly straightforward business. A few personal items to some of the staff and friends and any funds he had available went to Andersen Hall. But regarding you . . ." Clutching his case, Gillis held up a finger of his brown-gloved hand. "First, his prized book collection."

Marcus's heart skipped a beat. "He gave me his books?" His father had loved those tomes as if they were his flesh and blood.

"I had suggested that he donate them to the orphanage, but he wanted you to have them."

"I can't believe that he entrusted me with his library . . ."

"Two." Gillis raised another finger. "Your father gave you your mother's wedding ring, in the hopes that someday you would start a family of your own."

Catherine's lovely face flashed in Marcus's mind. It would be so fitting, so *right* for her to wear it. A lump formed in his throat. His father would have been so pleased about him and Catherine. Oh, how joyous Uriah Dunn would have been that they would have his grand-children . . .

Marcus coughed into his fist to hide his discomfiture. He refused to fall to pieces in front of Gillis. "What else?"

"A letter. He would not let me read it, but he told me that it was an—" The attorney cleared his throat, obviously displeased. "Apology. For what happened seven years ago. With it he included the only key to the master's closet. Therein lies your journal, hidden for the past seven years."

"Why didn't he burn it?"

"Said he couldn't. That it wasn't in his nature to destroy a 'masterpiece.'"

Dumbstruck, Marcus shook his head. "He called it a masterpiece?"

"Yes. He told me that he regretted that he'd driven you away and hoped that someday you could forgive him."

Something deep inside Marcus's chest twisted with bittersweet agony; his father was asking for his forgiveness. He let out a deep breath, astounded by these revelations. "When did he write this will?"

"The day after your return. He told me that the master closet had been sealed for years, but that he'd recently had the cupboard cleaned so that you could get to his hiding place when the time came. Miss Miller had just locked it and given him the key."

The Caddyhorn burglary was too perfect, too much his original style, and it was too much of a coincidence that the hiding place had been recently opened. Who had his journal?

He had been careful not to include anything personal in the book to mark it as his. So he doubted that anyone could know that he was the original Thief of Robinson Square. So who had assumed his nom de guerre?

Then it dawned on him. "Cobwebs," Marcus whispered. "Cat had cobwebs in her hair."

Timmy had complained about Cat tearing off in the night. She'd been carrying men's clothing. Covering his eyes, Marcus shook his head. Would she be so bold? So wretchedly reckless? But why?

"What does Cat, Miss Miller, know about my father and the Caddyhorns?" Marcus demanded, looking up.

"She knew about his efforts to stop the title petition . . ." Gillis's pallid cheeks blotched red. "And I suppose, I *may* have intimated that the Caddyhorns intended your father harm. I must confess since her visit I have been plagued by the horrible notion that they are somehow involved in your father's murder."

His insides turned to ice. The Caddyhorns. Not Renfrew. Could it be?

"Your father shared many of his secrets with Miss Miller, but I doubt he ever told her about you being the thief," Gillis avowed, then eyeing the doorway, lowered his voice. "Do you suppose that she discovered the journal and gave it to someone? Certainly Miss Miller couldn't be the burglar."

Marcus straightened. "Why the hell not?"

"Well, she's a female," Gillis huffed. "And, if you haven't noticed, she's lame."

Marcus shook his head, amazed at the man's obtuseness. Then he recalled how he'd pictured Cat when he'd first encountered her again in his father's study. He'd been a fool, he realized, not to see the magnificent woman she'd become. Moreover, he couldn't recall her leg impeding her in any real way. Thoughts of her perfectly formed porcelain calf flitted through his mind. No, she was sound in body and in spirit.

"Besides, it's not in Miss Miller's nature," Gillis added. "She's cautious. Understands the consequences of such foolish action. No." He made a downward, cutting motion. "There is no way on earth it could be her."

Gillis was right about one thing: Cat was cautious, and smart. It would take real inducement for her to embark on such a dangerous burglary. He'd done his larceny as a way of thumbing his nose at his father and all that he'd represented. That, and as a monumental challenge—just to prove he could do it. It had been a perfect training ground for his work for Wellington, he realized. But it had been reckless in the extreme. For Cat to undertake such folly she'd have to be compelled by something cataclysmic.

Did she really believe that the Caddyhorns were behind his father's murder? His lioness was most protective of those she loved. *Those she loved*. Jared . . . She'd never asked Marcus about his trip to Reigate. The Hartzes had told him that Sir John Winston and his son had returned to town. Marcus's anger seethed. If they had threatened Cat or her brother in any way . . .

Brother. A sister and younger brother. The thought flashed in his mind like lightning. The servant had said fifteen years ago. But if he'd been wrong . . . If it had been more like ten . . . And if Cat knew that his father had been investigating the Caddyhorns . . . The pieces slipped into place.

Cat had burgled the Caddyhorns' house.

His hands clenched and unclenched as he fought to contain his fury. The idea of her alone, climbing that rooftop . . . He was going to kill her.

What had she been thinking to place herself at such risk? And for what reward? Her life was worth more than a thousand jewels! But his Cat never cared for trinkets, she had no material ambitions. She was doing it for her brother, for his father and for herself, he realized. Her brother needed funds to pay off Thomas Winston; for his father, vengeance; and for Cat, some small semblance of justice.

He couldn't fault Cat. Hell, he admired the heck out of

her for her courage. His dear, lovely lioness had taken matters into her own hands, just as he himself would have done in her place. She had been doing so, apparently, for many years. She had to have been only twelve when she'd stolen her brother away from the Caddyhorns and found them a safe haven at Andersen Hall. Astute Cat had recognized the danger to them, it seemed.

Anger infused him. The Caddyhorns deserved a reckoning. Thomas Winston as well. And any other bastard who tried to hurt the woman of his heart.

Gillis's eyes lit up and he raised a stubby finger in the air. "I know who did it! Miss Miller must have given the book to the real Baron Coleridge and *he* must've executed the burglary!" Slowly, his finger drooped. "But that can't be. The real baron, if he were still alive, would only be about thirteen or fourteen or so."

Marcus gripped the attorney's arms, drawing his face close. "Don't say anything to anyone about the journal, the thief, anything! Do you promise? On my father's honor, do you swear?"

Gillis practically quaked, as he hugged his satchel to his chest. His eyes were wide with wonder. "On Uriah Dunn's honor, I swear."

Releasing him, Marcus spun on his heel and raced out the door.

Gillis watched Marcus rush from the portrait gallery, his eyes traveling over the closest painting on the wall.

"Dear Lord . . ." His paper case dropped to the floor with a *whoosh* of strewn foolscap.

The man had the look of Jared Miller. Older, bigger, but it was there if you knew to look.

Gillis pressed his hand over his mouth, tasting leather and bile. Uriah Dunn had been protecting the Miller children from their own relations!

With his heart pounding, Gillis got down on his hands and knees. Blindly, he picked up his papers and shoved them haphazardly into his case. Fury burned through him with righteous ferocity. "Vengeance will be yours, Uriah Dunn. I will see to it if it's the last thing I ever do."

Gillis knew he was going up against ruthless blackguards. But that didn't matter. He'd line up every resource, wield every weapon—

Gillis straightened. Realization smacked him on the head harder than Mrs. Nagel's broom.

Slowly, he stood, pushed up his spectacles and adjusted his coat. Then, leaving the rest of his papers scattered about the floor, Gillis went to find Solicitor General Dagwood.

Chapter 37

〜❦❦〜

"**F**or the last time," Clarence Kruger bit out, leaning over the green chintz sofa where his employers sat, "if you think that you're going to cut me out—"

"I swear I didn't take them!" Lady Frederica Caddyhorn shrieked, shaking her fat arms so wildly, they quaked like blubber.

Kruger knew that her purple gown and trimmings cost more than his month's wages and she was not about to bilk him. "I'm not a fool!" He pressed his fists so hard into the sofa's wooden border that his knuckles ached. "You slept with the damned jewels under your head. Who the hell else could have taken them?"

"The Thief of Robinson Square!"

"Don't give me that twaddle!" Kruger scoffed, crossing his arms so hard that his black coat pinched at the shoulders. "The thief hasn't burgled in years and suddenly he makes off with the loot that *we* were planning to steal?" Tilting his head, he confessed, "I'll admit the feather was

347

a nice touch, but no one, especially not anyone in this
room, believes that you slept through a man entering your
bedroom in the middle of the night." Lifting a hand he
studied his fingernails. "Why, it's been so long, you'd
have probably screamed with shock."

Dickey Caddyhorn shot Kruger an irritated look expressing, "Don't cause me trouble." Well, Clarence
Kruger would inconvenience his employers no bloody
end, if Lady Frederica didn't cough up his share of the
booty.

Lady Frederica's eyes narrowed. "How dare you—"

Dickey held up a hand. "Let me manage this, Kruger."
He turned to his wife, his sooty gray eyes imploring.
"Why did you move ahead with the plan, Freddie, dear?
The insurance certificates have only been in place for four
months. We'd agreed on six, at least, before we acted—"

"Someone else must have taken them, I tell you." Her
voice had taken on that high-pitched whiny tone that she
thought was cute. Kruger was sure that everyone else in
the world found it as annoying as he did.

Lady Frederica's gold turban slipped into her eyes and
she shoved it aside. "Perhaps that new maid—"

Kruger had had enough of his pinch-fisted mistress.
"Don't take me for a fool! I selected your new maid myself, because she's too beef-witted to cause trouble . . .
when we stole the jewels. We. Not you!"

Dickey scowled up at him. "Don't raise your voice to
my wife, Kruger."

"And I'm supposed to believe that she did this on her
own?" Kruger scoffed. "The lady doesn't fart without asking you first!"

Dickey stood, adjusting his maroon-and-fawn coat.
"There's no need for vulgarity, Kruger."

The man of affairs smirked. Even to the top of his dark curly hair Dickey was still a handspan shorter and had to crane his neck to look up at his employee. Well, Clarence was top-sawyer to his employer in more ways than one. "And murder's not vulgar?"

Dickey's cheeks reddened and his slate eyes lanced to the closed door. "Guard your tongue," he hissed. "The servants will hear."

"I have more dirt on your family than any headmaster can dig up in thirty years." Kruger banged his chest, demanding his just due. "I'm the one who found Furks. I'm the one who set it up—"

"If you're so peacock proud about it, then why did you insist that I be the one to pay him?" Dickey snarled.

"Leverage. Your hands are now as dirty as mine."

"I don't know that that's possible," Dickey muttered under his breath.

"Didn't you notice the name of the man accompanying the Solicitor General?" Kruger cooed.

Dickey frowned.

"No, of course you didn't, did you. All you heard was Solicitor General and your mind went to mush." Shaking his head, Kruger couldn't fathom what Dickey would have done without him over the last thirteen years. "Major Dunn. *Dunn*. Sound familiar?"

Lady Frederica's face drained of color. She looked to her husband. "Dickey?"

Dickey shrugged. "It could be a coincidence." But a new pinch of worry marred his dark brow.

"Now, why do you think a Solicitor General would bring a man named Dunn to your home?" Kruger needled.

"Look, Kruger." Dickey's tone was glib as he held his hands open wide and set a broad, yellow-stained smile on his face. He was drawing on his charming act, now. "We have always been in these things together. Equally involved—"

"Equally?" Kruger snickered. "Equally? You weren't the one draggin' through the snow chasing after those brats. You weren't the one cleaning up after your son's depraved messes, paying off every person with a greasy palm just so he didn't wind up dead in an alley. Beating whores, cheating at cards, even horse thievery! But I suppose pilfering runs in the family, eh?"

Lady Frederica's eyes narrowed. "Don't you talk about my Stannie that way!"

"Every charge you lay at our feet lands mud on your shoes, too, is all that I am saying." Dickey pulled out his gold snuffbox and took a pinch. "We are in this together."

"Then give me my share of the loot!"

Dickey sneezed twice and grasped the bridge of his nose, his eyes watering. Taking a handkerchief from his coat, he wiped his face. "We will get to the bottom of this, Kruger. I promise you."

"Bottom?" Kruger pointed to Lady Frederica's lardy rear. "There's your bottom!"

"I'm warning you, Kruger." Dickey glared. "Don't think yourself so above station that you can speak to my wife that way. No one speaks about my Frederica like that!"

Except for him, of course. Kruger had listened to Dickey complaining about his whining, overindulged squab of a wife for years. The litany of complaints ran so long a bloody bookkeeper couldn't tabulate them. Dickey had married Lady Frederica for her connections. She might be the daughter of an earl, but that obviously did not make her a great bed partner.

Thinking of all of the mistresses he had had to set up

and pay off over the years, Kruger's fury boiled. "You'd better make good, *Dickey*. Or there'll be hell to pay."

"Sweetling," Lady Frederica cooed, reaching for her husband's hand.

Dickey's eyes flickered down to his wife.

"I swear on my love for you that I did not take those jewels." She squeezed his wrist. "I wouldn't do that. Not without you."

Kruger recrossed his arms. "My point exactly."

Dickey's dark brows knitted and his wiry lips set in a hard firm line; a mulish look that Kruger knew well. "If my wife says she didn't take them, then she didn't take them. Now we just need to figure out who—"

"I've served you now for over thirteen years and this is how you repay me?" Kruger's voice had risen to a shriek, all of the anger and frustration of serving these grasping ingrates bubbled forth. "There's a Solicitor General downstairs. All I have to do is let him in on a few family secrets—"

"You wouldn't dare," Dickey sneered. "You'll land in prison. We've got connections, money for barristers. What have you got, Clarence Kruger? Nothing. You're nothing without us. And you'll swing for certain if you open your big mouth."

Lady Frederica hoisted herself off of the couch and turned her full form at Kruger. "How do we know that *you* didn't do it?"

"What?" he sputtered. "How can you think that?"

Crossing his arms, Dickey tilted his head and glared at Kruger. "Yes. You knew the plan. Perhaps you're the one who proceeded ahead of schedule."

"Why would I do that?" Kruger ground out, so frustrated he wanted to spit nails. "When the insurance certificates are in your name?"

"There's a fortune in jewels in that case—"

"Which I would get my share of, plus more, *when we made the claims.*"

Dickey wagged a stubby finger. "If I find out that you've double shuffled us—"

A knock resounded at the door.

Three pairs of eyes flew to the wood-paneled entry.

Lady Frederica grabbed her husband's arm, but he shoved her off.

"There's no need for melodrama," Dickey chided. "It's probably just Jenkins."

But Jenkins never tapped on the door like that. Rule of thumb in the Caddyhorn household was for servants to announce the presence with a call, "Jenkins at the door, sir." Then wait on their master's pleasure. All around the household servants walked about exclaiming their whereabouts. Unaccountably, the Caddyhorns thought that this lessened the possibility of eavesdropping. Notwithstanding, they routinely closed doors and stuffed keyholes with an enthusiasm that bordered on fixation.

Another tap reverberated, harder this time. "If I might have a word, Mr. Caddyhorn," came an unfamiliar male voice.

Lady Frederica's eyes widened. "What shall we do?"

Dickey frowned. "I can't believe that a Law Officer of the Crown would walk about our house unattended—"

Kruger checked his timepiece. "You've left him downstairs for over an hour . . ." His voice trailed off. Where had the time gone? A little stewing time was one thing for a guest, but over an hour? The man was probably furious.

"Dickey?" Lady Frederica whined. "What shall we do?"

Dickey swallowed, then set his shoulders. "Nothing, absolutely nothing. We are the victims here. We've done nothing wrong."

Kruger snorted.

Dickey shot him a glare. "If we keep calm and hold together, then it will all work out just fine. Remember, you are Lady Frederica Caddyhorn. Let us not let anyone forget who your father is. So mouths shut and follow my lead."

"Calm and together." She nodded, adjusting her slipping turban. "Mouths shut and follow your lead."

Dickey looked his way, and Kruger supplied, "I'm not stupid. Mouths shut. You do the talking."

"Very well." Clearing his throat, Dickey called, "Come."

Bit by bit, the entry yawned open and a dark-haired gentleman with sharp, almost black eyes peeked in. "Ah, here you are."

Where is a bloody servant when you need one? Kruger silently groused. But he pasted a servile smile on his face just the same.

The audacious man used his black cane to push the door open wider and step across the threshold. Kruger was fairly certain who the man had to be, but he held his tongue, waiting to follow his employers' direction.

The uninvited man looked at each of them in turn, his gaze assessing. He was dressed in a crisp navy coat with gold gilt buttons. Seeing the intricate knot of his tie and the shine of his black calf-high boots, Kruger noted that the gentleman was obviously of some means and fastidious about his appearance. Kruger wondered if he dealt with his legal responsibilities in the same fashion. He swallowed, tasting fear on his tongue.

Removing his tall black hat, the dark-haired gentleman nodded to the Caddyhorns. "Solicitor General Dagwood, at your service."

"He did it!" Lady Frederica shrieked, pointing a stubby finger at Kruger's chest. "He stole my jewels!"

"Why, you bloody hag!" Kruger leaped over the sofa and knocked the fat bitch to the ground, grabbing her fleshy throat in his hands.

Dickey jumped on his back, pressing Kruger obscenely against the lady's corpulent breasts. If he weren't so furious, Kruger would have been ill.

"Unhand her!" Dickey looked up at the Solicitor General. "He's a murderer! Can't you see? Help!"

"Get off me, you swine!" Kruger swung over his shoulder and cuffed his employer in the jaw.

The lout rolled over and crashed into the armchair, bleating like a goat. "He struck me!" Dickey shrieked, hugging his jaw. "Did you see that?"

Lady Frederica ripped her nails across Kruger's face, burning his flesh. "Bitch!" He slapped her, and her head whipped back, giving him so much satisfaction he wished he'd done it a few years before. She let out a whimper, then fainted dead away.

Disgusted, Kruger removed himself from the rotund mound and stood. He righted his cravat, adjusted his black coat, then stepped before the Law Officer.

Dagwood's countenance was the epitome of calm, as if witnessing such mêlées was common. "Who are you?" he asked, casually leaning on his black cane.

"My name is Clarence Kruger. I am Mr. Caddyhorn's man of affairs."

"I assume that you have a grievance with your employer?" the Law Officer supplied.

"They stole the jewels for an insurance claim."

"Don't listen to a word he says, Dagwood," Dickey cried, using the armchair to push himself up to stand. "He's mad. Has no idea of what he speaks."

Kruger stepped closer to the Law Officer. "I have records and all the proof you'll need."

"Lies!" Dickey adjusted his coat. "Fallacious nonsense! He's a madman. Didn't you see how he attacked my wife? I want the blackguard arrested immediately!"

A pudgy man suddenly appeared at the threshold behind Dagwood. His eyes widened as his gaze swept from Dickey leaning on the armchair to Lady Frederica sprawled on the floor. He stepped gingerly through the door, his rumpled brown coat, wrinkled breeches and scuffed shoes fairly screaming "dowd."

"These are the infamous Caddyhorns?" The disheveled man's tone was derisive.

"Who the hell are you?" Dickey snapped, rubbing his jaw.

Dagwood turned to the pudgy man. "You're not planning on representing these scoundrels are you, Gillis?"

Gillis. The lawyer. The one whose office he burgled. Kruger's armpits began to sweat, as the reality of his fix set in. His mind scrambled for any means of saving his hide.

"Not in a million years," Gillis answered Dagwood. He looked over at Dickey, declaring proudly, "I'm the man who's going to watch you hang, Caddyhorn. And ensure that you swing high." He stepped closer to Dagwood, his lips curled in disgust, as if sickened by the Caddyhorns. "They arranged Uriah Dunn's murder—"

"He did it!" Kruger pointed his finger at Dickey, knowing that if he had to burn, he'd take every last Caddyhorn with him. "He met with Conrad Furks—"

"Don't listen to a word he says, Dagwood! You can see he's round the bend! Crazy as a loon!"

"—at the Rose and Crown Tavern."

Dickey's fisted hands shook at his sides, but he was obviously trying to appear unruffled. "My wife's father, *the Earl of Ingham*, warned me about Kruger's propensities for flights of fancy. But I took pity on the poor man—"

"He paid Furks three hundred guineas! And I have record of the whole thing!"

"You kept records!" Dickey shrieked. "Records!"

"Just in case," Kruger smirked. At the murderous look on Dickey's face, he scrambled behind Dagwood for protection.

"I'm going to rip your black heart out!" Dickey charged.

Gillis stretched out his stubby leg and Dickey went hurtling, arms and legs flying, across the room, crashing into the pedestal cupboard by the door. The urn sitting on top of it teetered, almost as if swaying in a gentle breeze. Then it fell, crashing directly on top of Dickey's head. Dickey wore a crown of crumbly porcelain, dusting his dark mane a chalky white.

A hoarse laugh erupted from Kruger's throat. He cackled as Dickey floundered about, trying to stand on the broken porcelain pieces. The man's white-dusted hair was wild about his face like a crazed owl, and he groaned, "Kill . . . you . . ."

"Who's cracked now, Dickey?" Kruger cried, laughing.

Lady Frederica awoke with a start. "I'm blind! I'm blind!" she shrieked, her turban having listed over her face.

Kruger clutched his belly, hooting and laughing so hard he almost choked. And it felt so good, he almost didn't think about the hangman's noose.

"One wonders where the servants are with such ruckus going on," Dagwood muttered to Gillis. "And where are Kim and Kelly?"

Just then two Bow Street Runners charged into the room waving their tipstaffs and shouting for calm.

That's when the real trouble began.

Chapter 38

⎯⎯∾◦∾⎯⎯

Sitting on Marcus's bed in the guesthouse, Catherine stared at the snowy white pearls rolling around in her palm. Her mother's necklace; so lovely, like a luminous mound of teardrops. Her emotions felt like that strand, jumbled and knotted. She needed Marcus to help her untangle the perplexing feelings whipping through her with a velocity that left her quaking.

Where is he? It was growing late. Already a cool evening breeze drifted in through the window, carrying the scent of pine. Night was descending, the darkness unfurling into the day and blanketing the light.

The edifying Timmy had informed her that Marcus had taken off with an acquaintance of consequence, the Solicitor General. A gentleman named Dagwood. As they'd entered their coach, Timmy had overheard the Solicitor General tell his men that Marcus was assisting them. Catherine was impressed and wondered what it was about. But whatever he was doing, she prayed it wouldn't keep him from her for too long.

For the hundredth time in an hour, she stared at the shiny white baubles, trying to understand her confounding feelings. She'd accomplished a heretofore unimaginable feat, reclaimed some of her legacy, and gotten what she would need to save her brother. Yet it all felt so wretchedly *wrong*. The burglary had left her with a sour taste on her palate.

She realized now that Jared's predicament had provided the excuse she'd needed to go after the Caddyhorns. Deep down it was something she'd wanted to do for years but had been too afraid.

Until Marcus had resurfaced.

Since he'd returned, her life had gone from leaden gray to vibrant color. And she didn't want to live any longer under gloomy skies, waiting for it to pour. Instead, she wanted to kick off her shoes and dance in the rain. Chase after that rainbow.

It was his example that had moved her to don the mantle of the Thief of Robinson Square and make a claim for her destiny. He was so brave and selfless in ferreting out traitors for his country. It might have been the Thief's book that had guided Catherine last night, but it had been Marcus's spirit inspiring her onward.

But Marcus's deeds were heroic, motivated for the better good. Aside from paying off the Winstons (which didn't feel particularly laudable), what good had Catherine accomplished? All she'd done was to put the authorities on her heels and give herself something else to worry about.

Looking back, she realized that what she'd really wanted from the burglary was her deepest wish for the last ten years: for everything to be as it once was. Before her parents had died, before the Caddyhorns had taken over. But stealing the Caddyhorns' jewels did not bring back her parents. Possessing her family heirlooms didn't resuscitate her lost childhood. Granted, wounding the Caddyhorns where they'd suffer it most had felt really good . . . But the emotion had been surprisingly short-lived.

As the morning had stretched into the day and drifted into the evening, Catherine had realized a great many things, some of them inordinately disquieting. She'd been living in fear, she realized, thirsting for vengeance that could never be had, and in some respects, not living at all. She'd been *surviving*, existing until the next difficulty surfaced. She felt like she'd been going from one dilemma to the next, never once stopping to enjoy the beauty of the moment.

Jared had been right; Catherine had become a bitter old crone at the tender age of two-and-twenty.

Until Marcus. When she was with him she felt free. Safe from worry. Happy, even. He'd given her the pleasure of flying on his wind. To experience life and joy for the first time in so many, long difficult years. Whenever he was near she truly felt like the air she breathed was freer, the sun brighter and the world a richer place. Even before she'd shared his bed.

She had no regrets about losing her innocence with him. In fact, just the opposite. Something had changed for her this morning. The last vestiges of her restraint had slipped off. She felt like a caged bird suddenly set free to spread her wings and soar.

It wasn't just the bed-sport that had liberated her, she recognized. But the sharing of some deep part of herself that no one else had ever touched. For that moment, at least, she'd belonged to Marcus. And he'd been very much a part of her. Together what they'd shared had been . . . magical. She'd never felt anything like it, and wondered if he'd felt it, too.

"Cat." Marcus stood in the doorway, so handsome in his crimson-and-gold uniform he stole the breath from her throat.

"Marcus, I'm so glad to see you." Dropping the necklace, she jumped from the bed and rushed toward him. But at the strained look on his face, her steps slowed. "What's wrong?"

He stood uneasily, not advancing into the room. Slowly, he reached up and removed his crimson shako, the white plume waving gently in his hand. Cat was reminded of another feather, one left underneath Lady Frederica's pillow. She shook her head, overwhelmed by her folly. She could have lost her life, could have lost her only chance with Marcus.

But something was wrong with him. His face was flushed; guilt seemed to flash in his azure gaze and he seemed to be scrutinizing her as if she were a heretofore unknown entity. She felt like saying, "It's only me!" but instead held her tongue, waiting for him to tell her what was amiss.

Marcus set his shako on the dresser and removed his gloves. Then, walking over to her, he grasped her hand and led her to the bed. The feel of his touch was reassuring, but his mien was far less so. His handsome face was grave, his movements solemn. He pulled her down beside him, sinking the mattress with his brawny frame.

"We need to talk, you and I," he murmured somberly.

Ignoring the fear in her gut, she searched his dear face, trying to understand what was wrong. His usually twinkling eyes were filled with worry, his smooth, sweet lips pinched. He looked so upset and, she, seemingly, was the cause. She could see it in his bearing and how when he looked at her, he appeared somehow pained.

Marcus looked over at the necklace lying on the cover-let, distracted. "What's that?"

"My mother's pearls."

His face contorted with grief, and he shook his head. "I must have been blind not to see. I'm a cad, a selfish bas-tard, Cat. I never asked you about—"

"Stop insulting the man I love," she interrupted, squeezing his hand.

"But I've never even asked how you came—" He blinked, then his eyes widened. The vulnerability she saw in his gaze almost made her want to cry. "What did you say?"

"No one has the right to abuse the man I love. Even you."

"You love me?" He swallowed. "Truly?"

"I do. You are my wind."

His mouth worked. "Your wind?"

"Yes, when I'm with you, I fly free."

His brow furrowed, not exactly the response she'd ex-pected from her declaration. Granted it was more than a bit syrupy for a rugged man like Marcus, but still, it came from the heart.

"To me, love is about more than passion, Cat," he mur-mured gently. "Love is . . . so much more. It's about trust . . . sharing . . . honesty . . . Things we haven't really had enough of between us."

She swallowed, a sudden dread twisting in her belly. He was breaking it off. Trying to do it gently, but saying that it was time to go. Her heart wailed. Now that his mission was done, there was no reason for him to stay in London.

She recalled how long Marcus had held her at bay, not wanting to breach her maidenhead and get her with child. He'd made it perfectly clear that he'd never wanted entanglements. She was a fool to have expected more; she, the woman who'd always admired his free spirit. How could she have considered chaining him?

But that's exactly what she wanted. To bind him to her so that she'd never again have to live that colorless existence. Could she join him on his journey, perhaps? She knew he was fond of her. Her heart pinched that he didn't love her as she did him. But she loved him so very much; perhaps it was enough for the both of them?

Leave Andersen Hall, Jared . . . It might be a blessing to escape the authorities. They'd never find her. Jared could stay with Mrs. Nagel. Just for a while . . . Or perhaps he could come with them, too . . .

"I could come away with you," she murmured, not meeting his eye.

"To war?" he asked, seemingly incredulous. "You'd do that?"

Meeting those gleaming blue eyes, she explained, "I'm tired of feeling like a frightened mouse, Marcus—"

He squeezed her hand. "Darling—"

"No, let me finish."

Pursing his lips, he nodded.

"But there's something you should know, first. I've done something terrible."

"I know."

"You know?" she sputtered.

He nodded. "I visited the Caddyhorn residence today."

Her heart skipped a beat.

"I know what you did, and why you did it and I can't blame you." He shook his head. "I'm amazed at you, but I can't blame you."

Where was her hot-tempered overprotective bear? Dumbfounded, she bit her lip. "You're not angry with me?"

"No." He shook his head. "Not with you." His tone

hardened, the muscle in his jaw worked and his eyes blazed with fury. "But I will finish what you started and wreak vengeance on every last Caddyhorn who's ever hurt you or your brother."

The ferocity in his mien was enough to make a girl swoon.

"And," he added. "Sir John Winston and his son will never bother you or Jared again."

Raising her hand to her mouth, she asked, "What did you do?"

"Thomas Winston had apparently suffered from a lapse of memory. I simply helped jog it a bit. The man suddenly realized that his valet did, in fact, have Sir John Winston's watch and that, indeed, he had promised to discharge Jared's debt after that little prank."

"God, you're good," she breathed. The man had been back for only a few hours and figured out her every secret. Moreover, he seemed perfectly unfazed.

He smiled down at her. "And so are you, my lovely thief. The authorities haven't got a clue and I'll make certain they never do." He kissed the top of her head and she felt a heady rush of warmth for this special dear man. He would protect and keep her safe, she knew it with every fiber of her being.

"I have something important to tell you." He squeezed her hand reassuringly. "I don't want any secrets between us ever again. I've never shared this with anyone."

She looked up, holding her breath.

"I am the Thief of Robinson Square. Well, the first one, anyway."

Her mouth dropped opened.

"It's why I left for the army. Or was sent away, actually. It was a deal that Gillis brokered. On my father's behalf." He grimaced. "It didn't matter that the authorities didn't have a shred of evidence on me, or that I didn't want the blasted deal, Gillis met with Dagwood anyway."

She gaped, trying to process it all. "The Solicitor General?"

"He wasn't a Solicitor General back then."

"Oh, my God!" She covered her mouth. "He came to arrest you! He thought you'd robbed the Caddyhorns!" Tears burned her eyes. "I'll go to the authorities straight away! I'll confess to everything! I'm so sorry, Marcus! I won't let you hang!"

"Hush, Cat." Wrapping his brawny arm about her shoulders, he hugged her close. "No one is going to swing, least of all me."

She shuddered with fear. "What have I done? What have I done?"

"You've pulled off an awesome burglary, is what you've done. And I'll ensure that no one will ever find out that it was you."

"But what about you?" she cried.

"Dagwood knows I couldn't have done it. I was out of town, remember? And he's not about to tell anyone about my past."

Her shoulders sagged as relief flooded through her. "That's right. Thank heavens."

"Tell me about it, Cat. I'm dying to hear."

The suggestion took her aback. She peered at him sideways, wondering if he were jesting.

"Come on," he urged. "Tell me about the burglary."

She opened her mouth and closed it, then shrugged. "Well, it was fantastic, actually. The book, your book, well, it's bloody brilliant."

He grinned, so terribly pleased with himself.

"How in heaven's name did you ever learn about those trick knots?" She held up her hand and showed him. "You know, the ones where you flick your wrist and the rope slips free but it's tight as steel otherwise?"

Smiling, he shrugged. "My father. It was one of the many things he taught me."

Her eyes widened, as realization dawned. "Gillis brokered the deal with Dagwood that you didn't want. Your father was his client, not you. Heavens! He turned you in, didn't he? That's why you were so angry with him!"

His smile faded. "I was angry with him for so many reasons, Cat. And for so long. His turning me in was just the breaking point."

"I can't believe that your father set the authorities on you like that," she muttered, biting her lip. "It's just too awful."

"It's not as dreadful as it sounds."

She looked up, surprised. "You're defending your father?"

"I'm beginning to understand his reasoning. He wanted to make it impossible for me to continue with the thefts, and he wanted to save me from prosecution. So off to war I went. It was an ingenious plan, if I do say so."

"So he knew all along it was you."

"Not the whole time. He came upon my journal just as the anonymous donations to Andersen Hall soared. Despite everything, I believe he liked the incongruity of my stealing from the miserly prosperous to give to the less fortunate. And if you recall, I only selected the most parsimonious people for my targets. My father always had his own brand of justice."

"But the authorities—"

"My father held a certain magistrate's secrets over the man's head. In the end, he was more than happy for the arrangement."

"Righteous Uriah Dunn *blackmailed* someone?"

Would wonders never cease? Stunned, she shook her head. "So you went into the army and the Thief of Robinson Square disappeared."

"Yes. Until last night."

"Astounding." She shook her head. "But what I don't understand is why Headmaster Dunn would have the master closet cleaned when he knew that the book was there." She pressed her hand over her eyes, remembering. "It was hidden in a secret compartment. But the wood had rotted through. I never got a chance to tell him what I'd found!"

"He wanted to return it to me." His hands clenched and his face appeared stricken. "An apology of sorts . . . I almost can't believe it . . . It's I who owe him the apology." Blinking back tears, he bowed his head. "If only I'd understood him better . . . If only he knew . . . I never got to tell him how much . . . I loved him."

"He knew you loved him, Marcus." She squeezed his hand. "He knew it deep in his heart. Don't ever doubt it." Laying her head against his shoulder, she pressed a chaste kiss to his cheek. "He knew without you ever needing to say it."

"I'm not exactly a poet when it comes to expressing how I feel." Marcus sniffed, rubbing his eyes.

"Yes, and 'love is like the wind,' " she quoted her sappy self.

He chuckled. Then a rich laugh rumbled through him, reverberating deep in her soul. Shaking his head, he declared, "Oh, how you make me laugh, Cat Miller. You lighten my heart when I fear it turns to black."

"And you're no poet?" she teased.

"I suppose I am when you are near." His dear azure gaze met hers, sincere and filled with tenderness. "I love you, Catherine."

"I love you, too, Marcus." She smiled joyously, feeling

so jubilant she thought she might truly fly. Reaching up, she threw her arms around his shoulders and hugged him close.

"The world will have to find out about your being a Caddyhorn, you realize. For our marriage license to be legal, we must use your real name." He pulled back, his gaze searching hers. "You will marry me, won't you?"

She probed her heart, looking for that familiar apprehension. "I feel like everything I've done for the last ten years has been a reaction to the Caddyhorns, or my fears one way or another. Even refusing to marry." Deep inside of her, happiness welled. "But I'm not afraid anymore, Marcus," she marveled, beaming. "Yes, I'll marry you! Nothing would make me happier!"

His lips met hers, so sweetly and with such ardor, she melted into his embrace. This felt so perfect, so amazingly *right*, that her heart sang.

Realization struck and she pulled back, exclaiming, "Once we marry, Dickey Caddyhorn will cease to have legal guardianship over me."

"He's not going to be able to touch you, your brother or anyone else from his prison cell, I assure you."

"You really think he'll pay?"

"Oh, you can bet money on it, darling."

She bit her lip. "Do you think that Jared can come with us?"

Splaying gentle kisses along her jaw, he murmured, "To where?"

"The Peninsula."

He pulled back. "I'm not returning to duty, Cat. I'm going to sell my commission to my friend Luke Hayes."

"But the war, your efforts . . ."

"Seven years is enough, Cat. I'm done chasing traitors. I'm tired of the treachery, the lies. I've served my time, no one can dispute that." Leaning over, he pressed his lips to her crown. "And I'm tired of running away. I just want to be home."

"But you've always hated Andersen Hall—"

"Home is not the four walls. But here." He laid his hand over her heart. "This is my home. With you." His gaze met hers, filled with all the love that she imagined her own gaze reflected. "My father once told me that I'd come to cherish family. And he was right. What you have with Jared, the children, your friends . . . it's a beautiful thing and I want to be a part of it. I want to belong to your family. Here, with you."

A lump formed in her throat as tears burned the back of her eyes. "I love you, Marcus, and I'm so glad that you're mine."

"Not half as happy as I am," he murmured. "Now how about another kiss?"

"Only one?"

Their clothes were off in minutes.

This is the woman I love, Marcus marveled as he gently molded her naked breasts in his palms. "You were made for me," he murmured as he splayed kisses down her neck, inhaling the sweet scents of orange blossom interlaced with her desire. "As if crafted by the gods simply for my pleasure."

"For my pleasure, too," she breathed, opening her legs to receive him. "Please take me now, Marcus. I want you inside of me."

He needed no further urging.

Thrusting deep into her tight, hot core, he thought he might just expire from the ecstasy.

"So wet," he groaned. "So ready for me."

Trailing her hands over his shoulders, she hugged him

close, making made him feel cherished. "I love how you fill me, Marcus. Nothing . . . nothing compares . . ."

Slowly he eased out of her. "Even climbing rooftops?" he teased.

Her luscious lips spread into a wicked smile. "It comes close . . . but this beats it . . . by a nose."

He plunged deep into her wet core. "A nose, you say?"

Her breath hitched and her eyes widened. "Dear Lord in heaven!"

Drawing almost completely out of her, he murmured, "Care to reassess?"

"Marcus!" It was a command, a plea and a surrender.

Smiling, he drove into her again and again, relishing how her hips lifted to meet his, thrust for thrust. He couldn't imagine any other woman suiting him as well as Cat. She truly was his mate.

She grasped his face, drawing his lips down to hers and kissing him with a passion that left him breathless. She moaned into his mouth. Her inner muscles clenched around him, her breath hitched and her body tensed. Increasing his pace, he sent off a prayer of thanks, then flew with the woman he loved.

Epilogue

"**A**re you ready, my lovely wife of fifty-eight hours?" Marcus asked.

Catherine gave him a shaky smile. "Still counting?"

"Yes." He nodded sagely. "I like to think of it as coin in the bank."

"I hope you don't intend to make any withdrawals—"

"Never! I value my good fortune too much. Besides"—he kissed her white-gloved hand—"the credit is out of this world."

Catherine appreciated how he was trying to take her mind off the crowd waiting downstairs, but butterflies still fluttered in her middle and her mouth was dry as dust. "Perhaps I could have another lemonade?"

"You look beautiful, you know," was his only response. His gloved hand caressed her cheek. "That lavender gown makes your eyes shimmer. You'll be the belle of the ball."

Her hand slid over the sheer silk gown that had cost so much Lady Huntington had refused to allow her to know the price. "You really like it? It seems somewhat . . .

snug." For the hundredth time she adjusted the fichu of muslin at her breast.

"I'll confess that when I first saw it, I wasn't well pleased that so many men will have the benefit of such a view. But then Lady Huntington made me see the light."

"What light is that?"

"Every man in London will know just how very lucky I am."

His lips lifted into that charming smile that she adored and some of the tension inside of her loosened.

Sounds of a minuet drifted in through the closed door and Catherine's heart began to race. Not being afraid anymore was one thing, but a bit of nervousness at being launched into Society after ten years of a closed existence in an orphanage was another.

"Will you get a new uniform, do you think?" she dallied.

"What, you don't like my attire?" He waved to his costume.

"No, you are quite elegant, as a matter of fact." He was resplendent in his black coat, crisp white shirt, blue waistcoat, black breeches and shiny black-buckled shoes. She was particularly fond of how his coat was perfectly cut to show off his broad shoulders and lean waist. She sighed, hoping that she'd be able to get him out of the costume again before too long. "It's just that I like how dashing you look in a uniform."

"My superiors do not wish for me to make my connection with the Foreign Office too public. Napoleon's spies don't need to know that I am still on their trail. Besides, it's your night tonight, not mine." He held out his arm. "Shall we?"

Catherine took his proffered arm and together they stepped toward the door. "It was kind of Lady Huntington to host this ball for us."

"Kind? The lady is wallowing in her victory. Now she gets to show the world how she's been right all along about the wretched Caddyhorns. Besides"—he pressed a kiss to her cheek as if he couldn't help himself—"she's just glad to have some decent relations. She's had to live with the Caddyhorns for all of these years."

"She is quite taken with Jared." Catherine nodded.

"And he suffers her attention with good humor."

"Yes, well, she can be quite effusive," Catherine agreed, thinking fondly of the spirited matron who'd taken them all, including Andersen Hall, under her wing.

"I'm sure, in time, he will grow quite accustomed to all of the attention," Marcus assured.

The entry loomed large before them.

She bit her lip. "It's just so much change."

Marcus reached for the handle. "Come, darling, let us show polite Society all that they've missed." He threw open the door and the sounds of the minuet greeted them along with the buzz of many voices. Glasses tinkled, laughter chimed and the scent of many perfumes filled the air. Rose, lily, musk and thankfully, the beloved scent of sandalwood.

They stepped to the top of the stairs and a hush fell over the ballroom. Holding court in the far corner, Lady Huntington beamed.

Hundreds of faces looked up at them expectantly. Women in gold and diamonds and colorful gowns whose cost could feed ten children for a month. Men, mostly in black formal attire, just waiting to judge the lady who'd lived penniless in an orphanage for ten years. No amount of inheritance would ever make her feel like one of them, she knew. Jared probably felt the same, which is why she'd given him most of their legacy. She had a home, had Marcus by her side, and needed very little. Jared was going to have a difficult time ahead of him and would need every resource to fit into this very different world.

The voices began to hum. Fans wagged, monocles stared. People began to shift and mutter as the crowd grew restless.

Catherine fought the urge to turn and run.

Marcus leaned over and whispered in her ear, "Just think of all of those weighty purses down there, just waiting for us to lighten them."

"I thought we agreed," she muttered under her breath, "no more rooftops."

"For Andersen Hall, darling. We take from the rich and give to the poor. But now we're going to *ask for it first*."

Catherine blinked, as realization dawned. Her nervousness washed away like mud after the rain. She was an emissary, working for Andersen Hall, serving the needy children. Her uncommon story would be like a beacon inviting comment. Then she would have the opening to share the importance of the orphanage and its distinctive role in serving London's disadvantaged. It was a brilliant opportunity to draw supporters to the institution.

Catherine smiled up at her husband. "You always know exactly the right thing to say."

"I'll remember you said that."

"Are you with me, my partner in crime?"

Marcus lifted her hand to his lips and pressed a kiss on her palm. "Always."

Don't miss the heat in these sizzling new August releases from Avon Romance!

Love According to Lily by Julianne MacLean

An Avon Romantic Treasure

Lady Lily Langdon is ready to take matters of passion into her own hands. With lessons in flirtation from her American sister-in-law, Duchess Sophia, Lily means to seduce the object of her affection: the Earl of Whitby, a man who up to now has only seen Lily as a troublesome girl. He'll soon find that though she is still troublesome, she is no longer just a girl . . .

How to Marry a Millionaire Vampire by Kerrelyn Sparks

An Avon Contemporary Romance

Welcome to the dangerous—and hilarious—world of modern day vampires. There are vampire cable channels, a celebrity magazine called Live! With the Undead, and just like the living, vampires have dental emergencies. That's how dentist Shanna Whelan, a human female, meets the smolderingly undead Roman Draganesti, and finds her life turning absolutely, well, batty . . .

Daring the Duke by Anne Mallory

An Avon Romance

She once lived a secret life. He, a reluctant duke, once pursued that secret to the ends of the earth. Could he know her identity—and if he does can she trust the aid he offers? And what will happen to their growing passion when he discovers her final secret—the one that proves how powerfully they are connected?

Courting Claudia by Robyn DeHart

An Avon Romance

After a lifetime of chafing under her father's high expectations, Claudia Prattley is determined to please him by marrying the man of his choosing, but a dashing rogue is bent on foiling her plans. That rogue is Derrick Middleton, and he's so drawn to Claudia's enchanting combination of passion and trust that he knows he must take a chance on winning her love.

REL 0705